PRAISE FOR JOAN HESS
AND THE CLAIRE MALLOY SERIES

"Well-paced suspense spiced with wry wit."
—*Boston Sunday Herald* on *Closely Akin to Murder*

"Clever . . . irreverent murder and mayhem."
—*Baton Rouge Sunday Advocate* on *Closely Akin to Murder*

"Wickedly amusing."
—*Alfred Hitchcock Mystery Magazine* on *Busy Bodies*

"Intriguing . . . an amusing look at the universal human comedy." —*Fort Smith Times Record*

"If you've never spent time with Claire and her crew, I feel sorry for you. Stop reading this nonsense and hop to it. You'll see wit and humanity all wrapped up in a nifty murder mystery." —Harlan Coben

"Delightful . . . worthy of Hercule Poirot in the classic *Death on the Nile*."—*Publishers Weekly* on *Mummy Dearest*

"A good substitute for a trip to Egypt."
—*Deadly Pleasures* on *Mummy Dearest*

"Hess fans will find much to entertain them . . ."
—*Publishers Weekly* on *Damsels in Distress*

"Lively, sharp, irreverent."
—*The New York Times Book Review* on *Poisoned Pins*

"Larcenous shenanigans . . . breezy throughout."
—*Chicago Tribune* on *Poisoned Pins*

MORE . . .

"With her wry asides, Claire makes a most engaging narrator. The author deftly juggles the various plot strands . . . the surprising denouement comes off with éclat."
　　　　　—Publishers Weekly on *Out on a Limb*

"A winning blend of soft-core feminism, trendy subplots, and a completely irreverent style that characterizes both the series and the sleuth." 　　　*—Houston Chronicle*

"A wildly entertaining series." 　　　　　　*—Mystery Scene*

"Joan Hess is one of the best mystery writers in the world. She makes it look so easy that few readers and fewer critics realize what a rare talent hers is."
　　　　　—Elizabeth Peters, author of Tomb of the Golden Bird

"Joan Hess is seriously funny. Moreover, she is seriously kind as well as clever when depicting the follies, foibles, and fantasies of our lives. Viva Joan!"
　　　　　—Carolyn Hart, author of Dead Days of Summer

"Fresh and funny . . . her trademark humor is stamped on every page." 　*—Publishers Weekly, on* The Goodbye Body

"Breezy and delightful . . . Claire Malloy is one of the most engaging narrators in mystery."*—The Drood Review*

"Hess is one very funny woman."
　　　　　—Susan Dunlap, former president of Sisters in Crime

"Amiable entertainment with an edge." *—Kirkus Reviews*

ENJOY THESE OTHER MYSTERIES
FROM JOAN HESS

Strangled Prose

The Murder at the Murder at the Mimosa Inn

Dear Miss Demeanor

A Really Cute Corpse

A Diet to Die For

Roll Over and Play Dead

Death by the Light of the Moon

Poisoned Pins

Tickled to Death

Busy Bodies

Closely Akin to Murder

A Holly Jolly Murder

A Conventional Corpse

Out on a Limb

The Goodbye Body

Damsels in Distress

Mummy Dearest

The Merry Wives of Maggody

AVAILABLE FROM ST. MARTIN'S/MINOTAUR
PAPERBACKS

DEADER HOMES & GARDENS

JOAN HESS

St. Martin's Paperbacks

NOTE: If you purchased this book without a cover you should be aware that this book is stolen property. It was reported as "unsold and destroyed" to the publisher, and neither the author nor the publisher has received any payment for this "stripped book."

This is a work of fiction. All of the characters, organizations, and events portrayed in this novel are either products of the author's imagination or are used fictitiously.

DEADER HOMES AND GARDENS

Copyright © 2012 by Joan Hess.
Excerpt from *Murder as a Second Language* copyright © 2013 by Joan Hess.

All rights reserved.

For information address St. Martin's Press, 175 Fifth Avenue, New York, NY 10010.

ISBN: 978-1-250-01949-3

Printed in the United States of America

Minotaur hardcover edition / February 2012
St. Martin's Paperbacks edition / January 2013

St. Martin's Paperbacks are published by St. Martin's Press, 175 Fifth Avenue, New York, NY 10010.

10 9 8 7 6 5 4 3 2 1

For my beloved grandchildren,
Annabelle Hadley and Jack Benton King,
born July 8, 2010

ACKNOWLEDGMENTS

I would like to thank Dr. Brad Hall and Dr. Jinee Rizzo, who are the Chief and Deputy Chief of Toxology in the Travis County Medical Examiner's Department. Ms. Sarah Scott kindly helped with communication.

Dean James offered several significant observations, for which I am grateful. Dorothy Cannell and Elizabeth Peters tolerated my whines and moans for a very long time. Susan Rogers Cooper encouraged me in my bleaker moments.

Buy their books.

PROLOGUE

The weather had been milder than usual, but March was notoriously unreliable. Daffodils often struggled to keep their bright yellow blooms above a slather of snow. School administrators watched the weather forecasts and slept fitfully. Wet roads might be covered with black ice if the thermometer slipped a few degrees. Peach and apple crops could be destroyed by a single hard freeze. One never knew.

The stream, too small to be a river, careened down from the mountains and gradually settled into a meandering, listless rhythm. It had been deeper before the loggers had clear-cut swathes of hardwood trees. The consequent erosion had spilled soil and decayed matter into the stream, creating natural barriers that splintered the flow. What had been clear spring water now was muddy, obtuse.

The corpse remained submerged in the lethargic water for several days, its fingers combing the silt, its mouth clogged with detritus from the bottom of the stream. Its heavy clothing weighed it down like a burden of misfortune. The wound on the back of its skull had long ceased bleeding; more recent scrapes and cuts battered the face but drew no blood. Because of the coldness of the water, fish did only minimal damage. Had the temperature been lower, the body might not have surfaced for weeks.

A massive front swept up from the Gulf of Mexico, bringing rain and unseasonably warm temperatures. The corpse began to float upward as gas filled its cavities. The stream picked up its pace, agitating the deep, brooding pools and stirring the vegetation. The corpse rotated like an aged ballerina, snagging on underwater branches, then breaking free as it continued to rise.

The search party might have missed the dark blue bundle lodged in the roots of a tree on the far bank, had they not been methodically scouring every cranny of the stream. They gathered slowly and without enthusiasm. No one volunteered to find a way to cross the stream and examine what they supposed was the object of their mission. Someone would have to do so, they muttered to each other.

Eventually, someone did.

CHAPTER 1

"A house, a house, my kingdom for a house," I muttered as I crammed a pair of dirty jeans and several shirts under the bed. The bedroom floor still resembled an archipelago of discarded clothes. The hamper was draped with smelly socks and unmentionables. I tripped on a size-twelve sneaker, paused in midair to wonder if I could stuff it down the garbage disposal (had the garbage disposal worked, which it hadn't in a decade), and stumbled into the bookcase. Paperbacks felleth like the gentle rain upon the place beneath.

The bathroom looked as though it had been vandalized by hordes of Avon ladies and dental assistants. Since my darling husband, Peter, my egomaniacal seventeen-year-old daughter, Caron, and I now shared the space, there were at least three toothbrushes, shampoo and conditioner bottles, crusty toothpaste tubes, mouthwash bottles, towels, hair dryers, razors, and everything else deemed essential to roam hygienically in public. The addition of a third person to the household had proven to be a geometric rather than arithmetic progression in chaos.

After returning home from what turned out to be a

decidedly adventurous honeymoon in Egypt, we'd assessed the housing situation. Peter's house had one bedroom. My apartment had two. Caron had suggested that we put her up in a suite at a hotel, but the only suites to be found in Farberville were in university dorms and did not include maid service. Since I did not consider my marriage a temporary situation, I was not about to settle for a temporary solution. Neither was Peter, who, among his other talents, comes from the old-money aristocracy of New England. This is not to say that any of them was as handsome as Peter, who has molasses-colored eyes, a defined nose, and perfect white teeth. In situations best left unspecified, he blushes adorably. At the moment, he was in the living room, drinking coffee while he read the newspaper. I fetched coffee for myself and joined him.

"I heard you fall," he said without glancing up—or leaping to his feet to offer solace and a cool compress in case my leg was fractured and blood was dribbling down my pale face.

"Cosmetic surgery should help."

"That bad?" He turned to the sports page.

"Not yet," I said, "but it's a matter of time before one of us slips in the kitchen or runs into an open door. The closets and cabinets are packed with your stuff and my stuff. Caron's stuff is waist deep in her room. It's a whole new level of claustrophobia in here. My office at the Book Depot seems spacious in comparison, and that's with the boiler looming." I sighed as loudly and despondently as I could.

He finally put aside the paper to offer sympathy in a most charmingly amorous fashion. After making sure no bones were in need of splinting, he sat back up and ran his fingers through his hair. "We can't have Caron catching us in the middle of such unseemly behavior. She might get all kinds of ideas."

"She already has all kinds of ideas, most of which I

dearly hope I'll never discover. She and Inez went over to the campus to troll for fraternity boys."

"I thought she was dating that boy with the speech impediment."

"Joel does tend to mumble when you glower at him. Perhaps he'd speak up if you stopped growling. He's a sweet, well brought-up boy, which you already know since you checked to make sure that neither he nor anyone in his family ever received so much as a parking ticket." I took a sip of coffee and gazed at the mishmash of art, books, furniture, and doodads. "Isn't there a TV in that corner behind your fishing gear?"

Peter picked up the business section. "We need to find a real house."

"We as in the two of us?"

"If you want to wait six weeks." He folded the paper and tucked it under his arm as he stood up. "I've got piles of paperwork to dig through before a meeting at ten with the ATF task force. Next week, a four-day seminar, probably in Little Rock or Pine Bluff with the state and federal agents. After that, I'll be all over the region to coordinate communication systems and interagency cooperation. The governor's office is coming down on illegal weapons, as well as bootlegged whiskey and tobacco. You and Caron check out the housing market. When you've narrowed it down to a final few, I'll look at them." His voice rose as I began to sputter. "Whatever you like, darling. You have exquisite taste, and Caron will surely have lots of helpful comments." He made it out the door before I could tackle him. His size-twelves did not tread lightly as he escaped down the steps and out the front door of the duplex.

I ran out of spittle to sputter. That, and my coffee was getting cold.

* * *

Angela Delmond sighed, as did I. The contribution from
the backseat sounded like a death rattle. We were parked
in front of a very nice house, certainly functional, with a
nice kitchen and enough bathrooms to allow privacy for
all occupants and the occasional guest. It had a very nice
yard in a very nice neighborhood.

"Generic," Caron pronounced grimly.

Angela took her last shot. "There's a bakery just three
blocks away. They make wonderful croissants. It would
be lovely to sit on the patio on Sunday mornings and
share the newspaper."

"Be still my heart," said a lugubrious voice behind me.

I'd lost count of the number of houses we'd seen in the
last week. Along the way I'd also lost my mind. Angela
had been ebullient when we began the hunt, ecstatic over
walk-in closets, euphoric over bay windows, and raptur-
ous over wine racks. Now the car was thick with gloom.
Her spirit had deflated, but her exterior had not been
undermined. In her midthirties, her dark hair was styled
to soften her jaw; her chin was pointed, and her eyes were
slightly slanted, giving her a feline air. The wardrobe I'd
seen thus far cost more than my car. She'd told me one of
her purses was a steal. If I'd wanted it back in the olden
days, that's the only way I could have gotten it.

Angela's air of muted despair was a relief. She'd mastered the art of talking without pause to breathe, and I'd
been inundated with details about her personal life. I was
familiar with her fancy wedding at the country club, her
marriage to loathsome, despicable, deceitful, womanizing
Danny Delmond, and a divorce-in-progress that sounded
as though it might conclude with at least one felony. I was
impressed with her tenacious determination to succeed as
a single woman on a playing field strewn with chauvinis-
tic land mines. I'd been there, and it wasn't easy.

"Let's call it a day," I said to her. "This is a waste of

time for all of us. I really don't want to have to build, but it's beginning to seem like the only option."

"Do you know how long it takes to build a house, Mother?" Caron asked. "Months And Months. By the time you're ready to move in, I'll be moving out to go to college. No, I take that back. We'll all be living in a facility with padded walls. On Thursdays we'll paint birdhouses or cut out paper snowflakes. Not even Inez will visit us. Just kill me now and spare me the agony."

"The idea has crossed my mind," I said over my shoulder. "Something excruciatingly painful, like puffer fish sushi."

Caron snorted. "Golden poison frogs are more lethal, you know."

"You get a line, I'll get a pole," I sang, "and we'll all go down to the fishin' hole."

Angela delicately cleared her throat. "If I may interrupt for just a moment, Claire, there may be one last house for you to consider. I'd really hate for you to build. As Caron pointed out, it takes countless months. In the fall, it's slow because the workmen disappear for the various hunting seasons—turkeys, raccoons, deer, ducks, and who knows what else. Danny is nastier than a grizzly bear during the season, ranting about how the plumber had to wait for the tile man, who was waiting for the electrician, who'd gone hunting. One of his subcontractors was killed in a shooting accident. Not surprising, when you think about all these drunks armed with rifles, stomping around the woods. I gave Danny a rifle for his birthday two years ago and told him that only sissies wear orange."

I bit back a giggle. "One last house?"

"Made out of gingerbread," Caron said. "I'm not hungry, so how about you drop me off at the mall?"

Angela frowned. "I'll have to make a call and catch the owner. I'm not sure about certain legal situations."

She held up her hand before I could respond. "This house may be exactly what you're looking for. If the owner declines, you might reconsider some of the houses we've seen. Or I'll show you property, as long as you swear you won't use Danny as your contractor. As a child, he never mastered Tinkertoys. After the first storm, you'll be sitting on a pile of rubble."

I confessed that I had an aversion to rubble and was willing to look at the mysterious house. Angela discussed the finer points of joint custody of pets (specifically a schnauzer named Flopsy) until she dropped us off at the duplex, promising to call later. Caron, who now had a sensible Japanese compact and a notarized statement promising her the car of her choice (within reason) after high school graduation, headed for Inez's house to moan and whine about the abuse she'd suffered because of my maniacal insistence that she look at houses with me. I supposed I ought to go to the Book Depot and see how the new clerk had fared, but after a minuscule debate, I poured myself a glass of iced tea, picked up a mystery novel, and went out to my tiny balcony overlooking the campus.

Two days later, Angela called, and an hour later, I was in her car. "I am so excited!" she chirped like a sparrow on caffeine. "I know you'll love the house. It's perfect for you! Privacy, a lovely yard with a garden, four bedrooms, and four bathrooms. Although it was built in the eighteen-nineties, it was remodeled and updated three years ago. That's when the pool was put in. It comes with ten acres that slope down to a river. There's an apple orchard and a lovely view of the entire valley. As for the price—well, it's well below market value. I'd buy it myself if it weren't for this horrendous mess with Danny and his slut."

"Why isn't it on the market?" I asked.

"It's all very complicated, but nothing we girls need to

worry about. My broker has experience with estate and probate issues."

"The owner is dead?" I don't believe in ghosts, but I do believe in paperwork. When an elderly uncle had died intestate, other family members had come out of the baseboards to sue each other for years while their lawyers drained the assets. "One of Us Girls doesn't want to fall in love with something that's unobtainable." And Caron claims I never listen to her.

Angela, who'd endured several days with Caron's backseat commentaries, laughed. "Let's not get ahead of ourselves."

We drove to the north edge of Farberville and turned onto a blacktop road. A sign proclaimed the proximity of Hollow Valley Nursery. "As in small children?" I asked warily, imagining them darting around the woods like snotty-nosed elves.

"Trees and shrubs and flowers, but strictly wholesale. Well, they do have one sale in the autumn. I bought some red maples a year ago, and they're doing well. I'd planned to put in a row of crepe myrtles, but Danny's trying to force the sale of our house. Damned if I'm going to have work done in someone else's garden! He had the nerve to call this morning to tell me that he's taking that bimbo to our lake house this weekend. Can you imagine? I'd rather burn it down than have her sunbathing on my deck!" She ground her foot on the gas pedal as if it were the bimbo's face. Or Danny's.

I clutched my purse as we bounced over a pothole. I noticed a driveway on the right as Angela spun onto a narrow gravel road on the left. It wound through a wooded patch to the front of the purportedly perfect house. Which was, based on my first glimpse, darn close to perfect.

The house had the allure of a late nineteenth-century gingerbread manor, with gray siding and painted shingles and whimsical white trim. The front door had a transom, and the veranda stretched across the width of the front. A porch swing swayed in the breeze. Forsythia and japonicas bloomed in meticulously random beds. The trees soared beyond the second floor. Angela unlocked the front door. "It may be musty," she said. "I try to come out here to air it out, but with all these lawyer's appointments . . ." She continued talking, but I stopped listening.

In keeping with its Victorian heritage, the ceilings were fifteen feet high and trimmed with crown molding. Hardwood floors glistened. The living room was spacious and sunny. Centered on one wall was a native stone fireplace, with a mantel that supported brass candlesticks and a clock with a pendulum. French doors led to a terrace. The furniture looked as if it had been selected by a very adept designer who'd mixed period pieces with more contemporary styles. There were blank spaces on the walls where art had been hung.

Angela nudged me through a doorway into a dining room with an antique mahogany table and eight chairs. The crystal chandelier sparkled wickedly. "The furniture comes with the house—unless you don't want it. I'm sure we can find a thrift store to take it."

My mind was darting too quickly to reply. The kitchen had glistening appliances, a refrigerator large enough to stash a body, and a gas cooktop out of a four-star restaurant. I knew this only because I'd been flipping through magazines featuring the transformation of woodsheds to Tuscan villas with a few gallons of paint and fabric swatches. If I learned how to turn on the appliances, friends could sit at the immense marbletop island and watch me char vegetables and flambé turkeys.

Angela and I continued into the master suite, which was the size of my duplex, give or take a few square feet. The king-sized bed was covered by a ripply white silk spread with matching pillow shams. Another set of French doors led to the back terrace. His and hers dressing rooms, a marble bathroom with a complicated shower, a spacious bathtub, skylights, and heated towel racks. The library at the front of the house had floor-to-ceiling bookcases, a ladder on wheels (be still my heart!), and a serious desk where Important Things Could Take Place.

"You're beaming like a baby," Angela said.

I tried to compose myself. "What's upstairs?"

We toured three bedrooms, all large and sunny. One had a balcony that would suit a certain person who fancied herself as Lady Macbeth one day and Juliet Capulet the next. It also had a private bathroom with a Jacuzzi. A fourth room would serve nicely as another office, should I decide to write my memoirs—or a sewing room should I be struck in the head by lightning.

As we went downstairs, Angela's cell phone rang. She looked at it, grimaced, and in a curt voice said, "Go have a look at the garden and the pool. The apple orchard is farther beyond."

I left her hissing into her phone and went outside. The terrace was made of worn bricks in a herringbone pattern. The metal table, chairs, chaise lounge, and glider were nineteen-fifties retro in cheerful colors echoed by flowers and ornamental trees. A lovely place to sip a little something and watch the sunset (if my mental compass was accurate). I continued to the pool, which had a few leaves and sticks in the deep end. It wasn't Olympic sized, but there was a decent chance it was as large as that of Caron's nemesis, Rhonda Maguire.

The apple orchard had been there for decades; limbs were gnarled but strong enough to support the abundance of small green apples. The grass between the rows of trees was green and freshly mowed. The aroma was intoxicating. I continued to the far end, where a meadow led down to a lazy stream. Clumps of trees created shady patches that begged for a quilt, a picnic hamper, and a slim volume of poetry.

Indeed, it was the perfect house—if it was available. Even if it wasn't available, I thought morosely as I walked back to the terrace, it was the perfect house.

Angela was not waiting outside, so I opened the French doors and called her name. I looked in the kitchen, living room, dining room, and master suite. She was not in any of the upstairs rooms, including the bathrooms. I came down the stairs slowly, more irritated than concerned. Irritation turned into annoyance when I opened the front door and saw that her car was no longer there. At least I could stop searching for her, I told myself as I glared at the vacated space. Why on earth would she have driven off, effectively stranding me? To give me time to admire the placement of the linen closet? To stare in awe at the cabinets above the marble countertops? To dance with glee in the laundry room?

I harrumphed for a few more minutes, then went back inside. I'd left my purse in the kitchen, and I was trying to recall if I'd brought my cell phone when I reached the doorway—and froze.

The man standing in front of the refrigerator beamed at me. "Why, hello, hello. You're early, but do come in and have a seat. Do come in and have a seat. I was about to open a bottle of very nice Bordeaux. Will you join me? Won't you join me?" He waved a corkscrew at me.

I kept my distance. He appeared to be well over eighty years old, with etched wrinkles, liverish blotches, a nose ineptly carved out of blood sausage, and floppy wet lips. A grungy baseball cap covered most of his bald head. He wore a bowtie and a loosely tied plaid bathrobe.

"I am," the man continued as he took a bottle of wine out of the rack and attacked it with the corkscrew, "Moses

Hollow, great-great-grandson of Colonel Moses Ambrose Hollow, who bought this valley in eighteen sixty-six from President Ulysses S. Grant, despite being a colonel in the CSA. There may have been some funny business with the paperwork." He cackled as he filled two wineglasses and pushed one across the island. "A thousand acres of prime hardwood. Ol' Moses built hisself a lumber mill and made out like a bandit during Reconstruction. Let's toast Colonel Moses Ambrose Hollow!" When I failed to comply, he gave me a disgruntled look. "You a member of the Women's Christian Temperance Union? Why, when I wasn't more than eight years old, I'd go in the wagon with my grandpappy to deliver moonshine to the local saloons. Dodged the revenuers, Grandpappy and I did. Dangerous business, Grandpappy used to say when he was sober. Dangerous business."

His expression was darkening, so I picked up the glass of wine and took a swallow. "This is a lovely Bordeaux." I wasn't afraid of him, since I could topple him with one finger; I was curious. Also stuck at the house until Angela returned from her errand or whatever. "So you live in the valley?"

He turned around to open the refrigerator. He stuck his head so far inside that I wondered if he intended to find a nesting spot, but he emerged with a round wooden box of Brie and a bag of grapes. He located a cutting board, a knife, and a box of crackers. "Where do you think I live? Chattanooga? Chattanooga-choo-choo?"

I was quite sure a dormouse would waddle out of the microwave and request a cup of tea from the man, who was mad if not the Mad Hatter incarnate. "How many members of the Hollow family live here?" I asked.

He stuffed half a dozen grapes in his mouth and chewed vigorously. "Hard to say," he mumbled as grape pulp dribbled out of the corners of his mouth. "Moses had three daughters and seven sons. Five of the boys survived and got two hundred acres each, but a lot of it got sold over the years. These days most of it's for the greenhouses. Big greenhouses. Acres of greenhouses. I keep waiting for brimstone to hail down, so's all those pompous asses will find out what happens to people who live in glass houses. Or earn their living from them, anyhow." He drank the remaining wine from the bottle, belched, and ducked out of sight. "I tried to warn him, you know, but he thought I was a fool," his voice continued.

"Warn whom?"

"Love can be lethal. Even a fool knows that."

I stealthily opened my purse and took out my cell phone. Since I rarely used it, I rarely remembered to charge it. Peter insisted that I carry it, but he and Caron had long since stopped bothering to call me on it. Amazingly, life went on. At this point, however, I was disappointed to note that only electronic resuscitation could help it rise from the dead.

Moses had no such problem. He popped up from the far side of the island, holding another bottle of wine. "Let's try the merlot, shall we? My dear, you haven't touched the cheese and crackers. If we're going to continue our wine-tasting adventure, you really should eat something. We don't want to get tipsy, do we?"

He seemed to be more dedicated to getting sloshed. I said, "Merlot will be fine. If you'll excuse me for a moment . . ." I left before he could refuse to excuse me. There were no landlines in the rooms downstairs or upstairs. I peered out a window in case Angela might be parking in the driveway. Alas, she was not. Reminding myself that sobriety was my only hope of survival, I returned to the kitchen. The merlot bottle was half empty. I followed a trail of cracker crumbs to the living room, where I found Moses asleep on a wide leather sofa.

The situation was ludicrous, I decided as I went into the kitchen for Brie, crackers, and a glass of wine. I took my bounty out to the front porch and sat in the swing. Angela's phone call must have involved Danny, although if she was on the way to their lake house, I might have a lengthy wait. By no means was I panicky. Other people lived in Hollow Valley, some of whom operated a successful business. They might even have phones.

I decided to give Angela half an hour to reappear before I pondered my next move. I wandered around the yard, admiring the elegant simplicity of the landscaping. It helped, I supposed, to have a nursery nearby. Pine bark mulch kept the beds free of weeds, and even though the house was vacant, the grass was mown. I straightened up and eyed the house. It was whispering seductively to me, encouraging me to put my books in the library and my favorite bits of pottery on the mantel in the living room. Peter would have room to hang up his silk ties and align his Italian shoes on a shelf in his dressing room. Caron could have pool parties under my diligent yet dignified supervision. Cocktail parties on the terrace, and formal dinners abuzz with witty repartee and the clink of crystal (catered, of course).

Peter and Caron might object to the minor commute into Farberville's downtown area. I would suggest that they live in one of the generic houses and visit me on weekends and holidays. If Angela couldn't convince the buyer to sign over the house, my revenge would make her divorce seem like springtime in Paris.

It was approaching the time to take action of some sort. Unless Angela had communicated with her office, she was the only other person (besides Moses and me) who knew where I was. I wasn't all that sure myself. Hollow Valley had been inhabited since the post–Civil War era, but I'd been in Farberville for twenty years and I'd never heard of it.

Moses had rolled over but was still breathing. I picked up my purse and headed down the lane that led to the paved road. I did so at a leisurely pace, listening to birds and keeping an eye out for snakes and other evils that lurk in the darker fringe of nature. I was alarmed when a woman popped out from an unseen path. She was trim, dressed in shorts and a T-shirt, and had a frizzy brown ponytail restrained by a shoelace, and a broad face.

"Oops, I hope I didn't startle you," she said.

"I hope I didn't startle you."

"Nothing could startle me around here," she said, laughing. "I'm Natalie Hollow-Brown, but please call me Nattie. And you?"

"Claire Malloy. I came here with a real estate sales-woman to look at the house. Now she's vanished and I'm stranded."

Nattie raised her eyebrows. "Winston's house is on the market?"

"I'm not sure about its status, but Angela told me that she spoke to the owner."

"How very, very interesting," she murmured, "but none of my business. Have you happened to see an elderly man wandering around? I'm afraid I've lost him."

I gestured at the house behind me. "He found some wine and decided to take a nap on the sofa. I really need to make a phone call. Can you help me?"

Nattie glanced back at the house. "Let that old coot sleep it off where he is. He'll show up for supper. Or he won't, which is fine with me. You're welcome to come home with me and use the phone." She hesitated. "Are you going to call the police?"

"Actually, I am," I said, "in that my husband's the deputy chief of the Farberville Police Department. I need him to come pick me up. That way, he can have a look at

the house. I hope he'll be as excited as I am." I would see
that he was, if it meant we had to make love on the dining
room table. And in the meadow, and again on silk sheets.
Whatever personal sacrifices were necessary.

As we started walking in the direction of the paved
road, she said, "I'd better warn you about your potential
neighbors. I talk to my plants and read half a dozen fantasy novels a week, but I am by far the sanest of the lot—
even though the petunias talk back. It may be a genetic
flaw. Old Moses Ambrose Hollow was purported to be a
drunken tyrant. He was acquitted of murder charges
twice due to expeditious financial exchanges with judges
and juries. Before he died, he ordered a bronze statue of
himself to be placed in the area in front of the Old Tavern. It's still there, since nobody in the family has the
nerve to even suggest that we remove it. It gives me the
creeps whenever I'm near it."

"Because it might come to life?"

"Wait until you get a look at his seriously ugly face.
The gargoyles at Notre Dame are a damn sight more
handsome than he was. I doubt he'll stumble down from
his pedestal to terrorize the countryside and incite the
peasants to riot and burn down the mill. No, I worry that
a gust of wind will topple him when I'm too close."

When we reached the pavement, I pointed at the road
I'd noticed earlier. "Is that a driveway?"

"Yes, it leads to the Elysian Fields, where the wonders
of nature are constrained only by the horizon," Natty
said. "It ends at the home of Ethan Hollow and his wife,
Pandora Butterfly Saraswati. When they got married,
Pandora changed her last name from Kumari." She tried
to contain her amusement, but her effort was less than
convincing. "Kumari is the Hindu virgin goddess, you
see, and Saraswati is the divine consort of Lord Brahma.
I don't think we should assume Pandora was a virgin,

much less a virgin goddess. She and Ethan met at an ashram in Oregon."

"So she's a Buddhist named for Greek and Hindu goddesses? The theology seems a bit tangled," I said as I tried to visualize a woman dressed in traditional garb from three religions, along with gold wings and a tinsel halo.

"She's an egotistical flake," Nattie replied, "but harmless. Her children, on the other hand, are vicious weasels. Pandora believes in allowing them to run free in order to expand their consciousness to become one with the universe, or some nonsense like that. Their names are Rainbow and Weevil. Don't be fooled by their innocent smiles and guileless eyes. Remember the movie *Village of the Damned*?"

"I'll watch out for them. What about Ethan?"

Nattie thought for a moment. "He was a rather ordinary boy until he went away to college. He got involved with a radical environmentalist group and dropped out of school to save whales and hug trees. When his parents died in a car crash, he showed up with long, greasy hair and grubby clothes and a contemptuous smirk. I noticed that he spent a lot of time talking to his uncle, Charles Finnelly. I later found out it was about the family business, although I don't know the details. Six weeks after that, Ethan arrived with Pandora and they moved into what had been his parents' house. That was seven years ago. Now he supervises the production end of the business, while Charles and Felicia handle the commercial side. Margaret Louise does the bookkeeping and all the paperwork concerning taxes, licenses, and employees' paychecks. Hollow Valley Nursery is a big enterprise." She pointed at an area of pine trees and undergrowth on the right side of the road. "The greenhouses are over that way, along with outbuildings, cold storage facilities, pumps, irrigation systems, and a garage. There are four delivery trucks, but they won't be a bother because they use a road that leads east to some highway. HVN delivers to Missouri, Oklahoma, and Arkansas. Five years ago Ethan and Charles decided to start a twenty-acre Christmas tree farm. The first harvest will be this season. Each year they've planted four acres of seedlings, so there will always be a fresh crop for Christmas. I suspect it will be very lucrative." She picked up a rock and threw it in the direction of the greenhouses. "As if it matters anymore." Her cackle splintered the bucolic serenity. Unable to respond, I kept my eyes on the pavement and cursed my cell phone's untimely demise.

We turned left and continued up the road. I learned that the second driveway on the left led to the home of Felicia and Charles Finnelly, Felicia being the Hollow descendant. According to my guide, they were in their fifties, very conservative in matters of politics and religion, and tedious. "They both prance around like royals, looking down their snouts at those of us who are mere peasants. I keep waiting for them to whinny," Nattie said. "Beyond their acreage is the green, if you will. Margaret Louise lives in the mill. The exterior is original, but the interior has been remodeled and has two bedrooms upstairs and a lovely sitting room. Presiding over the green is the Old Tavern, where Moses and I reside. It's a dreary place, but I don't have the energy to do anything about it. At night, I hear voices from the original taproom. Nasty, sullen voices. I keep my bedroom door locked and a shotgun next to my bed. There were dozens of murderous brawls over the years, and—"

She broke off as we caught sight of the statue in the middle of the green. Colonel Hollow had his bronze arm raised to send his troops into battle or to order pioneers to go west. The body dangling on a rope tied around his arm did not appear to be going anywhere soon.

CHAPTER 2

Before I could so much as gasp, Nattie took off like a dog after a squirrel. A greyhound, to be more specific. I followed as fast as I could, although sprinting is not among my many talents. By the time I reached the grassy circle delineated by whitewashed stones, Nattie had her hands on her hips and was shouting, "Get down from there before I start paddling your fanny, young lady! We've had enough of your shenanigans! When I tell Ethan about this, he'll have you planting seedlings for a month of Sundays!"

I looked more closely at the body dangling in the breeze. It proved to be that of a teenaged girl dressed in a skimpy blue shirt, denim shorts, and sandals. Her hair was shaved on the sides and stood up in bright purple spikes from her forehead to her nape. She seemed to have a fondness for body piercings; she had silver rings through both of her eyebrows and nostrils, her lower lip, and her navel. The tattoo visible above her waist was a purple dragon with black wings. Her makeup had been applied with vigor. Her eyes were outlined in black, and her lips were purple (to coordinate with her hair, I assumed).

"I mean it, Jordan!" Nattie continued. "Undo that rig right now. Do you realize you would have given Aunt Margaret Louise a heart attack if she found you like that?"

When Jordan raised her head to scowl, I could see that the noose did not go around her neck but merely under the back of her collar. She unbuttoned her shirt and slid her arms out of a harness made of rope. It looked dreadfully uncomfortable, I thought, ordering myself not to appreciate her ingenuity. "Yeah, yeah," she said as she jumped off the pedestal and rubbed her armpits. "It was like a joke, okay? It's so friggin' boring out here that I decided to lighten things up. If Aunt Margaret Louise had a heart attack, at least we'd have some excitement. An ambulance, paramedic hunks, everybody screeching." She gave me an appraising look, dismissed me as boring, and saluted the statue. "Good work, Mo, but you need to do something about that bird poop."

"Put on your shirt, you fourteen-year-old hooligan!" Nattie said. "You'd better be here when Ethan and I get back. Or would you prefer to explain yourself to Uncle Charles?"

Jordan flopped down. "Like I care. Why don't you go ahead and flog me right now—or better yet, send me home. Banish me for life from the hallowed Hollow Valley prison camp."

Nattie shrugged. "Sorry, Claire, but I need to find Ethan. While he flogs Jordan, I'll take you in the Old Tavern to make your call."

"No problem," I said without enthusiasm. There was little point in returning to my dream house in hopes that Angela eventually would remember where she'd left me. The only other option was to wait where I was, despite the proximity of a sulky teenaged girl with a macabre sense of humor. I'd had more experience with pubescent lunacy than I'd ever wanted to have—and then some. Caron and her colleague in crime, Inez Thornton, had stolen frozen frogs from the high school biology lab, been arrested while wearing gorilla suits, broken into a local celebrity's house, and hidden an ancient Egyptian artifact in a hotel room closet. Peter's intervention was the only reason they didn't have rap sheets longer than those of Bonnie and Clyde.

"Who are you?" asked Jordan as she buttoned her shirt. "Did you come to this desolate place to buy potted plants? You're too old to be buying pot plants." She laughed merrily at her witticism. "Get it?"

It did not merit a reply. I looked up at Colonel Moses Ambrose Hollow, who was quite as ugly as Nattie had promised. He looked paunchy in his CSA coat, with beady eyes, bushy eyebrows, a beakish nose, and, below a droopy mustache, a scowl that mocked Jordan's best efforts. The sculptor had been drunk, vicious, or brilliant.

"You didn't come for the thrill of it," Jordan said. "The only thing less exciting than watching grass grow is waiting for geraniums to wilt. I'm supposed to water them, but I always skip a few. Do you think they silently scream when a leaf falls off?"

"Beats me," I said, having no desire to engage in conversation with someone whose idea of a joke was to fake a suicide (or a lynching). To the left of the green, there was a path that led to the old sawmill. The wheel towering behind it was at rest, unsurprising since the stream was lackadaisical. The window boxes were filled with blooms. The Old Tavern was more imposing, made of native stone with hewn wood door and window frames. The windows on both stories had heavy drapes. A bronze plaque beside the entrance asserted that it was built in 1868 and was of historical significance. I could easily envision horse-drawn wagons parked in the shade while logs were cut into planks and bewhiskered men guzzled whiskey inside the smoky tavern. There were no utility poles or satellite dishes in sight. A black Mercedes and a blue Mustang convertible parked under a tree were the only signs of the current century.

"Looks like a movie set, doesn't it?" Jordan tried again. "All pretense, no substance. If you peeked around the corner, you'd see that the facades are two-dimensional, just like the people who live in them. Problem is, it'd be a really boring movie, since nothing ever happens. Next time I may put the noose around my neck." She groaned for my benefit.

"All right," I said, "go ahead and tell me whatever it is that's ruining your life." I sat down on a stone bench and gave her a bright smile. Since Caron's life was ruined weekly because of a pimple or a spat with her first-ever boyfriend, I may not have sounded overly sympathetic.

"Well, I was forced to come here against my will. They almost had to put me in a straitjacket. The people here treat me like, you know, a slave. They're all the time ordering me to work in the fields, plant seeds, or even hose down the floors in the greenhouses. I barely get anything to eat, and I have to get up at like six in the morning. Aunt Margaret Louise won't let me watch any of my TV shows because she says they're vulgar. If she catches me on my cell, she like takes it away. No matter where she hides it, I always find it."

"Do you have it with you?" I asked optimistically.

Jordan snorted. "No, it's in the top dresser drawer in her bedroom. She took it away last night, and this morning decided that she had the sniffles and needed to stay in bed all day. I mean, who cares about the friggin' sniffles! She carried on like 'the sniffles' lead to pneumonia or the plague. When I took her a cup of tea, I thought she was asleep, so I happened to glance in her drawer. She squawked like a turkey." She lay down and stared at the sky. "But why should you care? Nobody else does."

"I didn't say I did care. All I want to do is make a call so someone will come pick me up. As for this slavery nonsense, there are no welts on your back, and you're hardly emaciated. Furthermore, I don't think jokes about slavery are amusing."

"I'm not fat!" Jordan squeaked.

I gazed at her. "No, you're normal, except for the hair, the tattoo, and the piercings. This current fad of self-disfiguration will be replaced by some other madness, and your look will be passé. Your hair will grow out and you can cover the tattoo, but you'll have facial scars forever. Explaining them away will be very boring indeed." I glanced down the road, hoping to see Angela's shiny silver SUV. I toyed with the idea of reporting her to some licensing bureau for real estate malfeasance, but then rejected it because I did want the house, the library, the terrace, the pool, the orchard, and the idyllic meadow. Feeling better, I said to Jordan, "Were you kidnapped by gypsies, who dumped you here when they could no longer bear your charming company?"

"I wish. No, my parents made a deal with Aunt Margaret Louise to make me stay here all summer. They think I'm like incorrigible. If I am, why do they think some doddery old lady can fix me in three months?" She plucked a few blades of grass and let them blow away. "Maybe I am incorrigible. I mean, all they do is yell at me and ground me for weeks at a time. Wanna know what they're going to do in September?" She did not give me a chance to respond with a firm denial. "Send me to some all-girls boarding school in Maine. Whoopee. They wear uniforms and go to chapel every morning. If I'm a good girl the first semester, the spring semester I'll be able to leave the campus on Saturday afternoons for all of four hours.

The next year, I get to go to a mixer every month and hang out with pimply morons from a military school. Punch, cookies, and chaperones." She made a face not unlike that of the Hollow clan's progenitor.

"What did you do to deserve this brutal punishment?" I asked. "Grand theft auto? Murder most foul? Failure to make the varsity lacrosse team?"

"How should I know? According to them, I screw up everything."

I saw Nattie come out from a dirt road that led to the greenhouses and fields. With her was a short, muscular man with a wispy billy-goat beard and ponytail, wire-rimmed glasses, and a red bandanna headband. He wore threadbare denim overalls. I assumed he was Ethan, somewhat more civilized but unlikely to join the Jaycees. He and Nattie were conversing in low, agitated voices. I heard Jordan mutter something best not repeated but reeking with contempt. If I'd been her parent, I would have found a boarding school in Saudi Arabia. In a burka, no one would see her body bling or hear her crude comments.

Ethan gestured to Jordan, who arose and trudged in his direction. She and Nattie exchanged dark looks as they passed. "Claire," Nattie said as she joined me, "please forgive the delay. That child is a mess, don't you think? I have to admit that I admire her spunk, but she's determined to make herself miserable. Come inside and I'll make tea while you call your husband."

The living room of the Old Tavern lacked the airiness of what I now thought of as my house. The furniture was heavy, and the low ceiling was oppressive. Nattie showed me the telephone and then disappeared down a hall. When I called Peter's cell, it went to voice mail, so I crossed my fingers and called the PD. The dispatcher recognized my voice and, after a few pleasantries, told me that Peter was in a meeting. I pleaded my case until she agreed it was most surely an emergency and went to extricate him.

"What's wrong?" he demanded with suitable urgency. "Are you okay?"

I felt as if I should respond like a princess warrior holding back the barbarians, but I doubted it would go over well. "I'm fine, darling. It's just that I'm stuck out here without a car and I need a ride home."

"Stuck out where?" he asked with a great deal less urgency in his voice. A less charitable person than I might have noted a tinge of irritation.

I explained the situation, tactfully omitting the drunk on the sofa and the pseudo-cide. "The house is absolutely perfect," I went on. "It has every last thing I could ever want. This'll give you the opportunity to see it before I buy it."

There was a moment of silence. "There isn't any point in arguing that I'm in a meeting with the county law enforcement department heads, is there?"

"No," I said, since I've always believed that honesty is the bedrock of a successful marriage. My first husband had not held that belief, although he might have changed his mind as a chicken truck plowed into his car, killing both him and a blond coed. I gave Peter directions, reminded him of how adorable he was, and was replacing the receiver when Nattie came in with a tea tray. "This is very kind of you, Nattie. My husband's going to meet me at the house in half an hour. Is there any chance you might remove Moses in the interim?"

"Of course." She poured me a cup of tea and offered a plate of cookies. "How long has your husband been a police officer, Claire?"

I gave her a recap of Peter's rise from lieutenant to deputy chief, careful not to mention his mysterious ties to the CIA. This is not to imply I knew much. Peter had informed me that the less I knew, the less inclined I would be to blurt out some juicy, top secret tidbit. My moderately piqued response had led to supercilious remarks about my undeserved reputation for meddling in crimes that were, in his esteemed opinion, none of my business. I'd begged to differ, pointing out my invaluable contributions to solving murders. After that, the conversation had not gone well.

Nattie nodded. "We'd better go back to the house. Moses could be licking the wallpaper or dancing naked in the yard. That may not be the best first impression for your husband."

I couldn't argue with that.

As we walked past the statue, I saw that the rope no longer dangled from the Colonel's arm. Jordan was not howling in the distance, so I supposed that Ethan had matters under his green thumb. I wondered if we might find Angela on the porch swing, berating herself for her thoughtless treachery. She was not, nor was Moses, to be found anywhere inside the house. Nattie continued toward the apple orchard. I put the empty wine bottles in a trash can, the grapes and Brie back in the refrigerator, and was headed for the porch when I saw Angela's slim leather briefcase on the floor under a table in the entry. I was surprised, since she wasn't careless.

Peter arrived a few minutes later. After he got out of the car, he studied the front of the house. I waved from the swing, like a demure country maiden. Without either of us speaking, I gave him the grand tour of the house, the pool, the orchard, and the view of the meadow and stream. We returned to the terrace and sat down on the glider. I waited with a goodly amount of trepidation.

"Well," he said slowly, "it will require a lot of maintenance. Mowing and weeding, the pool, the flower beds . . ."

"That's what checkbooks are for. The only blisters on the Rosen boys' hands are related to regattas and golf."

"True." He crossed his arms. "I didn't see a wine cellar."

"Because we didn't go down to the cellar," I said, willing to play his little game as long as I prevailed in the end. "The furnishings come with the house, unless we want to donate them to charity. It needs artwork, but we can always commission a Monet to hang above the mantel. Je suis sûr que Monsieur Monet would welcome les millions de francs."

"Je suis sûr qu'il est mort."

"Zut alors, we'll have to shop around."

"You're sure this is the house?" Peter asked softly.

My amorous attack served well as my answer. He admitted that the house was ideal for us and for Caron. Once we'd disentangled, he said, "How much, and when can we move in?"

"That's the tricky part," I said, then told him what Angela had said about possible complications. "We need to talk to her. She left her briefcase here, and it ought to have a business card with her cell phone number. I'll go dig one out and call her."

"While I investigate the cellar," he said as we stood up.

"To search for her body?" I gasped. In that her SUV was gone, I'd logically decided she'd driven away in it, à la Occam's razor.

"To search for wine racks."

He handed me his cell phone, and we parted ways. I took Angela's briefcase to the kitchen island and pulled out its disappointingly meager contents. There were several letters from her lawyer, but I'd already heard in great detail about the latest legal maneuvers. I put aside some manila folders and scrabbled in the bottom of the briefcase until I found her business cards in a monogrammed gold case.

I dialed her cell number and held my breath until it went to voice mail. I tried her office and was informed by a recorded voice that they were closed for the day. I replaced the files and letters and waited for Peter.

"Did you get hold of her?" he asked when he emerged from the hall.

"No, and her office is closed. I feel as though I should do something, but I don't know what." My characteristic stoicism was washed away by a wave of discouragement. "What if someone else is signing an offer at this very minute? I've looked at every house for sale in Farberville. Even if we have to build, we'll never find property with an apple orchard and a meadow. I've always wanted a meadow of my own."

Peter put his arms around me. "You told me the house isn't on the market. No one is going to buy it from under us. Angela will call tonight with an excuse about why she had to leave. You will accept her apology and tell her we're prepared to sign an offer immediately."

"Can you put up yellow tape and claim it's a crime scene? Then no one else can even look at it."

He winced. "The fact that Angela drove off without you isn't exactly a crime."

"Well, it should be." I took the briefcase with me as we went out to his car. As we drove home, Peter told me that he was flying to Little Rock early the next morning and Atlanta in the evening. I pleaded for him to wait until we located Angela and signed papers, but he countered with nonsense about the governor and the state's attorney general and his complete faith in me to handle the real estate transaction. I made several uncouth remarks about the state officials, the task force, and his exalted status with

unlimited power to reschedule lame, dreary meetings in
which everything was rehashed to the consistency of
mush, and went so far as to mention the name of Angela's
divorce lawyer. Peter spent the remainder of the ride ver-
bally stocking the wine cellar with Bordeaux and merlots
and champagne from les châteaux de whatever.

The next morning Peter left at dawn. I lingered in bed
until a more civilized hour, attended to the necessities to
begin the day, poured a cup of coffee, and called Angela's
cell number. I'd done so the previous evening every fifteen minutes until midnight without luck, and I wasn't
shocked to be informed that her message box was full. I
moved on to the real estate office, officially known as
Bartleby-King and Associates. The receptionist answered
with a manically friendly "Good morning! Welcome to
Bartleby-King and Associates! To whom may I direct
your call?"

"Angela Delmond, please."

"Ah, let me see if she's free." She put me on hold for a
minute. "No, Ms. Delmond is not available at this time.
Let me transfer you to one of our best agents, a recent
graduate of—"

"I need to speak to Angela."

"I'm sure you'll be just as satisfied with Gilda Can-
nella. Let me transfer—"

"Transfer me to the broker."

"Well, Mr. King's out of the country. I'll have to put
you on hold while I see if Mr. Bartleby's with a client.
Your name is . . . ?"

"Claire Malloy. I want to sign an offer on the house
that Angela showed me yesterday."

I was replaced on hold and allowed to listen to elevator
music for a good five minutes. When the receptionist
came back on the line, her bubbliness had evaporated.

"Mr. Bartleby just left for a closing. If you'll leave your number, he'll call you back in the next day or two."

This meant I would have ample time to read the entire *Encyclopedia Britannica* before I spoke to him. I gave her my number, then hung up and went to refill my coffee cup. Caron was staring at a cabinet crammed with boxes and cans.

She frowned at me. "If I try to extract my cereal box, I'll be buried alive by saltines and cornflakes. Don't put that on my headstone, okay?"

"Have some toast," I said. I could not prevent myself from comparing her to Jordan. Instead of a purple Mohawk and piercings, Caron had my curly red hair and freckles. Even her earlobes were unsullied. On the other hand, her expression was vaguely reminiscent of Jordan's (and Colonel Hollow's). "Very soon you'll have a kitchen with a dozen cabinets and storage shelves. You will never again live in fear of being struck dead by a can of corn."

"What does that mean?"

"I found the perfect house. It has four bedrooms, four bathrooms, a balcony from which to drop rose petals, a pool, a big terrace, an orchard—"

"You bought a house Without Consulting Me? What if I don't like it?"

"I invited you to come along yesterday, but you were too busy talking on the phone to Inez about Joel. You spent the night at her house, for pity's sake. Unless he proposed, it could have waited an hour." I saw no reason to mention that the hour had lasted more than three hours. "If I may paraphrase your remark, you said you didn't care what house we bought as long as you had your own bathroom."

"Of course I care! I have to live there for a whole year, you know. I'd be absolutely humiliated if I invited my friend over to a teepee or something. Does it have an attic with a resident psychotic who stumbles around in the house after we've gone to bed? I'll bet he has a chain saw."

"I believe it's a machete."

She stuck a piece of bread in the toaster. "That's a relief."

In the living room, I described the house in detail, emphasizing the glories of her private bathroom and walk-in closet. When I mentioned the meadow and stream, she interrupted. "There aren't any meadows or streams in Farberville. Just where is this house?"

"Not too far," I said glibly, "and the pool is enormous. You can have the best pool parties all summer. We'll get a grill so you can fix hot dogs and hamburgers."

Caron rarely bought my evasions. "How far?"

"Ten minutes or so." I was sure Dr. Spock would allow a parent to fib if it was in the child's best interest. "It's in a place called Hollow Valley."

"So it's hollow? It sounds more like a hole than a valley. Are there Hobbits?"

I gave her a brief rundown of the history of the place, omitting any references to the less-desirable resident members of the Hollow family. "We haven't signed an offer because Angela drove off, leaving me there. She won't answer her cell phone, and she's not at the office. At least I think she's not at the office," I said slowly, "but I do have her briefcase because she left it at the house."

Peter had propped it against a wall next to the small dining table, the table itself being piled so high with junk that it had alpine slopes. I fetched it, sidestepped a box of extraneous kitchen gadgets, and sat back on the sofa. I put the legal correspondence aside and began to examine the manila folders. The contents were mostly forms for offers, photocopies of signed paperwork and inspection reports, and bids from plumbing and tile businesses.

Apparently someone was demanding a remodeled bathroom before the purchase date. There was a booklet of listings, with terse comments written in the margin. The house in Hollow Valley did not appear on any of the paperwork.

"Maybe she's hiding at home," Caron suggested.

Her business card had only her office's address. "I guess I can try the telephone directory," I said.

"Stay here and drink your coffee," my darling daughter ordered. She went to her bedroom and returned a half minute later. Handing me a scrap of paper, she said, "Here are her home telephone number and address."

"How did you get these so quickly?"

Caron gave me a pained look. "On my computer, naturally. Nobody uses a telephone directory anymore, Mother. In a year or two, there won't be any telephone directories. You have a computer at the Book Depot. All businesses, even bookstores, have online sales. Do you even know what an e-mail is?"

I dialed Angela's home number, which greeted me with a male voice announcing that Danny and Angela weren't home but would return my call. I thought of several colorful Anglo-Saxon expletives but kept them to myself. "All I can see to do is drive to her house and pound on the door. If she's not there, I'll go to her office and find someone with information about the listing."

"Sherlock couldn't have come up with a better plan," Caron said as she headed for the bathroom. "Let me know if you find out anything."

"You have twenty minutes to get ready," I said to her back.

"Inez and I are going to the mall to hang out. Joel said he'd be there unless his mother pulls some obnoxious scheme to ruin his life."

"Shall I e-mail her and offer some suggestions?"

The bathroom door closed with unnecessary vigor, but not quickly enough to muffle the "Oh, Mother!"

We picked up Inez and drove to Angela's. I told Inez about the Hollow Valley house. She sounded excited, despite what I'm sure was a barrage of dirty looks across the backseat. Angela and the wretched Danny lived in a pricey neighborhood. Their house was a two-story brick mini mansion with imposing trees and ivied walls. I parked in the driveway and walked to the front door, keeping an eye out for twitching curtains or glimpses of an ashen face. Unlike in the black-and-white movies of yore, the windows remained blank. I rang the doorbell, waited for a moment, rang it again, and began to knock as loudly as I could. I kept this up for three minutes before acknowledging both the futility of it and the soreness of my knuckles.

Caron and Inez joined me. The former said, "We looked in all the ground-floor windows. I don't think anybody's home." Inez happily described the frilly decor and panoply of china vases and marble bowls, but I ignored her as I considered my next move.

"May I help you?" asked a Hispanic woman walking up the driveway. "I am the housekeeper. Do you want to leave a message for Mrs. Delmond? I can give it to her when she gets here."

"I'm a friend of Mrs. Delmond, and I'm worried about her. I've called and called, but I haven't heard back from her. We need to find her now. She could have tripped and broken her leg and be lying on the floor." Or worse, if Danny Delmond had lured her to their house with a mendacious claim concerning arson or vandalism.

The woman was not an easy mark. "You wait here and I'll see if she's home." She took a key out of her purse and unlocked the door, then went inside and closed it firmly. Caron and Inez took the opportunity to discuss Rhonda

Maguire's new haircut and the way she'd been snorkeling for compliments even though it looked like a pile of straw. I sat down on a step and tried to convince myself that no one was buying my house from under me.

The door opened, and the woman said, "Mrs. Delmond is not here, and her car is not in the garage. I do not think she slept here last night. I got to clean the house so I can get to my next job." As she closed the door, she added, "Majors Americanas stupids!"

I deduced that it was not a flattering remark. I ordered Caron and Inez back into the car and drove to Bartleby-King and Associates. "At least we know one place Angela isn't," I said.

"If she's driving at sixty miles per hour," Inez chimed in, "she could be over twelve hundred miles away. She'd already be in New York City or Miami, and close to Los Angeles. If she went to Chicago, she'd be back here by now."

Caron does not care to relinquish center stage. "Oh, like she'd drive round-trip to Chicago to buy a pizza or something. Give Me a Break!"

I was no more pleased than Caron to have the information. I parked in front of the office building that Bartleby-King shared with an orthodontist and an insurance company. I left Caron and Inez both texting with astounding alacrity and went inside, where I was greeted by a young woman. "I'm here to see Angela Delmond," I said with maternal steeliness.

She was clearly flustered. "Oh, you called earlier, didn't you? Angela's not here, like I said." She glanced at a closed door. "Mr. Bartleby's not here, either. I don't know when to expect him. If you want to write a message, I'll make sure he sees it as soon as he gets back from, ah, his closing. He may have scheduled a lunch appointment, and he usually goes to the bank on Fridays."

"Today's Wednesday. I do not desire to stay here until Friday afternoon, but I will. I prefer coffee with a splash of cream, and iced cake doughnuts sprinkled with coconut." I sat down on the couch and reached for a magazine.

The receptionist scurried down a hallway. I wondered if she was planning to go out the back door. I should have had Caron and Inez guard the exits so that we could, if the situation necessitated it, smoke out the office occupants one at a time. Peter most likely would be upset when he heard about it, I told myself as I watched buttons light up on the receptionist's phone. When it became evident that I wasn't getting any coffee, I opened the door in the corner.

A man looked up from his desk. "Mrs. Malloy," he said, no doubt having been warned via the intra-office phone line, "as Jennifer already told you, Angela Delmond is not here. Frankly, we don't know where she is. She failed to show up last evening to meet some clients, and again this morning. If you have any information concerning her whereabouts, I'd like to know." He glared at me as if I'd kidnapped Angela and was there to demand a ransom.

"So would I." I sat down in a leather chair and appraised him. His hairline was receding, and he was dressed in a dark suit, white shirt, and navy blue tie. He had the look of a staunch member of the chamber of commerce and the obligatory civic clubs. To his credit, he did seem worried about Angela. "Have you spoken to her husband?"

"No reason to. Danny's living in a condo near Thurber Street. He has plenty of friends in the building, since it's where all the middle-of-a-divorce boys camp out until the property is settled."

"He and his girlfriend?" I asked.

"I don't know anything about that," Bartleby said, pretending to be shocked at my insinuation. "You had an appointment yesterday afternoon with Angela?"

"She showed me a house, and my husband and I want to buy it." I told him about Angela's abrupt departure and my attempts to call her.

Bartleby beamed at me. "That's wonderful, Mrs. Malloy. Is Mr. Malloy here with you? Tell him to come on in and we'll get started on the offer. Don't you worry about Angela—I'll make sure she gets her share of the commission."

"My name is Ms. Malloy, and my husband's name is Peter Rosen. He's out of town, but I'm quite capable of signing the offer. The house is located in Hollow Valley. I don't have the address, but surely you do."

"Hollow Valley? That doesn't sound familiar." He took out a notebook and thumbed through it. "There's a lovely house on Holland Avenue, three bedrooms, two baths, and a fireplace. At the listed price it's a bargain, but we can try to get the sellers to come down a few thousand dollars—"

"Hollow Valley," I interrupted before he filled out an offer form and stabbed my hand with a pen. "It's at the northeast edge of Farberville, barely within the city limits. It has four bedrooms and four bathrooms, French doors, and is unoccupied but fully furnished."

"Nope, doesn't ring a bell. Maybe it just came on the market yesterday. You stay here while I check with the sales team. Somebody has to know something."

While he went in search of information, I gazed at the duck prints hanging on his office walls, along with all manner of framed awards and citations. The photo of the Bartleby-King Little League team members hinted at a less than victorious season, if their tiny trophies were indicative. Several years ago I'd been asked to sponsor a team, but the Book Depot didn't have enough cash to buy a baseball—even a used one.

"This is puzzling," Bartleby said as he entered the office. "This house you described isn't listed by anyone. Angela knows we have very strict guidelines about private sales. We have to keep a roof over our heads, don't we?" His chuckle was strained.

"Did you look in her desk?"

"Thoroughly searched." He leaned back in his chair to stare at me. "Did Angela mention a price?"

I shook my head. "Only that it was well below market value. What about her computer? It might have some information."

"It might, but we insist that our agents change their passwords weekly. There have been accusations of poaching clients and potential listings. I'm sure a hacker could get into her files, but our office policy forbids it. Trust is essential to team success."

He'd attended too many seminars on management techniques. I pictured him falling backward into his colleagues' protective arms—or cracking his head on the floor. "You're sure Danny isn't involved?" I asked.

"Danny's an outstanding member of our community. He served on the school board and organized the upcoming Babes, Boobs, and Bling biker rally. There's going to be a wet T-shirt contest and live music on Saturday. Good, clean family fun. Now you just let me take care of this, Ms. Malloy. Angela will pop up before too long, and then we can make sure you get that house you're so fond of." He stood up, in case I'd missed the cue to leave. "I've got an appointment in five minutes. Afterward, I'll go ahead and call Danny. If he knows anything, I'll pass it along."

I exited graciously, but I was fuming as I got in the car.

"I don't suppose either of you knows how to hack into a computer," I said as I leaned my forehead on the steering wheel. "Wait, I don't want to know the answer. It's likely to be a federal offense."

"It is," Inez said.

"So you might as well let us go to the mall," Caron added smugly. "Can I borrow twenty dollars?"

CHAPTER 3

"Let's go out to the Hollow Valley house," I suggested brightly. "Angela may be asleep in a bed, à la Goldilocks."

"I left my red hoodie at home," muttered Caron. "You go right ahead, Mother, but keep an eye out for a big, bad wolf. He might blow your house down. Please can I borrow the twenty dollars? I swear I'll pay you back tomorrow."

"With what?"

"With the twenty dollars you pay me for breaking into Angela's house. Fifty if the housekeeper's there. Please, Mother?"

Peter would not be happy if he got back to Farberville on the day of her arraignment. I dumped them at the duplex and went to the Book Depot to brood. The clerk whom Peter had hired for me was a grad student from the English Department. He'd told me that he'd been writing his dissertation for five and a half years on James Joyce's use of alliteration. As I came inside, he stuck a book under the counter and stared at me with disconcerting intensity.

I flinched. "Did we receive the shipment from that small press in Arizona?"

"Yes, Ms. Malloy. I went over the invoice and placed it on your desk." He consulted a notepad. "The sales rep for the college press dropped off the fall catalog. The fall reading lists from the area public schools and the college are on your desk. I wrote up the orders, and as soon as you review them, I'll submit them electronically. I've re-arranged the window display for this month. In mid-July, I thought we might run a sale on beach books—if you approve, of course. I repaired the leak in the lavatory. The exterminator is coming on Friday."

"Thank you," I said weakly. The Book Depot, my musty, unruly baby, was in more capable hands. My desk was neater than it had been in a decade. The filing cabinets' drawers could be closed without straining, and the habitual clutter atop them had been vanquished. My wastebasket was empty. As I sat down behind my desk, I felt as though I were intruding. Sighing, I reached for the order forms. Which were thorough and flawless.

A few customers came in to browse and left with paperbacks, study guides, or nothing whatsoever. My science fiction hippie, replete with scruffy hair, tangled beard, and pink flip-flops, shuffled inside and ducked behind a rack. After a while, I cornered him and frisked him with the diligence of a TSA officer. Once I'd removed the paperbacks he'd stashed in the pockets of his odiferous army surplus jacket, we chatted amiably as I escorted him out the door. If the Book Depot ever closed, I'd miss him, fleas and all.

I was accomplishing nothing. My beloved house was beginning to blur in my mind. Were the drapes in the master bedroom pearl or ash gray? How many bar stools were available should I desire to entertain guests with a demonstration of my cooking prowess (after a semester at Le Cordon Bleu)? Did the foyer have an umbrella stand?

If I couldn't deal with the elusive Angela or the pompous broker, I needed to cut out the flotsam in the middle and speak to the owner. I would simply tell him that I wanted to buy the house. No quibbling or bargaining required. He would accept the check and hand over the key. Nattie had said something about the house belonging to Winston. I opened the telephone directory. Winston was his first name; Hollow was apt to be his surname. Although my deductive skill was admirable, Winston Hollow had not deigned to allow his name to be published in such a plebeian locale, nor had any of his fellow Hollows. All the surnamed Winstons lived on familiar streets. I closed the directory.

Caron, bless her parsimonious heart, could have used her computer to locate him in the bowels of Tasmania or wherever else he was hiding from me. She would not be pleased if I interrupted her rendezvous at the mall, however. A rather clever idea came to mind. I went out to the counter, where the clerk was wiping the wood surface with lemon-scented polish.

"I need to find somebody," I said to him, "but I don't know how to search on the Internet. Will you do it for me?"

"I would prefer not to."

"Why not? I am your employer, you know. Do you have scruples that preclude Internet snooping? I'm not stalking someone. Please give me one good reason why you won't try."

"I would prefer not to."

"Not to explain your refusal?"

His expression was unfathomable, and I wasn't at all surprised when he said, "I would prefer not to."

I might have wrung his neck had it not been unseemly.

"Well," I said with a delicate harrumph, "I do hope that you would prefer not to end your sentences with a preposition!" I swept out the front door before he could respond and leaned against the hood of my car to regain my innate sense of decorum. Had Peter not been so thoughtless as to be incommunicado, he could have his buddies at the CIA find Winston in a nanosecond. I ran through my list of friends and acquaintances who were computer literate. Luanne, my best friend, was spending the summer in Greece, in search of Zorbaesque bimboys. The Haskells were on sabbatical in England, and Maggie Knott was visiting grandchildren in North Carolina. Babs Peabody was in rehab for the third or fourth time. I would have made some calls to others who might be in town, but I'd yet to recharge my cell phone—and I wasn't about to go back inside the Book Depot after such a magnificent parting shot.

The library was six blocks away. I parked, went inside, and asked for help at the reference desk. The twenty-something woman did her best to hide her disdain as she settled me in front of a computer, clicked hither and thither, and then showed me how to search for pretty much everybody and everything in the universe. Naturally, I typed in my name first, then spent a satisfying hour reading newspaper articles that mentioned my minor contributions to solving murder cases in Farberville. The events in Egypt were not noted, courtesy of various covert agencies.

I typed Winston Hollow's name in the box and waited. My eyebrows rose as I read the local newspaper's brief article concerning the accidental death of Winston Hollow Martinson. It had taken place in early spring, behind his home in Hollow Valley. Police had been called to the scene, where an unnamed relative had found the body tangled in branches at the edge of a river. Fishing tackle was found on the bank upstream, along with marks in the mud that indicated that the victim had lost his footing and been knocked unconscious as he fell into the water. His housemate, Terry Kennedy, was in Europe at the time, which explained why Winston Martinson's absence had not been noticed for a week. Case closed.

The obituary was not much longer. Winston, son of Victor Martinson and Sara Hollow Martinson, both deceased, had been thirty-six at the time of his death. He had a degree in fine arts from a liberal arts college on the East Coast and had designed sets for off-Broadway theater shows before returning to Farberville three years ago to focus on painting. He'd never married and had no offspring. There was no mention of a funeral or memorial service.

A psychic would be required to get in touch with someone currently resting in peace—or decomposing, according to one's beliefs. My beliefs precluded séances as a way to negotiate a real estate deal.

My first impulse was to drive out to Hollow Valley, but Nattie had not sounded as though she knew much about the house. Angela claimed to be in communication with the owner. That ruled out Winston, who must have inherited the property from his mother. I reread the article about the death, copied down the name of the housemate, and entered it on the computer screen.

Terry Kennedy's name generated almost nine hundred thousand results. The majority of them referred to a professional skateboarder, but others were lawyers, politicians, furniture dealers, and professors. I quit scanning pages and sat back. The highly overrated Internet was not going to print out a card that read: "Terry Kennedy, previous resident of Hollow Valley, close friend of deceased Winston Hollow Martinson, currently lives at such-and-so, with telephone and cell phones numbers as follows . . ." Nor would it tell me where Angela was or where she hid her house key.

I wondered if it might tell me the current owner of the house and the meadow that sloped gently down to the spot where Winston had died. I found the young librarian and requested more help. This time her expression implied that she questioned my ability to operate an electric can opener, but she sat down in front of the computer and located a Web site for the county assessor. I took the seat with great optimism. It faded into nothingness as I realized that I was required to enter bizarre information about sections, townships, blocks, lots, and subdivisions. About the only thing not required was my favorite color.

Confident that I was more effective with people than with machines, I drove to the courthouse and dutifully followed signs and arrows to the county assessor's office. An older man, wearing a name tag that identified him as K. Scott, listened to my abbreviated explanation and led me to a room with the ambience of a neglected warehouse. Dauntingly large plat books were piled on tables or on shelves that towered above my head. I sneezed, blinked, and then sneezed again.

"The dust," I said feebly, fighting back another sneeze without success. My eyes welled with tears as my lungs contracted.

"Allow me to assist you," K. Scott said, either eager to serve the public or terrified I might die on the spot and require him to remain beyond five o'clock. He asked questions about the route to Hollow Valley, which I answered between sniffs and sneezes, while he peered at a faded county map. He disappeared into the labyrinth of shelves and then emerged with a plat book. After asking more questions, he finally jabbed the pertinent page.

"Here it is!" He consulted his wristwatch. "Nineteen minutes and forty-five seconds! I do believe I've set a new record. Come along, dear woman."

I wiped my eyes with a tissue as I followed him back to the main office. He sat down in front of a computer, typed furiously, and then pointed at the screen. "Section seventeen, township nine, the northeast quarter of the southeast quarter and so forth. The owner of record is Terry M. Kennedy. It came to him through joint tenancy with right of survivorship."

"You found that out from the legal description?"

"Good heavens, no. He's a polite young man, and he told me when he brought in a modified deed to be filed. He had the necessary forms, all signed, dated, and notarized. I can't begin to tell you how many people barge in here without any idea how to—" K. Scott caught himself with the agility of an acrobat. "Would you like his address?" Without waiting for a reply, he turned his attention back to the keyboard, scribbled a couple of lines on a notepad, and then ripped off the page and handed it to me.

I felt as though I should kneel to accept the Holy Grail while a choir belted out the "Hallelujah Chorus." I managed to croak, "Thank you so very, very much, Mr. Scott. I am eternally grateful for your help. If you come by the Book Depot on Thurber Street, I'll give you an armful of books."

"It was my duty as a public servant," he said stiffly. "We are never allowed to receive private compensation."

I was relieved he hadn't said that he would prefer not to. I scampered down the hall, waited impatiently as the elevator creaked to the first floor, and barely kept myself from dancing across the parking lot to my car. Terry M. Kennedy lived in Key West, Florida. His house was a thousand miles from Farberville, but my telephone was only one mile from the courthouse.

Once at home, I went immediately to said telephone. I took a gulp of scotch before I picked up the receiver and prompted a cyber-operator to find Terry M. Kennedy's telephone number. The robotic voice recited the number and offered to dial it for a nominal charge. I wrote down the three-zero-five area code and the number, then put down the receiver before I dropped it on my foot. I tried not to salivate as I envisioned the house, furnishings, French doors, walnut bookcases, swimming pool, orchard, meadow, bucolic setting, elderly trees, and vibrant flowers. The tears that filled my eyes were not caused by an allergy but by a yearning that gripped me so tightly that I struggled to take a breath.

I stopped myself before I fell into a pose for the cover of a romance novel. My bosom was not heaving. Peter was not standing in the doorway, managing to both sneer and leer at the same time. I had an obligation to him, as well as to myself, to find an adequately spacious house. Pathos has no place in the real estate business, nor does melodrama. I was my own agent, negotiator, and broker. I flipped open a notebook and turned to an unsullied page. I found an extra pen in case it was needed. I refilled my glass and took a ladylike sip. I crossed my legs as I picked up the receiver. I waited until a ripple of dizziness passed and dialed the number.

"Hello," said a tenor voice.

"This is, uh, Claire Malloy and I want your house!" My words spewed out with the velocity of bullets, but I couldn't constrain myself. "It's everything I want and I've never had a meadow or a stream or a real library. I don't care about the price. I mean, I do care if it's millions of dollars, but I still want it and when can we move in?"

"My house doesn't have a library," he said cautiously. "The Gulf Stream originates in this region, but I don't think I can sell it to you."

"You have to! It's perfect! I looked at all the houses on the market, and not one of them is anywhere near as spacious and secluded and wonderful. Just tell me how much, Mr. Kennedy. You can't sell it to anyone else. You just can't!"

"Oh, I get it. You're not talking about my house in Key West. You're talking about the one in Farberville."

"Obviously," I said, wondering if he had suffered a traumatic head injury that impaired his mind. "Angela told me that you're willing to sell it. How much?"

"Let's take this slowly. Your name is Claire Malloy?" He paused until I acknowledged as much. "I've heard of you. You helped the police in a lot of murder investigations. Winston patronized your bookstore."

"All the more reason to sell me the house in Hollow Valley. Surely Winston would have approved."

"Are you or your husband related to any descendants of Colonel Hollow?"

I uttered an oath under my breath. "No, but I bet a genealogist could find a link somewhere in the past. I'm sure I had a seventeenth cousin somewhere who married a Hollow. Do they have Irish blood?"

"They have no blood, Ms. Malloy. No, I take that back. Winston was a warm, generous man who donated time and energy to charitable organizations. He loved music, art, literature, fine wine, and gourmet dining. He was offered the opportunity to design a set for a major Broadway musical, but he chose to move back to his boyhood home." Terry's voice was quivering with such emotion that his words were slurred. Had he been within reach, I would have patted his hand and blotted his cheeks with the pillowcase hem.

I gave him a brief moment to pull himself together before I said, "You have my warmest condolences. The mere mention of the house must cause you pain. I can understand why you feel it's time to sell it and get on with your life. As I mentioned, Angela showed me the house, but before I could sign an offer, she drove off. No one seems to know where she is."

"Did any of the Hollows know she was showing the house?"

"I have no idea. After Angela left, I spoke to a woman named Nattie. She was surprised to hear the house was for sale."

"It isn't."

My throat tightened. "Angela said that you're willing to sell it. I love the house, and so does my husband. You can't snatch it away like this." Desperation overrode morals. "My daughter is so weak from her treatments that she can hardly walk. Her only hope is fresh air and sunshine. If she could lie on a blanket in the meadow while I read to her from the shade of an apple tree, she might improve. Please, Mr. Kennedy. Only you can save her."

"Or Charles Dickens, presuming your daughter contracted consumption in the workhouse. I need to think about this, Ms. Malloy. I'll call you back this evening."

I retreated to the balcony to wait.

Caron and Peter were briefed on the situation. Peter, who was in Little Rock, offered all the usual platitudes, sprinkled with endearing remarks, and assured me that he was frantic to learn what Terry Kennedy said. Caron expressed her solicitude by heading out to a pizza place to meet her friends, one of whom was Joel.

I was perfecting my argument when Terry Kennedy called. "Claire," he began, "if I may call you that, I am willing to discuss the house, but we need to talk in person. I should be in Farberville by late tomorrow afternoon. As soon as I've checked into a motel, I'll call you."

"You're not going to stay at your house?"

There was a long silence. "Maybe I will," he finally said. "It could be interesting. In any case, we'll talk tomorrow. I was so startled by your earlier call that I didn't ask about Angela. She, Winston, and I were friends. You said that she disappeared?"

I told him what I knew, which wasn't much, then said, "Do you have any idea where she could be? She's divorcing Danny and it seems that she forgot all about me."

"Angela will come up with some crazy rationalization. I'll call you tomorrow afternoon."

I tripped over a box of Christmas ornaments as I went to the kitchen to find something for dinner. Ah, the perils of tiptoeing along the fine line between optimism and pessimism.

Caron was still asleep when I left the duplex the following morning. I drove to Angela's house and rang the doorbell, but there was no response. I'd already called Bartleby-King and Associates; Angela had yet to resume associating with them. She had been missing for almost forty-eight hours. It was premature to file a missing persons report. Since I had nothing worthwhile to do until Terry arrived from Key West, I decided to drive out to Hollow Valley on the off-chance she was there—and spend some time in my future home, counting bar stools and examining the bedroom decor.

Twenty minutes later, I turned at the Hollow Valley Nursery sign. Before I reached the driveway to my house, a willowy woman with hair so pale that it wafted around her face and shoulders like a cirrus cloud leaped out into the road and began to pirouette. Her oversized gauzy white shirt rippled like feathers. I hit the brakes before I mowed down the Swan Queen. In response, she wiggled her fingers at me before returning to her invisible lamentation of cygnets.

I tolerated the amateurish production for several minutes, then opened my car window and said, "That was lovely. If you'll be so kind as to move aside, I'll just drive around you and be out of your way."

"You're not bothering me," she trilled as she began hopping about, her arms swaying over her head. "I'm channeling the deities of Litha so we can prepare for the Midsummer's Eve bonfire and the appearance of Juno Luna, the goddess who blesses women with the privilege of menstruation. Come dance, whoever you are! The sun seeks its zenith. Free yourself and feel the warmth and perfume of nature!"

"Another day, but thank you anyway."

Pandora Butterfly, or so I presumed, gave me a wee frown. She twirled to a halt and said, "You won't dance with me?"

"I would prefer not to," I said solemnly, then clamped my lips together. A giggle erupted, followed by another and another, until I was sprawled across the front seat, tears streaking down my face, laughing so hard I was in danger of wetting my pants.

Pandora stuck her head inside the car. "Are you okay, lady?"

I stayed where I was until I could present a more dignified visage. She retreated as I sat up, although I could not contain an occasional snort. "I'm okay, and you're okay. You're Pandora, right?"

"Pandora Butterfly Saraswati," she said. "Who are you?"

"Just one of the minor Litha deities. I thought I'd come by early and examine the site of the bonfire. Last year the Wiccans in Omaha almost burned down an apartment complex."

Her pale blue eyes narrowed. "Are you looking for the nursery? It's a wholesale operation, so you can't buy anything except during the annual sale." Fine wrinkles around her eyes put her in her midthirties, although she probably fancied herself to be an innocent maiden. All she was missing was flowers in her hair.

In that she would be a neighbor of sorts, I got out of the car and said, "I'm Claire Malloy. My husband and I are hoping to buy Winston's house."

"Oh, really? Does the family know it's for sale?"

"I doubt it. It's a lovely house, isn't it?"

She tilted her head and stared at me. "The redness of your aura tells me that you are filled with strength, blending into the yellowness of optimism and enthusiasm. I also see a tinge of orange that indicates vanity. You may be a daunting combatant, Claire, but you must beware. Your aura is in danger of shifting into a fiery red that connotes raw passion and ruthlessness."

"Works for me," I said, politely overlooking the reference to vanity. I take pride in my modest, unassuming nature. I make it a point never to undermine Peter's masculinity by asserting that I am quite capable of carrying out the trash on a cold night.

Pandora tried a soaring leap that sent her into an oak sapling. She spit out a leaf and said, "Some days my aura is so light I can levitate, but today I am bathed in blue and green. I feel peaceful and nurturing, as well as spiritual. I should go into the woods and listen to the whispers of nature, but I shall wait until dusk. Would you like to come to my house for tea?"

It seemed like as good a plan as any, and she might have information about Terry Kennedy. I parked at the edge of the road, and we walked down her overgrown driveway to what would have been an elegant house had it not been painted in hues of purple and lavender. What would have been an ordinary yard was a maze of vegetable and herb gardens. Two small children were digging a hole; one wore shorts, and the other was naked. Their long, tangled blond hair and crouched poses hid their gender.

"Rainbow and Weevil," Pandora said proudly. "We encourage them to explore their environment without parental restraints. They often sleep outside, but they do appear when they're hungry." She clapped her hands to get their attention. "Come meet our new neighbor! She's a goddess of Litha."

Unimpressed by my rank, the naked child squatted over the hole while the other watched. After the hole was fertilized, they scampered into the woods. Pandora and I listened to their shrieks until they faded. I regret to say the image lingered in my mind. Had Caron been there, she would have locked herself in the car.

"I don't want to interrupt them," I said sincerely. I didn't want to go inside the purple house, either, since it was likely to reek of patchouli oil (Pandora did). Besides, if Rainbow and Weevil were as casual about body functions inside as they were outside, I wanted more than candlelight before I put my foot down. I sat down on a primitive wooden bench. "I just found out about Winston yesterday. It must have been stressful for the family."

"It was," Pandora said as she sat down beside me. "Ethan was so nervous while the police were here. He was convinced that they would demand to search the greenhouses for marijuana."

"Would they have found some?"

"You haven't met Charles, have you? He'd go ballistic if there was a single pot plant within a mile of the greenhouses. The workmen don't dare smoke cigarettes when he's there. Jordan was so disappointed that I had to dose her with my special green tea with ginseng, herbs, and lemongrass. Would you like some?"

"Why was Ethan nervous?"

Her arms swayed over her head as she began dancing around me, her eyes closed and her lips puckered like a dried rosebud. I was about to trip her when she came to rest. After a few pants, she said, "The poor dear was worried about his exotic plants. He has orchids, bromeliads, corpse lilies, Inca angel trumpets, and other stuff—all legal, but sensitive to light, humidity, and temperature. Some of them are rare and very delicate. When he's not talking about them, he's talking to them." Her head fell back so her face was bathed in sunlight. "Ethan and I are soul mates. We celebrate the earth with our love of all plants, whether they have beautiful blooms or prickly scales. A blade of grass is more complex than a play by Shakespeare. When people no longer are allowed to inhabit this glorious planet, the plant kingdom shall reign."

At which time I'd change my name to Violet, assuming I was a beautiful bloom rather than a cactus. "Did the police investigators cause botanical devastation?"

Pandora closed her eyes. "They didn't even mention the greenhouses. They just took photos, asked questions, and waited for the medical examiner. The whole thing was over in an hour." She opened one eye to gauge my reaction. "Not that the family wasn't really upset. We were all fond of Winston, and he was, after all, a Hollow. His mother and Felicia were second cousins, I think. We went to the Old Tavern to comfort ourselves. I was too sad to dance the next day. Ethan told me that some of the ferns had curled in response to our grief. Plants are incredibly sensitive. There's this kind of moss—".

"Terry must have felt horrible that he wasn't there at the time of the death," I said.

"He was in Italy. I don't remember why."

"Winston was fishing when he lost his balance?"

"That's the story," she said as she raised her head. "If

someone else had been with him, it could have been averted. No one was, though."

"The article I read claimed that he banged his head while struggling to keep his balance and was unconscious at the time."

Pandora sobered up from the heady drench of sunshine. "Why are you asking all these questions? Just because you want to buy Winston's house doesn't mean you have any business snooping around. Everybody in the family still feels bad about the accident." She stood up and crossed her arms. "Hollow Valley is private property. Until you actually own Winston's house, you're trespassing!"

Her small tirade reminded me of my exceedingly good reason for trespassing. "Have you seen Angela Delmond anywhere in the area? She's five-six, short dark hair, designer shoes and handbag, maybe driving a silver SUV."

"No, but this is the first day that I've ventured out of the house since Sunday. I was doing my monthly cleansing fast and restorative meditation. Now that I have rid my body of toxins and swept away the negative energy from the recesses of my psyche, I am free. You are trespassing."

"I'd best trespass back to my car," I said. "I hope we can avoid each other in the future. Have a nice day." I walked up the driveway, trying to decide if her act was credible. Despite all her gibberish about the glories of nature, I'd caught a glimpse of calculation. She and Ethan had met at an ashram, according to Nattie. I wondered if the ashram was a haven or a hideout.

When I arrived at my house, I was chagrined to discover that the front door was locked. Peter must have turned the button on the doorknob when we left. Or, I thought more brightly, Angela had been back to secure the premises. She could be at home or at her office while I was out beating the bushes for her. Metaphorically, in that I didn't trust nature not to retaliate with a swarm of bees.

I drove to the Old Tavern and parked within the pale of Colonel Hollow's glare. No one was about, but I could hear the muffled groans of heavy machinery from the direction of the greenhouses. I was less interested in tractors than I was in monthly cleansing fasts. I used the heavy iron ring to knock on the door. It echoed inside, but no one invited me in for tea. I was walking back to my car when Nattie emerged from behind the house.

"Claire," she called, "what a . . . surprise. I was working in the vegetable garden out back. Can I help you with something?"

"I'm still tracking Angela, and I wondered if she might have come back to Hollow Valley."

Nattie wiped her hands on her jeans as she joined me. "Well, if she has, I didn't see her. Would you like a glass of tea?"

"Spiked with ginseng and lemongrass?"

"I was thinking of Lipton. I gather you've met Pandora Butterfly. Ethan must have been on drugs when he married her. There're some chairs and a table in the garden. Make yourself comfortable while I make a pitcher of tea."

I strolled around the corner of the Old Tavern. The view was not of an orchard and a meadow. A barn that had once been red was the color of rust. There were two more outbuildings, and beyond them, a truck was rumbling across a bridge. Angela had mentioned that the delivery trucks used a back road. I had no idea how often they came and went, but they would not disrupt the bucolic serenity.

I sat down on an aluminum chair and idly watched the truck disappear into the woods. There were voices in the distance, presumably workmen doing serious things like planting and plucking. I had yet to meet four members of the Hollow family: Ethan, Charles and Felicia Finnelly, and Aunt Margaret Louise. If I was lucky, I might never run into them. I certainly wasn't going to invite them to a housewarming party. Nattie was agreeable. Jordan was a temporary blight. Moses might prove to be a nuisance, but I could handle him.

No, in my fantasy land Peter and I would sit on the terrace while Caron hosted pool parties. In the fall, I'd harvest apples to make applesauce and pies. When the weather turned cold, we'd snuggle in front of a blazing fire with mugs of homemade cider. We'd decorate for Christmas and have parties at which the local literati read poetry or debated politics. Later, Peter and I would sip champagne in the oversized bathtub, listening to mellow jazz and engaging in adult behavior.

I was so caught up in my blissful imagery that I almost fell out of the chair when Nattie said, "I'm so glad that you're moving to Hollow Valley, Claire. It can be lonely out here." She set a tray on the table and poured me a glass of iced tea. She'd also brought a plate of cinnamon rolls and a bowl of strawberries.

I helped myself to a cinnamon roll. "This is delicious, Nattie."

"I baked them this morning, along with several loaves of bread. As Jordan said, it can be boring out here if you let it be. I bake, garden, and often pack a sandwich and hike around the entire valley. I sketch birds and wildflowers. Yesterday I saw a Canada goose and four goslings. I also write in my journal every day. I've kept one since I was ten."

"Have you always lived here?" I attacked a second cinnamon roll, hoping she would produce a response long enough to let me slowly devour it.

"No, I grew up in a small town in Alabama. I've been back here for fifteen years. I had a difficult time in college.

So many demands, all those people pushing and shoving, the promiscuity—it was too much for me. I tried counseling, but the therapist was as bad as the others. My parents were furious when I refused to return after the third year. I found a menial job, but I knew I had to come here, where I would be safe." She made a vague gesture at the wooded slopes. "I spent my summers here. There were several of us cousins about the same age. Ethan, Sheldon, Ruth, Zack, myself, and of course, Winston. We swam in the stream, played hide-and-seek, went on picnics, and lay in the grass on hot summer nights, waiting for shooting stars. I lived for the summers." Her abrupt laugh startled me. "Reality sucks, doesn't it?"

"Sometimes," I said cautiously. "Once we're here, you can teach me how to make these divine cinnamon rolls. We'll go out to lunch every week."

"We might even have fun," she said, "if I can remember how. I picked the strawberries this morning. Tomorrow I'm going to hunt for blackberries. Are you a birdwatcher?"

"Not yet, but I'm willing to learn." I ate a strawberry while I considered how best to politely interrogate her. "May I ask you about Winston? He had a fatal accident while fishing, didn't he?"

Nattie regarded me over the rim of her glass. "You must have read the story in the newspaper. Winston was a very talented young man, and we were all saddened by his death. His mother taught high school math, and his father wrote long, wearisome tomes about the Napoleonic Wars. I did my best to read one, but after five hundred pages I was begging for Waterloo. Anyway, we saw very little of Winston after his parents sent him to a prep school in the East. He spent summers at a camp in Michigan or Minnesota. It changed him, turned him against us. During the holidays, he was polite but remote."

"Why do you think he moved back here?" I asked.

She glanced over her shoulder as if Jordan might be hunched behind the tomato plants. "I suspected he had some health problems—mental and physical. Last Christmas, he and Terry turned down my invitation for dinner." She shook her head. "That's understandable, though. I'm sure they had a much better time with pheasant and white wine than they would have had with Felicia's dry turkey, Margaret Louise's lumpy mashed potatoes, Pandora's pickled okra, and a glass of water. I know I would have."

"Even if he wasn't into the family thing, all of you must have been upset when he died in the fishing accident."

"It wasn't an accident," Nattie said as she popped a strawberry in her mouth.

CHAPTER 4

I choked on a mouthful of tea. Once I'd recovered, I said, "Not an accident?"

Nattie handed me a napkin so I could dry my chin. "The police investigators were happy to write it up that way, and the Hollow family was hardly going to disagree. Out of respect, the report didn't mention the two empty wine bottles. Those, coupled with the marks in the mud, satisfied them that Winston was inebriated when he lost his balance." She reached for the pitcher. "Let me refill your glass."

"Thank you. It still sounds like an accident, Nattie. If Winston consumed two bottles of wine, he easily could have slipped."

She gazed at the valley for a long while, gnawing her lower lip as though I'd said something profound. "I don't disagree with that, but . . ."

"But you don't believe it was an accident. Why not?"

"As I said earlier, Winston had problems. When I encouraged him to tell me what was going on, he was evasive. At first I thought he was missing his former life in

New York City. Farberville isn't exactly a hotbed of artistic excitement, and it must have been a devastating culture shock for him. Some people aren't meant to live in the countryside, where the loudest noises come from starlings and bullfrogs. I occasionally caught him during the remodeling, and he told me that he missed the clamor of garbage trucks, the incessant sirens, the honking horns, the kamikaze cabs, and the daily parade of pedestrians."

I heard something that was neither avian nor amphibian. "What's that thumping noise?"

She listened for a second and then said, "The clothes dryer in the basement. It's twenty years old and about to expire any day now. The washing machine sounds as if it's about to explode. Moses has a medical condition that causes him to change clothes often. He . . . uh, leaks."

I was sorry that I'd asked, and even sorrier that she'd answered. "Tell me more about Winston."

"When the house was finished, he and Terry invited all of us to a party. Felicia was apoplectic about the quantity of alcoholic beverages, and she and Charles stalked off after half an hour. In truth, it was uncomfortable for all the family members. The boys continued to have boisterous parties every week or so. I could hear them from the Old Tavern. However, the parties became less frequent and then stopped. I would run into Winston wandering in the woods, his shoulders slumped and his eyes dull. He seemed to become more depressed over the three years. The last time I saw him, he was sitting on a fallen tree trunk, staring at the ground. That was in early March. I was concerned because it was cold and he wasn't wearing a coat or gloves. He wouldn't even acknowledge my presence. I felt so helpless."

"You think he committed suicide?" I asked gently.

Nattie nodded. "I think he took the fishing gear as a

ploy so that it would look like an accident. He drank the
wine to rally his courage and then flung himself in the
freezing water."

"Did he own a fishing pole?"

"It's hard to imagine that he did," she said slowly. "He
never fished or hunted when he was a child. He hated to
kill things, even worms. That's a good point, Claire. The
only thing I can come up with is that Moses left a pole
and a tackle box down there. He loves to go fishing in all
weather. If it ever got so cold that the stream froze over,
he'd be out in the middle of it, cutting a hole in the
ice. Luckily for me, he never brings his scaly trophies
home. I'm not keen on cleaning fish."

Handling fish guts was not my idea of a pleasant pas-
time, either, so I returned to the pertinent topic. "Maybe it
was a ploy, as you suggested."

"Poor, sweet Winston. If only I could have convinced
him to tell me the truth about how he felt, I could have
helped him. We were so close once upon a time." She
sighed. "As they, whoever they are, say, 'Of all the words
of mice and men . . .'"

"Kurt Vonnegut, actually. You shouldn't feel responsible, Nattie. You tried."

"And failed. The Hollow family may not be able to
trace its lineage to the *Mayflower*, and there have been
more scoundrels than heroes, but I hate to see the family
reduced to suicide, dementia, feral children, and whatever
lies in the future. Once there are no more direct descendants to inherit the property, some real estate developer
will bulldoze the greenhouses and put in a fancy gated
community."

I sympathized with her bleak vision, but I wasn't in the
mood for maudlin sentiments. "Maybe Pandora Butterfly's children will grow up to become lawyers and engi-

neers, marry, and produce a new crop of happy little Hollows."

She laughed. "In a pig's eye. Pandora plans to home-school them, so the odds of them ever learning to read are minuscule. One can only pray that they'll end up in prison instead of being killed by a drug cartel. Well, this is my worry, not yours. You must have more entertaining things to do than listen to the creaking branches of the family tree."

"I enjoyed talking with you," I said as I stood up, "and I'm eager to learn how to make your cinnamon rolls."

She insisted on wrapping the remaining ones in a napkin so that I could take them home. I did not object. After a brief hug, I went to my car and placed my precious bundle on the passenger's seat. When I turned around to start the car, Moses's face was in the window.

"Whatcha got there?" he asked with a leer.

"Just something Nattie gave me," I said to let him know I wasn't about to share. "How are you today?"

He rested his arms on the windowsill. "Got a toothache, which is strange since I ain't got teeth. So you and Nattie were talking? Did she tell you a bunch of lies? I swear, that woman would try to persuade you that the sun rises in the west if she was of a mind to."

"She and I were having tea."

"Cinnamon rolls, too. I smell it on your breath."

I could smell liquor on his breath, but it didn't seem polite to point it out. "I have some errands to run, Moses." I put the key in the ignition in case he missed the hint. "Enjoy the sunshine."

"Did she tell you about Winston?" he asked with a snigger. "How we went to a party at his house and got snockered on fine whiskey? Well, I'll bet she didn't tell you half of what happened later."

"What's the other half?"

"That's between me and the Colonel. Look at him up there, waiting for the Yankees to come thundering through the valley." Moses stood up and stuck out his arm. "Into the Hollow Valley rode the six hundred! Cannon to the left of them! Cannon to the right of them! Volley'd and thunder'd! Theirs not to reason why, theirs but to do or die!" His ferocity startled a flock of cowbirds into abandoning their roost for a more peaceful perch elsewhere. A squirrel on the bench raised its bushy tail but hung on to its acorn.

Nattie came around the corner of the Old Tavern. "Moses, whatever is wrong with you? You're scaring Claire, who has better things to do than listen to you mangle poetry. How about a nice glass of milk and a slice of bread?"

"With honey?" he called back, his arm still beckoning the Light Brigade.

"With honey," she replied.

Moses lowered his arm and bent down to whisper, "She's not the only one who knows what happened to Winston. Other people have eyes, too. Don't let her fool you."

"I won't," I whispered in response. I started the car and drove carefully past him, not wanting to add crushed toes to his list of ailments. When I continued to the main road, I was relieved that Pandora Butterfly had taken her ballet troupe elsewhere.

Caron was still in her pajamas when I arrived home. She looked up from her bowl of cereal long enough to mumble, "Some guy called."

"Terry Kennedy? Is he already here?"

"No, Danny something. He wants you to call him." She briskly transitioned from spoon to cell phone and started texting.

I sat down before my knees buckled. "What did he say?"

"He said for you to call him, Mother. Are you developing ADD? That's attention deficit disorder, in case you've forgotten. Inez's parents decided that her little brother had it because he kept staring into space and walking off in the middle of conversations. They took him to a therapist and everything. It turned out that he was building a bomb in his room. What a hoot!"

I was impressed that she had not broken her texting rhythm during her remarks. "What happened to the bomb?"

She glanced at me out of the corner of her eye. "How should I know? He didn't blow up the house or his school or anything. Oh, and I wrote down the guy's number on the cereal box. He sounded anxious."

I took the box of pastel marshmallow rice puffs and the phone out to the balcony. The number proved to be that of Danny Delmond Enterprises Inc. The receptionist questioned me as to my identity and objective and then put me on hold. I waited impatiently until a male voice said, "Mrs. Malloy, I need information from you. Angela failed to show up to a deposition this morning, and I understand that you're involved in her pathetic charade as the innocent victim. Where is she?" His voice was brusque and accusatory, as if I'd stashed Angela under my bed. As if anyone could fit under it now that half of Peter's and my wardrobe was residing between the storage boxes of shoes, blankets, and sweaters.

"I have no idea where she is," I said, already disliking him.

"Don't give me that crap, Mrs. Malloy. My attorney can get a court order compelling you to produce her under penalty of contempt of court."

"Tell him to have at it. My husband can have your car

towed to the police compound to be searched for blood-stains." I despise bullies, and from what Angela had said about him, he was the worst kind. "It would be a shame if it got scratched, wouldn't it?"

"I'll sue you, your husband, and the police department if anyone lays a finger on my Jaguar. Now just tell me where she is and we can end this ridiculous conversation."

"Do you have a short-term memory problem? I don't know where she is, Mr. Delmond. If neither of us knows, it is indeed time to end this ridiculous conversation."

I put my finger on the pertinent button but paused when he said in a much more conciliatory voice, "I apologize, Mrs. Malloy. I'm worried about her. We're in the middle of a divorce, but we were married for ten years. I still have some feelings for her."

"Okay," I said, unimpressed. The only reason that he was apt to have been worried about her was that her absence interfered with the legal proceedings. His current girlfriend could have put down her foot and demanded that the divorce be finalized before she reached her twenty-first birthday. Or he'd won a twenty-million-dollar lottery ticket and was not inclined to share. "I haven't seen Angela in a couple of days."

"Neither has her office," Danny muttered. "I was told you were with her before she disappeared. Was she upset? Did she say anything about a relative or friend that suggested there was an emergency?"

"She mentioned something about your lake house."

"Oh, shit. Did she hear that . . . uh, I'm planning to use it this weekend?"

"I believe she did," I said, enjoying his discomfort. I wondered if visions of flames were dancing in his head. "Do you and she have a temporary agreement about the place?"

"That's none of your business. I'll send someone out there to look for her."

He hung up before I could ask him to let me know if she was there or not. I put down the phone and popped a pink marshmallow in my mouth. Two seconds later I spit it out and vowed to lecture Caron on the virtues of whole wheat and fiber. In a year, she'd be away at college, eating and drinking whatever she fancied. I would have an empty nest, but a glorious empty nest that I could feather with bouquets of wildflowers. If Terry Kennedy cooperated, that is.

When I went back inside, my nestling informed me that she and Inez were going to the park to play tennis. I skipped my lecture on nutrition and told her to have fun. Since I didn't know when Terry would arrive at the Farberville airport-of-sorts, I found a familiar mystery novel and settled down to read. Regrettably, I had the attention span of a toddler, but I assured myself it was not ADD. After indulging in fantasies about my little house in the valley (prairies are so dull), I replayed the conversation with Danny Delmond. Either he was the egocentric womanizer of whom Angela had spoken so bitterly, or he was a crafty schemer. Calling me could have been a ruse so that he would not be a suspect if something dire had happened to her. Maybe he'd already been to the lake house to bury her body. The call she'd received at Winston's house had displeased her. Danny perpetually displeased her, and a call from him might have sent her charging to confront him. Danny was a developer. He could have dumped her body in a hole that was by now covered by six inches of concrete. And I'd be on the witness stand, repeating the conversation he and I had.

At five o'clock I made myself a drink and pretended to watch the local news. If the anchorman had announced that a meteor would strike the planet within minutes, I missed it. If biologists in Brazil had captured a live fairy, I missed that, too. I would have paced had it been safe, but I'd stubbed my toes on a daily basis. Anxiety wasn't gnawing me; it was wolfing me down.

Which explained why I spilled my drink when the telephone rang. I lunged across the sofa and grabbed it. "Hello," I yelped.

"Claire?" Peter said. "Is something wrong?"

I struggled into a more dignified posture, although the front of my shirt was soaked and my hair hung in my eyes. "I was hoping you were Terry."

"Sorry to disappoint you, my dear. Husbands can be a nuisance when a wife is carrying on with another man."

"Idiot," I said. Since I'd told Peter about the previous evening's conversation, I did not feel obliged to carry on about his manly attributes and accomplishments. "I do want to keep the line open. Unless you've been appointed head of Homeland Security, I'll call you later."

"A quick word about Angela Delmond, and then I'll hobble back to the next round of meetings. I asked Lieutenant Jorgeson to let me know if her name appeared on any reports. Her car was found in Maxwell County early this morning. It was parked near a private landing strip. No sign of her, or any hint of foul play."

I sucked in a breath. "How long had it been there?"

"Jorgeson didn't say. He may be able to find out more tomorrow. I've got to go. Don't do anything too illicit or explicit just to persuade the guy to sell you the house."

"I haf my ways," I murmured in a German accent, then hung up. After I'd changed my shirt and poured another drink, I tried to make sense of what Peter told me. Maxwell County was no place for sissies. It held the state record per capita for homicides, violent domestic disputes, burglaries, illegal weapons, moonshine, and dubious hunting accidents. Well water was ninety proof. There were rumors that the chicken houses, conveniently devoid of chickens, were equipped with so many grow lights that no stars were visible in the night sky. It was decidedly not Angela Delmond's milieu.

The proximity of a private landing strip could mean nothing whatsoever, but I didn't buy that. Angela might have flown the coop, literally. The obvious question was who owned the airplanes that used the strip. Maxwell County lacked the terrain for crop dusters, and had the sheriff been interested in locating large marijuana fields, his search planes would have used a municipal landing strip. Some murky heir of Howard Hughes could have a compound in the middle of the forest, I supposed. Angela might have sold him the property.

I was itching to call Jorgeson, but I didn't dare use the phone. I dug through my purse to find my cell phone, but the charger had a life independent of mine and often crawled into dark corners or under piles of stuff. One glance into Caron's room erased any expectation of finding hers.

Time crawled by. Caron and Inez had informed me that they were going to Ashley's house after tennis; I didn't expect them until midnight. I tried to motivate myself to sort out the boxes on the dining room floor, but a silverfish slithered out from under one, and I fled to the sofa.

The phone finally rang at nine, just in time to keep me from leaping off the balcony. I licked my lips and said calmly, "This is Claire Malloy."

"Terry here. I was planning to call you earlier, but I went by to see some friends. How are you?"

I gulped back a sputter of outrage that he'd been chatting with friends while I chewed my toenails. "You're in Farberville?"

"I'm at the house. It's pretty late. Do you want to wait until tomorrow to talk about things?"

"I'll be there in ten minutes."

I hung up, grabbed my purse, and made it down the outside staircase without causing myself bodily harm. Angela could be in a private jet over China for all I cared, I thought as I drove at an imprudent speed through dark neighborhoods and busy intersections. There was a veneer of perspiration on my forehead when I screeched to a stop in front of the house in twelve minutes and forty-two seconds.

Terry Kennedy opened the front door. He was taller than his voice had intimated and very lean. His shaggy hair was long enough to get him hanged in Maxwell County. "Claire," he said, ushering me inside. "Do sit down in the living room. Would you care for a glass of wine?"

I shook my head but followed him into the kitchen to make sure he didn't disappear on me. Caron would have known the brand names of his clothing, but even I could see that the cotton sweater, jeans, and sandals were expensive. I would have preferred him to be dressed in yard sale chic, and therefore in need of cash. "Did you have any problems getting here?" I asked.

"Typical airline hassles." He poured himself a glass of wine from a bottle on the kitchen island. After we were settled in the living room, he propped his feet on the coffee table and gazed around the room. "Being back here is eerie, I must say. I feel as if Winston is about to come in from the terrace and challenge me to a game of chess. He wasn't very good, but I let him win once in a while. Math and logic were not his best subjects. I had to balance his checkbook and handle all the bills. He was all about colors and music, clouds, sunrises and sunsets, distant sounds. He had an incredible imagination."

I resigned myself to a eulogy. "He designed sets, I read."

Terry smiled, but not at me. "He loved the theater. He did sets for outlandish musicals and for avant-garde noir. We'd go out afterward with the cast and booze it up until the reviews came out, then celebrate or commiserate with champagne until dawn. We went to parties where we met August Wilson, Arthur Miller, and Wendy Wasserstein. We knew the trendy artists, too. We had a loft in SoHo, with a kosher deli on the ground floor and a bagel shop on the corner."

"Why did you move here?" I asked, trying to keep the focus on the present neighborhood.

"It is ironic, isn't it, that a set designer and a professional poker player would choose to live in a town in which the community theater group still puts on *The Mousetrap* and dance revolves around recitals featuring five-year-olds in tutus?" He went to the French windows and looked out at the darkness. "Not that Key West has a performing arts center. The only culture the tourists want is a cheeseburger in paradise."

"I understand that the Hollow family wasn't delighted when you moved here," I said bluntly.

He turned around. "No, I wouldn't say they were delighted. Winston insisted that we make an effort by throwing a party, but it was a disaster. I thought it was hilarious. All their little noses were twitching, and their eyes were as round as marbles. Charles could barely swallow a dab of very expensive caviar, and his wife went ballistic when I offered her a vodka and tonic, with a twist of lime. Those clichéd hippies tried to be cool, especially the airhead, but the guy was fuming. Nattie was okay once she found her rhythm with tequila shots; she passed out in a chaise on the terrace. Moses played charades by himself in the middle of the room. Oh, and dear Aunt Margaret Louise insisted on telling me truly peculiar stories about her wanton ways back in the sixties—and her fondness for chocolate truffles, which explained why she loaded her pockets with them before she left. She put the sushi slices and the cremini and goat cheese triangles in her purse, along with several pieces of silverware. At least she was more discerning than a New York City bag lady."

I laughed politely. I was almost certain why Winston and Terry had upset the Hollows, and in particular Charles and Felicia. Nattie had told me they were conservative, and I doubted they'd been prepared to party with a gay couple. I made a mental note to ask for the recipe for the cremini and goat cheese triangles. "So you didn't see much of them after they realized you were more than housemates."

Terry sat down on the sofa and primly crossed his legs. In a high, exaggerated voice that warbled, he said, "Oh, darling, they went to extremes to avoid us. I'm surprised they didn't put up gates to prevent us from driving past our turnoff. Nattie was the exception. She dropped by every week with fresh bread and pots of homemade strawberry jam. Her brownies were to die for." He abandoned his role of divine diva and said, "We were married in Connecticut the day after the law was enacted. The East Coast and the West Coast are open-minded, but Hollow Valley is a hidey-hole of homophobia. We made friends, both gay and straight, in Farberville. Angela came out to get drunk whenever her husband was shacked up with his latest girlfriend. I found it odd, since she ran with Farberville's elite and should have been crying in her martinis at the country club."

"It's hard to be around people who whisper behind your back," I said from experience. Carlton had been careful because of the taboo involving faculty and students, but his trysts in his office were a topic of conversation in the English Department for years. I had been fooled only briefly, and was contemplating my alternatives when he died. My only regret was that Caron knew about her father's Olympic record in philandering. However, both of us had survived, so I moved on to the pertinent topic. "I can understand that the house has disturbing memories for you. Angela told me that you're willing to sell it, but there may be legal complications. My husband and I will be glad to hire an attorney to sort things out."

"Ah, yes." Terry said. "The Hollow family is determined to keep it all in the family, so to speak. They've claimed that Winston was under undue influence when he signed the deed that gave the property to me on his death. I was the source of the undue influence, of course. Their story is that I badgered him until he folded, and that he was not in his right mind at the time. I'd never thought of myself as a gold digger, especially since I had a great deal more money than Winston. I majored in math in college and put my knowledge to use as a poker player. Big tournaments pay big bucks. I won a tournament in Monaco and went to Rome to celebrate with friends. Three days later I came home and learned about Winston's death."

"At this moment you own the house, though, right?"

"The deed's on file at the courthouse. I'm not sure about the status of the lawsuit, but my attorney says it could drag on for years. It may muddle the title." He arose with the elegance of a dancer. "Are you sure you wouldn't like a glass of wine?"

"I'm quite sure," I said. An exquisitely clever idea came to mind. "If you're not able to sell the house outright, you could lease it to us until the lawsuit is dismissed." I remembered something he'd said on the phone. "I can assure you that neither my husband nor I is related to any member of the Hollow family. We have gay friends, and we'll invite them for dinner parties as often as possible. My daughter and her friends will toilet-paper the statue of the Colonel and decorate him for holidays. The Hollows will hate us, I promise."

Terry grinned at me. "That's your best argument so far. I loathe those people. Winston's parents tried to protect him from their venom by sending him to boarding school, but he had to endure them when he was home. As a child, he was bullied and taunted by his cousins. As his sexual identity emerged, their parents treated him like a pervert. When he came home, he was naive enough to have hopes of reestablishing a decent relationship with them, since his mother was one of the dreaded 'direct descendants.' An army of zombies would have received a warmer welcome than we did."

He went into the kitchen, but I forced myself not to follow him. I did, however, listen for any wayward footsteps in the direction of an exit. He duly returned and said, "Their attitude distressed him, which I'm sure delighted them, but he'd worked on it with a psychiatrist for years and was ready to face them. We had plans for a trip to Rio after I finished my gig in Monaco. He was studying Portuguese and taking samba lessons at a dance studio. Nobody bothered to notify me of his death. I came home and—well, there it was. His ashes had been scattered in the wind. Nattie had the decency to tell me what had happened. I gave Goodwill all of his clothing and put all the personal items in storage. Two days later I left for Key West to stay with friends. I haven't been back until today."

"I read the article stating that it was an accident. Did you believe that?"

"In the same way I'd believe the world is flat and alchemy can solve the nation's financial crisis. Winston would never have gone fishing. There was no fishing gear in the house, and he preferred his fish to be filleted by an unseen hand. There is no way he would have even considered trying to catch whatever icky fishies might inhabit that sluggish excuse for a river. Can you imagine either of us eating catfish? The idea makes me nauseous."

I sought the most tactful way to broach Nattie's opinion without divulging her confidence. "Two empty wine bottles were found at the scene. That suggests Winston might have been disoriented when he slipped."

Terry grimaced. "Yeah, Nattie told me that she thought Winston had committed suicide. She was so upset that she went through a box of tissues. It was all I could do to remain civil. Did she tell you all that crap about finding him sitting on a tree trunk?" I nodded warily. "Well, it's utter nonsense. Winston would no more have moped in the woods than he would have gone to a biker bar in pink leggings. He wasn't the least bit depressed when I left. He was excited about the Rio trip. The last thing he said to me was 'Adeus,' which he swore was Portuguese for 'good-bye.' He had arranged to play with his amateur string quartet, and he'd invited some people for lunch that weekend. He was going to serve smoked trout." He began to pace around the room, throwing up his hands for emphasis. "He asked me if I thought he should serve a Reisling or sauvignon blanc. Does that sound like someone harboring suicidal thoughts? He didn't ask me which wine went well with suicide!"

"Then you think . . . ?"

"They murdered him. There's no way Winston would have taken fishing gear to the river and proceeded to get drunk. They must have held numerous tribal councils to work out a plan to kill him. He didn't have a heart condition or life-threatening allergy to bee stings or shellfish. If his body were found in his bed, the medical examiner might have insisted on an autopsy. That ruled out poison and suffocation. What's easier than a blow to the head and a shove? A tidy cause of death, no reason to check the alcohol level in his blood." He was pacing so fiercely that he was banging into furniture, and his face was as red as a poppy. "I don't know how they lured him down to the river, but they came up with something. I won't let them get away with it!"

I winced as his knee hit the coffee table, but I had sense enough not to attempt to placate him. We weren't going to have a civilized discussion about the terms of the lease until he had loosed all his anger. He was not my idea of an expressionless poker player who never twitched when confronted with four aces. It was easier to imagine him at a table in a grimy Old West saloon, where accusations of cheating led to gunfire. However, I was quite capable of presenting an unruffled visage while holding in outrage. Parenting had trained me well. Terry finally flopped down on the sofa. It was time to return to the matter at hand, which was in my arena of expertise.

"You're sure they murdered Winston? I can understand that they disapproved of your lifestyle, but why would they go to that extreme? It seems to me that they were doing a good job of ignoring the two of you for three years. Why not just let things continue as they were?"

Terry glared at me. "You don't believe me?"

"I do," I said hastily. "I've met Nattie, Pandora Butterfly, and Moses—who, by the way, has been sampling his way through your wine cabinet. None of them struck me as cold-blooded. Do you have any proof?"

His glare intensified until I felt a distinct pang of panic. "How could I have any proof? I was out of the country at the time. The police wouldn't have bothered to examine the fishing pole and bottles for fingerprints. They had a nice, neat explanation for all the evidence. They weren't going to waste any time investigating it."

I had to agree. "You believe that all of the Hollow family members were in on Winston's murder?"

"Maybe not," he said. To my relief, he gave me a less hostile look. "Nattie doesn't seem like the type, but she did tell me all that garbage about Winston's grand depression. No one would trust Moses to keep a secret. As for the hippie chick, she's been stoned since I met her. I tried to buy some pot from her, but she swore she was high on nature. Winston and I talked Nattie into giving us a tour of the nursery, but we didn't spot any suspicious plants. We even searched around all the outdoor plants and trees, just in case there might be a little patch concealed by the foliage. We subsequently found a dealer through a friend, so we stopped bothering. A nursery would make a good cover, though."

"That occurred to me, but sometimes a nursery is just a nursery, to misquote Freud. Aunt Margaret Louise doesn't sound like a suspect. That leaves Ethan, Charles, and Felicia. Still, it doesn't explain why they murdered Winston three years after you and he moved here."

Terry wiggled his eyebrows at me. "Well, if Winston announced that we were going to build cabins in the meadow for a summer retreat for gays and lesbians . . ."

"He didn't, though."

He took a gulp of wine. "I don't know why they decided to murder him when they did. I just know that they did."

I waited for a moment, preparing myself to bring up the issue of a lease, when I realized he was asleep. I covered him with a quilt and tiptoed out the front door. I was disappointed, but tomorrow was another day.

CHAPTER 5

It took me much longer to drive home. Caron was not back, and it was too late to call Peter. Terry's belief that Winston had been murdered was worrisome, to put it mildly. I made a cup of tea while I mulled over his assertions. It was clear that he had loved Winston, and grief can addle one's mind. Although I'd claimed to believe him, I'd done so partly out of diplomacy. If he'd cast me as an adherent of the enemy's position, I would have no chance of cajoling him into a sale or lease. Nattie was convinced that Winston had been deeply depressed. Terry might have omitted mentioning a spousal spat before he left to go to Italy. He'd dismissed it as trivial, but Winston might have blown it into a major conflagration with the potential for divorce. Both Nattie and Terry had talked about Winston's sensitivity. Maybe he had taken a walk to escape the painful scene and then replayed it over and over again.

I could think of other reasons as well. Winston might have suspected infidelity; Terry had not been there to defend himself. Nattie had mentioned Winston's health. Since there had been no autopsy, there was no way to determine if he'd received devastating news about a medical condition. He might have wanted to spare Terry from the relentless drudgery of taking care of a spouse with a multisyllabic terminal disease. Or, I thought as I went out to the balcony, he was ravaged by the rift with the family, despite all the therapy. Suicide was more likely than murder.

Either way, there wasn't much I could do about it. Peter would not have cases reopened on unsubstantiated allegations. That I knew from experience, which was why I'd been obliged to investigate them on my own. The police, including my beloved husband, are not big on imagination. Luckily for them, I am, but in this particular case, I was more interested in obtaining the house than in ferreting out all the dirty little secrets to determine the truth.

Caron arrived an hour later. If I'd expected an attentive audience, I was in the throes of self-delusion. I repeated what I'd heard, including the two scenarios, and waited for her to offer insights and point out discrepancies. She yawned several times, assured me that I would sort it out, and wafted away to her room. I bit back the urge to call Peter, put my teacup in the sink, and went to bed.

I was making coffee the next morning when I heard a knock at the front door. As mentioned previously, my immeasurably rich imagination kicked in despite the lack of caffeine. Angela, with a souvenir from Vegas. Peter, home from the conference with nary a dueling scar. Terry, bearing a ninety-nine-year lease. Nattie, with fragrant cinnamon rolls and freshly churned butter.

It proved to be Joel, who looked at me with a leery expression. "Good morning, Ms. Malloy. Caron wants to go to the lake for the day. Am I too early? Do you want me to wait downstairs? I don't mind, really." He stuck out the newspaper he'd picked up on my porch before he could be accused of petty theft.

What he wanted to know was if Peter was looming

behind the door, ready to interrogate him about his skill as a lifeguard, the amount of gas in his car, the precise time of arrival back home, etc. The fact that Joel made straight A's, was president of the honor society, and had been accepted to an Ivy League school had no bearing on his character, nor did his neat appearance and manners. Peter does not take his role of stepfather lightly.

"It's safe, Joel," I said as I gestured for him to come inside. "I'll tell Caron that you're here."

Said child was dressed and in the bathroom. I was impressed, since I'd heard her snoring when I got up. During my postpubescent years, I'd avoided the juvenile palpitations resulting from hormonal inundation, but I sympathized with her. I reported back to Joel, who had not moved since stepping inside, and offered him orange juice. He politely declined. At least Caron hadn't fallen for a football hulk who aspired to become a reality show celebrity. My sympathy extends only so far.

Caron emerged in white shorts (mine) and a yellow shirt (also mine), carrying a canvas gym bag (Peter's). They assured me that they had ample sunscreen, towels, hats, and bottled water and would be home before dark. I sent them along, then sat down with coffee and called Peter. His phone went to voice mail, which implied that he was already in a meeting and wasn't disposed to talk to me. I opened the newspaper to find out what twaddle had been spewed in Congress the previous day, as well as whatever dire news was crammed on the front page. I was grousing over the editorials when I heard another knock on the door. My imagination quickly added state troopers to the list of possible visitors.

I was relieved when it proved to be Inez. She was as mousy as ever, but now she looked like the sole survivor of a shipwreck. "Is Caron up? I thought we might go to the mall. There's a big sale on swimsuits."

I broke the news, which was harsher than anything in the newspaper. Inez's mouth drooped, and her hair seemed to lose what minimal curl it had. "That's okay," she said stoically. "I'll just go to the library and read. My little brother is messing around with his chemistry set, so the house reeks of rotten meat. I'm halfway through next year's AP World Lit reading list. I didn't have any trouble with *The Brothers Karamazov,* but Kafka's hard. Have you read *The Metamorphosis,* Ms. Malloy? It's way creepy. I mean, imagine if you woke up and you were an enormous, gruesome bug. Do you think there's something symbolic about him having six legs? With fewer legs, he had more freedom, but he couldn't adhere to the ceiling. Is that analogous to the glass ceiling experienced by women executives?"

Half a cup of coffee had not armed me adequately for a discussion of anything involving symbols or analogies. "Hey, Inez, if you want to skip the library, you can go out to Hollow Valley with me to see the house. While I talk to the owner, you can explore the orchard and the meadow."

Behind thick glasses, her eyes widened. "Are you sure I won't be in the way, Ms. Malloy? I was reading an article on the Internet about indigenous plants and herbal remedies. St. John's wort, black cohosh, evening primrose, and ginseng are good for menopausal symptoms."

"Do you think I'm experiencing menopausal symptoms?"

"Gosh, no, Ms. Malloy," she said, blinking earnestly. "They're also good for depression—not that you look depressed—and anxiety and all kinds of things. I never for a minute thought you're old enough to be going through—"

"Let me finish my coffee, and then we'll go."

Inez babbled about each and every Karamazov brother as I drove to Hollow Valley and turned onto the blacktop road. Pandora Butterfly was flitting elsewhere, thank goodness. Explaining her to Inez (or to anybody, for that matter) would be a waste of oxygen. I was annoyed that Terry's rental car was not parked out front. Inez, in contrast, was thrilled about every detail of the setting.

"Oh wow! It's fantastic!" she said. "It's classy and unique, and it somehow fits right into all the grass and trees and everything. The shingles look like scallop shells. My grandmother had a porch like that, with rocking chairs and a swing. I loved sitting out there on summer nights, watching the lightning bugs and listening to the cicadas." She scrambled out of the car and ran up to the porch. "This is so cool, Ms. Malloy. Way cool."

If Caron didn't physically resemble me, I'd have wondered if there might have been a mix-up in the hospital neonatal ward. I was eager to show Inez the interior as soon as the house was mine (and Peter's and Caron's, I amended grudgingly). "The owner must have gone to see his attorney, but surely he'll be back soon," I said. "Go have a look at the pool while I try to find out if he's spoken to any of the neighbors."

Inez zipped around the corner of the house as I got into the car. The only resident who might have information was Nattie, so I continued up the road and parked near the statue. I didn't notice Jordan until I walked up the path to the Old Tavern. She was hunkered under a shrub by the door, her arms wrapped around her knees.

"Hey," she said.

"Good morning," I responded with a polite smile. "Is Nattie here?"

"She went into town to buy groceries. I asked her to get me a pack of cigarettes, and she bawled me out for fifteen minutes. You'd think that I'd asked for a stick of dynamite and a box of matches."

"Do you smoke?"

She disengaged branches and crawled out onto the lawn. "No, but I was really, really bored. It's impossible to get a reaction from Aunt Margaret Louise. When I told her that back home I made money by stripping in the boys' locker room, she made this weird gurgly sound and put on the teakettle. I tried it on Aunt Felicia, but she just looked at me. Pandora wants me to go on some vegan cleansing regime and meditate in the moonlight. Like I'm going to subsist on grass and tofu!"

I looked at her for the first time. Under the piercings and Mohawk, I could see a fourteen-year-old girl with a lot of emotional problems. Her body had not yet begun to mature; she could easily pass as a prepubescent boy. I had a feeling that Jordan was not popular with peers of either gender. My pragmatic inclination was to dismiss her, but my maternal side butted in. "My daughter couldn't come with me today, but one of her friends volunteered. She's out behind Winston's house, hunting for herbs. You're welcome to join her."

Jordan sneered. "Like I want to hang out with some botany nerd? I can take care of myself."

"As you wish," I murmured. I was not surprised when she put her hands in her pockets and ambled ever so casually toward the mill, then faded into the woods in the direction of Winston's house. At the end of the day, Inez would have much more interesting stories to tell than who had the worst sunburn at the lake.

I was increasingly annoyed by people's inability to remain where I wanted them to be. First Angela, then Terry, and now Nattie had taken it upon themselves to complicate my agenda. All I wanted was the house. Once I succeeded, they were free to trek to Nepal or hole up in a resort. Or even go to interminable task force conferences in Atlanta. I sat down on the bench under Colonel Hollow's evil eye and called Peter. Voice mail. I brooded for a moment, then called the police department and asked to speak to my lone contact. Jorgeson had been Peter's minion since I'd first encountered them during a sticky situation involving the death of a local romance writer. Peter had behaved abominably, but Jorgeson had been detached and professional. Over the years, he had remained patient when dealing with me, albeit in a long-suffering manner emphasized by his drooping jowls and bulbous nose.

"Ms. Malloy," he said when he came on the line. "What can I do for you this beautiful morning?"

"A teeny-tiny favor, if you have a minute. Is there an update on Angela Delmond?"

"This came across my desk a few minutes ago. The sheriff's department is conducting a search of the area, but they haven't found anything. No body, blood, purse, shoe, anything like that. The dogs couldn't pick up a trail. The sheriff's going to find out who owns the aircraft that use the strip. It's their case, since her car was discovered in their jurisdiction."

"You don't sound as though you have much faith in the sheriff."

"It's not for me to comment, Ms. Malloy. Maybe they'll have something in a few days. The husband didn't file a missing persons report until yesterday afternoon."

I was impressed that Danny had gone to that much trouble. "As long as I have you on the line, Lieutenant Jorgeson, would you mind looking up an old case file for me?"

"You know I can't do that," he said with a martyred groan, as if he expected to be pelted with pleas and entreaties. I had no idea why.

"You're so clever that I'm sure you can steal a quick peek. Winston Hollow Martinson died in early March. It was ruled an accident."

"Then that's what will be in the case file, Ms. Malloy."

"Yes, but did the forensics people look for fingerprints on the wine bottles or the fishing equipment?"

"If they had cause, they would have done so. The case is closed. My wife says to tell you to come by and cut some flowers from the garden. We're being overrun by roses. Have a good day."

"Wait!" I yelped, but he'd already hung up. He'd been spending too much time around Peter, I thought with a sniff. All that pettiness about one skinny file containing a couple of sheets of paper. I hadn't asked for a list of the names of local businessmen who'd been picked up with prostitutes—and the telephone numbers of their wives. I hadn't asked him to fix a speeding ticket, or even a parking ticket. I was stewing when Ethan came across the green.

"You must be Claire Malloy. I'm Ethan Hollow. Welcome to the valley." He had on jeans, a dingy T-shirt, muddy boots, and the bandanna headband. "I'd offer to shake hands," he continued with a broad smile, "but I've been mucking in the field. Is there something I can help you with?"

"I came to visit Nattie, but she's not here."

"I think she went to the market. Would you like to tour the nursery while you wait for her?"

"Yes," I said, hoping he had a golf cart available for dignitaries. It was already a bit too warm in the sunshine.

"It's this way." He gestured at the path. "You must be the outdoors type, since you want to live in the country. I love it, or I wouldn't be here. It's a great place to raise kids. These days parents are reluctant to let their kids walk home from school or play without adult supervision. The kids don't have any time to be creative and spontaneous, what with sports leagues, music lessons, gymnastics, tutoring sessions, and God knows what else. They end up stifled in identical cubicles, with identical spouses and identical children."

He needn't worry about his children blending in with the bourgeoisie. "I met your wife yesterday," I said. "She wasn't at all stifled."

"Wife? Oh, you mean Pandora Butterfly. She didn't tell me, but her short-term memory is unreliable. Some days she remembers the addresses and zip codes of old friends and writes them long letters. The next day she'll forget where she left the car keys and we all have to search the woods."

"She was dancing on the road. I thought she might have been smoking something other than tobacco."

Frowning, he pulled off the bandanna and used it to wipe his neck. "I don't like to tell people this, but she was in a motorcycle accident when she was in college. There was brain damage. Once she got out of rehab, she got a job at an animal shelter and mooched off friends. When we met at the ashram, we knew that our lives were destined to be interconnected. One of the five precepts is that we abstain from alcohol and drugs. Now, I've been known to stray off the path for a beer, but neither of us has used drugs in ten years. Pandora Butterfly gets her high from nature."

Marijuana was as much a product of nature as the scattered oak trees on one side of us and the unidentifiable shrubs in neat rows on the other side. I wasn't in the mood to pursue the topic, since I didn't really care how high Pandora chose to hover. I became more concerned about my own physical well-being as Ethan dragged me through four greenhouses filled with pots of flowers and trays of seedlings and his exotic plants, acres of flowering trees and shrubs, the field of aspiring Christmas trees, outbuildings that contained engines for the irrigation systems and a generator, storage sheds, and many other things in which I had not an iota of interest. The humidity inside the greenhouses was sufficient for a steam room, and while I was admiring the red maple saplings, we were blind-sided by a sprinkler.

I am very fond of flowers and tidy lawns, but I prefer them to settle in with no questions asked. They need not explain their origin, their genus and species, their petty requirements, their strengths or their frailties.

My face was damp when we returned to the stone circle in front of the Old Tavern. Ethan had talked steadily during the hour-long tour, preventing me from asking him about Winston's tenure and death. I sat down, acting as though I had no need to catch my breath, and vowed never again to show even an infinitesimal speck of curiosity about the Hollow Valley Nursery.

"Thanks for showing me around," I said to Ethan. He was still amiable, if a bit distracted. I wanted to get his opinion about Winston's death before he returned to harangue some employees who were sprawled in the shade. I'd seen two women working in the greenhouses. The rest of the forty employees were marginally kempt men of varied ages. I'd received a few impudent stares and leers during the tour, but I knew I could handle them by myself, if the occasion arose. Which it wouldn't, unless I was overpowered by a fern-fueled compulsion to steal hanging baskets for the porch.

"Nattie should be home any minute," Ethan said as he started to turn away.

"Ethan," I said in a charmingly innocent voice, "could I ask you something? I realize you're very busy, but if you could give me a minute or two . . ."

"I can spare a few minutes. What's your question, Ms. Malloy?"

"There appear to be different stories about Winston's death, none of them verifiable. Do you know what happened?"

He sat down on a nearby stone. "Nattie said you were

interested in buying his house. Are you afraid it might be haunted?"

I gritted my teeth at his condescending tone but decided to play along. "Why would the house be haunted? He drowned in the stream. Did somebody die inside the house?"

"Somebody must have. What little remains of the original house is more than a hundred and twenty years old. It was a family home filled with grandparents, babies, children, parents, teenagers, and aunts and uncles and cousins, and until the road was paved, it must have taken a long time for a horse-drawn carriage to reach a hospital. You don't have to worry about Winston rattling his chains, though; you need to worry about the title to the property. It's going to take several years before anyone can buy or sell the house."

"Terry mentioned a lease," I said, watching his pale blue eyes.

They narrowed, although his smile stayed firmly planted. "So you spoke to Terry. Where is he these days? He left town in such a rush that he didn't leave a forwarding address. Did you get hold of him through his lawyer?"

I was a paragon of proficiency in the field of evasion; even Peter had acknowledged as much. "I have no idea which lawyer in Farberville is handling his affairs. Do you?"

Ethan shook his head. "Our lawyer has that information, but I haven't had a reason to ask him. Terry was . . . well, really upset when he got back from his trip and heard the sad news. He became so enraged that Nattie had to lock herself in the bathroom until he left. The legal business is best left to the lawyers until we go to court. I hope that she's able to testify with him sitting in the courtroom."

Nattie might not be capable of pinning Terry to the

mat, but she had not implied that she was afraid of him. I put that aside and said to Ethan, "Do you believe that Winston committed suicide?"

"I don't know," he said as he tugged on his wispy beard. "When we were little kids, we hung around together. As he got older, he kept to himself. I'd see him sitting on the swing with a book, totally engrossed in it. The only cousin he really talked to was Nattie, and only because she followed him like a puppy. By the time he went off to boarding school, he was a vague nobody who came and went. When we heard that he was moving back to Hollow Valley, I was kind of excited to see him. I'd escaped to California, and he'd escaped to New York. We had that in common." He stood up and stared at the distant bridge, his arms crossed. I was about to prompt him when he said, "It was tense. Winston acted like he was pleased to see me again, but I could tell that he remembered some of the childish pranks we played on him. It was like his face was behind a pane of glass. Make that bulletproof glass, and installed by none other than Terry himself. Every time I tried to get Winston aside so I could apologize, Terry was there with a snarky remark about me, like I was nothing more than a grimy redneck. It was humiliating."

"Did you know that Winston was gay?"

Ethan relaxed but remained standing in case he needed to dodge my questions. "I figured it out before he was sent away. My parents never told me, but all of the adults had what they thought were private family councils. In the front room of the Old Tavern, with the windows open. Back then, I bought into their bigotry, but once I got to middle school, I started thinking for myself. By college, I'd shed all those malicious attitudes and learned to love without boundaries. My first significant partner was a thirty-year-old Malaysian woman with three children. My parents cut me off financially, so I had to wait tables."

He may have been disappointed when I failed to applaud his act of defiance and the brutality of his parents' retribution. "College is an eye-opener," I said mildly. "The rest of the family must not share your tolerance for alternative lifestyles."

"You're talking about the party, aren't you? It may have been awkward, but it wasn't nearly as bad as Nattie remembers. Charles and Felicia—yeah, they were offended, but they're offended by the local weather reports. They tolerate Pandora Butterfly and me because I manage production. We don't socialize except for obligatory family meals on holidays, which are excruciatingly dull. They attend church without fail and then go out for Sunday dinner with their pet deacons. Charles told me that he never leaves a tip because the waiter's committing a sin by working on Sunday."

My face went from pink to red. "That's—that's repulsive! What a total hypocrite! I want to speak to him right this minute. How dare he stiff some working kid by—"

"He's not going to listen to you," Ethan said wryly. "You're a woman, so your opinion has no value."

"Go get him! I'll show him—"

Ethan put his hand on my shoulder and kept pressure on it until I sat down. "I feel the same way. The first time Nattie collided with one of his right-wing convictions, she kicked him in the shin. She said it was a reflex."

"My reflex might involve a fist," I muttered, then forced myself to cool off. "It sounds as though you had a problem with Terry, not Winston." When he shrugged, I added, "Did you think he was overly controlling?"

"From what I saw, yeah. Winston was always easy to manipulate, and Terry was a pro. I dropped by their house a couple of times with fresh vegetables, but Winston never came to the front door. It was always Terry, staring at me as if I were vermin. You'd think that after all the discrimination they'd encountered, they wouldn't be so quick to judge me. I guess I wasn't as well educated and as fond of the arts as their other friends. When Terry was away, Winston and I hung out sometimes, drinking beer on the terrace and talking. He remembered stuff from when we were kids. Once we hiked up the mountain to a cave that was our hideout during our train-robber days. Another time he wanted to go fishing. I found rods and a tackle box in the attic of the Old Tavern. We never caught anything, but it was nice. When Terry was around, I rarely saw them."

Ethan sounded very sincere, and wounded as well. I now had three versions of the relationship between Winston and the other Hollows. It was confusing, despite my talents in intuition and my keen sense of perception. I bluntly asked Ethan if he believed that Winston had been depressed and suicidal.

"I don't know. I do believe that Terry coerced Winston into signing the deed to the property. Winston was a Hollow by birthright, and he knew about the sanctity of his inheritance. My estate leaves my property to my children, just as all the past direct descendants made sure their estates went to their offspring. Other members of the family have always been welcome to live here, such as Nattie and that pain-in-the-butt Jordan. Have you seen her today? She vanished before she finished cutting back the japonicas."

"Jordan was here earlier," I said. "She went in the direction of the mill."

He growled under his breath. "She acts as if she were in a gulag, subsisting on crusts of bread and turnip soup. Did she try to sell you that yesterday? I'll bet she didn't tell you why her parents sent her here. She was arrested in Philadelphia for loitering in a park known for drugs and underage drinking—for the third time. She barely showed her face at school all year and was in danger of expulsion in April. Her parents pulled her out of school before anything was official. Uncle Sheldon and Aunt Joanne were ready to give up on her, but they called Nattie and she came up with the idea. Not that I think anything short of boot camp can turn Jordan around. Charles and Felicia forced her to go to church with them, but she was so disruptive that they had to slink out in the middle of the sermon." His lips curled slightly. "They never suggested that again."

"I imagine not." I felt a small twinge of trepidation, having sent the miscreant off to meet Inez. Inez's parents would not be pleased if their daughter came home with a pierced navel and a Kafkaesque tattoo.

He gave me a final pat on the shoulder and then walked in the direction of the greenhouses et al. I had no particular reason to think Nattie would show up in the immediate future, so I drove back to my house to see if Terry had returned. His rental car was parked in front of the house. Feeling much better, I got out of my car and walked toward the porch. The sound of laughter from the back of the house caught my attention, so I detoured accordingly. Terry, Inez, and Jordan were sitting on the edge of the swimming pool, their bare feet in the water. Terry said something inaudible to them. They both responded with whoops of amusement. Even Jordan had forsaken her perpetual sneer, at least for the moment.

"Hello," I called, delighted that Terry appeared to be in a jovial mood. The obvious reason would be good news from his lawyer, which meant good news for me.

"Ms. Malloy," Inez said, "did you know that there was an off-Broadway show called *Abraham Lincoln's Big, Gay Dance Party*?"

Jordan giggled. "That's the sort of thing we need to lighten up life around here. Ethan's already got the beard, so he can be at the front in the dance numbers. Can you see Uncle Charles and Aunt Felicia prancing onstage? Terry says we can stage the production on the front porch."

"Sounds divine," I said. "Terry, can we talk?"

Inez and Jordan found this hilarious. They clutched each other and brayed like possessed donkeys, making rude noises and in danger of falling into the pool. Terry stood up and grinned at me. "Of course, Claire. Shall we go inside?"

I sat on a stool in the kitchen and watched him make a pitcher of lemonade. He poured two glasses, then held a bottle of vodka over one and gave me a questioning look. I shook my head. He poured himself a rather stout shot. "So what shall we talk about? The latest flops on and off Broadway? The production of *The Sound of Music* in which all parts were played by drag queens?"

"How about the house? Did you speak with your lawyer this morning?"

Terry tasted his lemonade, grimaced, and added another shot of vodka. "That was my plan when I drove into Farberville this morning. Well, I also wanted to get a copy of the *New York Times* from that little news store on Thurber Street, and maybe some fresh bagels. I was stricken to discover that the bakery next to the pool hall had gone out of business. Roberta and Juniper were veritable artistes in the culinary world. Did you ever try their cream puffs filled with caramel mousse? To die for."

I took a deep breath and exhaled slowly. "Did you make it to your lawyer's office?" If he hadn't, I wouldn't be able to stop myself from making a suggestion about what he could do with the cream puffs. It would not be to die for.

"I did," he said. He took a drink of the much diluted lemonade. "Her name's Link Cranberry. Isn't that classic? She must have suffered in the schoolyard. 'Cranberry, strawberry, gooseberry pie, here comes Link with a tear in her eye.'" He noticed that I wasn't appreciating his drollness. "She said that I shouldn't sell the house until the Hollows' lawsuit is finalized. I can, however, lease it with the stipulation that the lease might be terminated."

"What did she say about the probable outcome of the lawsuit?"

"It's baseless, but the chancery judge is a die-hard conservative. If he's antigay, he may side with the Hollows out of spite. They'll all swear that Winston was not of sound mind, and that I forced him to sign the deed. Our friends will all swear that Winston was perfectly sane at the time. Who's he going to believe—a family that's been here since the nineteenth century or a bunch of faggots? The fact that Winston and I were legally married may annoy the judge all the more."

I had a feeling that his dire prediction might be right. The presence of Farber College added an element of liberal ambience, but it was only a teaspoon of water in a dark sea of social conservatism. "Green" was not an ecological movement; it was the color of money. "So Ms. Cranberry is not optimistic?"

Terry smiled. "I have unlimited financial resources to fight them, and for Winston's sake, I will. He wanted me to have the house if something happened to him. Murder may not have crossed his mind, but it should have." He drained his drink. "Damn, I forgot to pick up tonic water this morning. My official summer drink is vodka and tonic, with a squeeze of lime juice."

"I'll bring you a case of tonic water and dozens of limes after I've signed the lease," I said. "We agree to the stipulation. Do you have a pen?"

"Ms. Cranberry has to be in court this afternoon, but she'll draw it up first thing Monday morning. I can drop by your house and—" He broke off abruptly and put both hands on the edge of the island. "Something's wrong. I think I'm going to—" He concluded the sentence by vomiting on his hands. He tried to straighten up, but his arms began to twitch spasmodically. He vomited again.

With all due respect to Florence Nightingale, I have an aversion to sickness. I went to the sink and dampened a dish towel. "Here," I said as I averted my eyes. Had it been possible, I would have averted my nose as well.

Terry waved me back as he continued to retch. He lost his grip and slithered to the floor, moaning piteously. "I need help," he rasped.

I'd left my cell phone in my car. "Be right back," I said, then ran out the front door. I called nine-one-one, did my best to describe his symptoms, and gave directions.

"Is he on any medications?" the dispatcher asked.

"I have no idea! Just send an ambulance!"

"Does the victim have insurance? I'll need the name of the provider and the number of his policy."

My response was less than polite. Clutching the phone, I hurried back inside and crouched next to Terry. "An ambulance is on the way. Do you want some water?" I felt as useful as a flat tire on a rainy night. He was doubled up in a tight ball, his legs speckled with vomited debris. His moans were protracted. I put my hand on his back to keep him from banging his head on the low cabinet. I glanced up and saw Inez and Jordan in the doorway that led from the terrace. Their faces were white, their mouths open. Behind them, Moses's face hovered like an unsightly helium balloon.

"I've called for an ambulance," I said firmly, as if I were in control of some minor complication. "You'd better wait outside. Everything's going to be okay."

I didn't fool anyone, including myself.

CHAPTER 6

Paramedics stormed the house and surrounded Terry, who was alarmingly still. They were followed by a pair of uniformed policemen. Neither of the paramedics fell into Jordan's category of "hunk," but they were efficient and fast. I stood and watched as Terry was put on a gurney and taken to the ambulance parked outside. I followed to ask about Terry's diagnosis, but a police officer, who appeared to be Caron's age, stopped me in the entry hall.

"I need information about the patient, ma'am," he said.

All I could give him was Terry's last name and hometown. I described what had happened before the gastric attack. The officer eyed the vodka bottle on the floor. "So you both were drinking," he said as if accusing us of rampant alcoholism, "while the girls were in the vicinity of the swimming pool. Did you plan to drive home in your condition?"

"I can handle lemonade on the rocks," I said, "and the girls are hardly toddlers. You might want to take a sample of the vodka."

"Name and address, ma'am?"

"Claire Malloy, and my address is on record at the PD."

"You've been arrested in the past?" His hand shifted closer to his gun, prepared to react if I admitted that I'd robbed convenience stores and gunned down grannies on the street—and battered young policemen with liquor bottles.

The second officer, J. Bingsley, put his hand on the younger officer's arm. "Ms. Malloy is married to Deputy Chief Rosen. He'll vouch for her." He looked at me. "Do you think the vodka is responsible for the victim's condition?"

I shrugged. "He seemed fine when we came inside to talk. I have no idea what he ate or drank earlier, but his symptoms began after he'd ingested several ounces of the vodka. I drank the lemonade and I'm okay."

"Is he a friend?"

"I only met him in person yesterday. He came here from Key West to negotiate a lease for the property. My husband"—I pointedly did not add emphasis—"and I are hoping to buy it after a lawsuit is settled."

After Bingsley sent his partner outside to question Inez and Jordan, he went into the living room and made a call. Although I tried my best, I couldn't hear what he was saying, but I did catch my name—and I was pretty sure I heard a pained sigh from dear Jorgeson, who'd most likely planned to be sitting with his wife in their rose garden by late afternoon. I felt a pang of guilt for ruining his evening, but in no way was I responsible. "A policeman's lot is not a happy one," as Gilbert opined to Sullivan.

I went out to the terrace to escape the stench. Officer Teenager towered over Inez and Jordan, barking questions at them. I presumed Jordan had enough sense to refrain from mouthing off or bragging about her rap sheet. Moses had disappeared.

"I've called for the crime squad," Bingsley said as he came outside. "This is likely to be nothing more than food poisoning, but the scene has to be secured until the ER confirms the cause. If you prefer to leave, it's not a problem. Lieutenant Jorgeson went so far as to suggest that you do so." He eyed his partner. "Threadgill's a rookie. You'll have to forgive him, Ms. Malloy."

"For not knowing that I'm married to Deputy Chief Rosen, and therefore to be treated with deference? I am simply a witness and should be subjected to whatever it is to which witnesses should be subjected." I politely overlooked his bemused expression and continued. "I think you'd better test the vodka, but food poisoning is a possibility. He had breakfast in town a couple of hours ago. How long will it take to get lab results?"

"It depends on the backlog. Samples have to be sent to the state lab, in which case it may be weeks. Do you have a reason for thinking that the vodka was poisoned?"

I sat down to weigh the two scenarios. Food poisoning was not unknown in the cafés and restaurants in Farberville. Then again, Terry was not the golden child of Hollow Valley. I hadn't met Charles and Felicia, although from all reports thus far, I wasn't eager to do so. They had disapproved of Winston and Terry's lifestyle in all aspects, from their homosexuality to their consumption of alcohol. Ethan had made it clear that he thought Terry was conniving and manipulative. Almost everything I'd been told about Winston, Terry, the notorious housewarming party, and Winston's death had been contradicted by another source. I was trying to formulate a reply to Officer Bingsley when my cell phone rang.

I gaped at it as if it had stung me. "I'd better take this."

"What the hell is going on?" demanded Deputy Chief Peter Rosen.

"This is what you get for not taking my calls earlier," I

said, "but no, you were so busy with your silly meetings that you ignored my frantic efforts to keep you informed. I'd like to think you'll do better in the future."

"What the hell is going on?" Peter repeated, spitting out each word. "Who was taken to the ER? Why are you at what might be a crime scene?"

I grimaced at Officer Bingsley, who must have over-heard Peter's strident voice. "I'm fine, dear. I told you last night that I was coming to the house to talk to Terry about the lease, remember?" I went on to describe the events that had occurred prior to the call. "A very nice police officer named Bingsley is here with me now, discussing the possibility of food poisoning. It may turn out to be that it was something in the vodka . . ." I abruptly real-ized how close I'd been to having a nip in my lemonade. Had I done so, two gurneys would have been required. I might be in the ER, having my stomach pumped. It was a procedure not to be confused with recreation.

Peter was still ranting. I handed my phone to Officer Bingsley and walked toward the apple orchard, my arms wrapped around my shoulders, shivering. Food poisoning was more probable than sabotage. Terry hadn't offered me a pastry from his morning foray, or anything else that might contain *E. coli* or botulism. A surge of nausea overwhelmed. In spite of my efforts to control my stom-ach, I vomited, barely missing my feet. When the nausea passed, I sat down under a tree and assured myself that panic was the impetus, not something in the lemonade. As loath as I am to admit that I am not always unruffled, I was frightened. The apple trees began to resemble those in *The Wizard of Oz*. I certainly could use a bit of courage that I could not acquire by tapping my ruby slippers to-gether three times. I was wearing sandals.

Eventually, Officer Bingsley found me. "Are you ill, Ms. Malloy? Should I get the paramedics back here?"

I put out my hand and allowed him to help me up. "Delayed shock is all. Did Deputy Chief Rosen say anything of significance?"

"Mostly what he would do to me if I didn't escort you away from the scene in the next ten seconds," he said grimly. He gave me back my cell phone. "Do you want me to drive you and the girls home? Officer Threadgill can drive your vehicle."

"I'm quite capable of driving myself and one of the girls back to town. The other one lives nearby." I veered around a certain patch of grass as we went back to the terrace. Inez and Jordan were putting on their shoes under the belligerent supervision of Officer Threadgill. "Inez," I said, "we're leaving now. Jordan, you'd better go hide under Aunt Margaret Louise's bed. Ethan's looking for you."

I told Officer Bingsley that I would smooth things over with my husband, then beckoned Inez to follow me around the house to my car. Her face lowered, Jordan took off in the direction of the meadow. Officer Threadgill's rigid posture slumped as his prime suspects escaped from what might have been an interminable interrogation. When Inez and I arrived in the front yard, we were faced by an impromptu gathering of the property owners' association. Nattie, Ethan, Pandora Butterfly, and two unfamiliar people hovered in a clump, all looking worried.

"Claire," Nattie said, "what on earth happened? I saw an ambulance leaving when I turned off the highway. Are you all right?"

Ethan stepped forward. "Did Terry come back? Why didn't you tell me when we were talking about him?"

"You knew Terry was here?" Nattie asked accusingly, staring at me. "Did he say something about Winston? Is that why you've been asking me all these questions?"

"Of course not," I said. I felt as though I should apolo-

gize for eating cinnamon rolls under false pretenses. At the same time, I wondered if she'd been quite so truthful with me. Moses had told me that she lied.

"How lovely," Pandora said dreamily as she began to dance. She was wearing a richly embroidered kimono and stained ballet slippers. "Do you see the mockingbirds on the eave?"

Too many questions, I thought, resisting the urge to climb into my car, lock the doors, and drive off at a speed more suitable to an oval track. "Everything is under control. Terry flew in yesterday and stayed here last night. We were chatting when he became ill. It's most likely a case of food poisoning. When he recovers, the police will find out where he ate this morning and take it from there."

"He's going to recover?" Nattie asked.

"I'm sure he will." I squeezed Inez's shoulder to reassure her. I needed someone to squeeze my shoulder in the same manner. "He's young and healthy. He may be back by this evening."

A man with short, peppery hair and a hard look said, "His kind have despicable diseases because of promiscuity and illegal drugs. First Winston, and now this . . . this viper. He deserves to suffer for his sins."

I cleverly deduced that this was Charles Finnelly, spokesperson for the moral minority of Hollow Valley. His wife, Felicia, looked as though she'd been munching green persimmons. Her lips were so tight that they were scarcely visible. "No one deserves to suffer," I said, although I doubted that he cared about my opinion. At least he didn't keep his wife barefoot and pregnant. Not that he could, since she was in her fifties and probably wore a flannel gown and a platinum chastity belt to bed.

Nattie ignored the exchange and said, "Have you seen Jordan, Claire? Ethan said that she never showed up at the nursery this morning. Is she involved?"

I was not about to squeal on my Mohawked prodigy. "I saw her earlier and she was okay." Inez started to say something, but I increased the intensity of my grip on her shoulder until she gulped. "We need to go. The police will lock up the house before they leave."

"They needn't bother," trilled Madame Butterfly, who was now flapping her arms. "Oh, look at this dear little yellow butterfly! Catch her, Ethan, so I can release her in my garden."

I hustled Inez into the car, called a generic good-bye, and drove down the gravel driveway to the blacktop road. It took several minutes before I felt calm enough to say, "How did you and Jordan get along?"

"Okay, I guess," Inez said. "There are kids like that at school, but they're kind of invisible. They don't join any clubs or participate in class. They go to all that effort to be unique, but they look like clones. Anyway, Jordan was kind of nasty at first. After a while, she relaxed, and we went up the hillside to look for ginseng."

"The two of you must have had a good time. You were carrying on like a pair of drunks. Terry, too." I glanced at her and caught the blush on her cheeks. It was possible that the hormonal inundation had caught up with her at last. "He's handsome, isn't he?" I inquired delicately.

"He told us all these really wild stories about the theater people in New York. I thought I'd die laughing. Not that I did, of course." She began to giggle. "There are bars in Greenwich Village that put on beauty pageants for men who dress up like famous actresses. I kept picturing my father in a blond wig and an evening gown, wobbling across a stage in high heels." Her giggles grew so loud that I wanted to put my hand over her mouth. "And my brother in a bikini! He's so scrawny that he'd have to glue it on!"

It didn't sound as though she were infatuated with

Terry, I thought with relief. Although she must have been aware of alternative sexual orientations, I wasn't sure that she'd actually encountered any openly gay guys. Farberville High School's closet doors were locked with dead bolts. The lesbians and gays who came into the Book Depot were no more disposed to discuss their sexual activity than anyone else was. If for no other reason than to distract myself, I said, "Terry's gay, you know."

Inez stopped giggling to stare at me. "What difference does that make, Ms. Malloy?"

"None at all," I said. It was unfortunate (and inexcusable) that some of the Hollows did not concur. I let her ramble on about Broadway's wits and warts while I tried not to worry about Terry or dwell on what might turn out to be my closest call to date. I'd had some doozies over the last few years, but I'd never doubted that I could find a way to save my flawless skin.

I dropped off Inez at the library and went home. After a shower and a change of clothing, I called Jorgeson. "How's Terry Kennedy?" I asked.

"The man who had to be taken by ambulance to the emergency room? Officers Bingsley and Threadgill haven't reported yet, Ms. Malloy. As far as I know, they're still at the scene."

"Would you be so kind as to call the hospital? They're obsessed with privacy, and I'm not the man's sister. Well, I could claim to be his next of kin, but that would be a lie. I'd hate to upset Peter even more." I fluttered my eyelashes for the benefit of an unseen audience. "You know how he can be, Jorgeson."

"I'll call the hospital and then call you back."

"You're such a dear." I hung up and went into the kitchen to pour myself a small glass of Scotch. I jammed the bottle back in the cabinet and filled the teakettle, wondering how long it would be before I would be able to enjoy a cocktail. Days, weeks, months—as long as it took for the medical lab to determine that Terry had been stricken with food poisoning from a botulistic bagel or a salmonella-laden custard tart. I was spooning sugar in my tea when Jorgeson finally bestirred himself to call.

"Well?" I said by way of greeting.

"He lapsed into a coma in the ER and is hooked up to a ventilator and monitoring machines in the ICU. No diagnosis, but the prognosis is not good," he said. "The lab hasn't come up with anything yet. For now, they're assuming it's a case of food poisoning. We're searching his car for a receipt from one of the local eateries."

"He was in Key West yesterday. Maybe he ate something tainted before he left."

He sighed. "That's very helpful, Ms. Malloy. I'll ask the PD if they've had any cases down there. If you'll excuse me—"

"One more thing," I said, not at all ready to excuse him. "Has the Maxwell County sheriff found out any more about Angela?"

"The only airplane that uses the landing strip is locked in a metal shed. The owner is at his daughter's house, recovering from the flu. He has the only key, and there are no indications that anyone tampered with the padlock. Angela's car has been towed in to be examined in more detail. As for now, I'm dealing with two convenience store robberies and an escalating brawl on fraternity row. If I get any updates about Kennedy or Angela Delmond, you'll be the first to know." He had enough sense not to ask to be excused a second time.

I took the phone out to the balcony and called Peter. He listened to my recitation of the recent events, attempting to interrupt, until I'd covered everything that I felt was of consequence.

"I want you to stay away from Hollow Valley until this is cleared up," he began officiously. "I realize that you're focused on the house, but you'll have to wait until I get back tomorrow. This is not the time for meddling, however civic minded you like to think you are."

"Right now I am not the least bit civic minded," I protested. "I simply want the house, and I'm not going to let anyone stop me."

"What if I tell you to stay away from Hollow Valley?"

If ever a situation required tact, this was it. Besides, it would be cruel to allow him to worry. "There's not much I can do until we find out what caused Terry's attack. Jorgeson's quite sure it's food poisoning. I can't see myself snooping through garbage bins behind cafés, picking through rotten produce. Do you think we should rent a storage locker? I trip over a box every time I walk into the kitchen. We can pack up our winter clothes and—"

"Stay away from Hollow Valley." He launched into a very sweet lecture on how much I meant to him and how horribly he would suffer if something bad happened to me. When he ran out of hyperbole, I steered him into a romantic discussion involving his first night at home.

I was relieved when the conversation ended. I made a mental note to read some romance novels to increase my competency in verbal passion, then poured another cup of tea and sat down on the sofa with a notebook. The time had come to sort out the Hollows from octogenarian Moses to wee Weevil. Since I had limited knowledge of the lineage, it took only a couple of minutes. I sketched a map of Hollow Valley, with the blacktop road, the driveways, the residents, and the nursery. There were three houses: the Finnellys', Ethan and Pandora Butterfly's, and Terry's—which had been Winston's but was going to be mine. Aunt Margaret Louise lived in the mill, and Nattie and Moses lived in the Old Tavern. If Hollow hermits lived in caves on the mountain behind the nursery, no one had mentioned them.

The housewarming party would have been great entertainment for a disinterested observer. I smiled as I pictured Felicia and Charles in the dining room, overcome with self-righteousness as they viewed the debauchery. Oh, the horrors! Nattie thought that Terry was nice; Ethan thought that Terry was a con man. I knew that Terry could be charming, but also emotional. As for Winston, he had been either deeply depressed or eager to samba in Rio. He'd fished, or he hadn't. He'd slipped, jumped, or been propelled into the stream.

The whole business was a puddle of deception deep enough to provide a haven for catfish. I had only twenty-four hours to snoop around before Deputy Chief Rosen arrived home from Atlanta.

Before I could choose a course of action, Jorgeson called. He had checked with the hospital and reported that Terry's condition remained unchanged. I wished him success with the riotous Zetas, Thetas, and Betas. He failed to appreciate my witticism. There was no point in going to the hospital unless I was prepared to lie through my teeth, and even if I crept through a crack in the walls of the sterilized citadel, it would accomplish nothing as long as Terry was in a coma. The lab would not welcome my subtle hints that they step away from the vending machines and run the necessary tests to determine the cause of Terry's symptoms.

It was the middle of the afternoon. Surely the courthouse judges had stashed their gavels and retired their robes in order to enjoy the weekend. It was likely that Terry's attorney was back in her office, finishing the week's backlog of files to be filed and writs to be written. Her name was impossible to forget. I looked up her office address in the primordial telephone directory, grabbed my purse, and drove to a yellow-brick house within walking distance of the courthouse. What had been the living room was now a reception room. The desk was clear, and the receptionist was gone for the day. I prowled down a hallway until I found a door with the name CRANBERRY painted on the glass. The light was on, and I heard a voice. I tapped once and then went inside.

Link Cranberry was not what I'd expected, although in all honesty I had no expectations. It could not have been more than two or three years since she earned her law degree. She had black hair pulled back in a no-nonsense bun, and she wore enormous black-framed glasses. Her lips were scarlet. When she stood up, she was not as tall as the coat rack behind her desk. To compensate for her diminutive stature, she'd perfected a menacing glare.

"The office is closed," she said icily, the telephone receiver in her hand. It would have been far more impressive if she hadn't sounded like a squeaky, petulant child. "Call Monday and make an appointment."

"I don't know if you've heard what's happed to Terry Kennedy. He's at the hospital."

"Oh, shit," she said. She ended the telephone call with a few terse words. "I met with him only this morning. Was he in an accident?" She sank into her chair. "Are his injuries that severe? Is he in intensive care?"

"He's in a coma," I said, then told her what little I knew. "If it's food poisoning, it may not be fatal. Healthy people usually survive."

Ms. Cranberry rubbed her face and neck as she assimilated the information. "He's such a great guy. I should do something, but what? Does the hospital have the name of his next of kin? I may have it in a file somewhere." She took several deep breaths. "Give me a minute to find the file, okay? It should be in this stack."

I watched her fumble for a moment, then sat down and said, "I'm not convinced it's food poisoning."

She looked up. "Who are you?"

"Claire Malloy. I'm hoping to lease Terry's house until the lawsuit is settled. After that, my husband and I want to buy it."

"I recognize the name," she said. I waited for her to laud my modest contributions in the field of detection, but she found the file and pulled out a piece of paper. "Terry did say that he spoke to you. I'm supposed to draw up the lease Monday morning. I guess I ought to wait until he regains consciousness before I do anything further. Thank you for coming by, Ms. Malloy. I hope that next time the circumstances will be more pleasant."

I wasn't about to be sent away before I found out what I could. "Ms. Cranberry, I'm sorry to cause you more distress, but Terry may not regain consciousness."

"But you just said that healthy people can handle food poisoning . . ."

"That's true. However, his condition may not have been caused by food-borne bacteria. The police haven't ruled out the possibility that Terry unknowingly ingested another type of poison. I was talking to him this morning, after his appointment with you. I had lemonade; he had lemonade spiked with vodka. Five minutes later, he was writhing on his kitchen floor and I was calling nine-one-one for an ambulance."

"I can't believe it," she said. "I mean, why would somebody want to hurt Terry? Sure, the Hollows were unhappy about the transfer of the property to his name, but it's not worth killing somebody. I'm not one hundred percent confident that they won't prevail with their lawsuit."

"What then?"

She shrugged. "Winston died intestate, so his estate

will go to his closest relative, either a Hollow or a Martinson. It'll be a mess, but I won't be involved."

"Does Terry have a will?"

"Client-lawyer privilege prevents me from answering that."

"But he told you that he wanted to let me lease the property, didn't he? He asked you to prepare the lease."

Ms. Cranberry hesitated. "I suppose it's okay to tell you this much. We discussed your lease and the terms. He wants to let you and your husband lease it for a hundred dollars a month."

"We'll be happy to pay whatever the rental market dictates." My mood elevator raced to the top floor of a very high skyscraper, took in the panoramic view, but then plummeted to the basement. Terry was incapable of signing the lease, at least for the time being.

I promised to keep her informed. When I arrived home, I called Jorgeson, who said that Terry's condition was unchanged. Before I could ask, he added that the lab had not produced any results. In an amusingly opaque attempt to sidetrack me, he extolled the fragrance and beauty of roses begging to be cut and given a good home. I thanked him and hung up. I stared blankly at a pile of boxes, suddenly numbed with guilt. I'd sparked the mess by refusing to settle for an unremarkable house. Angela had tossed on kindling by contacting Terry, then disappearing, which had forced me to call him. He'd returned to Farberville, to end up in an ICU cubicle.

I would have gone back to Hollow Valley to talk to Nattie, despite Peter's pettiness, but I had no idea what to say to her. No one's opinion about Terry could help him until the appropriate antidote was administered, assuming there was one—and it wasn't too late. In a much more potent attempt to sidetrack myself, I tried to remember what I could about the vodka bottle that Terry took out of the lower cabinet. It was half full, as though he'd been nipping the previous evening—but, I thought, he'd been drinking wine, and vodka does not go well with le vin du jour. On the other hand (and there was always the other hand), he might have bought it when he arrived and shared it with friends. A less than amicable friend who added something on the sly.

Now all I needed was a list of the people he'd visited before he drove out to Hollow Valley and called me. That was a poser, in that he hadn't dropped any names. I went to the balcony and watched the Farber College students ambling across the green lawn. A significant number of them would head straight to their favorite bars to celebrate the advent of the weekend. I knew of one gay bar in Farberville, and it was well within ambling range. I told myself that I was making a ridiculous assumption, unworthy of my more pragmatic side. I told myself that over and over as I went downstairs and headed for Thurber Street.

The Toucan Lounge was tucked behind the performing arts center in what had been a laundry. I hesitated and then went inside. Blinds had been lowered to combat the afternoon sun, and it did not seem prudent to yank one open. The tables and booths were occupied by earnest young men and women and a few older ones. Most of the stools at the bar were taken. Although heads turned on my entry, no one seemed at all intrigued. I did not take it personally. I found a stool at the bar. The men on either side had their backs toward me; I felt as if I were in a crevice.

The bartender would most definitely qualify as a hunk in Jordan's mind. He put down a coaster and said, "What can I get you?"

It was encouraging to know my presence was tolerable, if not openly welcomed. "A glass of white wine, please." I gazed at the occupants, wondering which if any might know Terry. My assumption was not only ridiculous, but also inane and offensive. However, my motive was as pure as newly fallen flakes of dandruff, so when the bartender put down the glass of wine, I said, "Do you happen to know a friend of mine, Terry Kennedy?"

He did not return my smile. "You mean your gay friend, Terry Kennedy? Every liberal in town has to have one."

I struggled not to reach across the bar and poke him with a cocktail stirrer. "You didn't answer my question."

"You didn't answer mine." He sidled down the bar to take an order.

"Humph," I said in a low voice as I picked up the glass of what I suspected would not be vintage wine. I swirled it while I waited for inspiration.

"I know Terry," said the man on my right. His hair was gray, and he was of a more civilized age than the hunk/punk bartender. His round face and sparkly eyes reminded me of a naughty cherub. "He and Winston helped us with a performance at the college theater last summer. Winston was a fantastic designer. We had twelve scene changes and pulled them off flawlessly. So Terry's a friend of yours?"

I ignored a snort from somewhere down the bar. "We met last night for the first time. He came here to negotiate terms for me to buy his house."

"In Hollow Valley? Be careful what you wish for. My name's Bill Bobstay. Please call me Billy. I'm a professor of drama at the college. I met Terry and Winston through mutual friends, and I played in Winston's string ensemble. We made terrible screeches and never finished at the same time. God, that was fun."

Coincidences do happen, I thought smugly. "Were you scheduled to play that weekend . . . after the accident?"

"Yes, Winston made us all confirm the date and swear we'd come. The last time we'd met, the cello player backed out because he met someone. No one saw him for a week, the silly old bear. Then there was a time when we were on the terrace, and Hildebrand got so topsy-turvy that he fell in the pool. With his violin, no less. I thought Winston would throw a fit, not because Hildebrand was splashing like a calf, but because in all the excitement, he let the cassoulet burn."

"Did you see Terry late yesterday afternoon or this morning?"

"Why do you ask?"

My fishing expedition was going no better than Winston's had, although I hoped the results would not be similar. "He's in the ICU with what may be food poisoning. The police are trying to track down where he's been since he arrived in Farberville. If you have any information, Billy, it'll help determine the source."

"This is terrible news," he said, shaking his head. "Is he allowed visitors?"

"He's in a coma, so there's no point in attempting to breach hospital protocol. I'm Claire Malloy, by the way." I gave him a moment to react. When he failed to so much as raise an eyebrow, I asked again, "Did you see Terry yesterday or this morning?"

"I wish I could say that I had." Billy took my elbow and escorted me to a vacated booth in the back corner of the Toucan. "Please wait here, Claire. I'll see what I can find out. Trust me when I say that no one will disturb you."

I watched him as he moved from table to table, speaking quietly to the occupants. He then went to the bar, caught the attention of the bartender, and spoke with some urgency. When he returned to the booth, he said, "He was here yesterday around four o'clock and left with

Samuel to visit Loretta and Nicole. Would you like me to take you there?"

I slid out of the booth. "Yes, and thank you. I had a feeling I wasn't going to get much information here."

"Strangers have to submit an application and be vetted before anyone will tell them what time it is." He led me to a Volkswagen Beetle, circa nineteen sixty-something. What paint remained was light aqua; rust had eaten significant portions of the bumpers. He took a pile of books and papers off the passenger's seat and tossed them in the backseat. "The shocks died twenty years ago," he said cheerfully as he shifted into reverse and swung out of the parking space. "I don't know if Loretta and Nicole are home, but we might as well try. If they're not, we'll swing by Samuel's house. Don't you own the bookstore on Farber Street?"

I admitted that I did, and we conversed about books as the car bounced like a Ping-Pong ball. He drove past the football stadium and turned up a steep street to the top of the hill. I'd accepted the demise of the shocks, but I began to wonder about the brakes. Gravity dictates that going up requires coming down. I did not wish to land on the fifty-yard line in an eroded tin can.

The women's house was in need of tender loving care. The yard was overgrown, and the roof was littered with small branches. Billy and I went to the porch. He opened the door and called, "Hello? Anybody home? It's Billy Bobstay and a friend!"

A brown-haired woman in a long skirt came into the living room. "Billy! How are you, you old horny toad? We haven't seen you in months! Nicole and I adored the production of *The Taming of the Screw*. The original is so nauseatingly sexist. When Kate chopped off Petruchio's prick, we laughed so hard we slid out of our seats!"

"It was a masterpiece," Billy replied with a nod.

"Loretta, this is a friend of mine, Claire Malloy. Did you see Terry Kennedy yesterday?"

"He showed up about five with Samuel. When Nicole got home from her office, we sat around and talked about Winston. Terry got really upset. He hasn't begun to heal, and I'm afraid he may never get over it. We drank iced tea for a while and then had dinner here. He left at eight."

My heart thumped. "What did you have?" I asked, hoping they hadn't ordered a pizza.

Loretta gave me a puzzled look. "Is it important?"

"It might be."

"Loretta's a brilliant chef," Billy said, as if defending her from an imminent onslaught of culinary criticism. "She uses only fresh, organic produce. I absolutely salivate when I think about the chicken liver crostini with pickled eggs." His eyes welled with tears.

"It's important," I said to Loretta. "Terry had a ghastly attack this morning, which must have been provoked by something he ate or drank."

Her lips pursed as if she were sucking on a tiny straw. After a long moment, she said, "I didn't want to go to the store, so I used whatever I could find. We had salad, rosemary flatbread, and an onion and mushroom quiche. For dessert, we had fruit and cheese. No one else had any ill effects."

I zoomed in on the key word. "Mushrooms? Did you pick them yourself?"

"Billy, is she a lawyer? I'm not admitting to anything that might get me sued. I'm worried sick about Terry, but let me assure you that the mushrooms were safe. Remember the chanterelles in garlic butter? You carried on all night about them."

I held up my hand to prevent another gastronomic wet dream. "I swear that I'm not a lawyer and will never be one. I'm trying to identify the cause of Terry's condition. Did you pick the mushrooms, Loretta?"

"Yes, but I know which ones are edible, and I always double-check them." Her stare defied me to cast any doubt on her expertise. "I have several field guides if you'd like to look at them. Mrs. Pompy and I went out yesterday morning and gathered a basket of shaggy manes and chanterelles. She's at least a hundred years old, and she's gathered mushrooms since she was a child."

"Mrs. Pompy is blind, Loretta," Billy said. "When I drove up here last week to bring you tomatoes from the farmers' market, I saw her fumbling at her mailbox. I stopped and helped her pick up her mail. She tripped on her sidewalk and almost fell on her face."

Loretta crossed her arms. "She can still identify death caps and morels. Before I started making the quiche, I sorted through all the mushrooms. There were a couple of ink caps, which I discarded."

"Is there a remote chance that you missed one?" I asked.

"Of course not!" she snapped. "Samuel was peering over my shoulder. Why don't you go badger him?" She stepped back and slammed the door.

"Well, then," Billy said as we went back to his car, "shall we try to find Samuel?"

"No, I don't think so. I would appreciate it if you make sure he's not experiencing any symptoms, and give me a call." While we bounced and careened down the hill, I scribbled my telephone number on the back of a receipt. I asked him to drop me off at the Book Depot. Once the car shuddered to a stop, I gave him the scrap of paper and thanked him for his assistance.

"Anything for poor Terry," he said, clutching my hand. "Feel free to call me if I can do anything else. I'll spread the word about him and find out if anyone else saw him yesterday or this morning."

I went into the bookstore and swept past the clerk, who scarcely looked up from whatever he was doing on the computer. Loretta had field guides, but so did I. I took several to my office and made myself comfortable. After a lengthy foray into the world of mycology, I stumbled across a suspect. *Coprinopsis atramentaria* contained coprine, logically enough, which was usually nonfatal. However, consuming alcohol even twelve hours after eating them could cause vicious reactions.

I pushed aside the field guide and called Jorgeson. "I think I may have found out what's wrong with Terry," I said, trying not to sound insufferably smug. "Last night he ate a mushroom quiche. The mushrooms were picked by this woman who—"

"Terry died an hour ago."

CHAPTER 7

My eyes filled with tears as Jorgeson's words pounded in my head. I slumped back, overwhelmed by the tragedy of Terry's death, my culpability, and fierce anger. I removed myself from the battle waging inside my head and allowed my emotions to roil like a turbulent river. Once I could trust myself, I arose and went to the bathroom for a handful of tissues. Feeling steadier (and less soggy), I considered the entire scenario. Although I'd jumped on the possibility that ink caps were responsible for Terry's fatal attack, I knew that I was wrong. He'd been drinking the previous evening and had experienced no ill effects. Whoever had murdered him was accountable to me, too. All my idyllic fantasies would never become reality.

I do not accept defeat graciously.

Billy Bobstay might come across someone with a serious grudge against Terry, but it was unlikely. It would require a convoluted series of events. Terry had accepted the half-empty bottle of vodka from a so-called friend; neither of them drank it. Of course, he knew that he'd left behind a well-stocked bar and wine selection, minus whatever had caught Moses's fancy. The vodka brand was commonplace.

It was time to go back to Hollow Valley and determine who was behind the scheme to retain control of it. I hadn't precisely promised Peter that I wouldn't, and I was not about to let a mere man, albeit one to whom I was married, deter my determination to expose the perpetrator.

I heard two pairs of footsteps on the stairs. There was no sound for a minute, and then one pair went back down the stairs. The other pair continued into the living room.

"I am so sunburned," Caron said as she gingerly lay down on the sofa. Her nose was cerise, her cheeks pink. There were pale circles where her sunglasses had protected her, giving her the eerie appearance of an inverted raccoon. "I am going to require constant nursing if I am to survive, Mother. Cold compresses, aloe cream, herbal tea, whatever. I am In Pain."

"Sorry, dear," I said, "but I'm on my way out. Why don't you take a long, cool bath, then apply the aloe cream? I'll be back in an hour."

"You don't even care that I'm Pulsating With Pain. I'm feverish, you know. I could have second degree burns—or third, or even fourth degree, for that matter. When you get home, I'll be a charred corpse." She whimpered pathetically until she realized I had picked up my purse. "At least call Inez so that she can come over to administer last rights."

"You're not Catholic, and your cell phone's six inches from your hand."

I drove to Hollow Valley, taking my time as I did my best to formulate some sort of plan of attack. It made sense, I decided, to start with the Hollows I had not yet met: Charles, Felicia, and Margaret Louise. Charles had spoken earlier, although not necessarily to me. Felicia had been mute. As I turned onto the road, I decided to warm up with Margaret Louise before I tackled the pricklier ones. I parked at the top of the path and walked down to the mill. The wheel behind it looked like a Ferris wheel with bench seats; the first half of the ride would offer a panorama of the valley, but the second half would be watery. I knocked on the door. An elderly woman opened the door and said, "I know who you are, so don't try to pretend you're selling Girl Scout cookies."

Margaret Louise was not a sweet, white-haired granny in an apron, with a smudge of flour on the cheek. Her choppy hair was black, and she was wearing shorts and a T-shirt emblazoned with Mick Jagger's leering lips. A cigarette drooped from her lips. The only age-appropriate thing about her was her wrinkled complexion.

I wanted to dash back to my car, but I held my ground. "I'm Claire Malloy," I said. "I'd like to talk to you, if it's convenient."

"Yeah, okay." She turned around and walked away. After a moment, I followed her through the living room to a small deck. She sat down in one aluminum chair and flipped her hand at another one. "You've made a mess of things," she commented as if speaking of the weather.

"Yes, I have. Terry Kennedy died this afternoon."

"That's a shame. He really shouldn't have come back."

"It's his house," I pointed out. "Why shouldn't he have decided to stay there for a few days?"

"You'll have to ask Nattie. Shall I put on some reggae music? It's Saturday, and we should get it on, don't you think? Margarita time!"

"I'd prefer to talk," I said as I watched cigarette ashes trickle down her shirt. "What did you think about the relationship between Winston and Terry?"

Margaret Louise flipped the cigarette butt into the stream below us. "You mean because they were gay? I thought a helluva lot more about those chocolate truffles.

I don't care what they did in their bed. Back in my day, there'd be at least three or four people in the bed, all of 'em stoned out of their gourds. I was at Woodstock, and I saw the Grateful Dead at the Hollywood Palladium in 'seventy-one. I rode with the Angels one year. Two gay guys? That's as exciting as tepid milk."

I tried to keep my eyebrows from hitting the eave. "In perspective, I guess it is. I understand that the Finnellys were not as enlightened."

"They have tomato stakes up their butts," she said. "Splintery ones. Charles was the one who browbeat Winston's parents into packing him off to school. He thought that Winston's homosexuality was contagious, and that Ethan, Zack, Shelly, and the rest of the cousins would take to strutting around in tutus. He didn't have to make much of an argument—it was obvious that the kid needed to get away. I was sorry when Winston came back a couple of years ago 'cause I knew it wasn't going to be any better." She lit a cigarette and blew a smoke ring. "I saw it coming."

"Winston's accident?"

"That's a joke, right? He was dead drunk, in case nobody's told you, and probably sat on the bank and sobbed before he took the plunge. I hate to speak ill of the gay, but he was a wimp from the day he was born. When the boys teased him, I'd find him hunkered under this deck. I'd haul him up here, make him take a gulp of brandy, and send him back into battle."

"Then you believe that he committed suicide," I said flatly.

"Hush," she said in an exaggerated swoosh. "If the media hear of it, the scandal will be bigger than all of Elizabeth Taylor's divorces combined. Isn't every last soul in the country speculating about the death of Winston Hollow Martinson? I'm surprised that there aren't any conspiracy theories yet. The meadow could be the grassy knoll. Or maybe it was aliens. I've always liked aliens."

"Me, too." I took a minute to recompose my thoughts. "There is a rumor that Winston was pushed, Margaret Louise. Do you think that anyone out here would do that in order to keep the property in the family?"

She appeared to be more interested in a hawk on a branch across the stream, but she finally said, "You mean Charles, I assume. I did hear him muttering about tar and feathers, but he's nothing but hot air. Make that scorching hot air from the middle of the Sahara. I'd be surprised if they have to turn on their furnace in the winter. Felicia probably makes s'mores on the top of his head."

"Anyone else?" I had not forgotten her comment about Nattie.

"No, not really. Despite our eccentricities, we're really just an ordinary bunch of people running a family business. You can look at the Colonel's statue and deduce that some bad genes filtered down through the generations. Jordan has the record, as far as I can tell. Talk about a pain in the neck. I've never heard such an endless deluge of whines and complaints. This is no Sunnybrook Farm, and she's no Rebecca. Has she told you anything about me?"

"Nothing that matches reality." My cheeks tingled, perhaps from the late-afternoon sun.

"She and I play this asinine game. If you're in range later, you'll hear her shrieks when she discovers that I deleted all her names and numbers from her cell. And if she told you about my so-called sniffles, she was lying. I told her that I had a hangover, but that didn't fit into her script. Oh no, she wanted sympathy—and an excuse to skip out from the greenhouse when Ethan turned his back. I warned him never to do that. I told him the same thing about that Butterfly creature, and look where it got him. It's no wonder he works so late at the nursery. I'd rather kill myself than listen to her drivel." She clamped her hand over her mouth. "Oops, not a good phrase."

She didn't look all that embarrassed, and I suspected she was covering a smile. I said, "You don't think anyone in the family murdered Winston. What about Terry?"

"Like I said, he shouldn't have come back."

"And you said that I should ask Nattie about it. Does she know something?"

"Do I think she poisoned him?" Margaret Louise lit a cigarette and took a deep drag. "No, I don't. She was grief-stricken when Winston died, but Terry had nothing to do with that. He had the best alibi of all of us."

"Were you grief-stricken as well?"

"Why would I have been? I'm just the bookkeeper." She stood up. "I didn't realize how late it is, Claire. I must change into suitable drabness before Jordan and Ethan get back from a delivery. I keep losing my damn granny glasses. In the sixties, they were standard issue. I wore them to the March on Washington and listened to Martin Luther King Jr.'s speech on the steps of the Capitol."

"I believe it was at the Lincoln Memorial."

"Hey, I was stoned. It could have been the nearest McDonald's for all I cared."

She yanked off the black wig to expose thin gray hair as she went back through the living room to the front door. Once again, I followed her. I thanked her, but she was humming "We Shall Overcome" like a kazoo. I retreated to my car to consider what she'd said. I wasn't sure how much of it was true, or how much of it was permanent brain damage from hallucinogenics in the sixties. However, it didn't take much effort to imagine her in a graffiti-laden VW bus careening across the country, the windshield wipers slappin' time . . .

It was still early enough for a surprise visit to the Finnellys' house—unless they ate dinner at six o'clock so they could tuck themselves in bed at nine. I had a brief flash of them in bed with Margaret Louise and her merry pranksters and started laughing. As long as I could keep the image in mind, Charles could not intimidate me. Which isn't to say he could in other circumstances. I do not daunt easily. I drove around the green and turned down their driveway. Unlike the more primitive road surfaces, it was made of pricey aggregate. The house was a large redbrick rectangle, reminiscent of a Georgian manor. The landscaping was perfunctory; there were no cheerful flower beds or window boxes. I surmised such things were frivolous and therefore vanity. I vaguely remembered that Job had worried about vanity as well, along with the death of his family and other minor inconveniences. The new gold Cadillac was merely a basic necessity.

I pushed the doorbell and tried to look as if I'd been in Sunday school all day (which was harder than it sounds, it being Saturday; I certainly couldn't claim to be Jewish if I wanted to be invited inside).

Felicia opened the door with the same pained look I'd seen after the ambulance drove away. "You," she said. "Why are you here? We don't want to have anything to do with you or your kind."

"And what kind would that be?" I pictured her dressed in hot red lingerie, sprawled across a tangle of sweaty, hirsute bodies.

"You'll have to search your soul for the answer."

"I am kind of adorable, or so my husband says, and I'm kind to the elderly and the infirm. I'd like to talk to you about Winston's death. Is Mr. Finnelly here?"

"He doesn't want to talk to you."

I expected to be chased away with a broom, but she

continued to watch me as if she were a buzzard and I were a baby bunny. "Are you afraid to talk to me?"

"Most certainly not," she replied, although her eyes were shifting rapidly. Her puckered lips reminded me of a cat's derriere. She took several minutes to come to some kind of decision. I anticipated being ordered off her doorstep and was surprised when she suddenly smiled and said, "Wait here."

She closed the door, then locked it in case "my kind" stormed into any old house we chose. I watched squirrels leap from branch to branch for a good five minutes, prepared to stay on the doorstep all night, ringing the doorbell at random intervals. I had just dressed Charles in frayed cutoffs, with a peace sign on a shoelace hanging on his scrawny chest, when Felicia returned, her mouth tight. Her fleeting smile must have been a muscle spasm, I thought.

"We will give you five minutes. Please watch your language. This is a Christian household." She gestured for me to precede her into the living room. The furniture was as bland as she was, functional but unappealing. There were doilies on the arm rests of the brown sofa and straight-backed chairs. There were no photographs or artwork. I was told to sit down, so I complied.

She sat across from me, her hands folded in her lap. We looked at each other in uneasy silence until Charles Finnelly came into the room. He remained standing, his arms crossed and his stare contemptuous. Long live the king.

"You have five minutes," he said.

I wondered if he had a stopwatch in his back pocket. "Terry Kennedy died this afternoon from an unidentified poison. The lab is testing the contents of the vodka bottle."

"Oh, no," Felicia said, putting her hand to her mouth.

Charles handled the news without a twitch. "There has

never been a bottle of alcoholic beverage in my house. Drunkenness leads to depravity and degeneracy. That it led to Kennedy's death does not surprise me. He and Winston flaunted their perversity, and they died because of it."

"Okay. I understand that you didn't approve of their lifestyle. Let's not get into a debate about it. Do you think Winston committed suicide?"

"My opinion is none of your business."

I felt my chin edge forward. "It may not be any of my business, but it is police business. You'll have to go to the department tomorrow to make a statement about it, and about Terry's death. You'll miss church, and we must pray that no one sees you entering or leaving. You know how your kind are. They might think that you're involved in an ugly crime. Someone might start a rumor, and rumors tend to grow tentacles with every repetition. What would the congregation do if they heard you were accused of possessing child porn, for instance?"

"That's absurd!" Felicia said.

"Be silent," her husband commanded, then said, "Why is talking to you going to save me from further inconvenience?"

"I'm married to the deputy chief. He listens to me. If I tell him that you have no pertinent information, he may not send a squad car to pick you up in the morning." Odds were good that he wouldn't, since he'd be at the Atlanta airport. Besides, he never listens to me, even when I'm telling him what to buy at the grocery store.

"What I think about this suicide is not pertinent. We did not socialize with Winston and his 'friend.' He might have accepted the truth that he was an abomination in the eyes of God. Since he was unable to rein in his unholy lust, he did the only thing he could."

"So he killed himself out of remorse?"

"Sadly enough, God will never allow him to enter heaven. There can be no forgiveness for such a sinner."

"Amen," Felicia said under her breath.

Charles swiveled his head to stare at her. "Go to the kitchen and see to my dinner," he said sternly, then watched her scurry out of the room. "She forgets her place, as do other women." We both knew to whom he was referring.

"Terry didn't commit suicide out of remorse," I said. "He was poisoned by someone who lives in Hollow Valley."

"That is a false utterance, Mrs. Malloy. If you repeat it, I will sue you for slander. You won't be able to buy a trailer when I'm finished."

"So sue me. I'd like nothing more than to see this in the local paper. We might even warrant the front page. No, it's more likely to end up buried next to the church listings. That'll put the Hollow family in the spotlight, won't it?"

"It's my dinnertime, and I cannot abide overcooked chicken. Your five minutes are up. Allow me to escort you to the door."

"Do you have a key to Winston's house?"

"Of course not! Do not require me to be obliged to forcibly expel you." He maintained his stare as I walked across the room.

"I can't see Winston giving you a spare key so that you could water the houseplants whenever he and Terry were out of town," I said as I stopped in the doorway. My elegant nose was in peril should he attempt to slam the door, but I found a high level of satisfaction from irritating him. "However, no one seems to allow locks to thwart them. Moses has no difficulty getting inside the house. He prefers merlot, but he was into the whiskey yesterday morning. He may not be the only Hollow who likes to snoop."

Charles's face turned redder than Caron's. "Snoop?" he sputtered. "I do not snoop! I set foot in that house one time, and it was adequate to satisfy myself that it was a warren of perversity. The very thought of what went on in that house makes me shudder. I felt a moral compunction to go there the next day, but I stayed on the porch while I offered Winston the opportunity to repent and become a true Christian. He had the audacity to smirk, Mrs. Malloy. No one smirks at me. After that, I forbade my wife to acknowledge their presence in Hollow Valley."

"Were you angry enough to whack him on the head and push him in the stream?" I asked, battling the impulse to produce the most superb smirk he would ever see until he encountered St. Peter.

Felicia appeared at his side, a dish towel in her hand. "Charles, your dinner is ready. Please come eat while everything's hot."

"Everything had better be hot when I choose to eat. Go back to the kitchen and wait there." He did not see the glare she shot at his back as she left the room.

He deserved a dose of whatever had killed Terry, I thought as I clenched my fists. "Well, Charlie, were you that angry?"

Purple blotches spread on his face, and for several seconds, he was speechless. I was glad we weren't on the bank of the stream. "Mrs. Malloy," he managed to say, "leave my property immediately. Should you return, I will have you arrested for trespassing and harassment. I don't care if your husband is a five-star general. Go home and become an obedient wife. Your lack of modesty is shameful."

"Shameful? You haven't seen the half of it, buddy boy." Since I had no idea what I had just threatened him with, the best I could do was spin around and stalk to my car. I slammed the door, started the engine, and drove back to the blacktop. Had there been dust, I would have left a cloud.

There were at least two hours before sunset. My best-laid plan had gotten me nowhere. I now knew that Margaret Louise was someone with whom to reckon, and that the Finnellys were as Nattie had described them. I turned in the direction of the Old Tavern and parked in front of the door.

Nattie came outside as I climbed out of the car. "What's going on? Is Terry okay?"

I related the bad news. She stared in disbelief, then finally shook her head and said, "There's something terrible happening here. I don't know what to do. First Winston, and now Terry. I liked both of them. They made the sun shine on this dreary place." She began to cry and made no attempt to wipe her tears as they coursed down her face.

I put my arm around her shoulder and led her to the chairs in the backyard. "I wish I knew what to say, Nattie. I can't stop myself from feeling guilty. If I hadn't fallen in love with the house, Terry would be sitting in a bar in Key West, drinking a margarita while he waited for the sunset."

"He should have stayed there and left us alone to mourn for Winston." She gripped the chair arms with such intensity that her knuckles were white. "What painful memories he brought back with him."

I put aside my sympathy and said, "I don't know what happened to Winston, but Terry was murdered. Someone is responsible."

"It's frightening," Nattie said as she gazed at the distant bridge. "The whole thing was nothing more than a spat over Winston's house and acreage. Ethan told me that he and Charles spoke to Terry the day after he arrived home from Europe. They offered him a fair price, but he became hostile and ordered them to leave. Two days later, he was gone. They filed the lawsuit when they realized that he wasn't coming back."

"How did Charles and Ethan know about the deed?"

"You'll have to ask them. I certainly didn't know anything about it until Ethan told me. It was the day after Winston's body was found. He was flabbergasted that Winston hadn't wanted to keep the valley intact, and very hurt. We sat here and talked about it for a long time that afternoon. I agreed that Terry might be willing to settle the matter as quickly as possible. I was wrong about that." She tried to laugh, but it wasn't convincing. "It was a painful situation for all of us, including Terry. He came home from his poker tournament, eager to see Winston, and then learned about his tragic death. He cried on my shoulder. I felt like his mother, even though I'm only five years older. I kept thinking that I had to bake for him— bread, muffins, cinnamon rolls, something. I ended up burning a pan of brownies and dumping it in the trash."

"You did what you could," I said as I leaned over to squeeze her hand. I waited a few minutes to allow her to regain her composure while I mulled over what she'd said. "Did anyone try to get in touch with Terry after the death?" I'd long since stopped categorizing it as an accident, but I wasn't ready to use the other two theories: suicide or murder.

"How could I have done that?" asked Nattie. "All I knew was that he was in Europe."

"He would have left contact information with Winston, don't you think? Maybe on the desk in the library or on a kitchen counter."

She caught her breath. "It didn't seem right to go inside the house. Maybe someone should have, but we were in mourning. No one was thinking clearly. Charles took care of the funeral arrangements. Despite his antagonism, he was upset to lose a family member in such a horrible way."

"I've noticed how sensitive he is. You may not have been thinking clearly, but Ethan was. He could have been looking for guidance for the funeral service when he found the deed in a desk drawer or folder. It's public record at the courthouse, but he would have had to know the deed existed in the first place. Which nobody did, from what you said."

"Maybe Pandora had a vision while she was munching pokeweed berries," Nattie said. "You'll have to ask Ethan, Claire. I can't explain it."

I put that on my agenda, but I had a feeling I'd have no more luck with him than I'd had with Charles Finnelly. If I included Margaret Louise and Felicia, my batting average would send me back to the minors. Nattie excused herself and went into the Old Tavern. In the vicinity of the nursery, a truck rumbled to life. Minutes later I watched it drive across the bridge and around a bend. The driver must not have been thrilled to spend the remainder of the weekend delivering trees and shrubs to Missouri. I hoped he was getting overtime.

I was wasting time, I told myself sharply. I had less than twenty-four hours to find Terry's killer. Once Peter was back, it would be trickier to avoid violating his bureaucratic dicta while I sleuthed. There would be an official investigation once food poisoning was ruled out, although there might be a delay until an autopsy eliminated any kind of preexisting condition. Such things as blood clots and aneurisms could kill quickly. I knew perfectly well that Terry had been poisoned, but I also knew the police were sticklers for protocols and procedures. In the fable, the plodding tortoise won the race. I fully intended to be sitting on the finish line, nibbling a carrot, long before the investigation broke into a sweat.

There was one enormous hurdle in my path. No one in Hollow Valley knew that Terry had returned from Key West under the cover of darkness. The headlights of his rental car would not have been visible from the other houses, nor would the interior lights of the house. Billy Bobstay and his friends wouldn't have alerted any of the members of the family. I certainly hadn't. How long had the vodka bottle been lurking in the liquor cabinet like a brown recluse? Nattie knew about Moses's forays into Winston's house to drink whatever caught his rheumy eye. I'd seen him drink two bottles of wine. His tastes were likely to be eclectic, from absinthe to zinfandel. Other family members must have known, too. He was the reigning patriarch, for better or worse, and therefore to be protected—not poisoned.

I was not so lost in thought that I failed to see movement out of the corner of my eyes. "It must be uncomfortable sitting in that tree, Jordan. Come down before the starlings attack." In truth, I wasn't sure that it was Jordan, but it seemed like a logical guess. The Finnellys were having dinner, Margaret Louise was transforming herself from a well-worn flower child to a great-aunt, and Pandora Butterfly wasn't able to remain silent for more than a few seconds. I heard a thump, but I continued to watch the sunlight shifting on the woods beyond the bridge.

"I can't believe Terry's dead," Jordan said as she sat down in the grass. "I mean, what a bummer. I was thinking that he was cool and that I might survive the summer, as long as I could sneak over to his house sometimes. Now all I can look forward to is watching the geraniums wilt."

"Every once in a while, Jordan, it's not about you."

"Yeah, I know, but I can't show any weakness. If I do, they'll pounce on me like a pack of wolves. Terry was cool. He wasn't all snooty just because he'd lived in New

York and hung out with famous people. I guess they're famous. I've never heard of any of them."

"You might if you go to school," I said.

"Sure, and sit in a row of identical desks and listen to a teacher drone on and on about stuff that's never going to have anything to do with my life. When's the last time you did an algebraic equation, Ms. Malloy? If I have a job that requires me to explain the impact of the Industrial Revolution on current economic policies, I won't have to hang myself. I'll slowly disintegrate into a pile of sub-atomic particles and be blown away by a solar flare."

"I admit that doesn't sound too exciting." I wondered what would have become of me if Peter hadn't blundered into my life. I'd grow too old to manage the Book Depot and end up in a dusty little apartment with cats and the last remaining book made out of paper.

"You two don't look very chipper," Nattie said as she placed a tray on the table. "You're too young for wine, Jordan. There's a pitcher of lemonade inside."

A croak burst out of my mouth. A pitcher of lemonade, a splash of vodka, and an ambulance. "Thank you, Nattie, but I have to drive back to town in a few minutes. My husband will fix a squeaky door, but he refuses to fix my parking tickets. If I were picked up for a DWI, he'd line up to testify against me."

"Wow," Jordan murmured. "That's hard."

I hoped it wasn't true, although I wasn't positive. Peter had arranged for my car to be towed, simply because he was in a snit. He'd stationed an officer to prevent me from leaving my apartment, which had required me to come up with a devious escape plan. There have been moments when he seemed to be picturing me in a holding cell. "I've changed my mind, Nattie. I'd love a splash of wine. Would you like a piece of cheese?" I asked Jordan as I held out the plate.

She looked at me as if I'd offered her a ticket to Hawaii (or a get-out-of-jail-free card). She glanced at Nattie, then grabbed the plate. "Hell, yes. All I had for lunch was—" She caught herself. "Thank you."

Nattie nodded. "I'll make it my responsibility to see that you have a decent lunch break. Ethan gets so passionate about the plants that he forgets to eat. I've seen the workmen huddled behind an outbuilding, eating lunch."

"And chain-smoking," Jordan said. "They're real careful to pick up the butts so Ethan won't find them. When he caught Mariposa sneaking a quick cigarette near the red maples, he yelled at her until she burst into tears. I don't know if he fired her, but she never came back. I wouldn't have." She produced an admirably dramatic sigh. "I don't have that option. Ethan yells at me all day, no matter what. If I do a good job, he tells me that I was too slow. If I try to hurry, he tells me that I was sloppy and makes me do it again. When I get incarcerated in that boarding school, I'm going to read up on child labor laws."

I retrieved the plate of cheese. "Run along, Jordan. Aunt Margaret Louise is expecting you."

"Expecting me to do what? Clean the bathroom? Scrub the floor on my hands and knees?" She stood up. "I am so out of here. I wonder what language they speak in Oklahoma."

Nattie waited until Jordan was out of sight. "An idle threat. She stowed away on a delivery truck a while back. After six hours of bouncing into pines and holly trees in the dark, with no air-conditioning, bathroom facilities, food, or water, she concluded that it was a poor idea. She was lucky that the driver let her sit in front on the ride back."

"The workers loading the truck didn't see her?"

She carefully poured herself a glass of wine. "Apparently

not. She might have crawled in at the last minute, just before they closed the door. For all I know, she could have been wearing a black ski mask to cover those ridiculous rings and studs—and that hair. Looking at her makes me feel old, Claire."

"I feel sorry for her. It sounds as though she and her parents are trapped in a futile cycle. They get mad at her for something, so she retaliates by doing something even worse. I hope she still has a few square inches of unsullied skin before she reaches maturity." Thinking about Jordan's angst-ridden adolescence reminded me of a question. "Nattie, from what I've heard, everyone in Hollow Valley knew that Winston was gay by the time he became a teenager. Did he announce it?"

"I knew Winston better than anyone, including his parents. We were practically soul mates, but I sensed that he wasn't completely open about . . . certain things. Some of his poems hinted at his confusion and pain. I still have them in a box in my nightstand. I shall always treasure them." She realized she'd wandered off track and said, "I only came during summer vacations, so if there was a formal announcement, I missed it. I think maybe there was a vicious rumor at school. Ethan and Esther must have repeated it to their respective parents."

"Who's Esther?"

"Charles and Felicia's daughter. She's a year older than Ethan."

I was less than excited to hear that there was yet another Hollow. "Where is she? How did she escape from her parents' piety?"

"She ran away when she was seventeen. It's a touchy subject, especially for Felicia, so we never mention it."

"Nobody knows what happened to her?"

Nattie shook her head. "All I can say is that I don't know what happened to her. I hope she's living in a million-dollar condo in Manhattan or with a disgustingly rich marquis in Tuscany. Anyone who survived seventeen years under Charles Finnelly's tyranny deserves all the worldly wickedness she wants. She and I talked quite a bit. She told me that she had to come straight home from school, wasn't allowed to participate in any outside activities, and was dragged to church twice a week. She had long braids and wore dresses that covered her arms and knees. I felt just awful when I thought about her, and the other kids, too. They were required to put in fifteen hours a week at the nursery."

"It sounds pretty dreadful," I murmured. The last time Caron had worn braids was in kindergarten. I still remembered the day she brought them home in her lunchbox. "Did the police conduct a search?"

"Ethan told me that Esther's friends were candid with the police, who figured they weren't going to have much luck tracking down a runaway."

I sat back and took a discreet sip of wine. Now I had too much information to even begin to assimilate on my own. Peter was not a potential confidant, due to his obsession with the rules. "Okay," I said as if I were about to say something of profound significance, "what do you think about all this? I know that you believe Winston committed suicide, but Terry was adamant that he didn't. He said that Winston wasn't depressed and was looking forward to their trip to Rio. I met someone who played in Winston's string ensemble, and he told me that Winston was definitely expecting them that weekend. Have you considered the possibility that you caught Winston at a bad moment, or maybe misinterpreted his actions?"

"Two days ago I was convinced that Winston did indeed commit suicide, but after Terry's death . . . well, we both know that he didn't poison himself." She gave me a perplexed look. "I suppose we know that. I've read that combinations of prescription drugs or illegal substances can be toxic. The police have searched the house and his luggage, haven't they?"

"I'm sure they have. In any case, he didn't spike the vodka with some caustic cleaning solution; the symptoms would have been immediate and obvious. An overdose of a prescription medication takes time to get into the system. The poison was strong, obviously. The lab will identify it sooner or later."

"I've tried my best to figure out who might have had a motive to kill Terry." She held up her palms before I could launch into a tirade. "Yes, you're convinced that everyone out here is so fixated on keeping Hollow Valley in the family that we were lined up at his front door, each with a weapon."

"Why else would someone kill Terry—and Winston? Did either of them express any interest in the nursery business? Did they expect a share of the profits? They must have been in good financial shape to remodel the house with such style. I can't picture them in overalls, with dirty fingernails."

Nattie smiled. "They weren't good ol' country boys. When Winston's parents died, he signed over his interest in the Hollow Valley Nursery to the corporation. He said that he didn't want any responsibility or liability. The nursery's profitable, but a percentage goes to maintaining stock, and the remaining profit's split four ways. Jordan's father sold his interest to the corporation about five years ago."

"Why?" I asked.

She glanced over her shoulder, then said in a low voice, "A midlife crisis named Chiffon. Jordan's mother said that she'd accept either a divorce or a six-bedroom villa in Aruba. Jordan says it has a wonderful view of the beach."

My head was beginning to ache. I put down the glass

and said, "I need to go home and feign sympathy for my daughter, who has a sunburn."

Nattie stood up to give me a hug. "I'm really sorry about the house, Claire. I know how much you wanted it, and I was looking forward to having someone remotely sane to talk to. I loved it out here, but now it feels . . . well, menacing. Someone murdered Terry. I don't see how it could be a random sociopath." She gave me a heartrending look. "What do I do, Claire?"

"Let the police investigate before you do anything," I said. "There may be some screwy explanation that we haven't begun to consider." I didn't add that I intended to consider every last screwy explanation, including aliens, delivery truck drivers, and treacherous cave-dwelling mutants from the family tree. I told her that I would keep her informed about the police investigation and went to my car. When I reached the driveway that led to what should have been my house, I couldn't stop myself from turning. If I found a way to get inside, it was not likely that I'd find a confession on the kitchen island. I could, however, take a quick look in the desk.

Dusk was settling in as I got out of the car. I was on my way to the porch when I heard an outraged screech.

CHAPTER 8

I did not go thundering around the corner of the house to rescue some hapless female from the jaws of a bear, nor did I bust through the front door to find an ax before I thundered around the corner of the house to rescue any hapless body. I took the wiser course and stopped where I was. The second screech was more of a yelp. Biting down on my lower lip, I cautiously headed for the back of the house. I heard frantic whispers and splashes. I regret to say that I recognized the voices, so instead of dialing nine-one-one to report a burglary in progress, I merely stepped into sight and said, "What are you two doing here?"

Caron, dressed in shorts and a T-shirt, was treading water in the middle of the pool. Inez clutched a long pole with a flat basket on one end. Neither seemed eager to answer me. "Well?" I said.

"Swimming," Caron said blithely. "Does it look like I'm riding a bicycle?"

Inez held up the pole. "This is in case Caron gets a cramp and I have to pull her out of the water before she drowns. We ate hamburgers on the drive. My mother always makes me wait for an hour before I go in the water."

I wanted to take the pole and bop Caron on the head. "Swimming while fully dressed? Isn't it a bit cumbersome? Inez, put down that thing before you poke yourself in the eye." I watched Caron as she swam to a ladder and pulled herself up. "Let me try again. What are you two doing here?"

Caron shook herself like a wet dog and then meticulously fluffed her hair with her fingers while she concocted a plausible story. She has a talent for mendacity that has been honed since the day she filched her first teething biscuit. "I don't see what the big deal is," she began. "I mean, what are you doing here? Aren't you trespassing?"

"That's the best you can do?" I asked. "Were you and Inez stalking a unicorn when you lost your balance?"

"It wasn't a unicorn," Inez said.

"My mother was being facetious, for pity's sake," Caron said to her. "At least I hope she was." She blinked at me. "You have been acting Quite Odd. Is there something you need to tell me? Does it have anything to do with Peter? You can't divorce him, Mother. He promised me a new car next June, a convertible if I want. All you'd give me is that pathetic thing you drive." She buried her face in her hands as though overwhelmed with grief. Her shoulders actually trembled.

"I was thinking about a used bicycle and a helmet. You'll get to select the color."

Caron flopped down on a chaise. "Inez told me how really cool the house is, so we came here so I could see it. It really is cool. It's kind of far, but if I get the car this summer instead of waiting, I won't care that it takes At Least twenty minutes."

"Which isn't that bad," Inez said, "if you take into consideration the fact that the average commute time for New York City is thirty minutes. In Los Angeles, commuters spend an average of seventy-two hours stuck in traffic every year."

I looked at her for a moment, then at Caron. "There's a problem, dear. We can't have the house. The title is unresolved, but it belonged to either Winston or Terry. Sadly, neither of them can sell or even lease it to us. Winston died three months ago, and Terry died this afternoon." I turned back at Inez, whose eyes were wide. "I'm sorry. I know you liked him. He lapsed into a coma and never came out of it."

Caron stood up. "What do you mean we can't have the house? Just buy it from whoever inherited it from whoever owned it. Did you see the size of the closet? I could hide a dozen unicorns in there! And the shower has so many faucets that I'll never figure out how to turn them all on at the same time. You never let a murder get in your way. How many hours till Peter gets back? We need to solve this before he starts ordering you to stop meddling."

"I think we should make a list," Inez said. "We can have two columns—one for the improbable suspects and another for the probable ones. Then we can categorize them by motive and opportunity, and rank them accordingly."

I sighed. "We are not going to use the Dewey Decimal System to solve this, Inez. These people aren't that obliging. Inez, did you tell Caron about Jordan?"

"She sounds egotistical and immature," Caron opined with a sniff. "She's probably in one of those gangs where everybody has the same tattoo. She wasn't here in March when this Winston person drowned. I see no reason to waste time on her."

"She's kind of interesting," Inez countered meekly. "She plays guitar in an all-girls band."

"For all I care, she can play the oboe with her toes."

"You can't even play solitaire without cheating."

"I can count to ten on my fingers."

"Sometimes, if you're lucky."

I intervened before the inane spat escalated. "There's no point in sitting here, debating digital prowess. I didn't see your car when I arrived. Where did you park it?"

"At the edge of the front yard, behind some trees," Caron said. "I figured you'd be lurking around out here. All I wanted to do was have a quick look at the house."

"Why did you jump in the pool with your clothes on?"

She averted her eyes. "I slipped."

"Yeah," said Inez. "You about jumped out of your skin when you saw that creepy old guy and fell over backward. I guess that's like slipping."

"Moses?" I asked Inez. When she looked blank, I added, "The bald man who was here this morning."

"This morning? Who are you talking about, Ms. Malloy? Jordan was here, and then Terry arrived. You and he went inside to talk. After that, there were the paramedics and the two police officers. I'd never seen the old guy until a few minutes ago."

Moses was beginning to seriously annoy me. I would have questioned my sanity had not Nattie seen him, too. His corporeal subsistence did not seem to interfere with his ability to vanish when it suited him. "You both saw him, right? Where is he now?"

"Inside," Caron said. "He sort of popped out of nowhere and scuttled into the house like a hermit crab. Inez and I were going to find him as soon as I recovered from my shock. My heart is still pounding, and I feel weak."

"Put your head between your toes," I said as I headed for the French doors. Moses was not in the living room, nor was he in the kitchen, the master suite, or the delectable library. As I went upstairs, I heard a shower running. This presented a dilemma: I wanted to find Moses, but I

most assuredly did not want to find Moses-in-the-raw. My
mind recoiled from the involuntary image. I ascertained
that he was in what Caron claimed was her bathroom. A
pair of trousers and a short-sleeved shirt were piled next
to the bed. This implied that when he emerged from the
bathroom, he would be wearing a towel—or not.

I went downstairs at a brisk clip. Caron and Inez were
poking around the kitchen cabinets, commenting on the
alphabetized spice bottles and the obscure gourmet ac-
coutrements. "He's taking a shower," I told them. "You
need to run along before he comes down to give you big,
fat, slobbery kisses. He's very affectionate."

Caron slammed a cabinet door. "Let's go, Inez. I can't
wait to tell Joel about all of this. It is such a hoot." Inez
shrugged and put down what appeared to be olive tongs.

I walked with them to the front door. "One question
before you leave. Did Moses use a key to get inside?"

Inez shook her head. "He came out of the orchard,
singing a crazy song like he was drunk. When he saw us,
he shouted something and then just went inside. That's
when Caron . . . slipped."

I waited on the porch until they left in Caron's car. It
was tempting to follow them, but I squared my shoulders
and went back inside to wait for Moses. I busied myself
turning on lights and opening stray drawers. I wanted to
search the library, but I didn't want Moses to amble out
the French doors before I talked to him. It was well past
my dinner hour, and I couldn't remember if I'd eaten
lunch. I found the half-wheel of Brie in the refrigerator
and a box of crackers on a counter.

I perched on a stool and began to eat. Eventually, I
heard a door open in the room above me, followed by a
series of thumps. Moses might be an expert in the gentle
art of picking locks, but it sounded as though he were
less adept at putting on his trousers. When I heard his

footstep in the foyer, I called, "Moses, come join me for a snack."

"Snick-snack, paddywack," he said cheerfully as he materialized in the kitchen doorway. "Shall we have a little snort?"

"Help yourself. It might be prudent to stick to unopened bottles. You saw what happened to Terry."

"Damn shame." Moses ducked behind the counter and reappeared with a bottle of peppermint schnapps. He smacked his lips as he wiggled out the cork and poured several ounces into a glass. "Want some?" he asked as he lunged for the cracker box. "It'll put some pep in your schnapps, that's for sure."

I shoved the box within his reach. "I saw you here this morning when the paramedics and police arrived."

"Nothing like a grand brouhaha to get the juices flowing. Yep, I saw it all. I was in the orchard when that pretty little miss with the spectacles walked down to the stream. She was talking to herself something fierce. Then along skulks Jordan, acting like she was a Russian spy. I was hoping to see a real hissy fight, but they went across the stream and into the woods. I thought real hard about following them."

"Why didn't you?"

"I didn't want to get briars all over my britches. Nattie doesn't like to pluck 'em off before she does laundry." He took a gulp and wiped his mouth with the back of his hand. "The other reason I didn't go after them was that I wanted to have a word with Terry when he got back from wherever he went. Turns out I was too late. Too late for a date, too late for Miss Prissy. She said if she caught me inside this house she was gonna get me in trouble. I reckon at my age there ain't no trouble I haven't already been in—up to my neck. I can't recall the number of nights I spent in jails over the years. When I wasn't but thirteen, I got caught stealing a pack of cigarettes at the general store. If the doctor hadn't made me swear I'd give up smoking, I'd be smoking three packs a day."

I tried not to smile. "You might be surprised at the cost these days. One of my friends had a fit when the price for a pack topped six dollars. After she calculated that one pack a day would cost nearly two hundred dollars a month, she quit cold turkey."

Moses chortled. "Wouldn't cost me a dime a month. Did you see any cookies in a cabinet? Peppermint schnapps always gives me an itch for chocolate chips."

"I'll try to find a box if you answer my question. Who's Miss Prissy?"

"Don't know her right name. You're the one who ought to be answering my questions. Who's Miss Prissy?"

He knew the names of all the distaff members of the Hollow family. Caron and Inez had not said a word to him. "This woman drives a silver SUV, right?" I asked him. "She has short, dark hair and carries a leather briefcase. Angela Delmond is the real estate agent who showed me this house earlier in the week. Do you know where she is?"

"No," Moses whispered, staring at me. "Where is she?"

He was more than seriously annoying, I thought as I cut a sliver of cheese. He was extremely annoying—and then some. There was something cagey about him. Interspersed with his seemingly random remarks were nuggets of truthfulness. All I needed to do was identify them. "You said that Miss Prissy, also known as Angela, warned you not to come inside. When did she do that?"

"Morning, noon, and night. She's a tough little broad, a real spitfire. One time she bristled like a darn hedgehog. I laughed so hard that I split my britches. Nattie stitched them up, but she was testy for a week. I told her that she was being stupid, since I have enough money in the bank to buy a rack of trousers. I reckon I could have more shoes than Winston and Terry had in their closet, and lemme tell you, their shoes didn't come from a discount store. What's more, they had so many silk ties that they could wear different ones every day of the month."

"You were in their closet?"

"Are you accusing me of something?" His hand clasped the neck of the liquor bottle.

"No," I said, "and let go of that before you knock it over. Did you run into Angela when she came here to visit Winston and Terry?"

"Did I run into her or did I run over her? I may not be the saltiest peanut in the bag, but I ain't senile. I used to see her after Terry ran off to Florida, and I saw her the day that you were here with her. She was real upset when she got out to the porch. She was still jabbering on her cell phone when she drove off." He dribbled the last of the peppermint schnapps into his glass. "What we need is some wine, 'specially if you're gonna keep on whining all night. I was thinking a pinot blanc might be tasty. Sit a spell while I go look in the cellar."

"Moses, please let me ask you one more question. You told me that you've seen Angela in the last couple of months. What was she doing here?"

His lips parted as he gazed blankly at the ceiling. I was ready to shake him back into reality when he blinked and said, "Laundry."

"She came all the way to Hollow Valley to do laundry? Think, Moses. Did anyone come with her? Did she bring an overnight bag?"

"Who'd you think brought the cheese and fresh fruit? Once there was half of a cheesecake, covered with plastic wrap. It wasn't as good as Nattie's, mind you. She puts fresh blueberries on top. Another time there was leftover steak."

My lips may have been slightly parted as I considered what he'd told me. "You never saw her with anyone?"

"I thought you said you had one more question. You're up to four, and I'm in the mood for pinot blanc, not some goosey game show. Next thing I know, you'll be demanding my Social Security number and date of birth." He left the kitchen and opened a door in the hallway. "See you later, crocodile!"

I reexamined the contents of the refrigerator. In the drawer where I'd retrieved the Brie, there were sealed packages of Gruyère and Gorgonzola. Moldy cherries were in a plastic container in a corner of a shelf, and apples were in the bottom drawer. I couldn't tell the age of the condiments in the door shelves. The collection of condiments in my refrigerator might well have been served at the picnic after my wedding to Carlton. I moved on to the freezer, where I found sturdily wrapped filet mignons, a pair of lobster tails, and an assortment of frozen appetizers. I looked at the grocery label on the package of steaks. They had been purchased not in January or February but in May. Steaks, cherries, and imported cheeses were not the makings of a business lunch.

It seemed likely that Angela, who'd carried on for hours about Danny's infidelities, was having a cozy affair of her own. I had no way to identify her lover, who could be any suitable male in her social circle or in a much wider circle. I toyed with the possibility that the culprit was Bartleby, but it was a stretch to envision them closing a real estate deal between silk sheets. The house was an ideal place for a tryst. It wasn't visible from the blacktop road, and none of the Hollows had a reason to encroach. The exception (a glaring one), was Moses, who seemed to be a master of random acts of insignificance. He might have seen Angela and her lover arriving, cavorting, or leaving.

I would have questioned him had I not heard the front

door bang closed. By the time I reached the veranda, he had disappeared into the darkness. I felt a twinge of pity for Nattie, who was obliged to hunt him down on a daily, if not hourly, basis. If I were in her position, I'd make him some sandwiches for the road. Luckily, I was not in her position, nor did I feel any responsibility to go after him. I returned to the kitchen to finish the Brie while I pondered Angela's assignations in the house that was meant to be mine.

The call that she'd received had led to my abandonment. Danny claimed that he hadn't called her, and I had no judges stashed in my back pocket who could be cajoled into signing a subpoena to have his phone records examined. From what she'd told me, the two of them communicated through their respective lawyers. If one of her friends had called to remind her of a social engagement, she wouldn't have reacted with such urgency. Even a call about a relative's health crisis, as distressing as it might have been, was not enough to send her racing away without a word to me.

That left the theory that her nameless lover was the caller. For reasons known only to her, Angela felt as though she could not offer me even a curt explanation. She'd jumped in her car and driven to . . . Maxwell County. It made no sense. Her car was found by an airstrip, but she had not leaped into a jet to be whisked away for a romantic interlude on a beach. The sheriff's dogs had not been able to follow a trail from her car. Assuming the dogs hadn't been smoking Maxwell County's number-one cash crop, the obvious explanation was that Angela had not gotten out of the car on her own two Gucci-clad feet.

I crammed a cracker in my mouth and crunched fiercely. Someone had driven her car to Maxwell County, and a second someone had been there to collect the driver. If Angela had been a willing participant, she'd chosen a peculiar moment to launch the deception. Had she wanted me to assume that she'd been kidnapped? If that was the case, why hadn't there been a ransom demand or some sort of communication? It was a very poor way to go about it, I thought as I dug another cracker out of the box. Danny worked in an office, so he probably had an alibi for the afternoon. On the TV cop shows, the prime suspect was always home alone on the pertinent night. I had a feeling Danny was rarely home alone. With a sigh, I scratched him off the list.

Coconspirators are not easy to find, particularly in matters of murder. They don't advertise their credentials and availability, or even their fees. They don't gather on corners in hopes of picking up odd jobs. Very few of us have friends who are obliging enough to commit a felony as a favor. I decided that Angela's lover had to be one of the participants, although I lacked a compelling argument, much less proof. There was no way to slap a name on him, much less handcuffs. The only person who might have the information was Moses Hollow.

I put my cell phone in my pocket, locked my purse in my car, and started walking in the direction of the Old Tavern. I could have tried to follow Moses, but I was not inclined to risk encountering anything that growled, hissed, or nipped. As I passed the Finnellys' driveway, I caught a glimpse of light through the dense foliage. I doubted they were rollicking on the floor or even watching depraved TV shows in which people behaved in an indecorous fashion (which eliminated ninety percent of them). No, Charles would be reading scriptures while Felicia knitted scarves for missionaries in Africa. I wished them both a sleepless night of heartburn and flatulence.

I slowed down as I remembered what Nattie had said about their daughter. Esther had run away from home, which was hardly astonishing. She and Ethan had been about the same age, so she was now in her midthirties. I wondered if she'd rebelled so vehemently that she joined a circus or took up with a motorcycle gang as her aunt had done. An unpleasant thought came to mind. Had she run away from home, or was that a cover story for something appalling? If she was incarcerated somewhere in Hollow Valley—or buried somewhere in Hollow Valley—it would explain why the family was so determined to keep their domain intact. Ignoring the inexplicable small noises coming from the woods on either side of the road, I stopped to examine the idea. Winston had known her when they were growing up. She could have confided in him, since they were both alienated from the clan. Later, he had begun to question the more benign account of her disappearance. Maybe after his return three years ago, he'd asked some uncomfortable questions and eventually found evidence that would lead to an obtrusive police investigation. Nattie had described how she'd encountered him in the woods one day, and how he'd been too distracted to acknowledge her. Stumbling across an unmarked grave would explain his reticence to speak. If Nattie had mentioned it to a family member, someone had a strong motive to murder him. His death had been staged as an accident, with the empty wine bottles handy should a second version be needed.

My brilliant theory explained several things. Nattie had misinterpreted Winston's behavior as depression (although it would be depressing to discover that someone in one's family committed murder). Terry had been correct when he claimed that Winston had been murdered. I felt as if I were in a haze of means and motives that needed to be dissected carefully. It took no leap of imagination to picture Charles Finnelly assaulting his daughter with such sanctimonious fury that her skull cracked against the hearth. Rather than calling for an ambulance, he'd chosen to conceal his crime. Had Felicia held the flashlight while he dug the grave? Charles had brainwashed his wife. Could he have brainwashed the entire family? Certainly not Nattie, I told myself, and Pandora and Moses would have been problematic. As for Ethan and Margaret Louise, I had no clue. Charles might have concocted a plausible reason why outsiders posed a risk to the family business. For all I knew, he had persuaded Ethan that the exotic plant collection would suffer from the proximity of anyone lacking the proper genes.

I was so impressed with my acuity that I felt radiant. I resumed walking while I tossed around scenarios. Clearly, the first order of business was to find the grave. I doubted that Jorgeson would send a convoy of CSI officers to start digging up the hundreds of acres of woods, nursery plants, and greenhouse floors. Peter would go so far as to imply that I was flinging about random accusations to compensate for the loss of the perfect house. I was quite sure I wasn't.

As I approached the statue of Colonel Hollow, I heard droning noises and voices from the direction of the greenhouses. There was enough moonlight to make out the path, but I had no interest in watching ornamental trees and shrubs being loaded onto trucks that would drive through the night to retail nurseries in the adjoining states. If I was spotted, I would be required to defend myself from allegations of nosiness.

I turned toward the Old Tavern, hoping that Moses would be more cooperative with Nattie there to prod him. Someone coughed from behind the house. I detoured across the yard to the table and chairs. A small red circle was visible, and the redolence of tobacco smoke reached my delicate nostrils. Jordan's silhouette was impossible to misidentify. She was draped in a chair, her bare feet crossed.

"I thought you didn't smoke," I said.

She scrambled to her feet and stuck the cigarette behind her back. "Who said I was smoking?" she asked, managing to sound both startled and surly. She needed lessons from Caron, who could convey a plethora of unspoken criticisms in a single word.

"My mistake," I answered politely. "I smelled smoke. There must be a fire in the tobacco field. Should we try to find fire extinguishers?"

"There's no reason for sarcasm." She stubbed out the cigarette and placed the butt in the pack. "I wanted to find out what it's like, that's all. It's really nasty, but it'll be worth it when I light up in front of Aunt Margaret Louise. Do you know what she did? She screwed up my cell phone. Now I can't call anyone on the outside. They might as well put me in solitary confinement for the rest of the summer."

"In chains, while the rats gnaw on your toes," I said as I sat down. "Where'd you get the cigarettes?"

She sat down in the chair farthest away from me. "I stole them from one of the workmen, an ugly old dude named Rudy. He's usually drunk by the middle of the afternoon, so it's not like he'll figure out what happened. Why are you still here?"

I was surprised that Ethan would tolerate a drunk handling his precious azaleas and rhododendrons. However, experienced drunks could be deceptive. "I want to talk to Moses. Have you seen him?"

"No, but that doesn't mean he's not crouched under that table. He's creepier than Gollum from *The Lord of the Rings*. He's the one who should be in solitary confinement—for the rest of his life." She coughed again.

"Why do you want to talk to him? You must be really desperate for conversation."

"I need to ask him some questions," I said as I gazed at the stars. Without the light pollution from streetlights and neon signs, the stars were vivid. Had I any knowledge of constellations, I would have had a wondrous view of scorpions and horses and whatever else was up there. A meteor streaked across the sky. I felt sad that Peter and I would never sit on our terrace, commenting softly on the vastness of the universe and speculating about life on distant planets. Whoever had snatched away my dream would pay the price, I thought as the sadness gave in to anger. "You prowl around, Jordan. Did you ever see a short woman with dark hair at Winston's house?"

"What's in it for me?"

"For starters, I won't rat you out to anyone who might give you a well-deserved spanking. If you tell me anything useful, I'll ask Aunt Margaret Louise if you can come spend the night with Caron and Inez. We're talking pizza and the mall."

Jordan jerked her head around to gape at me. "Do you think she will?"

"We're not there yet. I need you to answer my question."

"Is it a big mall?"

"Yes, and whatever toppings you want on the pizza. Please don't tell me about your preferences in pepperoni, olives, and sausage. Did you ever see the woman?"

"I saw someone like that near the greenhouses a couple of weeks ago, talking to Ethan. When I asked him who she was, he told me that she wanted to know about flowering pear trees and catalpas, whatever they are. I was so fascinated that I yawned. Does the mall have a Gap?"

"Considering the current economy, it's possible there are numerous gaps," I said as I thought about what she'd told me. Angela had said that she wasn't going to do anything to enhance her landscaping until the divorce was finalized. That did not preclude the possibility that she assumed she would end up with her house and was researching future improvements. She had mentioned the autumn sale at the Hollow Valley Nursery, too. "Is that the only time you saw her?"

Jordan grimaced. "Yeah, except for when she almost ran over me on the road. Scared the holy bejeezus out of me. I was walking to the highway to see if there was any hope I could hitch a ride out of here. I literally threw myself into a thicket, and I have the scratches to prove it. By the time I freed myself, she was long gone. Uncle Charles would have convulsions if he'd overheard what I yelled."

"When was that?" I asked.

"The day you showed up. I was still mad, so I decided to sort of hang myself on the statue to prove I wasn't completely invisible. It was too bad that Nattie found me first. I was hoping for Aunt Margaret Louise or Aunt Felicia. That would have made for an awesome scene." Her teeth glinted in the moonlight. "Well, at least I wasn't invisible anymore."

That neatly fit into the timeline, but it wasn't much help. "This happened where the driveway meets the blacktop?"

"It wasn't where the Tigris and the Euphrates meet," she said with a muffled snort. "That's in Egypt."

"I gather you didn't ace the geography final. There is a certain value in education, Jordan. You don't want to end up working alongside Rudy." I paused as I heard an engine start. "Why is there so much activity at the nursery?"

"Because the retail nurseries do big business on Sundays, and they want fresh stock. There is a certain value in common sense, Ms. Malloy."

I clenched my teeth while I reminded myself that she was an unhappy fourteen-year-old. Caron had been no worse at that age. "All right," I said, "I'll have a word with Margaret Louise about a brief parole. She may be delighted at the idea of having you out of her hair for a night."

"Which hair?" Jordan asked. "The black shag or the dusty brown dreadlocks?"

I was too tired to stop myself from laughing. "She's not a little old lady with a dozen cats. Don't think for a second that you're fooling her."

"Anything to keep from dying of boredom. Would you like to know about aphids, mealy bugs, spider mites, and thrips? Ethan made me look at pictures of the icky things so I can raise an alarm if I see one. Now that's exciting."

"Hello?" called Nattie. "Who's out there?"

"I'll speak to your aunt tomorrow, Jordan." I went to the front door, where Nattie was hovering. "I was talking to the Mohawk princess," I said. "Is Moses inside? I want to ask him a few more questions before I go home."

"Come on in," she said. "He may be asleep by now, but I'll check. Would you like coffee and a piece of fresh blackberry pie? Let me get you settled in the kitchen, then I'll go upstairs." I accepted her invitation with the eagerness of a famished coyote. She led me along a hallway to a spacious kitchen. The enormous stone fireplace could easily roast a pig on a spit, which presumably it had in the past. The heavy cast-iron andirons and tool set looked authentic. The table was made of long planks of oak that gleamed in the light. A coffeemaker gurgled on the tile countertop. "Sit here, Claire. Do you take your coffee with cream or sugar?"

"Black, please."

She set a steaming cup on the table along with a large wedge of oozy, delectable pie. "You saw Moses earlier?

I apologize if he was pestering you. I'm fond of him, but some days he drives me crazier than a bucktoothed rooster. There are times when I think he's faking his dementia just to get on my nerves. If so, he does a fine job." She glanced at the high, smoke-stained ceiling. "You might have more luck talking to him in the morning. He's more lucid then. What are you going to ask him? Please promise me that you won't get him started on the Colonel's half-assed military exploits during the Civil War. I may strangle him to preserve what little sanity I have."

"I admire you for your patience," I said sincerely. "When Peter's distracted, there have been moments when I've weighed my options."

"I'm the 'designated daughter,' even though I'm a second cousin twice removed. Felicia should have been stuck with the old coot, but she outmaneuvered me by marrying Charles."

I grinned. "I'd take Moses over Charles in a nanosecond."

"Good point." She hesitated, then said, "I'll go look for him—Moses, not Charles. I don't recall having ever looked for Charles. If he gets lost in the wilderness for forty days and forty nights, I won't be in the search party. Try the pie while I go upstairs."

It was heavenly. I tried not to gulp it down, but the temptation lingered with each bite. I was preparing to lick the plate when Nattie reappeared.

"He's not anywhere to be found," she said with a shrug. "He gets agitated when the men are loading the delivery trucks. He's probably spying on them from behind a tree, convinced they're Yankees stealing Confederate gold. Or the Light Brigade organizing their charge on whatever they charged."

"The Russians, in the Battle of Balaclava," I said. "I was an English major."

"Balaclava? An old friend of mine went to a college named Balaclava. She dearly loved it. I'm sorry Moses isn't here. Perhaps I can answer your questions while you have another piece of pie."

A well-mannered lady does not gorge herself in other people's company. "Fine idea," I said. "Just a sliver, though. Moses told me that he saw Angela carrying food into Winston's house. I'm hoping I can get some more details out of him."

"Angela?" Nattie asked blankly.

"The real estate woman who showed me the house last Tuesday. I think that she might have been conducting an affair there. The refrigerator was stocked with cheese, grapes, and cherries." I stopped cold. "Maybe the toxic vodka was meant for her. Someone put the bottle in the liquor cabinet. I don't know what Angela drank, but it could have been vodka and tonic, or screwdrivers."

"Wait a minute," she said. "Your mind is bouncing around like Moses's does, and he has an excuse. Are you on medication?"

"It makes sense," I continued, declining to respond to her ridiculous question. "Angela was the target, not Terry. Only two people knew about the love nest, and one of them has disappeared under mysterious conditions. I wish I had a clue to the identity of the second." I sucked on the fork tines while I worked on my latest brilliant theory. "Have you ever seen unfamiliar cars on the blacktop road? Angela has a silver SUV."

She was staring at me as if I'd defied gravity and was rising out of the chair. "On occasion people drive up here, wanting to buy plants. Ethan deals with them, not me. As for a silver SUV, I can't say." She went to the counter and poured herself a cup of coffee. "Well, about a month ago I happened to see a car coming out of the driveway. It was dark blue or black, splattered with mud, maybe a Toyota

or a Honda. I wasn't paying much attention. I'd taken
Moses to a doctor's appointment, and he was complain-
ing loudly about having to have blood drawn. You'd
think the nurse had cut open a vein and stuck a garden
hose in it."

I finally felt as though I'd learned something of significance. Now all I needed to do was convince Jorgeson to
track down all the owners of black or blue Toyotas or
Hondas in Farberville and Maxwell County and compare
their fingerprints to those in Winston's house—and
search the entire valley for Esther's grave.

So many bodies, so little time.

CHAPTER 9

I walked down the road to my car, dug my keys out of my pocket, and glanced at the house that would fade away in a quagmire of legal fights and probate hearings. A light shone in the library, a light that I had not turned on earlier. I was too exhausted to rally much enthusiasm as I went to the porch and tried the front door. It was locked. However, that had not kept Moses from going inside whenever he wished. I continued around the house to the French doors, which were conveniently unlocked. As I entered, I heard a female voice muttering rather vulgar expletives.

Angela might have returned, I thought cautiously, or Esther might have emerged from her hideout in the basement. The latter was a stretch. Peter had examined the wine cellar. If he'd found a one-cell apartment, he would have at least commented on it. Furthermore, it was an absurd idea brought on by desperation and mental fatigue. The house had been remodeled three years ago. Esther was not the contemporary prisoner of Zenda, nor had she a reason to dawdle in Hollow Valley for fifteen years.

I went down the hall to the library and was astounded to find Pandora Butterfly sitting in the leather chair behind the desk, her feet propped on a rung of the ladder. Her kimono had been replaced by short shorts and a semitransparent blouse that allowed observers to note her lack of anything underneath it. A glass of red wine was next to an ashtray with a smoldering cigarette. She looked up at me with slitted eyes, then deftly closed her cell phone. "What are you doing here?" she demanded.

"An excellent question. I have no reasonable explanation for being here. What about you?"

"I needed some privacy." She realized that I was staring at the ashtray. "It's not pot, if that's what you're thinking. It's an organic cigarette, made with additive-free natural tobacco."

"That's good to know. Shouldn't you be out communing with nature beneath the starry sky?"

"I told you that I needed some privacy. The children can track my scent, so the only way to escape is to come over here. They're afraid to cross the blacktop. I warned them that Dearg Due, an Irish vampire, prowls the woods for children. When he catches one, he sucks its blood. Whatever works. If you don't mind, I'd like to enjoy the solitude for a few more minutes." She blew a stream of smoke at me.

I sat down in a leather armchair and said, "As long as we're here, let me ask you a question. Have you seen any unfamiliar cars in the driveway?"

"I pay no heed to the mindless monstrosities from Detroit. They're nothing but crass metal cages for those who care nothing for the environment. They growl and spew noxious fumes into the air."

"So you walked here from the ashram in California?" I asked. "I'm impressed with your commitment to the environment. You might want to have a word with your husband about those delivery trucks."

Her voice thick with exasperation, she said, "Yeah, right. Why don't you run along home now?"

"I haven't been in training for a marathon, and I loathe blisters. I prefer to sit right here and have a lovely conversation with you. You sounded upset while you were on your cell phone. Do you need sympathy or advice?"

"Let me give you some advice, lady. Eavesdropping is rude, and so are you. I feel a migraine coming on."

"Oh, Pandora Butterfly, do let me apologize for causing you stress. Let's go gather some herbs and berries to make you a soothing cup of tea. That is among your talents, isn't it? We are weyard sisters. Perhaps we can find a lizard's leg and an owlet's wing to spicen up the brew." I leaned back in the chair and crossed my legs. "Or you can answer my question. I have all night."

She shot me a dark look. "Okay, I saw an SUV turn down this driveway a couple of times. Some woman was driving. I thought maybe she'd been hired by Terry to clean the house periodically. Are you satisfied?"

"Are you certain that you didn't see any other vehicles?"

"Ethan sends workmen down every once in a while to take care of the yard. I have no idea why he bothers, but he said he does it out of respect for Winston. Like Winston cares if the grass is shaggy. His ashes are in the Gulf of Mexico by now." She rolled her eyes like a particular seventeen-year-old I happened to know. "The men come in a pickup truck. Other than them, I haven't seen anybody else around here."

We both heard the sound of a motorcycle as it neared the house and then stopped. I hoped it was a motorcycle, anyway; for all I knew about Dearg Due, he might ride a leaf blower. "Expecting company?" I asked her.

"Yeah," she said as she leaped up and made it out the door before I could stop her (had I intended to do so, which I hadn't). She continued out the front door. Almost immediately, the engine roared. I arrived in time to see Pandora clinging to the driver as the motorcycle sped in the direction of the blacktop. Seconds later, the noise began to wane.

"Humph," I said as I returned to the library to turn off the light. Pandora's cell phone was on the desk. Unlike mine, which was designed for time travelers from the fifteenth century, hers had a myriad of buttons, arrows, and keys. When I pushed the ON button, a screen covered with quaint doodads came to life. I squinted until I spotted a tiny rectangle that implied it would redial the last number. Impressed with my techno-triumph, I made myself comfortable in the leather chair, took a breath, and hit the button.

"Devil's Roost," a man said. The words were barely discernible over blaring music and shouting in the background.

"I apologize for bothering you," I said loudly, "but were you speaking to Pandora Butterfly about five minutes ago?"

"Who?" he shouted. "You have to speak up. It's damn crazy here, what with the band screeching like hogs gettin' butchered. Rowena! Get over to that booth afore they take to wiping the floor with those college boys!"

"Pandora Butterfly!" I shouted as loudly as he had.

"Ain't no butterflies here!"

For a split second, I wished I'd been a cheerleader in my past. I did my best to turn up my volume. "I'm talking about a woman with long blond hair! She calls herself Pandora Butterfly!"

"You mean Pandy? No, she ain't been here since I kicked her out on her butt. I got enough trouble with the cops without that bitch selling drugs. If you're a friend of hers, you ain't welcome neither!"

The band ended its cacophony with a chorus of atonal howls. There was still plenty of noise from what must have been a very inebriated crowd, but I was relieved to be able to speak in a more normal voice. "Let me make sure we're talking about the same person. This woman named Pandy—about five-seven, frizzy blond hair that hangs to the middle of her back?"

"Who's this?" he countered.

Although I had no scruples about lying to him, I wasn't going to win his confidence if I claimed to be her friend. "She's no friend of mine," I said firmly. "She owes me money. Five minutes ago she was talking to somebody at this number. Was it you?"

There was a pause. "This is a pay phone, honey. I don't keep tabs on the customers who use it. Hang on and lemme see if Rowena noticed."

I listened to men and women shrieking at each, mostly in words of one syllable that they had not learned at their mothers' knees. Some of the lewd propositions sounded anatomically implausible. I had no idea where the Devil's Roost was but reminded myself to find out so that I could stay outside a ten-mile radius. I was becoming engrossed by an exchange between someone named Jude and his girlfriend, Izzy, who was perturbed that someone named Tiawana was crawling all over him, when my confidante came back on the line.

"Rowena says she saw Zeppo on the phone a while back. He jabbered for five minutes, then took off."

"On a motorcycle?" I asked.

"He's got a banged-up standard chopper with a sissy bar. He claims it can hit a double ton, but he's an idiot."

"Okay," I said, mystified by the jargon but fairly certain that he'd referred to a motorcycle. "Thanks for your help."

"Any time you're out this way, stop by and ask for Jimmie John. You and me can get to know each other better. I got the—" Babeldom drowned out any elaboration of the invitation, which was for the best.

"I'll keep it in mind." I turned off the cell phone. I hadn't bought Pandora's pretense earlier, and it was gratifying to know that my intuition was as flawless as always. I hadn't cast her in the role of a drug dealer, though. Nattie wasn't aware of Pandora's double life. If Charles and Felicia Finnelly had known, they would have demanded an old-fashioned Salem witch trial. Ethan surely wouldn't have tolerated her jaunts to the Devil's Roost, no matter how profitable they were.

I turned out the light in the library and went to my car. I was too tired to try to even remember everything that had happened during the previous twelve hours, and it took all of my energy to drive safely. When I arrived home, I said good night to Caron and Inez and went directly to bed. I did not pass Go or attempt to collect two hundred house keys.

I was nursing a cup of coffee when Inez and Caron joined me in the living room. They watched me like a pair of hyenas, waiting for me to expire on the sofa. I ignored them as long as I could, then said, "You're wasting your time. We won't get the house, no matter what happens. Go outside and play in the sandbox. I'll bring you cookies and juice in an hour or two."

"We don't have a yard, Mother," Caron said. "I suppose we could go play in the Dumpster behind the sorority house next door. Maybe we can find some food."

"Like rotten vegetables," Inez added.

I very carefully put down the cup. "There's no point in getting angry at me. I want the house more than you do. You'll go away to college in a year. I had dreams of living out my golden years in a meadow, reading Emily Dickinson to the larks and the bluebirds. I was going to learn how to cook gourmet dishes sprinkled with fresh herbs from my garden. All my favorite books would be on the highest shelf in the library so I'd have to use the ladder. It's not going to happen. On Monday I guess Peter and I will start looking for a lot and an architect. We should be able to move into our new house by Christmas, if there aren't any glitches."

Caron sighed. "Can't you Do Something? What if everybody in that weird family is a coconspirator in Terry's death, and when they all go to jail, you can buy the house from them so they can buy gum at the prison canteen?"

"It doesn't work that way," I said wearily.

"How about this, Ms. Malloy?" Inez said suggested. "You find out that they're guilty and blackmail them?"

"I don't think that we'd be comfortable knowing that all of our neighbors have a reason to murder us in our beds." I gazed at their identical woebegone faces, wondering how long they'd practiced in the mirror the previous evening. "Give it up, girls. Why don't you clean out Caron's closet? Maybe you'll come across Barbie's Dream House. You can play make-believe all day long."

"I torched it when I was in fifth grade, remember? I wrote a report on arson," Caron said, then frowned at me. "Are you really going to let those people get away with it, Mother?"

I thought about it for a long while. "I don't want to let anyone get away with anything," I said at last. "The whole thing is so incredibly confusing. There should be a logical way to connect the dots, but I can't even figure out where to start."

"Start at the beginning," Inez murmured.

It was better than brooding for the next six months, I

told myself. I looked at Inez and said, "Get a notebook and a pen. This may take a while."

It took over two hours, as it turned out. Inez carefully noted names, relationships, estimated dates, presumptions, facts, and fanciful hypotheses based on nothing whatsoever. We took breaks for food (chips and crackers), beverages (coffee and sodas), and trips to the bathroom (best unspecified). They turned off their cell phones. When Inez's hand cramped, Caron took over the secretarial duties. By the time we gave up, we had a dozen pages of scribbles, arrows, stars, and deletions. The margins looked as if spiders had dipped their legs in blue ink and danced with abandonment.

The three of us were reduced to numb despair. I went out to the balcony, as frustrated as I'd ever been, and waited for a lightning bolt to energize me. Caron came out and leaned her head on my shoulder. I knew it was a ploy, but I appreciated the gesture all the same. "Damn it," I said, "I am not going to let the guilty party get away with it. Maybe it's true that revenge is best served cold, but it's not going to be served freeze-dried on a tarnished platter."

"Go for it," my darling daughter said. "You can do it."

I drew away to smile at her. "Now you're my number-one fan? My ratings must have shot sky-high to warrant this pretense of loyalty."

"So I want the house—okay?" She pursed her lips to emphasize her displeasure at my lack of gullibility. I longed for the days when she'd merely stuck out her lower lip and rolled her eyes.

I found myself mimicking her expression. It was as if I'd been whacked on the head by a sense of déjà vu, but I couldn't put my finger on the déjà or the vu. Caron gave me a perplexed look as I struggled to snatch a vague memory from my mind. "Loretta," I said slowly. "It has to do with Loretta. Why does it have to do with Loretta?"

"Hold that thought," Caron said. She went back into the living room to consult with Inez.

I couldn't hold a thought I didn't have, but I remained on the balcony, oblivious to whoever might be walking across the campus lawn. I finally decided that my only hope was a jolt of caffeine and went inside.

Inez cleared her throat. "Loretta is the woman that made the mushroom quiche for Terry the night before he died. You said that it didn't have anything to do with his death. Her housemate's name is Nicole. You rode with—"

I cut her off. "I'm going to have another cup of coffee and then pay her a visit. I don't know why, but I'll come up with something." The phone rang before I could do anything. I picked it up with reluctance. "Hello?"

"I love you, Claire Malloy," Peter said. "You are the most alluring woman since Helen of Troy, and she pales in your charm."

I let him continue for a minute and then inquired in my most sultry voice about the purpose of the call.

"I'm in Atlanta. My flight to Nashville is delayed, so I may miss my connection. The next flight will get me there at midnight. I'll take a cab from the airport, but you'd better be waiting up for me. I'm going to arouse you with the details of every meeting, then overwhelm you with the latest policies concerning the regulation of gun show sales. You'll melt when I outline the procedures for coordination between the feds and regional law enforcement officers. I will write the outlines in whipped cream on your writhing body and slowly lick them—"

"I get the idea," I said, "and I'll pick up a carton of cream. I'll see you at the midnight hour." A moment later my goofy grin was replaced with a steely stare. Peter's call was more catalytic than a random bolt of lightning. I had approximately twelve hours to assist the police before Sherlock shut me down.

I decided to forgo the coffee, gave Caron enough money for bagels, and went to my car. I was energized, but I was still baffled. I had no clue why I was determined to talk to Loretta, which meant I had no clue what to say to her. I was driving on automatic and operating on raw instinct. It was just as well there were no pedestrians strolling across the street, cell phones glued to their ears.

Loretta opened the door. Her eyes were red, and she clutched a damp tissue in her hand. "You again. Am I going to be arrested for misidentification of local fungi? You'd better read me my rights before you slap on the handcuffs."

"I came to apologize," I said with a rueful smile. "I have a bad habit of thinking out loud under stress. Have you heard about Terry?"

Her face slackened, and she gestured for me to come inside. "Yes, and I feel like crap. I cried half the night. I have one of Winston's paintings in the bedroom. As soon as I looked at it this morning, I lost it. Winston and Terry were so dear to me. I can't believe what happened. Please tell me that I didn't . . ."

"Terry's death had nothing to do with mushrooms," I said. "The police think it was caused by food poisoning."

"Let's go to the kitchen," she said, her voice unsteady. "I baked oatmeal bread this morning, and we have organic honey. Tea or coffee?"

I opted for coffee and did not protest when she set down a plate of bread slices, butter, and honey. "I don't quite know how to say this, but there's something about you that puzzles me. It has nothing to do with your reaction Friday night. That was understandable, and I apologize again. Can you help me, Loretta?"

"You don't suspect me of anything?"

I slathered butter on a slice of bread, took a bite, and studied her face as I ate. "Why would I? You don't have any connections to the Hollow family. You liked Winston and Terry, so you wouldn't have a motive to hurt either of them." The twenty-watt bulb in my head finally clicked on, but the illumination was poor. "Do you have any connections to the Hollow family, Loretta?"

"Not anymore."

"Now I see it. You and your mother have the same mouth. When she's annoyed, she puckers her lips just like you did the other afternoon. You have the same chin, too."

"None of the mousiness, though. Yes, I used to be a simpering, pathetic little wimp who was too afraid to make eye contact with normal people. I'm over it."

"When you ran away from home, you didn't go very far."

"Yes I did." She stirred a spoonful of honey into her tea. "After Winston was shipped off, he wrote me letters. He sent them to a friend of his, who passed them to me at school. When I got fed up with my father's abuse and my mother's timidity, I took a bus to New York City and stayed in a shelter until Winston had an opportunity to come get me. He arranged for me to live with a family until he started college. His parents thought they were paying for him to live in a dorm, but he used the money for an apartment. After he graduated, we moved to the city and lived in crappy apartments until he started making big bucks as a set designer. At first, I thought we could live happily ever after, but I got tired of the traffic and the incessant noise and the frantic pace. I knew my parents didn't care where I was as long as I didn't disrupt their facade of respectability. I make a point not to shop on the other side of town, or get plowed and stagger into their holier-than-thou church. I've been back nearly eight years."

"I thought that you were dead, and they'd buried you in their backyard," I admitted. "I was going to demand that the police take cadaver dogs and scour the entire valley until they found your decomposed body. It's comforting to learn that I was misguided."

Loretta shivered. "My father's not that evil. I'd throw boiling water on him if he showed up here, of course, but I don't sit around all day trying to find a way to make his life as miserable as he made mine. When he was a child, he probably planned to be a senator or a governor. Instead, he squeaked through college with borderline grades and ended up working in the family business. Some people crave respect like junkies crave crack. The only two places he could get any were at home and at that awful church. My father had the most expensive car and the loudest voice, so he got to be on the board. He used to strut around the house on Sunday afternoon, condemning members of the congregation for their lapses. If I defended anyone, he'd slap me or grip my arms until I cried." She looked out the window for a long moment. "Maybe I *should* be thinking up ways to make him miserable. Any suggestions?"

"I didn't come here to stir up latent anger," I said. "Let's talk about Winston. Why did he go back to Hollow Valley? Surely he wasn't nostalgic for the good old days."

"He told me that he needed to come to grips with his childhood, that his psychiatrist had urged him to face his family and show them that he was no longer a victim. He wanted to make them understand that they'd never had the right to demean him. On another level, I think he wanted to piss them off. The best way to accomplish that was to establish his legitimacy in Hollow Valley by building a house and living there in flagrante delicto."

"Was this aimed at your parents in particular?"

She snickered. "My father was the commander of the gulag, but the rest of them mindlessly obeyed his orders. He encouraged the other boys to harass Winston. They did ghastly things to him whenever they caught him alone in the woods. Aunt Margaret Louise, Nattie, my mother, Aunt Joanne and Uncle Sheldon, Aunt Misty and Uncle Syd sat in silence while my father vented his outrage at family meetings. Nobody said a word in Winston's defense, not even his parents." She noticed my confused expression. "Aunt Joanne and Uncle Sheldon are Jordan's parents. They moved to Pennsylvania when she was a toddler. Aunt Misty and Uncle Syd were Ethan's parents."

I made no effort to add their names to my list of suspects, since they no longer resided in the "gulag." "Was it worth it to Winston? From what Terry told me, they had a great life in Manhattan. Couldn't he have confronted them for a long weekend?"

Loretta refilled my coffee cup and sat back down. "He wanted them to know that he had a right to live in Hollow Valley as a direct descendant of the old fart. They didn't intend to live in the house for more than a year, but Winston discovered that he had a talent for landscapes. His paintings were a contemporary version of French impressionism. He wanted to put a lily pond out in back and cover the meadow with sunflowers. Terry flew to his poker tournaments. They had a lot of close friends. The last time I talked to Winston was the weekend before his death. He wanted me to take samba lessons with him. I said no."

"And when you heard about his purported accident . . . ?"

"I cried all night."

"Then moped for a month," said a woman in the doorway. She was tall and lean, dressed in sweats. "I'm Nicole.

Loretta, we promised Samuel that we'd go to Joplin with him in an hour. I need to jump in the shower. Have you fixed food for the picnic basket yet? He's counting on chicken salad, crudités, marinated mushrooms, Camembert and tomato sandwiches, and blueberry tarts. Billy bought the champagne yesterday."

Loretta shrugged at me. "I guess I'd better get to work, Claire. For reasons known only to himself, Samuel demands a well-equipped entourage when he makes a dash across the border to buy cheap cigarettes. Because of the grueling one-hour drive, we have to spend the entire afternoon singing show tunes in the van and picnicking at a particular rest stop that has a splendid view of cows. Winston used to bring his pastels and do wicked caricatures of us." Her lips were pursed, but her eyes were filled with tears. "Can you come back tomorrow? There is one thing he said that may mean something."

"What?"

"I'm not sure. Let me think about it. The tarts need forty minutes in the oven, and I have to get started on the pastry right now. Samuel throws a fit when everything's not exactly as he commands. I ought to make peanut butter and jelly sandwiches one of these days." She stood up and turned on the oven and then opened the refrigerator. "Tomorrow, okay?"

"Thanks for talking to me," I said. "I'll be back in the morning." I gave her a brief hug and went out to my car. I'd solved one crime, or noncrime, anyway. In a perverse way, I was a little disappointed that I couldn't point my finger at Charles Finnelly and accuse him of murder most foul. Maritodespotism was not a crime in the eagle eyes of the law, and the statute of limitations for child abuse had long since expired. I made a note to myself to ask Caron to come up with tips for Loretta to punish him someday in the future.

When I reached the bottom of the hill, I pulled into the stadium parking lot to think. One motive could be dismissed. Charles had not killed Winston because of a shallow grave in the woods, and it was hard to imagine that he had killed him because of his own religious fanaticism. Winston had not communicated a grisly secret to Terry. Therefore, Charles had no motive to kill Terry.

I moved on to the revelation of Pandora Butterfly's secret life as a drug dealer (and other things). There was not one leaf of proof that she was selling marijuana grown in a greenhouse in Hollow Valley. I'd been dragged over every damn inch of the place, and I knew what marijuana plants looked like. I wouldn't have missed acres of poppies or a coca plantation surrounded by tropical trees. Still if Jimmie John had been truthful, she was selling something illegal. It was Sunday, and the bar was closed. I felt Peter's breath on my neck. I had less than twelve hours, and the clock was ticking. What I didn't have was a clear-cut course of action. The idea of going back to Hollow Valley made me queasy. There was no reason to drive all the way to Maxwell County to talk to the sheriff. Angela's car had been found there; Angela hadn't. The sheriff would not take kindly to being interrupted during Sunday dinner, and I couldn't so much as hint that his deputies were incompetent or I'd find myself in jail for impudence.

A skateboarder swooped by my car and cut a wide circle in the bottom of the lot. Seconds later, a veritable horde of them were skimming by my car so closely that I could see their acned faces and orthodontia. Their message was easy to comprehend. I was an invader and would be targeted until I removed myself from their sacred ground. I waved as I exited the lot and drove toward the campus—and toward Hollow Valley. I'd intended to search the desk in the library, but Pandora's presence had distracted me. I doubted that I'd find anything to justify my effort, but I was down to ten hours and fifty-two minutes.

I hate deadlines.

I parked in what had become my personal parking space. There was no indication that anyone was present. That meant nothing, I told myself as I went around to the doors in the back. If the goddesses were on my side, Moses was sitting down to roast beef and mashed potatoes at the Old Tavern. I went to the library and paused to soak in the aroma of furniture polish and leather-bound books. There were empty spaces where Terry must have taken his treasured books to Key West. I found a complete set of Jane Austen and another of Dickens. An entire shelf was filled with biographies and histories. The collection of poetry included all of my favorites. First editions were shelved with battered classics from my childhood. I sneezed with delight as I thumbed through a worn edition of nursery rhymes. I would have died on the spot as long as someone was there to turn the pages.

It was not my time to rest in this blissful bed of literature, alas. I replaced the book and sat down to search the desk. The top drawer contained standard paraphernalia. There were enough paper clips to make a chain to encircle the house. Rubber bands nestled in profusion. Scraps of paper had illegible notations, e-mail addresses, and telephone numbers. The stapler lacked staples. When I pricked my finger on a thumbtack, I closed the drawer and moved on. Terry had overlooked a manila folder crammed with receipts for art supplies; oil paint was pricier than I thought. Another was dedicated to travel vouchers, creased boarding passes, and hotel bills. It hadn't occurred to me that artists and professional poker players took deductions for business expenses. I smiled to myself as I pictured Winston tossing such trivial things on the desk for Terry to sort and file. A successful couple requires a word person and a number person. The poetry books most likely belonged to Winston, and the mathematical theory books to Terry. The odds were good that they'd been happy together.

The bottom drawer held a carton of cigarettes, minus one pack. I was dumbfounded, a reaction that I experience very rarely. When I'd first toured the house, I hadn't seen any ashtrays inside or on the tables on the terrace. I hadn't noticed any lingering odor of stale smoke in the drapes or rugs. I attributed the missing pack to Pandora. The carton might have been hers as well. I examined a pack, but there was no stamp advising that it was best used by such-and-so date. Cigarettes didn't expire, but their users often did. Not that I was an authority, I thought as I replaced the carton and closed the drawer. Ethan could have found the deed among personal items that Terry subsequently removed. Winston had owned a current passport. Most people have copies of their birth certificates, car titles, piles of old bank statements, records of credit card purchases, and other things required to avoid the wrath of the IRS should they descend to audit. I didn't, to Peter's oft-vocalized distress. Some of us value poetry over mundane concerns.

I rocked in the chair, waiting for inspiration. When none came, I made sure that everything was back in its place and went out to the terrace. As I looked at the stream, I remembered what Moses had said about Inez and Jordan's trek in the distant field. I found it hard to believe that Jordan would volunteer to lead a search party in pursuit of medicinal berries, or volunteer to do anything that required exertion. I could be wrong, I told myself, however improbable that was. Jordan might have been so desperate for a friend that she would have climbed a mountain. Inez was older, which mattered in the contorted teenage world, and she wouldn't have hidden her disdain for Jordan's hair and piercings. Or she'd hypnotized Jordan with an elaborate analysis of entomological metamorphosis.

I didn't know if I was stewing over details of no consequence. Inez and Jordan had taken a walk, and Pandora had hidden her cigarettes in a safe place. I couldn't pin down the correlation between Winston's death in March and Terry's death the previous day, but there had to be one. Charles and Felicia Finnelly weren't going to offer me further information. Nattie had already told me what she knew. Unless a squirrel pegged Moses in the head with a two-ton acorn, his babbles would remain enigmatic, and I didn't have time to dissect them. I couldn't bear the thought of another round with Aunt Margaret Louise, who'd savor the opportunity to tell me how she was a Grateful Dead backup singer and slept with Eric Clapton every other weekend and six weeks in the summer. That left Ethan, and Pandora if she'd come home to braid daisies in her hair.

My only recourse required exertion. I drank a glass of water in the kitchen, looked sadly at the island over which I would never reign, and contemplated the best route to the greenhouses. When in doubt, snoop.

I made it across the blacktop road and into the woods that lay between the Old Tavern and Ethan's house. I encountered no lions, tigers, or bears, but I had to fight through thorns, fallen branches, stumps, and holes concealed by leaves. I definitely preferred the Nature Channel to nature. By the time I emerged into neat rows of saplings, I'd accumulated an assortment of scratches on my bare arms and face, and dried leaves in my hair. My ankles were itchy. Worst of all, I was sweaty.

No one seemed to be working. I stayed in the minimal protection of the baby trees until I had a better view of the greenhouses and outbuildings. One delivery truck was parked nearby. Painted on its side was a depiction of the arched sign in an oval of flowering vines. Beneath that were an e-mail address and a claim that Hollow Valley Nursery had been established in nineteen sixty-four. Their fiftieth anniversary was approaching. I wondered if they'd give each other a dozen rosebushes to commemorate the occasion. Champagne would not be served within range of Charles's sanctimonious nose, but blueberry tarts might be on the menu.

I sat down on a concrete block to pick the leaves out of my hair and to examine the red bumps on my ankles. Caron had blundered into a patch of chiggers when she and Inez had taken a shortcut home from school, and she'd spent the weekend with her feet in a bucket of hot water and Epsom salts. My maternal impulses had been sorely tested. Peter's amorous intentions for our midnight assignation would require imagination (and agility) if I ended up in the same situation. I was grinning at the idea when I heard a delivery truck rumble up the hill from the bridge. I slipped behind the back of a greenhouse and peered around the corner. The cab door opened, and the driver grunted as his feet hit the ground. He glanced around and then flicked a cigarette in my direction. I did not take it personally, since I was operating on the theory that he couldn't see me.

A minute later, Ethan called, "About damn time, Rudy. What happened?"

I resisted an urge to dive into the weeds and put my arms over my head. I wasn't breaking the law, I reassured myself. I hadn't scaled a fence or blatantly disregarded warnings not to trespass.

"Had to wait on Coop," Rudy said. "I wasn't gonna load the stuff by myself, was I? He said he overslept, but he looked worse than something the dog dragged in. He stank to high heavens and was real ornery."

"You don't smell all that good yourself," Ethan responded. "If you get stopped for a DUI, you'd better be across the border before I hear about it. Grab the nursery receipts and come in the office." He disappeared into a building that I'd been inside during my grand tour. It housed a desk, a filing cabinet, a squeaky ceiling fan, a wall calendar sporting the HVN logo, and a coffeepot so filthy that Mr. Coffee himself would have wept in shame.

"Neither do you, boss," Rudy muttered as he stomped to the cab of the truck. He retrieved the documents and went inside the building.

I risked standing up, a move greatly appreciated by my knees. I wasn't interested in the truck, so I had no reason to make any furtive attempts to gain access. However, I wasn't sure why I was there or what I'd hoped to discover. I was feeling rather foolish when I was tapped on the shoulder.

My response shall remain unrecorded for posterity.

CHAPTER 10

"Are you here to talk to Aunt Margaret Louise?" asked Jordan.

Justifiably startled, I reeled around, then gaped at her. "What have you done?"

Her hair was no longer purple, nor was it aligned in a rigid row across the top of her head. It resembled a shaggy brown pelt, but it was an improvement. The bling had been removed, exposing small holes that she'd attempted to cover with makeup. The rest of her face was clean. "Better?"

"Good grief," I said, "did Uncle Charles convert you?"

Jordan blushed. "Not likely. I just decided I was too old for the goth crap. It took a lot of time to pull off, and after the initial horror, nobody seemed to care. Why are you looking for Aunt Margaret Louise here? She's at the mill, getting ready to go play bridge with her cronies. We need to catch her before she leaves." She tugged on my arm. "Please, Mrs. Malloy. You promised."

"I'll take care of it, Jordan. If your aunt has gone, I can clear it with Nattie. Wait for me by the statue." I took a peek around the corner of the building.

Her voice dropped. "What are you doing? If you want to steal ornamental trees, you ought to wait until dark. The root balls are heavier than you think. Do you want azaleas or anything like that? I can grab a couple and carry them to your car for you."

She was clearly in the throes of mall withdrawal and cell phone deprivation, both potentially fatal to teenagers. I shook my head. "Thanks for your offer of assistance, but I'm not here to steal anything." I would have elaborated, but nothing came to mind. To distract her from asking the obvious question, I said, "Have you seen Pandora Butterfly this morning?"

"No, and I'd better not!"

"You have a problem with her?" I did, but I wasn't going to proffer it as a topic of conversation. As much as I appreciated Jordan's efforts to join civilized society, I didn't trust her.

"No, it's nothing," she replied hastily. "We're fine. It's just that, uh, her kids made off with a book I left outside. It's probably in shreds."

"Oh," I said. I wasn't a poker player, but I could read the mendacity in her eyes. I chose not to pursue it. Pandora's fan base was small, and I wasn't surprised that Jordan was not a member. Since Ethan was otherwise occupied, it seemed logical that Pandora was at home with her wee beasties. "Jordan, if you want me to arrange for you to come home with me, you need to wait for me at the statue. I'll be there in no more than half an hour. Got it?"

Her upper lip started to curl into a sneer, but she caught herself. "Okay."

Once she'd trudged away, I wound my way through the saplings and stayed at the edge of the field until I found a well-beaten path that I assumed led to Ethan and Pandora's house. The path was littered with sodden piles of discarded clothes and muddy shoes. A headless doll had been nailed to a tree. I did not allow myself to conjure up horrific images of pagan rituals.

The beasties were not in sight when I reached the yard. Pandora was seated on a railroad tie, her head lowered. When I stepped on a particularly crunchy leaf, she looked up. "Are you stalking me? Go play with Dearg Due. He's got a thing for scrawny, meddlesome redheads."

I politely overlooked her lack of appreciation for the difference between scrawny and svelte, as well as between meddlesome and inquisitive. In sunlight, my hair has red highlights, so I couldn't accuse her of total ignorance. "You look dreadful, dear. Do you have a hangover?"

"From one glass of wine?" Her laugh was nasty. "You must be a cheap date."

"Zeppo took you to a church revival? Charles will be tickled pink."

She nearly lost her balance as she stood up. "What are you talking about? The guy on the motorcycle owed me some money. I got off at the highway and came home, if it's any of your business. I don't even know his name, and I've never heard of anybody named Zeppo. That's stupid."

"I don't guess he took you to the Devil's Roost," I continued, refusing to flinch as she glowered at me. "Jimmie John said you're not welcome there anymore."

I had her full attention. Her fists tightened as she turned away, and I could hear her cursing in a low voice. "My cell phone," she said abruptly.

"It begged me to hit the redial button, and I didn't want to hurt its feelings. Jimmie John had quite a lot to say about you, Pandy."

"That's a violation of my privacy! It's like reading somebody's diary or opening their personal mail."

"Equally enlightening, too. Does Ethan know about these little jaunts with Zeppo? For the record, I do agree that it's a stupid name. He should consider changing it to Harpo or Chico."

"What do you want from me?" she asked with a groan.

"An explanation would be a good start." I sat down on a splintery railroad tie and waited for her to fabricate a remotely plausible story.

The hangover was too much for her. She sat cross-legged in the grass and sighed. "You cannot believe how boring it is out here. Yeah, Jordan whines all the time, but she's only been here a month. I've been here for ten tedious years. All Ethan talks about is the nursery, and he's up there all day and half the night. Am I supposed to have intelligent conversations with Rainbow and Weevil? All they do is snuffle and snort like filthy little pigs. What am I supposed to do? If I didn't get a break, I'd lose it."

"What happened to the free-spirited lily of the valley? Can't you commune with the goddesses, or have they cut you off? They may not approve of your participation in the drug business."

"Jimmie John's full of it. He's a runty old alcoholic who runs a bar for losers. I may have been there once, but I didn't stay. I dance and flutter and act like an idiot because it keeps the rest of the family away. The last things I want to do are drink tea with Nattie and listen to her talk on and on about poor, confused Winston. It gets old. There were times I wished that I could drown her out with a mantra."

"What were you doing at an ashram?"

"There was a warrant out on me, and it was a safe place. Then Ethan showed up in his tree-hugger sandals, all eager to meditate and starve himself on brown rice and seaweed. He was so squishy and sincere that I wanted to puke. Then he started talking about his inheritance and

the nursery, and he looked a helluva lot more attractive."
She shoved her hair back and closed her eyes. "We had
this wonderful scheme how we'd take over one of the
greenhouses and get serious about growing pot. He wove
my wedding ring out of slivers of bamboo. We mumbled
a lot of nonsense out in a pasture, with goats nibbling on
the hem of my dress and a monk in a purple robe." She
held out her hand to allow me to swoon over an emerald
ring surrounded by diamonds. "I replaced the bamboo
thingie with this. I can always sell it if I need to. It's worth
eighteen thousand."

"Your grand scheme didn't work out so well. There's
no marijuana in the greenhouses."

"Once we got here, Ethan got all excited about growing trees and flowers. He said we couldn't put the nursery
at risk. It has to comply with state regulations and be in-
spected at least once a year. Then there's dear old Uncle
Charles. Ethan didn't tell me about him until we got here.
He does his own inspection several times a week. Felicia
trots behind him with a notebook, assiduously writing
down his grumbles and complaints. One of these days I'll
bake him a batch of brownies that will make his toenails
tingle!"

"How are you planning to do that without marijuana?
As fond as I am of Duncan Hines, he doesn't seem like
the sort to arouse tingles." I paused for a moment. "You're
growing it out in the woods, aren't you? Did Ethan give
you any suggestions for an irrigation system, or is he un-
aware of your horticultural endeavor?"

"He may suspect, but he wouldn't dare take a hit and
imperil his karma. Then again, he gets totally drunk
when it suits him and boasts about all the money he's
stashed away. We could be living in Florida in one of
those ridiculously expensive houses with plate-glass windows looking out on a white sand beach. You know, hur-

ricane bait. Who cares how much it costs after your roof tiles end up in the Everglades?"

"You can't convince him to move away from here?" I asked. "He can't be having too much fun if he puts in so many hours at the nursery."

Pandora's mouth curled. "He swears we'll leave every year, but then there's the spring planting season, and the fall planting season, and the rush at the beginning of the summer, and the rush before Christmas. 'One more year' is his mantra. I've heard that for a bloody decade!"

Nattie had told me that the nursery did well, but Pandora was talking big bucks. It didn't sound like the family members were scraping by on their shares of the profit. They did have expensive cars: Charles's new Cadillac, the Mercedes, the Mustang convertible. The sleek, cocoa-colored Jaguar parked on the far side of the yard had not come from a used car lot in Maxwell County. Pandora's kimono had been hand-embroidered with silk. I hadn't realized that holly berries were worth their weight in dollars. Living in a duplex does not require extensive expertise in landscaping. Weeds bewilder me, and grass is grass.

"I need water," Pandora said suddenly. "Don't say anything to Ethan about last night, and I'll bake you some brownies." She struggled to her feet in preparation to escape my stare.

I had principles, but one of them involved using whatever worked. In this case, blackmail would do nicely. "Wait a minute, Pandy," I said, laying emphasis on her alias. "I'll agree to forget about the Devil's Roost and Zeppo, but you have to give me something more helpful than a vague promise of brownies. Don't bother to offer me a little plastic bag of pot. My husband's a cop, and he might ask me where I got it."

"What do you want? I can have the children's bags

packed in three minutes. You can deliver them to whatever agency will take them. I can tell Ethan they're hibernating under the house. He won't care."

I do not hold grudges, but I was still rankled by her attitude in the library. "Let's start with Winston's death. Tell me what you know."

"I don't know anything," she said, rubbing her temples. "He fell, he jumped. I didn't like him or Terry. They were always polite, but I knew they were laughing at me. I wouldn't have sold them a friggin' aspirin."

"What did Ethan say about it?"

"He said it was suicide and not to worry about it. To be honest, I wasn't paying much attention. It's not like I'm a member of the family. To them, respectability is like the Nobel Peace Prize. When a journalist comes here to do a piece for a magazine, the kids and I aren't allowed to leave the house because we don't fit into the image of a wholesome, family-owned business. I tried to leave once, but Charles and Ethan came after me like drooling bloodhounds. They'd put computer chips under everyone's skin if a veterinarian would do it. Esther's the only one who escaped for real."

"You know Esther?" I asked, trying not to sound as perplexed as I felt.

"I know about her," she said. "Charles gets on his pulpit and carries on about her treachery and sinfulness at least once a year. He intersperses that rant with ones about homosexuals, promiscuous teenagers, drunks, dopers, disobedient wives, unruly children, and whatever other bug he has up his butt. We all sit there with our hands in our laps and nod on cue. What a jolly time to be had at Hollow Valley!"

"They can't force you to stay here."

Pandora looked in the direction of the nursery. "I know that. This is my final year to tiptoe through the tulips. I'm out of here on January first, with or without Ethan and the kids, and I'm cleaning out the bank accounts before I go. You know what this place needs? A flash flood that carries everybody downstream all the way to whichever ocean is handier. Maybe they'll end up on an island where they can grow coconut trees and sell them to the cannibals."

I'd gotten more information from Moses than I had from her. I scratched a red bump on my ankle, then got up. "Does the nursery really make that much money?" I asked bluntly.

"There's half a million dollars in Ethan's savings account," she said as she started for the house.

"Your children ate one of Jordan's books," I called to her back.

"Let's hope it wasn't a cookbook. They get diarrhea if they eat anything with meat in it." The front door closed.

I deftly inferred that she no longer desired to talk to me. Instead of wading through the woods to my car, I walked down the driveway to the blacktop and turned in the direction of the Old Tavern. As I ambled, my mind was racing. Two of the dots on the scribbled notes found a possible connection. Jordan and Pandora Butterfly made an odd couple, but I was willing to bet they had one thing in common.

Jordan had climbed the statue of Colonel Moses Ambrose Hollow and was sitting on his shoulders. She waved her arms at me. "Mrs. Malloy!"

I felt like a ship coming to the rescue of a dehydrated traveler adrift in a lifeboat. "Yes, Jordan," I said with minimum enthusiasm. "You can come down now."

She slithered down his back. "You can't see anything from up there, except at night. Then I can watch Nattie put on pajamas and putter around her bedroom. If she was having a mad, passionate affair with one of the workmen, that'd be worth the bird poop on my butt. Mostly she reads. Aunt Margaret Louise left five minutes ago. When you talk to Nattie, don't tell her about what I said or anything, okay?"

It seemed as though potential blackmail victims were flinging themselves in my path. Pandora had Zeppo, and Jordan had a nocturnal affinity for the Colonel. "I won't bring up the subject, but I never lie." I could almost hear Peter's brays of laughter. "Unless it's in the best interests of the community, and it usually falls into the category of omission, not commission."

"Whatever you say, Mrs. Malloy."

I knocked on the heavy door. Nattie opened it and tried to hide her dismay. "Claire . . . do come in. Moses and I have finished eating, but you're welcome to a piece of chocolate cake." Her mouth fell open as she spotted Jordan. "Oh, my goodness, what have you done with Jordan? Did you replace her with a real child?"

"I'm fourteen years old," Jordan said sullenly.

Nattie shook her head. "You're attractive. Who would have thought it? Let me have a closer look at you, Jordan. Are those your real eyelashes?"

I let Jordan squirm while Nattie fussed over her, then poked her. "Go ahead and ask her, dear."

She stammered out a convoluted but mostly coherent request that covered Aunt Margaret Louise's absence, Caron and Inez's maturity, and her solemn promise to behave impeccably the remainder of the summer and pick gallons of blackberries or raspberries or blueberries or whatever Nattie wanted. She finally ran down. "Can I, Nattie?"

I expected Nattie to smile and send her off with me, so I was a bit mystified when she said, "I don't know, Jordan. Aunt Margaret Louise is the one who should make that decision. Discuss it with her tonight, and maybe you can spend the night at Claire's house later in the week. I hope you understand, Claire. Jordan's parents made the arrangement with Margaret Louise."

When Jordan turned around, her face looked almost as contorted as it had with the garish makeup. She swept past me, cut across the mill's lawn, and disappeared into the woods.

"That didn't go well," Nattie said. "I have no idea how you convinced her to wash her hair and remove those rings and studs, but I thank you from the bottom of my heart."

"Let me give you my home telephone number so that Margaret Louise can let me know what she decides. Jordan deserves a treat, and we'll take good care of her."

Nattie found a notepad and a pencil. I wrote down my number, said good-bye, and drove toward the highway. I'd instinctively put on my blinker when I stomped on the brake. I'd been so befuddled by Nattie's refusal that I'd forgotten about the missing link. I managed to back up far enough to turn down the driveway to the house that should have been my house. I purposefully slammed the car door loudly enough to startle a flock of blackbirds into an amorphous black cloud. I went around to the terrace and made myself comfortable in a chaise lounge. Within five minutes, Jordan plopped down on a nearby chair and said, "You should have let me go with you, no matter what Nattie said. It's not like she's my nanny. Aunt Margaret Louise would have been thrilled to get rid of me for a night. She hates me, just like everybody else in this miserable place does."

"They don't hate you, Jordan. They're tired of putting up with your attitude and posturing. Show Aunt Margaret Louise a smidgen of respect when you plead your case, and she'll grant you a furlough."

"It would be so cool if you lived here, Ms. Malloy. At

least there'd be someone to hang out with. Caron, I mean, and Inez. Adults are all about money and their precious gym memberships and golf tournaments and crap like that." She paused as she realized what she'd said. "I didn't mean you. I was talking about Uncle Charles and—"

"I'd rather talk about pot, and I don't mean the kind that hold potting soil and plants. Where's your patch? If you won't show it to me, I'll drag Inez out here and make her lead me to it. Your lack of cooperation will be noted."

She bristled at my implied threat. "It's not my patch. I've only been here a month, remember? I found it by accident. If you want to see, I'll take you there. Just don't blame me if you step on a snake. I've seen three copperheads on the path in the last week."

"Snakes don't scare me," I said truthfully. They didn't scare me; they terrified me. It was unfortunate that Winston and Terry had not been fishermen. Otherwise, they might have waist-high waders in a closet somewhere. My civic duty to solve Terry's death overcame my reluctance to play hopscotch with writing reptiles.

Jordan led me across the meadow and along the stream until we came to a tree trunk that made a very dubious bridge. She bounded across it and then waited while I sidled inch by inch. The minnows resembled baby piranhas, and the dragonflies came at me like kamikaze pilots. When I arrived at the far bank, I was breathless. I closed my eyes until the panic faded. "How much farther?" I asked.

Jordan fought to maintain a passive expression, but her voice cracked as she said, "Not far. Would you like to rest? You look kind of pale."

"I'm fine," I said grimly.

By the time we arrived at a clearing in the woods, I was quite sure we'd hiked for several miles. If this was a pot patch, it was a great deal less productive than Hollow

Valley Nursery. The soil had been churned and trampled. Dead leaves, branches, and rocks constituted the entire crop. "This is it?" I asked her.

"Now it is. A month ago I pulled up some old plants and hung them to dry, and planted their seeds in such straight rows that Ethan would have been proud. I should have had a nice little crop by the end of the summer, but no. I came here this morning and found this mess! Pandora must have done it. She stole the dried plants and then did one of her goofy dances to trample the seedlings. I can see her, totally stoned, flinging leaves in the air while she pretended she was a nymph. I can't even start another crop."

"Am I supposed to offer my condolences on the loss of your illegal industry?" I asked as I tossed a branch into the woods. "All you have to do is clean this up, and then you can make a hut out of twigs and straw. If you're patient, maybe Hansel and Gretel will come play with you."

"Is that supposed to be funny? It took me hours and hours to turn over the soil with a trowel. I had a big blister on the palm of my hand and cuts all over my knees."

I smiled as I envisioned Pandora's amazement when she found her patch primed for a new crop. Once she'd eliminated Demeter and fairies, it couldn't have taken much thought to realize that Jordan had done the dirty work. Why would she have destroyed it? Neither of them would rat on the other.

"When were you here last?" I asked.

Jordan frowned. "This morning, when I discovered what she'd done. It's so unfair. If I accuse her, then all she has to say is that she didn't know anything about the patch until she found it. She had no choice but to destroy it, naturally. My name will come up, and I'll be in big trouble."

One of Moses's garbled remarks came to mind. "You

were here yesterday morning, weren't you? You and Inez, that is. You had to show her how clever you are. Was she impressed?"

"She was talking to me like I was a kid. She wouldn't last five minutes in my neighborhood. My friends don't care about reading books or doing homework. They care about surviving. Too bad there's not a field guide to avoiding crack houses and spotting cops."

I studied her for a minute. "I didn't realize that you live in a ghetto. It's no wonder your parents sent you here to romp in the sunshine and be safe from drive-by shootings. You poor baby."

"So I don't live in a ghetto. I get so fed up with all the preppie snobs who worry about which Ivy League schools will accept them in four years. They have tutors and private coaches so they can excel at the proper sports, use the right forks, and work on their résumés. I hang out with real people."

"Drug dealers and pimps? Good for you, Jordan. If and when you grow up, you can savor the joys of soup kitchens, shelters, grime, rats, and jail." I cut short what was going to be a lengthy lecture and knelt in the dirt. I brushed aside leaves and twigs to pick up an expensive pen. I knew it was expensive because Peter had pitched a fit when Caron borrowed his. Angela had mentioned that hers was a Montblanc, a mere trinket that she'd bought herself to sign the divorce decree. It was too clean to have been buried, or even exposed to the elements. "Is the trowel here?" I asked, my voice shaking.

Jordan knelt beside me. "What's that? I've never seen it before."

"Is the trowel here?"

"I took it back before Ethan noticed that it wasn't in its proper place. He's a royal pain about his precious tools. Do you want me to go get it?"

"Yes," I said, although I was reluctant to be alone. Jordan had claimed to be tough, but she didn't need to be with me when I began to dig. I waited until she was gone and then found a flat rock to serve as a shovel. I scraped the dirt, repeatedly telling myself that I was wrong. I threw rocks and twigs over my back, yanked out stands of roots, and scooped loose dirt out of the deepening hole. Sweat dripped down my face and pooled in my armpits.

I was ready to give up and concede that my only error was thinking that I'd made one. My final scrape uncovered a few inches of a black plastic sheet. I'd inadvertently made a slit that exposed part of a hand. I scrambled backward until my back thumped against a tree. This was not a forgotten family burial plot, and I hadn't discovered the remains of anybody's ancestors.

Jordan had crossed the log and was trotting toward the clearing as I met her. I grabbed her wrist. "Wrong way," I said. "Did anyone see you?"

"Forgive me for saying this, but you're weird, Ms. Malloy. What about the pen? Do you know whose it is?"

"I have a pretty good guess," I said as I dragged her behind me. I was so distraught that I failed to have a second panic attack while I teetered back across the log. The meadow sloped up to the house. By the time we reached the terrace, I wanted nothing more than to sit down and put my head between my knees. I gestured at Jordan to hand me my purse. My cell battery was low, but there was hope. I didn't want to get into an extended conversation with the nine-one-one dispatcher, so I called Jorgeson.

"Ms. Malloy," he said with a mournful sigh, "how can I help you this fine afternoon?"

CHAPTER 11

Jordan and I sat on the terrace, waiting for the invasion. I'd made coffee, and she'd found a can of soda in the refrigerator. I was angry at whoever murdered Angela and buried her body in a plastic tarp, and I was angry at myself for all the uncharitable thoughts that I'd had about her. She'd had a legitimate reason for not calling me with a blither of apologies. It's hard to dial when you're dead.

"Who is it?" Jordan asked timidly.

"Until the investigators extricate the body, we can't be certain. I'm assuming that it's Angela Delmond, the real estate agent who showed me this house on Tuesday. She stranded me, and Nattie agreed to let me use her phone to call for a ride. That was when we saw you pulling that childish stunt. Death isn't funny. You might remember that next time you get the urge to stir up some excitement."

"Yeah, I know. Who killed her?"

I shrugged. "That was the last time I saw her. I don't know where she went or what she did after she drove away—or when she died. The medical examiner will order an autopsy to estimate the time of death." I did not elaborate on the intricacies of decomposition and the analysis of insect eggs and maggots. "Does anyone besides Pandora know about the pot patch?"

"I doubt it," she said with a grin. "Otherwise, I'd be wearing an ankle monitor and working eighteen hours a day at the nursery. That's if Uncle Charles didn't dump me in the nearest jail cell. He'd be sputtering like a constipated camel."

"As if you know what a constipated camel looks like."

"Sure I do. It looks like Uncle Charles."

I couldn't hold back a giggle, despite the solemnity of the situation. "What about Aunt Felicia?"

Jordan gave the question serious consideration. "A white lab rat, waiting to be injected with a lethal virus or be dissected. If you watch her carefully, you'll see that she's got an eye on the lookout for the nearest exit, and she'll trample anybody who gets in her way."

I raised my eyebrows. "Aunt Felicia strikes me as a mushy sponge without an original idea left in her mind after all those years with Charles." I recalled the glare she'd shot at his back. "Maybe I'd already made up my mind. I'd like to talk to her without Charles looming."

"You can try when he's at the nursery."

"I have a feeling I won't be out here anymore—except to pick you up, of course. The police have archaic rules about civilian participation in their investigations."

Car doors began to slam in the front of the house, and male voices barked. I made a face, then settled back for the ordeal that was to come. I recognized some of the members of the CSI team from past encounters, and one of the detectives. The same paramedics appeared with a gurney and equipment bags. Jorgeson was the last to arrive, and he was rather grumpy. Everyone else stepped aside to give him a clear path that ended at the chaise lounge.

"I informed the deputy chief about your call," he said. "He'd like you to call him at your first opportunity. In the meantime, Ms. Malloy, why don't you tell me what this is about. Your stories never fail to impress me. You and the young lady found a body that you think is Angela Delmond?"

It was tricky to decide where to start, so I limited myself to the basics. Jordan had told me about the vandalized pot patch, and I'd asked her to show it to me. I had not suspected anything of significance until I found the pen. I showed him my dirty fingernails and described what I'd unearthed. Jorgeson and I eyed each other for a minute.

"We can continue this later," he said at last. "We need to go to the crime scene."

I graciously allowed Jordan to lead the party. No one looked delighted when we arrived at the fallen log. Jorgeson sent an officer to look for a more suitable place to cross the stream. After grumbles, muttered discussions, and debate, we trekked downstream and waded through ankle-deep water. Our shoes squished over hill and dale until we arrived at the clearing. Jordan and I watched mutely as the investigators took photos, examined the ground, and carefully began to extricate the body. An officer pulled back a corner of the plastic tarp, and I identified Angela. When Jordan whispered that she was going to be sick, I asked Jorgeson's permission for us to wait at the house.

As soon as we were back, we took off our shoes on the terrace. Jordan headed for a bathroom. I scrubbed my hands at the kitchen sink and then set out crackers, cheese, and a jar of jam. We sat at the island to eat, neither of us inclined to talk. Jordan offered to clean up and put away the remaining food. I took my cell phone out to the front porch to call Peter. With luck, he was in an airplane somewhere between Atlanta and Farberville. I was preparing to record a bright message when luck failed me.

"What is wrong with you?" he demanded. "I talked to

you—what, six hours ago? You were supposed to stay home and do the Sunday crossword, not go to the blasted place and dig up a body!"

"I was saving the crossword to do with you," I said. "Furthermore, I didn't dig up a body. I simply found it and called Jorgeson."

"Why were you even at Hollow Valley? You promised me that—"

"I made no such promise. Why aren't you in midflight? Are you still stuck at the Atlanta airport?"

He made a rude noise. "We'll discuss this later. No, I'm not at the Atlanta airport. I'm at the St. Louis airport, waiting to be picked up. A truck was hijacked last night, and the feds have jurisdiction because it crossed state lines. I'm supposed to work with the regional ATF office until it's cleared up. I don't know when I'll get home."

"I'm sorry," I said. "You must be exhausted."

I commiserated with him until my cell began to beep. Seconds later the connection broke and the screen went dark. So much for the miracle of technology, I thought as I continued to swing. I tried to come up with a time frame that began with Angela's departure and concluded with an unknown figure burying her body. Presumably, only two people had known the location of the pot patch: Jordan and Pandora. Unless I'd failed to notice a psychotic glint in Jordan's eyes, she was not a suspect. Pandora could not be as easily dismissed. She could, to quote Muhammad Ali, "float like a butterfly, sting like a bee."

I was trying to recall the conversations I'd had with Angela when Jordan came out to the porch. Her eyes were pink, her cheeks damp.

"The cops want to talk to you," she said. "I had to tell them about the pot. Am I in trouble?"

I stood up and put my hands on her shoulders. "As long as you're truthful, you'll be okay. You didn't actually produce a crop. However, if you have a stash, this would be the time to dispose of it. The police are here to investigate a murder, which overshadows trivial offenses." I gave her an encouraging smile. "For pity's sake, don't mouth off when they question you."

Deputy Chief Peter Rosen might not be pleased that I was counseling a pot grower on how to avoid incriminating herself, but I felt responsible for exposing her misdemeanor. Or felony, I amended with a flicker of uneasiness.

The next two hours were excruciatingly dull. Jorgeson was occupied issuing instructions and delegating, and the detectives must have been warned to stay away from me. The paramedics wheeled the gurney across the yard. Jordan answered the same questions over and over again but held her sarcasm to a minimum. I perked up when Moses wandered inside and regarded the officers with a cheery grin.

"To whom do I owe the pleasure of your company?" he asked. "Have you come for tea? Have you come for me? This calls for a drink!" No one said a word as he squatted behind the kitchen island and reappeared with a bottle of bourbon. "If we had mint, we could all have a julep! A hint of mint! Praise the Lord and pass the ammunition."

"Hold on, sir," a uniformed officer said. "Who are you?"

Moses opened the bottle and took a swig. "I am the great-great-grandson of Colonel Moses Ambrose Hollow. I come in peace. Identify yourself, sir!"

Jorgeson came in from the terrace and looked at me. "Can you help us out here, Ms. Malloy?"

"I would prefer not to," I blurted out before I could stop myself. I muffled a snort. "Yes, of course, Jorgeson. This is Moses Hollow, who resides at the Old Tavern. He's the family patriarch, I suppose."

"Moses opposes what you supposes," the object of discussion said with a cackle. He tilted the bourbon bottle and drank greedily. Liquor dribbled down his chin and neck like droplets of amber.

Jorgeson moved to my side, and in a low voice, said, "Does he know anything that might be helpful?"

"I hate to say this, but he most likely does."

"I am sorry to hear that, Ms. Malloy," Jorgeson said, his face sagging. "We're finished with the young lady, for now anyway. There's no reason to take her to the PD. What do you suggest we do with her?"

"Let me take her to Nattie, who'll take care of her." I gave him a brief rundown on the valley's residents and their residences. "Are you finished with me?"

"How can I be finished when I haven't even begun? I fear that you and I will be in my office well into the evening. The sandwiches will be soggy and the coffee bitter. Mrs. Jorgeson will dine alone, and later retire with a book. For the time being, take the young lady to the Old Tavern and wait there. When we're finished here, I'll send an officer to let you know."

"What about Pandora?" I asked.

"Detective Greer talked to her. She swore that she has no knowledge of any marijuana in this area and has never been near the crime scene. I'll have her come to the PD to make a formal statement tomorrow, but we don't have cause to detain her."

"What if she takes off with her biker buddy?"

"A vehicle with two officers will be parked at the turn-off from the highway. No one is going to leave without my permission. Now if you don't mind, Ms. Malloy, I'd like to get back to work."

I drove Jordan to the tavern green. The Mustang had not returned, but Jordan assured me that she would stay at the mill. As I watched her walk away, Nattie came outside.

"Claire? I thought you were going home," she said, clearly irritated. "There's really no point in discussing your invitation to Jordan. Margaret Louise will call you later."

"It's complicated. Do you mind if I wait here until the police send for me?"

Her lips parted as she stared at me. "Are you going to be arrested? Charles told me that he was going to call the police if he saw you at Winston's house. He claims that you're trespassing, which is nonsense. The property doesn't belong to him."

"Charles may get his wish, all the same. The police want to question me about the murder of Angela Delmond."

"Come sit down and tell me about it. Can I offer you iced tea, or something stronger?"

I was beyond adhering to cocktail hour etiquette. "Scotch and water, please."

She steered me to the backyard and insisted that I put my feet on a stool. I could see that she was frantic to hear the details, but she went inside and returned shortly with my promised drink and one for herself. "Angela Delmond is the real estate woman, isn't she? You were asking earlier if I'd seen her. She's been murdered? The police want to question you?" Irritation had transformed into bewilderment.

I was reluctant to throw Jordan and Pandora under a bus, but their complicity would be made known soon. I described my recent encounter with Pandora, Jordan's admission, and my subsequent discovery of Angela's body. My theory about Angela's trysts sounded feeble, even to me, but I needed to verbalize it.

"Whoa," Nattie said, her hand unsteady as she set down her glass. "Jordan was wrong about Hollow Valley. It's not boring. I can't believe Pandora Butterfly has been making jackasses of us for so long. Ethan will be devastated, the poor thing. He truly cares about the nursery.

When Charles hears about it, well, I don't want to be there. We'll have to call in a bomb squad to defuse him. Two deaths in less than a week . . ."

"Plus Winston's, three months ago."

"This is beyond incredible." She sat back and gazed at the valley and the bridge, nibbling on her lower lip and humming tunelessly. She sniffled but blinked back tears. I felt remorse that I'd shattered any remaining vestiges of pretense that Hollow Valley was her sanctuary. I was about to offer lame words of comfort when she said, "Whoever did these horrible things must be caught and made to pay. Angela used Winston's house for her assignations. I hate the very thought of it! She violated our privacy and took advantage of dear Winston's suicide. Who could have been her lover? Some man from her office, maybe her boss?"

"They'll collect fingerprints from the house, especially the bedroom. They can eliminate Terry and Winston's friends and the people out here. It'll take time, though. There aren't any old guest lists in a desk drawer." I paused. "I did find something odd in the bottom drawer. Did Terry or Winston smoke cigarettes?"

"Not that I know of. Winston told me that he liked a cigar and a nip of brandy after dinner, but only once in a while. Terry gave him a box of Cuban cigars for his birthday last October."

"Why would they have a carton of cigarettes in the house?"

She shook her head. "I can understand having basic toiletries for unexpected company, but not cigarettes. Maybe someone left it by mistake, and they were holding on to it until the person came back to visit. Until you told me about Pandora, I didn't think anybody out here smoked except Margaret Louise." She forced a smile. "At least Jordan doesn't smoke cigarettes."

I didn't want to disillusion her. One cigarette doth not a habit make. "Should you tell everybody else why the police are at Winston's house?"

Yes," Nattie said, "but they can wait. I'm getting a horrible headache, and I need to go lie down. Please excuse me."

She went through the kitchen door. The washing machine or the dryer—I couldn't remember which—was still thumping from inside the building. It would not have been my first choice if my head was already thumping. I finished my drink and put down the glass. I wandered around to admire the flower beds and the vegetable garden. The shed had shelves of stacked flowerpots, scattered bulbs, soil-encrusted boots, several pairs of cotton gloves, and hooks that held tools. Shovels and rakes were propped in a corner behind a rough wooden table. I browsed through seed packets with depictions of ripe vegetables.

It was the shed I would have had in the garden I would never have. Unlike Nattie, I was unable to blink back my tears. I wanted Peter's arm around me, his lips tickling my neck, his voice murmuring in my ear. I allotted myself a minute to feel incredibly sorry for myself, then firmly closed the shed door. Jorgeson would be occupied for at least another half hour, I told myself as I took off in the direction of the nursery.

The delivery truck I'd seen earlier was still there. Ethan was either at home or riding shotgun with a payload of fruit trees and flowering shrubs. I was disappointed to find padlocks on the greenhouse doors and the outbuildings. Was he worried that garden club guerrillas would make off with his ferns? I walked across the empty parking area to the edge of the Christmas tree farm. The time would come when the elders would be toppled with a chain saw, tossed into trucks, and eventually drop their needles on someone's rug. Although I was not a tree-hugger, I would have embraced them had I not been worried about insects and spiders.

There was nothing else to see, so I walked back toward the path to the Old Tavern. When I glanced at the truck, I noticed the front door was ajar. Out of nothing more than curiosity, I climbed up to the driver's seat. The seat was concave from hours of punishment from hefty derrieres. The cab smelled of sweat, onions, stale smoke, and banana peels. The floor was cluttered with fast food wrappers and paper cups. A dirty T-shirt exuded a pungent odor that made my skin itch. Between the two seats was a recessed catchall. A road map was so creased that its folds were frayed. When I set it aside, I saw what must have been the driver's prized collection of matchbooks. I picked up several of them. Arkansas had towns named Paris and England, but Missouri could claim Lebanon and Cuba. I replaced the matchbooks, amused at the idea of a Missouri Empire with colonies.

It took me a moment to gather the courage to climb out of the cab. I took my time to find footholds and arrived on the ground with minimal fuss. If I ever found myself unemployed and desperate for work, I could rule out truck driving as a potential vocation. I walked around to the back of the truck and tugged at the corner of a door until it squeaked open. The interior was littered with leaves, berries, smashed flowers, and dust. I sneezed as I peered into the depths. It was not as vast as I'd estimated, but it would do well as an echo chamber. Prudence dictated that I not test my hypothesis.

Having learned only that Missouri had an international flair, I walked back to the Old Tavern. A police car was parked behind my hatchback, and an officer stood next to it, his face stony and his arms crossed. "Lieutenant Jorgeson sent me up here to find you, ma'am. He instructed me to follow you to the PD."

"Everybody loves a parade," I said as I got into my car. I caught a glimpse of Nattie in a second-story window as I drove away.

Jorgeson had accurately predicted the amount of time he and I would spend in his office at the PD. I'd told him everything numerous times, but he seemed to have trouble following my logical speculations about possible scenarios. By the fifth time he asked me to repeat myself, I was becoming confused as well. I'd made assumptions about the motives behind Winston and Terry's death, but Angela's death did not fit neatly into place. I was especially sorry to acknowledge the fallacy of my theory that Charles had murdered Esther and Winston had found her body. Jorgeson was beginning to whimper, so I tactfully retreated to the ladies' room while he pulled himself together. There was no graffiti to distract me, so I entertained myself by visualizing the goodies that Loretta had packed in the picnic basket. She, Nicole, Samuel, and Billy Bobstay were back in Farberville by now, well fed on Camembert and tomato sandwiches, marinated mushrooms, and blueberry tarts. I'd dined on a carry-out sandwich that was even soggier than Jorgeson had envisioned. No one had offered champagne.

When I emerged, I heard Danny Delmond's irate voice. Feeling much better, I joined him in Jorgeson's office. Danny was expensively coiffed and clad. He was attractive in the overly polished manner of a politician, but potential voters would have been alarmed by his furious expression. I was charmed.

"So we were still officially married," he bellowed, "but I didn't care if she was sleeping with a caddie! How should I know where she went or what she did? I didn't care, Lieutenant Jorgeson. I didn't care if she drove off a cliff! All I wanted her to do was take a reasonable settlement and get out of my life!"

"Sounds like a motive to me," I said as I sat down. "Now you don't have to give her anything. It's all yours."

Danny jabbed a finger at me. "You were the last person to see her alive. Maybe she changed her mind and decided to buy the house herself. That's a motive if ever there was one. Bartleby will testify how obsessed you were with the house. You'd do anything to get it, wouldn't you? I know all about you, honey. You interfere with the police, you badger people, you fake evidence so you can claim to solve crimes!"

"How dare you call me honey?" I asked indignantly.

"That's the best you can do? Listen up, *honey*—you won't be so huffy when I sue you for slander and defamation!"

Jorgeson intervened before I could respond. "Sit down, Mr. Delmond. I realize that you must be in shock over your wife's untimely death, so I'll disregard this attack on Ms. Malloy. All I'm asking for is your cooperation. This won't take long. Please account for your whereabouts yesterday and last night."

"Why don't you ask her?"

I gave him a sweet smile. "I always cooperate with the police. Do you have a teensy problem with an alibi, Mr. Delmond? Has your girlfriend gone off to cheerleader camp with her little friends?"

He took several deep breaths, but his jaw was quivering. "I had planned to entertain a guest at my lake house, but she canceled at the last minute. Since I had nothing better to do, I drove there late Friday night and spent two days working on a deal for a new development. No one bothered me. Last night I grilled a steak and drank a bottle of wine. I came back this morning and went to my office to revise some figures."

While Jorgeson dutifully wrote down the statement, I studied Danny Delmond. He was a womanizer and a misogynist, I decided, but he was a shrewd businessman at heart. Developing property for houses was a risky business in the current economy. Many of his competitors had gone bankrupt over the previous five years. If he was struggling, he would be ruthless.

"Where's this new development?" I asked.

He looked at Jorgeson. "Why is she here? Shouldn't she be twiddling her thumbs in an interview room or a holding cell?"

"It's hard to explain, Mr. Delmond," Jorgeson replied. "Is there something about her question that bothers you?"

"No, it's just none of her damn business. There is no new development until the deal comes together. It's in the preliminary stages, and nothing's been signed. I don't want to talk about it because the negotiations are private. Get a subpoena if you want to know the details."

Jorgeson tapped his pen on the notebook. "That's all for the moment, Mr. Delmond. The medical examiner's office will let you know when they'll release the body so that you can make funeral arrangements."

Danny stood up. "Put her back where you found her. I gave you her parents' information. They can handle it." He stormed out without so much as a word of farewell.

"I think a subpoena is a wonderful suggestion," I said. "He was hiding something. Maybe he wants to develop Hollow Valley. He has a verbal agreement with Charles, who can coerce the others into selling. The only property—"

"I am very tired, Ms. Malloy, and you must be, too. Please go home and make yourself a nice supper. Read the Sunday paper, or watch TV. Have a pleasant night. We can resume in the morning when you're . . . less enthusiastic."

I opted to leave with dignity before he had me escorted out to my car. As I drove home, I worked on my inspired theory. Nattie had said something about a gated community, but I couldn't remember the context. Hollow Valley could offer spacious, wooded lots with beautiful views—or quarter-acre lots with rows and rows of modest homes. The Old Tavern would be converted into condos, and the green space replaced with a community swimming pool. Danny Delmond would make millions of dollars. The thought appalled me. The only property, as I'd tried to tell Jorgeson, that was out of Charles's control was that which had belonged to Winston. It now belonged to Terry Kennedy's estate. Danny must have been hoping that either the family's lawsuit would prevail or Terry would sell.

Angela had thrown the proverbial monkey wrench into his plan by contacting Terry, who'd given her permission to show me the house. She might have done so intentionally, if she knew about the proposed development. Someone in the Hollow family had seen us and called Danny. He panicked and then came up with a way to trick her into leaving. I needed to find out how he'd done it. That, and who'd helped him move her car, hide her body, and dig her grave. Danny would not have sullied his manicured fingernails by grubbing in the dirt.

I realized that I'd made it home and was parked in the garage. I went upstairs and opened the refrigerator. I found leftover pizza, which was less appealing than the sandwich at the PD. I stuck a slice in the microwave, ate it in the middle of the kitchen, and then took a hot shower.

I was toweling my hair when I heard Caron's and Inez's voices in the living room. I put on a bathrobe and walked down the hallway cluttered with boxes. I'd called Caron from the PD to let her know why I would be late, but I'd skimped on the details. I braced myself as I sat down.

"Did they arrest somebody?" demanded Caron. "Was it that despicable Charles guy? Why'd he do it?"

"He was having an affair with Angela, wasn't he?" Inez inserted. "I knew he was the one. Do you remember that televangelist who got caught—"

"No one has confessed or been arrested," I said, "and Charles didn't murder his daughter. She lives on the hill past the football stadium."

"The woman who fed Terry the nonpoisonous mushrooms?" Caron asked, looking confused. "I'd like to think you didn't eat anything she made. It's so disgusting when people throw up. You aren't going to, are you?"

I massaged my neck as I ran through the story that I had repeated endlessly to Jorgeson. Having some knowledge of the players, they remained quiet until I finished.

"Okay," Caron said, "then all we have to do is prove that Danny Delmond is conspiring with Charles to buy up all the property."

Inez blinked solemnly. "We also have to prove Danny killed Terry and Angela, and maybe even Winston." She glanced at her watch. "What time is Mr. Rosen getting home?"

"Probably not for a few days," I said. "He was diverted to St. Louis for another case. It doesn't matter. Hollow Valley has been effectively sealed off by the police. I am not going to buy a camouflage jumpsuit and crawl through the woods. I've had more than enough nature to hold me for several years. Jorgeson will sort it out. I'm going to make a cup of tea and read in bed. Good night."

I was doing just that when I heard the back door close softly. I closed the book, switched off the reading light, and promptly fell asleep.

CHAPTER 12

The telephone woke me from an uncomfortable dream that involved a firing squad, Fidel Castro, and Winston, who had golden hair and was smoking a cigar while he awaited my execution. A string quartet performed while Loretta passed a plate of canapés. I pulled a pillow over my head until the ringing stopped. I had no desire to face the day. I knew Jorgeson would request the honor of my presence at the PD so that I could reiterate my activities at Hollow Valley ad nauseam. I'd wanted Peter to put yellow tape around the house. Now the entire valley was off-limits.

I crawled out of bed, avoiding the hazards on the floor, and rummaged through the crammed closet for jeans and a blouse suitable for interrogation. Caron and Inez were sound asleep. I was relieved to know they had done nothing that ended with a request for bail. I tidied myself for the day and started a pot of coffee. The light on the answering machine was blinking, but I wasn't in the mood to deal with anyone, including my irate husband.

I went downstairs and picked up the local paper. The discovery of Angela's body was not mentioned, since it had happened late in the day. With the majority of Farber

College students gone for the summer, the newspapers and local TV coverage were stuck with burglaries, missing geriatric patients, and fender-benders. Bad news was better than no news. Bad news was even better than good news, as far as the media were concerned.

After I'd had ample caffeine, I pushed the button on the answering machine. Jorgeson's hoarse voice informed me that I was welcome to return to his office early in the afternoon, since he would be in a meeting with the chief and unspecified others most of the morning. I debated calling Peter, but he was likely to be in a meeting as well—or conducting interviews at truck stops. I was not eager to talk to him until he'd simmered down.

Caron and Inez came into the living room, both of them yawning. Caron ran her fingers through her mussed hair as she said, "So what are you going to do now? Read the newspaper while a murderer escapes?"

"That was not my plan," I said mildly.

Inez sat down and looked at me, although her lenses were so smudged that I could barely see her eyes. "You said that Danny Delmond killed his wife, but you don't have any evidence. We need to find some."

"That's a better plan, but how are you going to do that?"

"Search Angela's house," Caron said. "Is there anything to eat before we go? I'm starving."

"Wait a minute," I said. "We can't search her house because we don't have permission. That's the gist of breaking and entering. The police take a very dim view of that, as do judges. Then again, prison doesn't charge tuition every semester, and you won't have to buy books for classes. It'll be a challenge to find meaningful careers with only a GED degree and a record."

"We're not going to Break Anything, Mother. You're the one who wants to paw through her papers."

I reminded myself that I was a role model. "I might have said something about her files, but I did not imply that I was willing to commit a felony to satisfy my curiosity. Besides, the police have the house under surveillance."

"No, they don't," Inez murmured as she went into the kitchen. "Can I make some toast?"

Caron's lower lip was out. "What about the house? Don't you want it anymore?"

"Yes, I do, but it's not going to happen," I said. "Even if I figure out who's behind this dreadful mess, the house is in Terry's estate. Probate can take years. And don't forget the Hollow family's lawsuit. That may take years, too." I paused. "Inez, how do you know the house isn't under surveillance?"

Inez appeared in the kitchen doorway. "Well, I don't know for sure if it is now. It wasn't three hours ago."

I turned back to Caron, who was curled up on the chair in an attempt to make herself invisible. "Three hours ago?"

"Close enough. We sort of went over there after you went to bed. We didn't break in, if that's what you're getting freaked over. There was a darling little dog in the backyard. He was so happy to see us. I guess a neighbor was feeding him and giving him fresh water."

"Her name is Flopsy," I said. "Please continue."

"I told you so," Inez called from the kitchen.

Caron made a face. "So he's a she. No big deal. While we were there, we happened to notice there was an alarm system. When I touched the patio door, it started whooping. We didn't know what to do, so we hid behind the doghouse. Ten minutes later, a cop and this other guy, maybe from the security company, came in the backyard and tested all the doors and windows. They went on around the house. All the while, the alarm kept whooping.

Then a light came on inside, and the alarm stopped. The cop and the other guy left, and the neighbors turned off their lights."

"I don't want to hear this," I said. "It was a mistake, and thank goodness you left without getting caught. Prowling is against the law, too."

"We didn't exactly leave," Inez said as she came into the room and handed Caron a piece of limp toast. "We waited half an hour and then did it again, just to see what would happen. The second time, the cop was surly and the security guy was on his cell phone with some technician. They opened and closed the patio door a bunch of times. They went inside, set the alarm, and left."

"So we did it again," Caron said through a mouthful of crumbs. "You should have heard the cop. He made such a fuss that the dog ran over and nipped him. It was so incredibly funny. This big old cop, trying to defend himself without kicking the dog, was hopping around the patio like a drunken kangaroo. He finally yelled at the security guy to deactivate the alarm. The security guy said he couldn't without the owner's permission, and the cop threatened to arrest him for some trumped-up charge, and then the dog bit the security guy and they both left."

I struggled to maintain my maternal steeliness. "Don't ever do anything like that again—and I mean it."

Caron smiled smugly. "Why would we? The alarm is off and the patio door is unlocked. Are you coming with us or not?"

I went into the bathroom and stared at my reflection in the mirror. I lacked Fagin's scraggly hair and poor posture, but I was as guilty as he'd been. He'd recruited orphans to become thieves and pickpockets. I'd reared one. If she made it through college, her only hope was to become a politician. I splashed water on my face, squared my shapely shoulders, and mentally rehearsed my lecture as I went back to the living room.

They were gone. I ran through my list of Anglo-Saxon profanities as I hurried down to my car and drove to the neighborhood of faux Tudors, contemporary antebellums, and stately pleasure domes. Caron's car was parked a block away from Angela's house. I parked nearby and walked along the sidewalk, feeling so far out of my comfort zone that I needed a passport. I went to the front door and knocked, waited for a moment, and then dodged around the corner of the house to a gate. I let myself in and was immediately greeted by a hysterical dog that believed I was Anubis incarnate.

"Down, Flopsy," I said sternly as I closed the gate behind me. Caron and Inez were nowhere in sight, which was not good. The patio door was slightly open. Flopsy continued to jump on me and splatter my ankles with slobber as I went inside. "Caron! Inez! I'm going to call the police myself if you two don't get in here right now!"

I hurried through the sunroom, the kitchen, and was in the foyer when Inez came bounding downstairs. "You've got to see her shoes, Ms. Malloy! There must be two hundred pairs of them on special shelves in her closet."

"I have no desire to look at shoes. Where's Caron?"

"In the office upstairs."

I continued to the second floor. The master bedroom was royal purple, violet, lavender, and all shades in between. The four-poster bed had a canopy of tapestry with dribbly fringe and mounds of carefully coordinated throw pillows and shams. The next bedroom was decidedly green, and the next pink and pinker. Winston and Terry had not solicited her decorating advice. The last room had been converted into an office with a large desk, filing cabinets, shelves of supplies, an array of computer equipment, a printer, and arcane wonders.

Caron was sitting on the floor, surrounded by stacks of papers and manila folders. "About time," she said with a sniff. "I have no idea what I'm looking for. This real estate stuff is stupid. I can't believe they use paper. Do you realize how many trees died just because she didn't keep all these records on her computer? We're talking entire national forests."

"Put it all back where you found it so we can leave," I said with impressive self-control. "If you're so concerned about trees, volunteer on Arbor Day. Let's go—now!"

"Yeah, we're not going to find anything." She began to cram papers back into folders. "I didn't see anything marked 'Hollow Valley' or 'love letters.'"

Inez came into the room, holding Flopsy in her arms. "Nobody writes letters. Let's check her old e-mail."

I looked out the window at the street, where a white van was backing out of a driveway. Cars cruised sedately by, and children on bicycles ventured into the street. "We are not going to do anything to her computer. The security company may be sending over an electrician to search for a faulty breaker. It will be hard to explain why we're in the house, ransacking Angela's office."

"I did not ransack anything," Caron said as she rose to her feet and sat down in front of the computer. "This will only take a second, Mother. Why don't you go play fetch with the dog?" Her fingers began to flit across the keyboard. "I need a password. Inez, see if you can find her passport or birth certificate. A lot of people use their birthday or maiden name for their passwords."

"Try Flopsy," Inez suggested.

I was mesmerized by Caron's fingers. Her handwriting was illegible, but her manual dexterity was superlative. Evolution was in high gear. Kindergarten children would never learn to hold a pencil or memorize the multiplication tables. Why bother, when computers and calculators

replaced their pudgy little hands. Emotions would be reduced to emoticons. As an anomaly from the twentieth
century, I would not be LOL.

"I'm in," Caron announced. "There must be a hundred
e-mails. She has more document files than the Library of
Congress. This will take forever." She leaned forward as
she continued to type. "Garden parties, fashion shows,
dinner invitation list, charitable contributions, business expenses, photos from at least ten different addresses, lawyer
stuff, travel destinations, somebody's baby shower
registry—this is ridiculous!"

Inez put Flopsy on the floor and peered over Caron's
shoulder. "Look at all the kennels that sent information.
Oh, and there's a file from a private detective agency.
Open that one."

I raised an eyebrow. "Does it concern her husband?"

"Yeah," Caron said, "but the last report is dated six
months ago. What a sleaze her husband is. Can you imagine staying at the Chez Amigos Motel? There are bullet
holes in the door."

I let them gasp and giggle while I looked around. There
were no plats pinned to a wall or rolled up in a pile.
The lack of tangible evidence did not negate the theory
that Angela knew about Danny's plans for Hollow Valley.
I noticed that the answering machine was blinking fre-
netically.

I pushed the button. The messages concerned an upcoming fund-raiser for the local symphony orchestra, a
bridal shower for someone named Penelope, and a reception in honor of a dean at Farber College. Angela was invited to be on a steering committee, arrange flowers, pick
up Sylvia's coffee urn, tell Jessica to stop being such a
bitch, shop for shoes, and have lunch at an absolutely fabu-
lous new café. In the middle of these, my messages began
to intrude. The receptionist at the real estate company left

perky messages; Bartleby's messages were blunt. The last twelve messages were from me.

"Mother," Caron said, "come read this. It's an e-mail from her husband from a week ago."

I took her seat in front of the computer. The e-mail had been sent the previous Tuesday morning, less than an hour before Angela had picked me up to show me the house. It read: "This is a waste of time and money for both of us. I will agree to the settlement proposal already on the table. You can have the damn house if it's such a big deal, and the furnishings except for my personal stuff. I'll take the lake house. You get the country club membership. I get the season football tickets. I don't give a shit about the jewelry, so sell it or whatever. Take the damn dog, too. The financial assets will be divided as laid out in the proposal. You're getting every goddamn thing you want, Angela. The only thing you have to do is stay the hell out of my business. If you screw up the development, this offer's off the table. You mess with me and you can kiss your ass good-bye. Danny."

"I wish he'd been more specific," I said, disappointed. "Even his threat is vague."

Caron nudged me aside. "Let's see what she e-mailed him. It'll be in her sent-mail box, most likely the evening before he sent her that one." She tackled the keyboard. "Okay, here it is. This ought to be enough to nail him."

Angela's e-mail read: "Guess who I talked to tonight—Terry Kennedy. He's willing to sell his house to one of my clients. Put that up your nose, jerk."

I grinned at the screen. "That's it! She got to him, and he was so desperate that he capitulated on the divorce settlement. We have his motive. Now Jorgeson can subpoena all the paperwork concerning the Hollow Valley development. Danny doesn't have an alibi for Saturday or Sunday."

"Did he murder Terry, too?" asked Inez.

"It makes sense," I said. "He thought that kidnapping and murdering Angela would solve all of his problems. Then I found a way to get in touch with Terry, so his precious plan was still in peril. He snuck in the house and left the poisoned vodka."

"How did he do that, Ms. Malloy?" Jorgeson asked from the doorway. His smile was strained and his voice chilly.

"Didn't your mother teach you to knock?"

"I might ask you the same question. I'm not implying that you didn't knock, Ms. Malloy, but only as a gesture. You knew that no one was here to invite you and the young ladies to come inside and hack into this computer."

"We did not hack," I said in an offended voice. "Hacking implies violence. We did nothing more than turn it on. Shouldn't you be having one of your men print out the e-mails?"

Jorgeson gave me a glum look. "We'll print them out, but they can't be used as evidence at a trial. The defense will claim that they might have been tampered with by a civilian. If we'd taken the computer to the PD, our tech would have opened them. The only fingerprints on the keyboard would have belonged to the victim."

"Okay, okay," I said. "I'm sorry. However, you know perfectly well that we didn't tamper with anything. We found Danny's motive, Jorgeson. All you have to do is find out who tipped him off Tuesday afternoon that Angela and I were at Winston's house."

"I fear that I have other things to do as well." He looked at Caron and Inez, who had backed into a corner. "For the moment, you two may go home and stay there. I will do what I can with the city prosecutor, but the decision is his."

"I can't stay home," Caron protested. "I'm going to the lake with Joel. He borrowed a kayak from his uncle."

Jorgeson shrugged. "Then I apologize for the inconvenience. You are free to choose whether you prefer to remain at home or accompany us to the police department. I must warn you that the soda machine is broken and the reading material is limited to hunting and car magazines."

Caron rolled her eyes. "C'mon, Inez. Let's go to my house and do some online research about the legality of detaining juveniles." She stomped out of the room, with Inez following obediently.

"As for you, Ms. Malloy," he said with a long-suffering sigh, "you and I need to resume our interview in my office. Please give your car key to this nice young officer. I am reluctant to let you out of my sight until Deputy Chief Rosen is back."

I raised my eyebrows. "Why, I'd be delighted to ride with you, Lieutenant Jorgeson. Is there a chance we might swing by a coffee bar on the way for lattes and biscotti? My treat, of course."

I did not get my latte and biscotto. Once I was seated in Jorgeson's office, I forgave him for his petulance and said, "What did the medical examiner determine about Angela's time of death?"

Jorgeson took his sweet time before responding. "She's unable to do more than offer an approximation. The body was kept in cold storage for some period of time, so the standard measures are unreliable. She was killed elsewhere more than five days ago, and put in the ground within six hours of discovery." He put up his hand to stop me before I could blurt out the obvious question. "Blunt force trauma to the back of the head. Something heavy with a flat surface. Bits of dirt and debris in the wound. No indications that she fought back."

I was amazed at his willingness to share the medical

examiner's findings. Peter would not have offered an observation on the weather. "Does Danny have an alibi for Tuesday afternoon and evening?" I asked.

"Yes, and it's been verified. He was at his office until five and then had drinks and dinner at the country with a group of friends. His, uh, friend says the two of them spent the night at his condo."

"Then his accomplice did it," I said. "A couple of days later, Danny and the accomplice drove Angela's car to Maxwell County to muddle things."

"Well done, Ms. Malloy. If you'll give us the name of the accomplice, we'll have this wrapped up before the evening news."

I was not amused by his flippancy. "The Farberville Police Department has adequate resources to identify the accomplice, while I, a civilian of no great consequence, am powerless and can only watch with awe and respect. Is that all, Lieutenant Jorgeson?"

It was not. I offered Jorgeson a multitude of means, motives, and opportunities that could be applied to every last person I'd met since the day Angela showed me the perfect house. Some plots required convoluted conspiracies, bribery, blackmail, psychotic breaks, and/or sexual misconduct. I gave him grudges galore. After I finished a theory in which Nattie was Bartleby's ex-wife and Jordan was their love child, Jorgeson suggested that we take a very long break.

"What about Caron and Inez?" I asked him. "I am more than willing to sit here the rest of the day and explain why it was necessary for them to gain ingress, however the means, so that—"

Jorgeson's gaze was a wee bit unfriendly. "I will make a note that they went inside to rescue the dog. The computer hacking need not be mentioned as long as I don't come across their names in any future reports. Is there any hope that you and I can settle for the same arrangement?"

"Of course," I said merrily. "There is one thing, though. I promised Jordan that she could come spend the night with Caron and Inez, so I'll need a letter of passage to pick her up."

He scribbled out a note that ensured my safety behind enemy lines. His parting words were desultory, leading me to wonder if he was unwell. The previous day had been exhausting for both of us, I thought as I drove home and parked next to Caron's car. She and Inez were cross-legged on her bed, texting silently like Zen adherents. There seemed to be so many texts zipping through the atmosphere that it was a miracle there was adequate oxygen for respiration. If everyone was sending them, who had time to read them?

I called Peter and was composing a message when he said, "Claire, is something wrong?"

It was a poser. I opted for innocence. "Everything's fine. I told Jorgeson what I know, and now it's his headache. We're not going to get the house, so I've decided to move on. Later, I'll go get some magazines with house plans. But how are you? Do you know how long you'll be stuck up there?"

"No idea. Most of the agents are out in the field. I'll meet with the brass from the trucking company and their insurance people and then participate in a conference call with the feds. The truck driver's not talking. I could be here for at least a couple of days." He stopped for a moment. "I've got to go. Can I trust you to stay out of the investigation just this once?"

"You can always trust me, darling."

I made a peanut butter sandwich and poured a glass of iced tea. I was brooding on the balcony when Caron came out.

"If I'm going to prison, I'm not going to bother with the summer reading list," she said. "It's not like we'll sit around in a cell and discuss *No Exit*. Do I need to start packing anytime soon?"

"Jorgeson said that he'd overlook our minor escapade if we keep a low profile."

"Can I go to the lake with Joel? Inez wants to come, too."

"Yes," I said, "but you have to be home at four, and not one minute later. I promised Jordan that she could come spend the night. You can take her to the mall, and I'll give you money for pizza. After everything that's happened out there lately, she deserves a respite. She was with me when we uncovered the body."

"Cool," Caron said. "Yeah, we'll be here at four. Inez says that Jordan has body piercings and a tattoo. I've never met anyone like that. She probably has some really neat stories."

The peanut butter solidified in my stomach. "Don't even think about it. If you so much as draw on your skin with an indelible marker, you're grounded for the rest of the summer. I mean it, Caron. You are not going to make the same mistakes she made."

Caron grinned, then went to her bedroom to confer with Inez. I drowned my worries in iced tea, calling good-bye to the girls as they went downstairs. In a year, I reminded myself for the umpteenth time, Caron would make her own decisions. If she made the wrong ones, Peter and I would not leave a forwarding address.

Rather than descend into depression, I turned my thoughts back to the matter at hand. Danny Delmond claimed to have alibis for the day when Angela disappeared and for the six-hour period when her body had been transported and buried. Angela's low opinion of the young woman was less than impartial. She might be a respectable sort, who had a good job, called her parents every week, and sang in a church choir. Or she might be a slut. Jorgeson had not mentioned her name, and he most likely would not do so if I called him.

I'd agreed to keep a low profile, but I hadn't promised to spend the next few days polishing silver. Angela had told me that she'd amended the divorce petition from the standard "irreconcilable differences" to the ever popular "adultery," and named Danny's girlfriend as a corespondent. I found Angela's briefcase under a chair and took out the documents from the lawyer. All things *Delmond v. Delmond* were covered, including property division proposals, vitriolic notes from Angela that contained references to Danny's manhood, conciliatory letters from her lawyer, D. W. Hendrix, and preliminary rulings. Not one listed the name of the corespondent.

I found D. W. Hendrix's office number in the directory and dialed it. When a receptionist answered, I launched into an impromptu speech. "I'm with KLMNOP, your local all-news station. As you surely have been informed, Angela Delmond's body was found yesterday, and the police are investigating it as a murder. To give depth to our report, we're running background stories about Mr. and Ms. Delmond. I've located the divorce petition filed by your office, along with the amendments. If you could just give me the contact information for the corespondent, you'd save me a trip to the courthouse." I paused and then lowered my voice. "You know how bosses can be. Mine thinks I can drop everything to fetch him coffee or run errands. Last week I had to take off a day because my child was ill, and I nearly got fired."

The receptionist was immune to my offer of feminist camaraderie. "In that the information is a matter of public record, her name is Nanette Campbell. I have no further information concerning her. What station are you with?"

"Thank you so very much," I said and hung up. I held my breath while I looked up the name in the directory, then exhaled when I spotted it. Nanette lived in what I suspected was an apartment in the historic district. It was unlikely that she was home in the afternoon, but I had nothing better to do. A few minutes later I parked in front of a house with four mailboxes next to the front door. Nanette resided in 1-A. I knocked a couple of times, then gave up and paused on the porch to decide whether I should leave a note in her mailbox. The odds that she would call me were close to nil.

A portly man with a furled umbrella came up the steps. "May I help you?"

"I'm looking for Nanette Campbell."

He gave me a disappointed look. "Oh, yes. She works at the local library. Would you like to come in and wait for her? We could have a glass of sherry."

"No, thank you." I surprised both of us when I gave him a kiss on the check, then went back to my car. She might work in the children's area, I told myself without optimism. There was no reason to assume that she'd peeked over my shoulder while I read about the Terry Kennedys on the computer. Even if she had, she wouldn't recognize the significance of the name. I could have asked about deeds for a genealogy project. Furthermore, not everyone lunged to conclusions with the agility of a gazelle.

I went inside the library and stopped at the main desk. "Nanette Campbell?" I asked quietly.

I was directed to the reference desk, where the same young woman who'd helped me almost a week ago was seated. She recognized me. "Good afternoon. Do you need to use a computer again?"

"No," I said, "but I'd like to speak to you about another matter."

"If you need assistance in the genealogy department, Caroline will be happy to get you started. She has a great deal more experience than the rest of us. Let me go find her for you."

I sat down next to her. "Have you heard about Angela Delmond?"

Her eyes narrowed. "I heard she was murdered. One of the patrons saw it on the news and passed it on. Ginger, who's a volunteer, burst into tears in the break room. Why are you asking me about it?"

"Because of your relationship with Angela's husband. You're named as a corespondent in the divorce." I smiled brightly. "You were, anyway. Now the divorce is no longer an issue."

"Is that so?" She didn't seem surprised.

Considering my reputation as an amateur sleuth, I was getting tired of the question. "You've already spoken to the police about Danny's alibi last Tuesday night. Are you certain about the date and time? I'd hate to see you cited for interfering with a police investigation or committing perjury on the stand."

"Are you helping the police?"

"In a manner of speaking," I said firmly. "Danny told the police that the two of you met for drinks and dinner, and then you spent the night at his condo. Will that be your testimony at the trial?"

"What trial?" She was beginning to squirm, and she glanced around to make sure no one was within earshot before she said, "Danny isn't going to be charged with anything. He said that the police don't have any evidence that he did anything wrong."

"That depends on your testimony, doesn't it? Subverting justice is a serious crime, and perjury can result in up to five years in prison."

If her office chair had had wheels, Nanette would have

been pedaling backward as fast as she could. "I didn't lie about anything! Danny and I were together from six o'clock in the evening until we left for work the next morning. There's no way he could have left the condo without waking me up. I'm a very light sleeper."

"Okay, then what about the weekend? You were supposed to go to the lake house with him, but you didn't." I felt as if I were a shark circling in on her, one ripple at a time. I would have bared my teeth had it not been unsightly.

Perspiration glinted on her forehead. "That was the plan, yeah. I'd bought sunscreen and a new bikini, packed a suitcase, and was waiting for him when he called to say he couldn't make it. I was royally pissed. A friend had an extra ticket to a rock concert in Tulsa, but I'd turned it down. I was stuck home all weekend."

I patted her knee. "What a crappy thing to do to you at the last minute. Where does he get the nerve to ask you to lie for him? Men!"

"He didn't ask me to lie," she muttered. "If he had, I would have told him what he could do with it."

"Did he bother to send you flowers after you told him about my computer search last Wednesday?"

Nanette swept back her hair with a dramatic gesture. "Our library has a strict rule concerning confidentiality. We never discuss our patrons."

I nodded. "Of course not. The Patriot Act should not override our right to privacy. Still, surely you pass along amusing little anecdotes about techno-idiots like me. It must drive you crazy to put up with us. We can barely turn on the computers."

"I did think it was kind of funny that you spent so long reading about yourself," she admitted with a giggle. "You looked like you were posing for paparazzi. You practically patted yourself on the back a couple of times. I looked you up after you left. You've got a reputation for meddling, Ms. Malloy."

"Is that what you told Danny?"

"He didn't know who you were, either. He was more interested when I said that you were a middle-aged skateboard groupie. The idea of someone like you in a helmet, balancing on a skateboard, your arms flapping—I laughed so hard that I fell off the couch. Then Danny got this idea about putting a walker on two skateboards, and—"

"It must have been a delightful conversation," I interrupted before I said something uncouth. "What did Danny say when you told him about my struggles with the county clerk's site?"

"I, uh, don't remember exactly. It's really easy for him because he does it all the time." Nanette glanced over my shoulder. "Mrs. Mendlehoff is waiting for me to help her find a law book. She was arrested for picketing at the federal courthouse, and she wants to sue the government for violating some constitutional amendment."

I sat on a bench beside the library's small flower bed, once again mired in guilt. Danny might have believed that disposing of Angela on Tuesday would sour any chance of a deal involving Winston's house, but Wednesday I'd gone to the library and, under Nanette's tutelage, searched for Terry Kennedy. Unless Danny sorely underestimated me, he could have guessed that I'd head for the courthouse for more information. I might as well have called him after I spoke to Terry.

Now all I had to do was prove that he'd spiked the vodka.

CHAPTER 13

I looked at my watch. Proving that Danny had murdered Winston, Angela, and Terry (in that order) would have to wait until I picked up Jordan. Peter may have believed that I wouldn't dream of setting foot anywhere in Hollow Valley, but I had a hall pass from Jorgeson. The turnoff to HVN was lined with TV vans and vehicles. Reporters shouted questions at me, but I merely waved as I drove past them. I handed the note to a uniformed officer, who read it with a skeptical expression. He conferred with his partner, who made a call from inside the police car. The random roar of the crowd increased to the point that I felt sorry for the wildlife. Those with camera crews primped in preparation for "live breaking news." It was nice to be recognized.

I continued up the road to the Old Tavern. The Mustang and the Mercedes were parked in the shade. I wanted to talk to Nattie but decided to hold off until I fetched Jordan, who might gnaw off her leg at any moment. No one answered the door at the mill. I retraced my route and knocked on the door of the Old Tavern. I waited for several minutes, knocked again, and finally went to look in the backyard. It was unoccupied. It was challenging to come up with a reason why Nattie, Margaret Louise, and Jordan would be at the nursery, and impossible to come up with one that included Charles Finnelly's house.

As I came back around the corner, Nattie opened the door. "Claire," she said in a chilly voice. "I thought I heard a knock, but we were in the kitchen. Can I help you?"

I had no idea why she was regarding me as if I were an aphid out to ravage her vegetable garden. "I came to pick up Jordan. Margaret Louise isn't home. Are she and Jordan here?"

Nattie came out to the stoop and closed the door behind her. "Yes, but there's a problem. Because of everything that's happened, Margaret Louise prefers that Jordan remain under her supervision for the time being. Why don't you come back next week? I'm sure Margaret Louise will relent once the police have concluded their investigation."

"You're okay with that?" I asked incredulously.

"Margaret Louise is taking her responsibility seriously. What if Jordan were to shoplift or attempt to run away? You must admit that she's not trustworthy, no matter what she says."

I couldn't deny that Jordan was capable of most anything, but it didn't seem fair that she had been judged and found guilty at the tender age of fourteen. "My daughter and her friend will keep an eye on her. They'll make sure that she doesn't do anything to disgrace the family name." At least I hoped they would, as long as I persuaded them that it was in their best interest. Bribery and threats, in a proper ratio, can accomplish miracles.

"Maybe next week." Nattie put her hand on the doorknob.

When it suits me, I have a strong sense of social justice. I ducked under Nattie's arm and went inside. I took no notice of her protests as I hurried down the hallway to the kitchen. Margaret Louise sat at the table, a cup of coffee in her hand. Jordan was slouched in a chair, radiating fury. I'd missed the meltdown, but I was definitely in the contamination zone.

Margaret Louise was at her dowdiest, dressed in a print housedress, her spectacles perched on her nose. Her expression was far from dowdy, however. She raised her eyebrows. "What part of 'no way' has you baffled? The spitfire stays here. She may believe she ain't gonna work on Maggie's farm no more, but she's a minor and I'm her custodial guardian. Isn't that right, Jordan? Running away is a status offense. No one wants you to spend the next four years in a juvenile detention facility."

"Shut up," Jordan muttered.

"I called her parents last night," Margaret Louise continued, "and they assured me that they will support any decisions I make about Jordan's immediate future. I decided that she's staying right here for the rest of the summer."

I looked at Nattie, who shrugged in response. Margaret Louise was slurping coffee and humming an unrecognizable melody. I was afraid to so much as glance at Jordan, who was undoubtedly harboring some unflattering opinions of me. I rallied all my dignity and said, "We'll just see about this, won't we?"

Nattie did not offer to show me out. I left briskly, as though I were on my way to the governor's mansion to tattle on them. Since he didn't owe me any favors (or know me), he might not overturn the parole board's decision. I stopped under Colonel Moses Ambrose Hollow's outstretched arm to concoct a wily scheme that did not include kidnapping, abetting a runaway, or grinding a blackberry pie in Margaret Louise's face. I reminded myself that I was a mild-mannered bookseller with an unblemished reputation for sense and sensibility.

I called Jorgeson, was put on hold to twiddle my toes, and was getting testy when he finally said, "Ms. Malloy."

"Have you taken Jordan Hollow's formal statement yet? In case it slipped your mind, she is the one who showed me the pot patch. She's a material witness. I'm concerned that she may be under the influence of certain members of the Hollow family who are attempting to taint her perception of the events."

There was a silence. "Who might they be, these members of the Hollow family?"

I was so irate that I had no compunctions about throwing Nattie and Margaret Louise to the wolves. I explained the situation, perhaps embellishing the story with references to dark stares and whispered conversations. "They're brainwashing her," I continued earnestly, if a shade mendaciously. "She's only fourteen."

"With a Mohawk, a tattoo, body piercings, and a juvenile rap sheet. She's not fragile, Ms. Malloy. I appreciate your concern, but I'm busy."

I needed to stall. "Did you get the lab report about the poison used to kill Terry Kennedy?"

"The ME has ruled out food poisoning, prescription drugs, and garden-variety poisons like cyanide, arsenic, strychnine, aconitine, and atropine. Now it's up to the state lab. If you're bored, may I suggest you call Deputy Chief Rosen? He'll be interested to hear about this purported brainwashing. He may have been trained in the techniques being used as we speak. He might even send a black helicopter to rescue the young lady."

I closed my cell phone. Jorgeson was obviously under a lot of pressure, since he rarely resorted to sarcasm. He needed help. Since Peter was out of pocket, I had a moral obligation to ease poor Jorgeson's anxiety. It could not be a coincidence that I was in Hollow Valley. Clotho, Lachesis, and Atropos had best be on alert, since I was preparing to tempt fate.

Danny Delmond had an alibi for the evening that Angela had disappeared, but his alibi for the weekend was as squishy as an overripe melon. Nanette hadn't canceled their plans. He'd left her at the curb. Conveniently alone at the lake house, he could come and go with impunity, but he still required an accomplice—someone clever enough to lure Angela away in a panic, bash her on the head, conceal the body, and ultimately help him bury it. The workers at the nursery were apt to be muscular. Jordan had mentioned one named Rudy, but there were others.

I didn't want to leave my car in sight of the Old Tavern. I drove to the perfect house and parked away from the gravel driveway. This might be the last time I saw it, I thought sadly. I wanted to grind a dozen blackberry pies in Danny's face. Slowly and thoroughly, until every one of his orifices was clogged with purple pulp.

Getting inside the house did not seem to pose a challenge to anyone. I walked around to the French doors and jiggled a handle. The door opened. Having solved one mystery, I went inside and wandered around, looking for clues that someone had been there since yesterday afternoon. The police investigators had left a fine mist of black dust here and there, and they'd probably come up with scores of prints left from parties. It occurred to me that Loretta, aka Esther, might have attended some of them. Her parents were a mere hoot away, whining about the noise and damning the miscreants.

The thought gave me great satisfaction, as it surely did for her. It did not, however, move me an inch closer to the solution, and I had limited time before the police officers at the gate began to wonder where I was. I remembered that I'd wanted to talk to Felicia without Charles's presence. I sat down at the kitchen island and took out my cell phone. I called information and asked for a number for Charles Finnelly. A computer obliged. If Charles answered, I would hang up. My heart was thumping uncomfortably when Felicia said, "Hello?"

"Don't say a word," I said. "This is Claire Malloy, and I have information about Esther. I'm at Winston's house. Now I want you to say, 'We're not interested,' and hang up. I'll wait for fifteen minutes."

I dropped my cell phone in my purse and resumed prowling around the house, looking for something the police had overlooked. The carton of cigarettes was still in the bottom desk drawer. No one had scrawled any bloody messages on the walls or left a written confession on a bedside table. I returned to the kitchen. Felicia's time was running out. If she didn't show up, which was a distinct possibility, I was going to have to decide on my next move. If she'd told Charles what I'd said, I could expect a police officer at the front door.

I admit I was somewhat nervous. I did not want to face Charles, Jorgeson, or Peter. I went out to the terrace and forced myself to breathe deeply. I was nearly hyperventilating when Felicia came out of the orchard and made her way to the pool area. She eyed me for a moment, then came around the pool and stood in front of me.

"Well?" she asked.

"Why don't you sit down," I suggested. "This will take a few minutes. Did you have any problems with Charles?"

Her expression thawed. "Yes, I had a problem with Charles. Luckily, he was going to the nursery to talk to Ethan, so I had to wait. He demands to know where I am every blasted minute of the day. If I visit Margaret Louise, he wants to know what we talked about. If I go shopping, he checks the receipts to make sure I didn't buy

myself a treat." She glanced inside. "Is it possible to have
a glass of wine? I'm terrified of what you're going to tell
me. I can't face any more bad news."

I tried to conceal my astonishment. "Certainly. Do you
have a preference?"

"Anything."

I found an unopened bottle in the cabinet and attacked
it with a corkscrew, trying all the while to readjust my
opinion of her. She was not the woman who'd referred to
me as "your kind." She appeared to be warm-blooded,
unlike her reptilian mate. I filled a wineglass and went
back to the terrace. I handed her a glass and said, "My
news isn't bad, Felicia. Your daughter is fine, and she currently lives in Farberville."

Her face turned pale. "Oh, my God. Are you sure that
it's really Esther? Can I see her?"

"I'm sure as I can be," I said gently. "She told me about
her childhood and where she went after she ran away. I
can't tell you anything more about her without her con-
sent. Shall I let her know that you want to meet with her?"

"Of course I do. She's my daughter." She hesitated.
"Tell her that I'll come alone. Charles will never know.
When will you see her?"

"I'll give her your message tomorrow."

She covered her face with her hands and began to cry.
I would have felt more sympathy had I not known that she
allowed Charles to abuse their daughter. If she hadn't
allowed it, she had let it happen. She'd had options. She
could have called the police or taken Esther to a shelter.
Instead, she'd played the role of a meek, obedient wife.

"What happened to you?" I asked in a somewhat angry
voice. "Why didn't you protect your daughter?"

She looked up at me, her face wet. "I can't explain.
When I met Charles, he was kind and polite. My parents

were delighted with him and pressured me into marrying him. He owned a drugstore, and we lived in an apartment upstairs. Everything was fine until he joined that . . . that church. They're bigots and hate-mongers. They distort the Bible to suit themselves. I fought as hard as I could, but Charles dragged me into their quagmire. I had no choice. You believe me, don't you?"

She looked so pathetic that I eased off, although I doubted that she had no choice. "Okay."

"It's the family," she said, gripping the arms of the chair. "You don't understand about the family. I was taught from infancy that the family comes first. When my father died, we moved here to Hollow Valley. Charles took over his duties at the nursery, and I cared for my mother until her death. He became more of a Hollow than I ever was. The wealth and power corrupted what was left of him. I shrank until I was a shadowy presence."

"Hollow Valley doesn't seem to be overflowing with wealth or power. Sure, everyone has a big house and an expensive car, and I gather the nursery business is good. Nobody seems to be jetting off to luxurious resorts or floating their yachts in the stream. Does the family own a vast corporation or a senator?"

Felicia downed the wine and held out her glass. I went inside and brought out the wine bottle. She was likely to be unaccustomed to alcohol, and I had no reservations about exploiting her weakness. I refilled her glass and waited.

"Not that kind of power," she said with a ladylike snort. "One can have the power to flaunt authority. And just because we don't wear mink coats and diamonds doesn't mean we're not richer than a corporate law firm. Charles's watch cost six thousand dollars. He never wears it to church, but you can bet he wears it to chamber of commerce meetings. He's a nasty old hypocrite." She finished the wine in her glass and, with some fumbling, managed to pour herself a very full glass. "It was a damn shame about Winston. I felt sorry for him when he was a kid. He taught Esther how to use watercolors, and they would sneak off whenever they could. Charles was furious, of course. The first painting that Esther brought home so incensed him that he ripped it into shreds and made her put in an extra ten hours at the nursery."

"Do you believe that Winston committed suicide?" I asked.

"About as far as I can fart," she replied with a giggle. "Want a demonstration?"

"Not really. What do you think happened to him?"

Wine dribbled down her blouse as she took a drink. "I'd like to think that Charles murdered him and that you can prove it. Drag the bastard off to jail! Unfortunately, that's only in my dreams. Charles had the flu and could barely haul his sorry ass out of bed for a week. He complained the entire time. I should have held a pillow over his face."

"If Charles didn't murder Winston, who did?"

"How should I know? I was home making chicken soup and rice pudding. Charles was the only one out here who was upset about Winston and Terry's relationship. I thought Terry was a snob, but I liked Winston. Don't tell a soul, but I used to come here every now and then while Charles was away at a church meeting and Terry was out of town. Winston and I drank wine and talked about the old days. I'd go home, gargle with mouthwash, and be asleep when Charles got back." She hiccuped with delight. "The good old days, when I still had Esther. How is she? Does she need money? I have some in a box in the closet. Her toys, too. She had a doll named Heloise and a stuffed monkey with one eye. What was his name?"

She was way too close to slipping into a maudlin reverie.

She had the wine bottle in her lap, and retrieving it might send her over the edge. "She's doing fine," I said, "and she didn't appear to need money. Do you know anything about a real estate deal that involves Hollow Valley?"

After a few misses, she managed to put her finger to her lips. "Can't talk about it. Big secret."

"Did someone named Danny Delmond ever come here to meet with Charles?"

Felicia gave me a lopsided grin. "Hairy Danny. Whenever business is discussed, Charles orders me to stay in the kitchen. Mostly church business. Once they heard gossip that the choir director was having private sessions with underaged girls from the congregation. You should have heard them carrying on like a flock of biddy hens. Cluck, cluck, cluck! They finally decided to punish the girls for telling sordid lies. The choir director quietly resigned and left town."

"Danny Delmond is a developer."

"Good for him. I'm the great-great-great-granddaughter of Colonel Moses Ambrose Hollow. I live in the middle of nowhere and am married to an evil-tempered dictator. My own daughter despises me. You despise me. Everyone else just feels sorry for me—humorless, spineless Felicia Hollow Finnelly." She began to cry again, this time embellished with noisy gulps, moans, and whimpers.

I realized that I would hear nothing more from her that was remotely coherent. She presented a dilemma. If I left her alone, she might stumble into the pool and drown. I had opened the wine bottle, and I hadn't wrested it away from her. I didn't want to carry her home, where Charles might notice that she was drunk. He would not be amused.

I was sitting there, watching her for any indication that she might stop crying in the foreseeable future, when the shriek of a siren grew closer. I went to the front yard in time to see flashing lights streaking toward the Old Tavern. My throat tightened. Jordan had been furious. Had she done something outrageous that resulted in injury? Margaret Louise was at the top of her hit list, with Nattie in the second slot. I was a contender for third, but I wasn't easily available. I wanted to chase the ambulance, but I couldn't leave Felicia. I returned to check on the dilemma. The wine bottle was on its side, also empty.

"Is Esther here?" she bleated. "I want to see Esther. Will she forgive me? Oh, Esther, I'm so sorry!"

I grasped her arm and encouraged her to stand. "Let's go inside, Felicia. You can rest while I look for Esther." She sagged as if she'd been punched. I put my arm around her back and tried to keep her moving. "A nice nap is what you need. When you feel better, we can talk about Esther's one-eyed monkey."

We made it to the master bedroom. I gave a tiny shove that sent her sprawling facedown across the bed, then rolled her over and took off her shoes. She wiggled until her head bumped a pillow, fluttered her fingers at me, and passed out. I closed the blinds and made sure the French doors were locked. The rhythm of her breathing became slower and deeper. When she began to snore like an asthmatic dog, I tiptoed out of the room and went to the front porch.

Either the ambulance had departed without fanfare or it was still at the Old Tavern. I walked to the blacktop road. After a moment of deliberation, I went down the driveway that led to Pandora and Ethan's house. Rainbow and Weevil were in the garden, pulverizing tomatoes with a hammer. They were too engrossed in destruction to look up as I took the path to the nursery. My plan was to skirt the greenhouses and approach the Old Tavern with the stealth of a ferret.

Two delivery trucks were parked near an outbuilding. I heard voices, but the words were indecipherable. Several men emerged from the back of a truck and headed in my direction, talking and laughing among themselves. I'd seen some of them when Ethan had given me the grand tour, but I most certainly did not want them to see me. I checked the ground for errant snakes, then scrunched behind a clump of scrub trees and brush. The men came within twenty feet of me but continued to the rows of ornamental trees and began to carry them back to the trucks. I was stuck between a rock (under my knee) and a hard place (an oak tree), and I had no idea how long it would take them to load the trees. A man with a clipboard periodically shouted instructions about flowering pears, hollies, redbuds, and whatever. The workmen cursed as they staggered under the weight of the trees with burlap root balls. Leaves rustled nearby. I bit down on my lip to hold in a squeak of terror. The only weapon at hand was a spindly branch no thicker than my thumb. I anticipated a snake with the diameter of a fire hose. Although I knew that anacondas and pythons were indigenous to South America, I wasn't sure they hadn't acquired the proper visas to grant them temporary residency in Hollow Valley.

The rustling noise seemed closer—and louder. No one had reported seeing an alligator within three hundred miles, but that did little to reassure me. I'd never seen a purple cow, but I could not swear under oath that purple cows did not exist. The workmen chose that moment to take a break. Their alarming proximity overpowered my nebulous fear of skunks, raccoons, and rabid possums. The men sat in the dirt or leaned against the truck, some of them smoking. A bearish man with a red face said something that the others found hysterically funny, then walked straight at me. His hands fumbled with the zipper of his jeans.

I tucked myself into the smallest ball possible and gritted my teeth. The splatter on the leaves echoed like a deluge. The smell caused me to gag. I closed my eyes and did what I could to distract myself until the last droplets hit the dust and I heard the sound of a zipper being restored to its proper place. Only then did I risk a breath. The men resumed talking. I opened one eye and peered around the tree. Most of them had their backs to me, including the one whose mother had failed to instill in him a sense of decorum.

I was trapped for a quarter of an hour before the man with the clipboard announced that they were finished. As they headed for the office, the bearish man looked over his shoulder and winked at me. I was so astonished that I would have fallen back on my derriere if I hadn't been concerned about spiders. He might have assumed that we were compatriots, but he was wrong. I do not make alliances with men who expose themselves to Mother Nature.

I finally stood up. My knees were embedded with dirt and flecks of composted debris, and my back had tread marks from the bark of the tree. All I'd learned was that the woods were more dangerous than I'd ever imagined. One of the workmen was likely to be Danny's accomplice. None of them was likely to admit it to me. I still had no idea what had transpired at the Old Tavern, which had been my goal when I took the devious route. I was about to plunge back into the woods when Ethan came out of his office. Charles stalked behind him, as if he were the Grand Inquisitor of his petty bishopric.

Ethan began to designate drivers and crews for the trucks. The trucks were going south and east in Arkansas. He rattled off a list of stops, some in cities and some in unfamiliar towns. I was surprised that landscaping was prevalent in places called "County Line Liquor" and "the Redbird Bar and Grill." I recognized the name of a town in Maxwell County, only because one of my customers at the Book Depot had described it in unflattering terms.

"Beerbelly's" would soon be surrounded by flowering pear trees and crepe myrtles.

Another truck appeared from the road that crossed the bridge. A woman in jeans and a T-shirt slid out of the driver's seat. She stretched her muscular arms above her head and arched her back. "Drove straight through," she said. "Gotta use the can." She entered the appropriate outbuilding.

"Rudy, you and Wayne get this unloaded," Ethan said. He stopped to consult with Charles. "We'll use it for the county run later today. Miguel, make sure you get a good variety of healthy plants this time. I don't want to send out a single spider mite, so hand check every leaf."

This was not the time to congratulate Ethan on his beautification project. I crept behind the buildings until I came to the path to the Old Tavern. I made it to the fringe of the grass without raising an alarm. The ambulance was parked near the door. I dashed across the open space and hid behind the Mercedes. A white van with an official decal on the door was parked behind the Mustang; presumably the medical examiner was present. A police car was nearby. People moved in the living room, but they were indistinguishable in the dim light.

When the front door opened, I risked poking my head up far enough to watch the exodus. The two police officers who were stationed at the gate went to their car. The medical examiner, Nattie, and Margaret Louise came out, their expressions subdued. Following them were two paramedics pushing a gurney. The body bag was zipped. A jolt of fear stabbed my gut. I curled my fingers and waited for Jordan to appear in the doorway. Surely no one would be unruffled by the death of a fourteen-year-old, I told myself. The body was loaded into the van. The medical examiner spoke to the police officers, who then drove away. The paramedics left in the ambulance. I heard Nattie thank the medical examiner for his promptness. Margaret Louise simpered at him and clutched his hand. He said something that made them smile.

I had only a few seconds before he drove away, the body bag secured in the back of his van. I took a deep breath, stood up, and called, "Hey, Nattie! Did you find my cell phone in your kitchen? I was sure I had it with me, but I've searched my car and my purse." I approached them rapidly. "Aren't you the medical examiner? We met at a banquet last year, one of those obligatory police department banquets. Such a bore! I'm Claire Malloy, and my husband is Peter Rosen."

"Ah, yes, of course," the poor man stammered, having never even seen me before that moment. "Peter Rosen, good man. Those banquets are ghastly, so I avoid them when I can. Rubber chicken, green beans. Gives me indigestion for days. It's nice to see you again, Mrs. Rosen."

Nattie and Margaret Louise resembled a couple of goldfish in a glass bowl. Their eyes were round, and their lips moved silently. I rewarded each of them with a warm smile and turned back to the medical examiner. "I gather that you're here in your official capacity. Who died?"

"The old gentleman died in his sleep," the medical examiner said with proper gravity. "Based on what I've been told about his health problems and advanced age, I'll notify his doctor for confirmation and then rule it death by natural causes. Have the funeral home director call my office tomorrow. My condolences, ladies." He got in the van and drove down the blacktop road to the gate.

"What are you doing here?" demanded Margaret Louise.

"Offering my condolences, obviously. Moses died in his sleep. I guess that's the most serene way to go. I'm very sorry for your loss."

Nattie frowned. "I thought you left Hollow Valley after

our previous conversation more than an hour ago. You're not lingering to give Jordan a chance to conceal herself in your car, are you? I'm disappointed in you, Claire."

I refrained from pointing out which of us was more disappointed in the other. Maybe I didn't appreciate how much thicker blood was than water. "Where's Jordan?"

Margaret Louise shook her head. "She claimed that she was too upset to be here while the body was removed. That does not concern you, since she is not to leave with you under any circumstances. The police officers at the gate have been advised to search your car."

"Rats," I said. "They'll find the Picasso, the Matisse, and the Modigliani I stole from the Museum of Modern Art in Paris a couple of years ago. Do you know how difficult it is to get a fair price on the black market? The best offer I've had to date was a measly hundred million."

They backed away from me. I advanced, taking credit for the theft of a Corot and a Degas from the Louvre, King Tut's golden death mask from the Egyptian Museum, and a neighborhood kid's basketball from his front yard. I kept it up until they reached the door, went inside, and locked it. The manic verbal attack had exhilarated me, but the adrenaline ebbed as I thought about Moses's death. He'd annoyed and frustrated me. The majority of his babbling had made no sense. I felt sad, but I was not enveloped with grief. If he hadn't died from system failure, cirrhosis would have caught up with him soon.

Jordan could be anywhere. I looked in the backyard, then at the bridge, the road, and the wooded mountains. If she was escaping, she had a healthy head start. I had no intention of beating the bushes, figuratively or literally. The delivery trucks had not yet driven away to distribute botanical bliss across the state. Jordan might have found an opportunity to hop in the back of one. She had experience, if not expertise, in that form of transportation.

Without the Mohawk and the bling, she had a chance of blending into a large town or a city. She had street skills. It was a discouraging thought.

I tucked in my blouse, pulled a twig out of my hair, and walked back to the nursery. I wasn't sure how to approach Ethan, if Charles was still lurking nearby. When I saw the two of them, I waved. They waited in silence, as unflinching as the columns at the Karnak Temple near Luxor.

"I came to offer my condolences," I said. "Moses was . . . quite a character."

Ethan nodded. "Thank you. I'll miss the old coot."

"Do not speak ill of the dead," Charles said sternly. "Moses was the great-great-grandson of Moses Ambrose Hollow, the patriarch of our family. We have suffered a painful loss on this day."

Not so painful as to interfere with business as usual, I amended mentally. "I see that the trucks are being loaded. This is a busy season, isn't it?"

"Yes," Ethan said, his forehead wrinkling. "Is there something I can do for you, Claire? I want to get the trucks on the road as soon as possible. The drivers are waiting for me to do a final inspection to see that we have everything on the order list."

"How fascinating. Do you mind if I tag along?"

Charles harrumphed. "This is not a playground. You have no legitimate reason to be here. As the CEO of Hollow Valley Nursery, I demand that you leave the premises immediately."

"Or what? Are you going to have me arrested for trespassing? I look forward to answering reporters' questions at the gate. Whatever I say will be both entertaining and enlightening, and might hint at illegal activity. Is that what you want, Charles?" The final word was laden with derision.

Ethan intervened. "There's no harm in letting you see how efficiently we operate." He took my arm and led me toward the nearest truck. He held up the clipboard and read the names and quantities of the trees, shrubs, and flowers. A workman inside the truck responded to each with a curt confirmation. I listened intently for a telltale gasp from an unauthorized passenger. As we started for the next truck, he slowed down and said, "Pandora told me what happened the other night. I'm sorry you had to see her at her worst. She'd always thought of herself as an earth mother, raising children in an open setting and embracing nature. After a couple of years, she began to unravel."

He may have been thinking of her as a pile of mohair yarn, but I saw a bale of barbed wire. "So you don't mind her nocturnal activities?" I asked.

"I can't put her in a cage. It's awful to say this, but I tolerate her unacceptable behavior for the sake of the children. We love them dearly." He wiped away a tear. "She's agreed to therapy. If it doesn't help, well . . . I'll have to do something."

We arrived at the second truck. Ethan told one of the workmen to climb into the back. He and the workman ran through the routine, although it appeared that three more hemlocks were required. There were no gasps. While we waited, our backs to Charles, he added, "Please don't tell anyone else about . . . what happened. They're already worried about her. If they found out the truth, they'd go ballistic. You'd be able to hear Charles in the next county."

"Okay," I said, "as long as you tell me the truth about something. Are there any plans to turn the valley into a housing development?"

"That's ridiculous. Hollow Valley has been in the family for a hundred and fifty years. It's our enclave, our business, our heritage. No one would consider selling a square foot of land to some developer."

"Terry Kennedy wasn't a member of the family," I pointed out. "He was free to sell his acreage to anyone he wanted. Before he was murdered, that is."

"The land was never rightfully his," Ethan said with a trace of anger. "He was a poker player, wasn't he? He took a gamble when he intimidated Winston into signing that worthless paper. Our lawyer has assured us that there will be no problem convincing a judge to find that Winston was under mental duress, and therefore incapable of entering into a legal contract."

"It's a shame that Terry won't be in court to present his side of the story. He might have presented a compelling version of the events prior to the signing of the deed. The executor of his estate won't be able to call any witnesses."

"Yeah, it's a damn shame. I need to get the guys on the road." He slammed the back doors of the truck and went to the cab to talk to the driver.

I was relieved to know that Jordan was not a stowaway on either truck. I looked over the workmen, wondering which one was Danny Delmond's accomplice. The one who was responsible for his unseemly behavior grinned at me, but I shot him down with a withering stare that singed his nose hairs. Several of them looked as if they would fit the role of a hit man, and I couldn't rule out the woman truck driver with the bulky biceps. I failed to acknowledge Charles as I went back to the Old Tavern. Jordan was not perched in a tree or snoozing in the backyard. I continued down the road and turned at the driveway to Winston's house, or Terry's house, or Terry's heirs' house. Not my house, alas.

Caron and Inez were sitting in the porch swing.

"What are you two doing here?" I asked as I came up the steps.

"Mother, do you know there's a woman passed out in the master bedroom?" Caron demanded.

"Oh, good."

"What does that mean?"

"Trust me," I said with a sigh. "It's very, very good."

CHAPTER 14

"Isn't she that tight-lipped woman who lives around here?" Inez asked.

"Yes, and it's better if she stays where she is," I said. "We have a problem. Jordan's disappeared, and I'm concerned." I gave them a puzzled look. "So what are you doing here?"

Caron shrugged. "You told us that we had to be home at four o'clock so we can babysit this juvenile delinquent. We waited Forever. I tried to call you, but you didn't answer. You're supposed to keep your cell phone handy, you know. We finally decided to come out here and see what's going on. It's really crazy at the turnoff."

"So crazy," Inez added, "that we drove down to some little dirt road and parked and then came across the pasture. Caron wanted to see where that lady's body was buried, but there was yellow tape."

I gave them an account of my conversation with Margaret Louise and Nattie, and Moses's death. "Jordan was furious the last time I saw her. She may be disturbed about Moses. I never heard her say much of anything about him."

Inez clung to the spotlight, despite Caron's growing displeasure. "She liked him because he didn't give her a hard time. They used to sneak down here so he could get into the wine. He even let her have a glass, but she said it tasted nasty. He was like really old, wasn't he? When my great-grandmother died, my parents forgot to tell me for a week. It was sad, but not tragic like when Bambi's mother died."

"Bambi!" Caron said with a sniff. "You can be so immature, Inez."

I moved them to the ends of the swing and sat in the middle. The chains creaked in an ominous fashion but held our collective weight. "Let's figure out where Jordan may have gone. Did she have any favorite spots, Inez?"

"Just the pot garden."

An image came back to me—Terry, Jordan, and Inez, laughing ever so merrily as they sat by the pool. "Inez," I said carefully, "I don't want to hear another word about that. Not one word."

Caron leaned forward to look at her. "You got stoned? That is way cool."

"It is in no way cool," I said. Now I wasn't so enthusiastic about finding Jordan, who could introduce the girls to things that I didn't want to think about. "I promise you that this will be discussed later—and at length."

We swung for a few minutes. I tried to keep myself from composing the lecture I would deliver in the near future, but I had a difficult time trying to focus on Jordan's whereabouts. She could be anywhere in the valley, sitting under a tree while she devised how best to seek revenge. She could be hitchhiking to Philadelphia in a rusty pickup truck driven by a fugitive from a chain gang. Or a street gang. She'd mellowed over the previous week, but she could have relapsed.

A voice from inside the house disrupted my meanderings. "I hear my drunk," I said as I stood up. "It's too soon to try to sober her up, but I'm afraid of what might happen to her if she staggers home in her current condition." They expressed no interest in assisting me. I went to the master bedroom and found Felicia struggling to stand up.

"Got to go," she mumbled. "Got to make dinner."

I put my hand on her shoulder and pushed her down. "You don't have to go anywhere. Charles can make himself a sandwich."

She chewed on that for a moment. "No, this is Monday, I think. We have meat loaf on Monday, fried chicken on Tuesday . . ." Her hands fluttered in the air. "On Wednesday, we have a salad because we have to go to church and sit on a damn pew and listen to the choir mangle some hymn, and on Thursday we have spaghetti, and on Friday I'm gonna bake a great big humble pie and make the old fart eat it with his fingers!"

"Good job on menu planning," I said. "Why don't you lie down and dream about picking humble berries in the meadow?"

"I thought they grew on trees," she said, sniggering as she fell back. "Doughnuts grow on bushes. All you have to do is plant Cheerios in the spring. Bet you didn't know that, did you?" She was giggling so wildly that her feet flopped on the end of the bed. "When Esther was a little girl, she and I planted a chocolate chip. A few weeks later I made a batch of chocolate chip cookies and told her that I'd picked them off the bush. She loved it, my sweet little girl. Is she here yet?"

We were back to the teary thing. I sat down and held her hand while she rambled about Esther's innocence and talents and so forth. She tossed in a few remarks about Charles that were not complimentary, and surprisingly creative. I heard Caron and Inez come inside, and shortly thereafter the sound of the refrigerator door being opened. It reminded me of Angela, who'd stocked the refrigerator for her lover. I still had no clue to his identity—assuming the lover was male. I toyed with that for a while, still holding Felicia's hand and murmuring soothing noises. I replayed what I could remember of Angela's monologues and concluded that she was as straight as a sorority reception line.

Felicia finally dozed off. I extricated my hand and went into the kitchen. Caron and Inez had found canned sodas, crackers, and a jar of peanut butter. They watched me as I went to the French doors and looked out at the pool and the meadow. Jordan did not come hopping through the clover like a little punk bunny. She was safe from Danny, who would not risk coming to Hollow Valley. His accomplice might be within the confines, however. After some thought, I decided that Jordan wasn't at risk. She had no control over her father's property, since he had deeded it to the family. She was in Philadelphia at the time of Winston's death. She and Inez had been present when Terry drank the vodka, but they hadn't seen anything that aroused their suspicion.

Moses had been there as well. He was no longer available for questioning, however futile it might have been. The medical examiner would consult with Moses's doctor and declare the death a result of natural causes. Unlike Winston, he would merit a funeral, and presumably a spot in the family plot. The phrase disturbed me, although I wasn't sure why. I nibbled on my lip, which was getting sore, as I turned around and sat down on a stool by the island.

"Did Jordan mention a family plot?" I asked Inez.

She wiped her mouth with a paper napkin. "You mean

where they bury people? Yes, it's on the other side of the river, near the bridge and the back road. She said that the headstones are mossy and there are weeds all over the place. She found out that she had a great-great-aunt named Ethiopia. Isn't that wild?"

"It's dumb," Caron said. "Was her husband's name Cameroon?"

"Lloyd, I think."

"I want the two of you to go find the family plot and see if Jordan's there," I said. "I can't leave Felicia alone."

Caron winced. "You want us to swim across a river and hike through the woods just because Jordan might be hugging a headstone? I forgot to bring my bathing suit, boots, compass, and camouflage T-shirt. What if we get shot by deer hunters?"

"Bullets can travel more than two miles," Inez contributed helpfully.

"It's not deer season," I said, hoping it wasn't. "You can get across the stream on a fallen tree trunk, or go farther downstream to a shallow place. Worry about poison ivy, not lions and tigers. Call me on my cell when you get there."

"What's the point of that?" Caron asked, one eyebrow raised. It was a skill I'd yet to master, making it all the more annoying. "Do you even know how to answer it?"

"If I don't hear from you in thirty minutes, I'll call the police and report you as runaways. That's a status offense. I'd hate for you to spend your senior year in a juvenile detention facility."

"You are So Not Funny," Caron said as she and Inez got up. They went out the French doors, leaving a redolence of indignation behind them. I reminded myself how endearing she'd been as a toddler.

I found my cell in the bottom of my purse. Terry's

lawyer, Ms. Cranberry, had left a message asking me to contact her. Her office had closed two hours ago, so there was no reason to call back. I made a pot of coffee, looked in on Felicia, and returned to the kitchen for a peanut butter cracker. Sleuthing plays havoc with normal meals. A drop of Scotch sounded divine, but I wasn't about to drink anything in the liquor cabinet that had not been put through a rigorous round of tests. Jorgeson had told me that the poison was not among the usual suspects. In mystery novels, the antagonist has access to African tree frog sweat or bamboo curare, purchased in a quaint corner chemist's shoppe next to a tearoom. The rest of us are obliged to buy weed killer at a discount store. I'd never tasted the stuff, but it had a pungent odor that vodka and lemonade would not mask.

Anyone who knew the location of the house could have planted the bottle. I doubted that preference for vodka and tonic was a secret. He'd upset Felicia when he offered her one at Terry's party. Had Charles not been there, she might have snatched the glass from his hand and drained it. She was a gifted actress. She'd fooled me, and all the family members, too. I nearly choked on the cracker in my mouth. Unless her husband preferred to tolerate her weakness, as Ethan did with Pandora Butterfly. His church was inflexible and willing to blame the innocent along with the guilty. Charles would no longer be the Grand Pooh-Bah of the congregation. The only way to test my theory was to send her home, but I wasn't that confident.

I wasn't that confident about anything, I thought morosely. Although anyone could have planted the bottle, he or she couldn't have known that Terry had come back to Hollow Valley. If the tainted vodka bottle had been in the cabinet for three months, Moses would have drained it and died in the kitchen instead of his own bed. The medical examiner wouldn't have been quite so eager to declare the death due to natural causes. Nattie and Felicia had looked appropriately sad when Moses's body had been wheeled out on a gurney. When Terry's body had been dealt with the same way, the family members had looked stunned. If I recalled accurately (and I always do), I'd been accused of not telling them that Terry had returned. They'd been downright testy about it, as if I had an obligation to knock on their respective doors and enlighten them.

The coffeepot stopped gurgling. I went into the master bedroom to find out if Felicia had recovered enough to drink lots of black coffee. She'd had a couple of hours of sleep. The alcohol was still in her bloodstream, but if she could be induced to move around and take her caffeine like an adult, I might be able to mask the worst of her symptoms. It was time to confront the shower.

I took off her clothes, wrestled her into the shower stall, and turned on four showerheads to blast her with cold water. She did not enjoy the experience. I helped her dress, clutched her arm, and maneuvered her into the kitchen. Under my stern supervision, she drank three cups of coffee.

Felicia waggled her finger at me in reproach. "You didn't have to do that. I wasn't inebriated; I was tipsy. There was something about Esther, wasn't there?"

I repeated what I said and promised to contact Esther the next day. "You're going to have to deal with Charles," I continued. "You're miserable being married to him. You can't pretend that you're staying together for the sake of your child. She's long gone, and happier for it."

"Divorce Charles?" she asked, shocked. "I could never do that. He wouldn't survive without his position at the nursery. That and the church are the only two things he really cares about. The church does not condone divorce. It's considered blasphemy because marriage vows are sacred. Wives are not permitted to complain about their husbands, even if the bastards are having affairs on the side."

"Like Charles?" I held my breath.

"Hardly," she said with a snigger. "No one would put up with him. If I'd believed in premarital sex, I would have dropped him like a molten rock and married the next man I met at the grocery store. He has his secrets, though." She slid off the stool and grabbed the edge of the island until she regained her balance. "I need to go home. Will you please let me know what Esther says? Whatever she wants. We can meet at a café or a park. Five minutes is better than never."

I stood on the terrace and watched her until she wobbled into the orchard. I'd made an unsuccessful stab at playing marriage counselor. She would return to her abuser again and again, like so many battered women, before she accepted the simple fact that he would never change. I wished her well, then went inside to check the time. Caron and Inez had been gone more than thirty minutes. I carried my cell while I searched the house for nooks and crannies large enough to conceal a teenager. I forced myself to go down to the basement. The wine racks had numerous empty slots, courtesy of Moses. Beyond that was a large, unfinished room. I mentally equipped it with a wet bar, comfortable seating, and a billiard table beneath a rectangular stained-glass light fixture. Now all I needed was a conservatory, a lounge, and a ballroom.

My cell phone chirped. I opened it and said, "I was getting worried about you. Did you find Jordan?"

"Who's Jordan?" said Deputy Chief Peter Rosen.

"Hello, my love. How are you?"

"Who's Jordan?"

I needed to get him off the line, which required a certain amount of evasion. "One of Caron's friends. You haven't met her. When are you coming home?"

"Tomorrow night. We're getting nowhere. The state police are still looking for witnesses, but it's an impossible task. The feds insist on endless meetings in which everybody says the same things over and over. The governor's up for reelection, so he calls a press conference three times a day. The big guns from North Carolina left this morning."

"Quite a dither over a hijacking," I said. "I'm in the middle of something, so why don't I call you back later?"

"In the middle of what?"

I was getting tired of his rash assumptions that I was meddling in official police business. "Stir-fry," I said. "It's very healthy. Oops, the broccoli is smoking. I'll talk to you later." I'd never actually made a stir-fry dish, but I'd glanced at a recipe that had an extensive list of vegetables to be sliced and diced and set aside in separate piles. It was an apt description of my muddle. I had three murders, numerous motives, and an unknown number of suspects. If only I could toss all of it in a wok, stir and fry, and end up with one simple dish. It would not be humble pie.

It had now been forty-five minutes since Caron and Inez headed out on their mission. I resigned myself to wet shoes, chiggers, and whatever lay in wait for me across the river. There was no reason to lock the house. I was halfway out the door when my cell phone chirped. I crossed my fingers and answered it.

"Sorry it took so long," Caron said. "We were being careful not to be seen by the reporters on the road. Anyway, Jordan is not in the graveyard. We found Ethiopia's headstone. She was born in eighteen ninety-three and died when she was a hundred years old. Lloyd died almost forty years before she did."

"Fascinating."

"I'm sick and tired of tromping around in the woods, which happen to cover miles and miles of rocks, stumps, and bugs. I nearly stepped on a snake. I'm spending the night at Inez's house. See you tomorrow."

She switched off her phone before I could respond. I considered calling her back, but I didn't want to hear any more whining. I had no inclination to step on a snake. If Jordan didn't want to be found, she wouldn't be. I had never hiked farther than Luanne's shop on Thurber Street.

I cleaned up the kitchen and straightened the bedspread in the master bedroom. I had no reason to stay in Hollow Valley any longer. My time would be better spent in battle with the boxes in every room of the duplex. I made sure I had my cell phone and then went out the front door. As I peered into the back of my car to make sure I wouldn't have an extra passenger, Nattie came across the grass.

"Claire, I'm so glad you're still here. I want to apologize for my behavior at the Old Tavern. Margaret Louise called Sheldon and Joanne last night. When they heard about Terry and Angela, they had a fit. They wanted Jordan on the next flight to Philadelphia. Then they remembered that they were leaving in less than a week for a vacation in Aruba and backed off. Margaret Louise promised to watch Jordan like a sharp-shinned hawk until they get back. She was angry at me for telling you that Jordan could spend the night at your house. I assured her that you would take very good care of her ward, but I couldn't persuade her to change her mind. Poor Jordan was infuriated. Please forgive me."

"I was miffed, but I accept your apology. I am sorry about Moses. He was entertaining, in his way. I couldn't decide when he was telling the truth and when he was spewing nonsense. The Light Brigade will miss him, too."

Nattie laughed. "All six hundred of them. Moses had dementia, and his medication made it worse. Last year he claimed that the valley had been infiltrated by Nazis. For at least a month he sat in a tree, binoculars around his neck, prepared to sound the call to arms. When he was hungry, he hollered for me to bring him rations. He dangled a cord so I could tie the bag to it, and then he'd hoist it up. At least I knew where to find him."

"Caron did that for a day when she was seven. She was on the lookout for Captain Hook and his pirates, although Farberville's five hundred miles from the Gulf of Mexico."

"If I were you, I wouldn't believe anything Moses said." She glanced around the yard. "Have you seen Jordan?"

I shook my head. "Not since I was in the kitchen at the Old Tavern."

"Margaret Louise will throw a fit if Jordan doesn't show up before dark, especially after talking to her parents last night. There have been times when she frightened me." She gave me an appraising look. "You wouldn't lie about this, would you? I know you feel sorry for her."

I met her gaze. "I have no idea where Jordan is right now. I have not seen her since I was at the Old Tavern several hours ago. If I knew where she was, I'd tell you. I'm worried about her, too."

"Okay," Nattie said. "I'll call you when she drags home."

"Thanks." I got in my car and drove down the driveway. The reporters, the TV vans, and the gawkers were gone. The police officers waved me through the gate, not having received the memo to search my car. I appreciated the silence when I arrived home. The boxes had bred in my absence; there were twice as many shoe boxes in stacks in the hall. I went out to the balcony. The afternoon had not been profitable in terms of piecing together any of the fragments that were banging around in my mind. It had been interesting, though. Felicia was not as timorous as

she pretended to be. She'd said that she and Winston
drank wine on occasion. I wondered if she had found her
way to the wine cellar after his death. After Terry arrived
on the scene, with rumors that he might sell the house,
the access would cease. It wasn't much of a motive for
murder.

She had confirmed that Danny Delmond had been to
her house, admittedly in a vague manner. In a very vague
and oblique manner, I corrected myself. She had said that
Charles's life was his church and the nursery, and he
would be devastated to lose either one. Although I'd yet to
see it, Danny might be able to transform himself into an
affable, charismatic businessman whose one goal in life
was to house homeless souls. Ethan and Nattie had told
me that they knew nothing about a development at Hollow Valley. That made sense, since Danny would start
with the alpha dog. Pandora Butterfly was the omega dog,
and Felicia was a chi or psi dog at best. If Charles was
even considering Danny's offer, he would have to convince Margaret Louise and Ethan. Moses would surely
have named the family corporation as his heir. Terry
wouldn't have agreed to anything that would benefit the
Hollows. Winston might not have, either. The first step
would have been to kill him. When the deed with right of
survivorship popped up, the second step was to kill
Terry—and it had to be done before he sold the property
to the wife of the deputy chief of the Farberville Police
Department. Angela had been in the way, requiring yet
another step.

I wanted to call Jorgeson and shout, "It's Danny Delmond! He did it! Lock him up and bury the key in your
rose garden." It was not probable that he would oblige. He
was methodical and overly attentive to procedure. Lacking imagination, he might ask for proof. Which was a

problem. Breaking into Danny's office was not a possibility, even with Caron and Inez's devious assistance. Inez's little brother could build an incendiary device to shatter the door, but I would have only a minute or two inside before I was arrested. Peter would not react well if his wife was accused of terrorism, no matter how minor the offense.

I had given up for the moment and was watching the sunset when I heard someone whistling "Three Little Maids from School Are We," a song from *Mikado*. I leaned forward and saw Billy Bobstay ambling by with an ornate walking stick.

"Hey, Yum-Yum," I called.

He stopped and squinted up at me. "I beg your pardon. My name is Pitti-Sing."

"Would you like to come up for a drink, Pitti-Sing?"

"At your service, Peep-Bo. Perhaps we can harmonize as the sun drifts below the horizon and night falls on the palace in Titipu. How should I scale the wall?"

"Try the front door and the stairs," I said, smiling. I was delighted to have a distraction. I went inside and opened my door. He was panting when he reached the final step, and his ears were pink.

"Thank goodness I didn't have to climb the ivy. It gives me a rash."

I fixed him a drink, and we went out to the balcony. "How was your jaunt to Missouri? The food must have been scrumptious," I said.

"Oh, yes, Loretta told me you were at her house yesterday. The trip was tedious, I must say. Samuel has taken up the accordion. He found it in his grandfather's attic. He swears that when he picked it up, he had a spiritual revelation that he'd been chosen to keep up the tradition. I dislike the accordion, but I absolutely loathe it in the hands of an amateur. We forced him to do all the driving,

but we did stop for lunch. Cars driving by honked in
protest. The cows in the pasture fled for the barn. Their
milk will be curdled for days."

"I trust the mission was accomplished without any
fatalities."

"As always," he said with a melodramatic sigh. "We
do this every few months so that Samuel can buy cheap
cigarettes. He simply refuses to admit that the cost of
gasoline negates any savings. It's the principle of the
thing."

"Cigarettes are cheaper in Missouri?" I asked. "Why
is that?"

"State tax. Nasty things, cigarettes. I much prefer
healthy vices." He grinned at me. "What are your vices,
Peep-Bo? Singing in the shower? Chocolate? I see from
the slight blush on your cheeks that you're thinking of
something naughty."

"I was thinking of Yum-Yum," I said, ducking my
head. "Do you mind if I ask you a question?"

He held out his empty glass. "I will ponder it, and
when you return I shall have come to a conclusion. Students have been asking me questions all day. My assistant
asked if he could take his vacation in July, of all things.
That's when we do our summer production. I told him if
he went on a cruise with his pretty boy, he might as well
buy a cabana in Cancún or some ridiculous place like
that." I tried to grab his glass, but he was waving his arm
to emphasize the implications of such treachery. "July,
mind you. We're doing *The Boys in the Band* this year.
I would be honored if you choose to attend."

I finally snagged his glass and went into the kitchen.
Billy had found a captive audience on my balcony and
might stay until midnight. All I could do was persevere in
hopes I could steer him in a more useful direction. I
handed him his drink and sat down, but before he could

continue discussing his next production, I said, "Did Loretta tell you what we talked about?"

"Are the two of you up to no good? I should warn you that despite her penchant for rebellion, at heart she's conservative. She likes men. I like men as well, but of a different sort."

"We talked about Winston," I said before he could elaborate. "Did he ever say anything to you about his relatives at Hollow Valley?"

"He resented them for the way he was treated as an adolescent, but he didn't despise them. I wish my parents had sent me to a boarding school when I came out to them. Instead, they hugged me. It was such a letdown. I'd envisioned a dramatic scene with tears and anguish, along the lines of *Who's Afraid of Virginia Woolf?* I got the von Trapp family. I would have begged to be sent to one of those British prep schools where the older boys flog the younger ones on their bare buttocks."

"It's never too late to apply. Did Winston say anything about selling his property to a developer named Danny Delmond?"

Billy blinked. "Why would he and Terry sell their new house? They enjoyed living here. I might prefer a house in Tuscany, with my own vineyard. A glass of vino, a plate of pasta, a houseboy named Guido—what more could anyone want?"

"You never heard Winston mention Danny Delmond?" I persisted.

"The name is not familiar. He did say that an uncle tried to buy the property. Apparently the uncle was a teensy bit uncomfortable having a gay couple for next-door neighbors. Winston and Terry thought it was hysterical. They said whenever the uncle tried to talk to them in a civilized fashion, his eyes bulged like golf balls." Billy widened his eyes and goggled at me.

I grimaced. "I've met the man, and received the same look. Did you talk to Terry after he came back from Italy and learned about Winston's death?"

Billy was quiet for a moment. "Yes. He came to Loretta and Nicole's place while I was there. He was in a rage. We were afraid he might hurt himself. I drove down the hill and bought a big bottle of vodka, tonic water, and a dozen limes. We drank with him until he passed out from exhaustion. Jet lag, and then the dreadful news. It was a very bad day."

"Yes, it must have been."

We sat for a long while, watching the sunset. Pedestrians walked by the duplex, heading for the restaurants on Thurber Street. Eventually the streetlights came on. I should have been thinking furiously, but I was too befuddled to bother.

Billy cleared his throat. "Winston told me something after they'd been living in the house for six months or so. It may be insignificant. One night he went for a walk, and when he reached the silly statue of Colonel Mustard, he heard a great deal of noise at the nursery. He concluded that the moonflowers and evening primroses were being shipped out under the cloak of darkness. I told him that was utter balderdash. He had a very self-satisfied expression on his face, but he refused to explain himself. Frankly, I doubted that he could. Now, my dear Peep-Bo, I must continue to my humble abode for a bowl of soup and a torturous evening of grading papers written by earnest nincompoops who have no idea about the importance of being earnest."

I waited at my front door until I heard him go out to the porch. He resumed whistling as he headed home. I could understand his displeasure at grading papers; I'd been a TA for three years and had groaned through many a mangled essay. I locked the door and made myself a sandwich. Like Winston, I'd heard noises from the nursery after dark. Moonflowers and evening primroses had not come to mind. With deliveries going to three states, the trucks would be on the road continuously. It was a busy season for dedicated gardeners and professional landscapers. My busy seasons, which weren't all that busy, occurred at the beginning of the fall and spring semesters, when unenthusiastic students dragged in with empty backpacks and shiny credit cards. I was as appalled as they were at the prices of textbooks, but I was smiling when they dragged out with laden backpacks and tarnished credit cards.

After I finished eating, I rinsed out the glasses and left them in the sink. It was getting late, and time flies whether or not you're having fun. I crawled into my bed and resumed reading a mystery. Scotland Yard was on the wrong track, convinced that the light at the end of the tunnel was the solution. It was too obvious, the amateur sleuth explained tactfully. They were in the wrong tunnel. Lord Brandywine had not murdered his wife for the insurance money. It was all about the estate.

CHAPTER 15

The next morning, braced with coffee, I called Attorney Cranberry's office. Her receptionist told me that Ms. Cranberry would be in court all day. I asked her to let Ms. Cranberry know that I'd called. I ate a piece of toast and called Jorgeson, who probably wished that he could hide in court all day.

"Ms. Malloy," he said flatly.

"Good morning," I said. "I suppose you heard about Moses Hollow's death yesterday. It's getting to be dangerous out there, isn't it?"

"Yes, I was informed of the death from natural causes. Surely you aren't going to suggest that it was murder."

That stopped me for a moment. "I wasn't, but it's not inconceivable. He might have seen something suspicious, you know. He was a free-range pain in the neck." I heard a drawn-out sigh that hinted of exasperation. "Have you heard anything new from the state lab? What about the fingerprints at Winston's house?"

"I have heard nothing from the state lab, Ms. Malloy, and I don't anticipate hearing from them for days, if not weeks. The only prints on the vodka bottle belonged to

the victim. This gives credence to the theory that someone tampered with the bottle and wiped off all the prints,
unless Kennedy was compulsive about hygiene. Elsewhere
we found numerous fingerprints, but none of them are in
the database. We have nothing to compare them to, unless
you'd like to come in and give us yours. That will rule out
half of them."

"Goodness, Jorgeson, you must have had trouble sleeping last night. Have you tried warm milk?"

"No, I have not," he said. "I will make a note of your
suggestion. If there's nothing else, I have a large pile of
reports to get through before a meeting at eleven."

"Wait!" I yelped before he could get rid of me. "I have
useful information for you. Danny Delmond lied about
his alibi for the weekend. His girlfriend did not stand him
up at the last minute. He stood her up so that he could be
alone at his lake house."

"I realize that this may be an alien concept for you, but
he may have wanted peace and quiet so that he could
work. There is no evidence that he is involved, Ms. Malloy. You dislike him. That does not give us cause to question him further. Why don't you buy some nice decorating
magazines to occupy yourself until Deputy Chief Rosen
gets back to town?"

I ended the call without a fond farewell. My face was
flushed from frustration, and my blood pressure was in an
elevator on its way to a penthouse. I stomped around until
I stubbed a toe on a box of dishes and had to hop to the
sofa. Jorgeson was not my ally. Conforming to police procedure would keep him occupied with paperwork and
meetings while the culprit chortled over his success.

There is a time to sit back with a magazine and a time
to charge ahead. The Light Brigade had not faltered in the
face of certain death. I would not falter in the face of contempt from Danny Delmond. If I called for an appointment,

I would not be invited to set foot in his office during the next decade. I was dressing myself in a black skirt, demure blouse, and black blazer when the phone rang. I do not care for eerie coincidences. I stared at the phone for a moment before I answered with a curt "Hello."

"Oh, Ms. Malloy, I'm so glad I caught you," said Inez's mother. She was a pleasant woman, dedicated to all things librarian. She always sounded slightly out of kilter with reality, and oblivious to her daughter's long history of brushes with the law. I do not believe in rocking other people's boats. "Would you please remind Inez that she has a dentist's appointment at eleven?"

"Inez isn't here," I said, trying to disregard the bells and whistles going off like fireworks on the Fourth of July. "The girls stayed at your house, didn't they?"

"Inez told me that they were staying at your house. Should I be worried?"

My eyes narrowed. "No, Ms. Thornton, I'm pretty sure I know where they were last night. I'll give Inez the message when I see her. It will be very soon." *My* house, in my dreams.

I managed to hang up without shattering the receiver. I called Caron's cell phone. It went to voice message immediately. I took off my shark-attack clothes and put on jeans and a T-shirt. I had driven to Hollow Valley so many times that I recognized individual weeds in the ditches and pockmarked county road signs. The reporters had lost interest, having nothing new to report. Mercifully, there was no police car parked by the arched sign. I drove very slowly to Winston's house, parked, and went around to the French doors.

No one was in the kitchen. I went down the hall and peered into the master bedroom. The king-sized bed was accommodating three prone bodies, all of them breathing. I made a pot of coffee and went out to the terrace, relieved but angry at Caron's deception. When I spoke to her via cell phone, she had said that Jordan was not in the graveyard. I'm sure she hadn't been at that particular moment. The three of them were elsewhere.

I let them sleep while I drank coffee and watched honeybees and butterflies feasting in the flower beds. Eventually I went into the bedroom and roused them with unnecessary zeal. Inez scrambled to find her glasses, and Jordan tried to hide under the tangle of sheets and cotton blankets. Caron slunk into the bathroom to work on her opening statement to be presented to a jury of one.

I waited in the kitchen, drumming my fingers on the countertop. Inez glanced at me as she went to the refrigerator and found a canned soda. Jordan avoided eye contact as she did the same. Caron opted for a defiant look. She perched on a stool and said, "It Wasn't My Fault."

Inez gaped at her. "Well, it wasn't my fault, either."

Jordan did not offer a disclaimer. I looked them over for a long moment, then said, "Would you care to explain? Please don't pretend that the Dearg Due chased you in here."

"Who?" Caron asked, her nose wrinkled.

"Never mind. You told me that you were spending the night at Inez's house. Inez, your mother called to remind you that you have a dentist's appointment at eleven. Jordan, there may be an APB out for you. Nattie's worried about you."

"So what?" Jordan asked.

Her flippancy impressed Caron and Inez. It did not impress me, however. "As soon as we conclude this little discussion, you are to go straight to the mill and apologize to Aunt Margaret Louise. You will then apologize to Nattie. Got it?"

"Yeah, sure. There's nothing more fun than being lectured for an hour—and that's if I'm lucky. Too bad Aunt

Margaret Louise can't put me on a bus home. My parents will have to cancel their vacation so they can drag me to a shrink. Been there, done that. The last one was this really old guy who could barely keep his hands off me. The one before that was a woman who wanted to be my BFF."

I waited until Caron translated it for me. "Then talk to me," I said. "Why did you disappear yesterday afternoon? Were you that distressed about Moses's death?"

"You don't get it, do you?"

"Get what?" asked Caron. "You promised to tell us everything."

Jordan shrugged. "That was last night. I'm tired of being accused of lying and exaggerating. I'll go get down on my knees in front of Aunt Margaret Louise and beg for forgiveness. I will follow all of Ethan's orders for the rest of the day, and possibly tomorrow. I will set the table and offer to do the dishes. I may hang around for Moses's funeral. He's the only one who treated me like a human being."

"Instead of unpaid labor," I said. "I understand why you're angry at them. I would be, too, if I were in your position."

"You're *not* in my position, Ms. Malloy. I may be a kid, but I'm not brain-dead. They think I am. They can keep on thinking that while I'm on the road to Springfield or wherever. When the driver stops to make a delivery, I can slip out and hitch a ride to Canada. I'll become a famous fishing guide and charge hundreds of dollars to take a bunch of guys out to the middle of nowhere."

"Fishing guide?" echoed Caron. "That's kind of yucky."

"You could become a supermodel," Inez said. "You'll be like really skinny if you live in the wilderness. You have great cheekbones."

Jordan touched her face. "Do you think so?"

I cut in before they started debating designers. "Yesterday I watched trucks being loaded. Unless you have the cheekbones of a boxwood, you won't have much luck escaping on a truck."

"You don't get it," she said again.

I was beyond frustration. "What don't I get?"

"You should have asked Moses," she said with a smirk.

I calculated the distance between us. I would have to pole vault across the island to grab her by the shoulders. In that I lacked a pole and the ability to vault, she was relatively safe. "How did you stow away on a delivery truck the first time?"

Caron and Inez were transfixed. Their eyes were locked on Jordan, who'd raised the bar to a much higher level—despite being three years younger. I was sure that they were comparing their antics to hers. She was rebellious and rude. She'd hung around street corners after dark. She had a tattoo.

Jordan looked at me. "I disguised myself as a flowering pear tree. I stuck some petunias between my fingers and held my breath."

She was still mad at me because I hadn't slain the dragons and rescued her from the dungeon. I was not unaccustomed to teenagers holding grudges. Caron still complains about being bested in the middle school science fair, even though the winner had analyzed chemicals in the local aquifer and Caron's sweet potato had rotted in a glass of water. I hastily revised my plan.

"You're so clever," I said admiringly. "Tell us how you did it."

She held out her arms and fluttered her fingers. "Use your imagination, Ms. Malloy. Pandora does a really good weeping willow. It brings tears to my eyes."

I retreated to the terrace before my baser instincts could kick in. Nattie had told me that Jordan had managed to stow away on a delivery truck. I'd watched two trucks being loaded. Unless Jordan was in cahoots with a workman, she could not have made herself invisible. Unless there was another way. I realized that I'd needed to inspect the trucks more carefully. Only Ethan, Charles, and forty workmen would present a problem. I revised my plan for the second time.

"Jordan," I said as I came back into the kitchen, "get off the stool and go to the mill right now. Caron and Inez, we have many things to talk about, but we shall do so later." I clapped my hands like a hard-hearted headmistress. "Move it, all of you!"

Caron made a final plea for the defendant. "You can't send her back to Those People. What about the Geneva Conventions? Aunt Margaret Louise destroyed her cell phone. She can't even tweet!"

"Neither can I," I said. "Tweeting is best left to songbirds. Don't forget your appointment, Inez. As for you, Caron Malloy—go to the Book Depot and give it a thorough cleaning. Sweep the floor, scour the bathroom, and dust the bookshelves. The new clerk can tell you what else needs to be done."

"That is so Not Fair," she protested with a squeak.

"Would you rather spend the day at the nursery? Ethan can find lots of jobs for you, such as picking spider mites off the begonias and spreading fertilizer."

"I didn't lie. You asked if Jordan was at the graveyard, and she wasn't. We really were going to Inez's house, but we stopped here to rest after that nightmarish hike. We were all covered with bugs and dead leaves and mud. We got in the pool for no more than half an hour, and then Jordan found a quiche in the freezer. It was going to go to waste, so we heated it and ate it. By then, it was too dark to go slogging across a pasture littered with cow poop and who knows what else."

"No zombies surrounding the house?" I asked sweetly.

Caron crossed her arms. "I am telling you the truth, Mother."

"I am not a priest who will hear your confession and absolve you on the spot. You did not call me—and don't pretend your cell phone died. The Book Depot or the Hollow Valley Nursery. Choose one."

Jordan snorted. "I'd rather scrub the urinals at a bus station than put up with Ethan yammering at me. Uncle Charles acts like he's seated on a throne, commanding the peasants to dig potatoes with their bare hands. Last week I snuck into the office to hide, but Uncle Charles caught me. He was so pissed off that spittle was flying everywhere while he yelled at me. I thought he was going to hit me."

Ethan had shown me the office. It was unremarkable. Magazines and brochures were stacked haphazardly in corners. There were maps on the wall of Arkansas, Oklahoma, and Missouri. A photograph of the family members preparing to cut a ribbon was hung in a place of honor. Other photographs were of Charles, Ethan, Nattie, and Margaret Louise in varied combinations at trade shows. The wall calendar depicted a cottage garden on a sunny day. It was very ho-hum.

"You'll be fine at Aunt Margaret Louise's house," I said to Jordan. I told Caron and Inez that I would drive them to the place where they'd parked the previous day. We left through the front door. Jordan took the path toward the Old Tavern and the mill. There was no conversation as I drove the girls a half mile down the county road and dumped them. It was not yet noon. I went to the duplex, changed back into my black suit, and drove to the square.

Delmond Enterprises Inc. occupied rooms on the second floor of a bank. I had no idea what to say that would elicit a confession. I had no choice but to trust my wits to keep me afloat. A woman with too many teeth smiled at me as I entered the reception room.

"Good afternoon," she said. "May I help you?"

"I need to speak to Danny Delmond."

She looked at her calendar. "I don't seem to have you down for an appointment today. Mr. Delmond is a very busy man. Would you like to schedule an appointment for later this week? He's free on Thursday morning. What time is convenient for you?"

"Right now," I said. "Please let him know that Claire Malloy is here."

Her smile withered. "As I said, he's a very busy man."

"Yes, you did say that." I sat down and opened a copy of *Architectural Digest* to photos of a modern atrocity, with a massive vaulted ceiling, exposed beams, and glass walls. There were no bookcases to distort the geometry. The expanse of hardwood flooring reminded me of a basketball court. I did not look up as the receptionist stood up and went down a hall. I turned to an ad for glossy black leather furniture on a pure white carpet. It would remain so only if the occupants had no feet. Peter and Caron invariably left a trail of grime when they came home. I was picturing Peter in a peculiar cup-shaped chair when the receptionist returned.

"Mr. Delmond will see you now," she said with icy disapproval.

I replaced the magazine and followed her to Danny's office. His diploma and contractor's license hung on the wall, along with photos of himself with golfers, politicians, obscure celebrities, and dead animals. A table was cluttered with blueprints and site maps. The room reeked of cigar smoke and masculine odors.

"Ms. Malloy," he said, "I've been wanting to talk to you. Please don't bother to sit down, because this will be brief. Stop meddling in my business. You may have menopausal notions that I am involved in the deaths at Hollow Valley, but I am not. Furthermore, stay away from my acquaintances."

I sat down. "Nanette is a nice girl, and she'll make a radiant bride. Have you set the date? For appearances' sake, you might wait until after Angela's funeral. You don't want to offend your friends at the country club." It was not wise of him to irritate me so early in the game. If "menopausal notions" was the best he could do, he might as well be the fish in the barrel.

"You're a real pain in the ass, Ms. Malloy. How can I convince you that I had nothing to do with Angela's death?"

"I'm not sure you can," I said bluntly. "You had motive, means, and opportunity. That's all it takes. You might be able to blame some of it on your accomplice, but you'll bear the brunt of it."

His face contorted in peculiar ways as he tried to control his temper. He gripped his coffee mug with such ferocity that I waited to see if it shattered. I was sorry that I didn't have a cell phone that could make a video. He glared at me from beneath his lowered brow. "Nanette told me that you questioned her about the weekend. I canceled our plans at the last moment because I wanted to spend some time with another woman. She is married. I will not give you her name so that you can pester her, too. I hope that satisfies you. As for a development at Hollow Valley, I did approach Charles Finnelly after a chamber meeting. He told me that the idea was preposterous. I redid my budget and went to his house with a rough draft of the development and a high offer. He turned me down again. When I got Angela's e-mail about Terry Kennedy, I admit that I was annoyed that she was even out there, but I had no motive to kill her, Ms. Malloy. The deal was already in the crapper unless Finnelly had an epiphany."

"Will he confirm this?"

He picked up the telephone receiver. "Want to call him and ask?"

"Maybe you're planning to kill him next."

He sneered. "Yeah, and then all the other family members, one by one. The police might not notice, but the heirs would be a tad suspicious. Then I'd have to kill them, too, and the next generation and the next generation. I do not intend to pursue the project into my eighties. I've made a bid on a forty-acre parcel on the other side of Farberville. Interested in a two-acre lot?"

"Why should I believe you? You lied to the police."

He would have thrown his hands in the air had they not been attached. "At this point I doubt I could convince you that I'm not Islamist with a bomb factory in the basement." He stood up. "Let me show you the drafting room."

We went to the next room. Roles of long paper poked out of bins. The fluorescent lights made me wince. Plats and survey maps were taped to the walls. The large drafting table dominated the space. A man with bushy eyebrows looked up as we came in. "Yeah?"

"Brad, Ms. Malloy has a deep interest in our business. Please show her the plans for Clover Creek. She's looking to build a new house." Danny poked me in the back. "Don't be shy. You have your choice of lots. I think you'll like the ones at the back. Wooded, and private."

I looked at the plat, with its streets, utilities easements, and neatly delineated lots. Writing in the corner declared it to be Clover Creek Planned Unit Development. "What about the Hollow Valley Development?" I asked Brad.

He put his fingertips on his forehead. "Jeez, I don't know where that stuff is. You can look in the storage closet. I can't promise we saved anything, though."

Danny gave me a patently fake smile. "Unless you want to do some digging, you're out of luck. Shall we return to my office?"

I desperately tried to come up with a theory to explain away Danny's account. Unless his employee was lying, he had given up his plan involving Hollow Valley. People did murder their spouses in the middle of hostile divorces, but usually when millions of dollars were at stake. From the size of Delmond Enterprises Inc., I could tell that any financial settlement would not make the front page of the *Wall Street Journal*. When we sat down in his office, I said, "Did you know Winston Martinson and Terry Kennedy?"

"I knew who they were. Kennedy didn't have a bat's chance of winning the lawsuit. There's not a judge in this town who would rule in favor of a faggot. His claim to the property was a bunch of baloney. Charles is the one who killed the project—not Kennedy, not Angela. I've never met any of the others."

I was beginning to deflate, but I wasn't going to display a wisp of doubt. "I will take this under consideration before I speak to Lieutenant Jorgeson. However, I insist on knowing the name of the woman who spent the weekend at your lake house."

Danny shuffled papers on his desk for a minute. "If I tell you, you have to swear not to repeat it to anyone. If you ask her, she'll deny it. Our reputations in this town will be destroyed if it gets out. I'll go broke in six months."

This woke me up. "I promise that I won't tell anyone unless it's relevant to the crime."

"Susie Bartleby," he said without looking at me.

"The real estate broker's wife?"

"We met at an office party. Things took off from there. If Bartleby finds out, he'll come after me like a bulldozer. She told him that she was visiting her college roommate."

It wasn't germane, but it was interesting. Since he'd withdrawn his fangs, I moved in. "I think Angela was having an affair. Do you have any idea who he might be?"

He wasn't overwhelmed by my observation. "Good for her. She was going to need someone when the plastic surgeons admitted defeat." He tapped a pen on his desk while he thought. "I haven't heard any gossip, so I don't think it was anyone in our social circle. She didn't have time to go out of town; she was at her damned lawyer's office almost daily. I can't help you, Ms. Malloy. Please show yourself out."

I did so. The town square had extensive flower beds, fountains, and benches for weary shoppers. I bought a cup of iced tea and sat in the shade. There had been one hitch in my brilliant theory, one that I'd chosen to overlook. Angela had e-mailed Danny the night before she disappeared. She hadn't told him that she was showing the house the next day. Fate was not so twisted that he'd called her at the house and arranged for his accomplice to be outside at the pertinent moment. What could he have said that would send her to her car without telling me? A bomb threat would have propelled her out the French doors to alert me, surely. Buyers are worth their weight in commissions.

The tea was watery by the time I faced the possibility that I was mistaken about Danny Delmond. He was vain and overly impressed with himself. Angela's harsher sentiments might well be true. What he wasn't, I thought glumly, was intelligent enough to formulate a complex plan in a limited time. This made for a substantial setback in my determination to solve the case before my adorable husband arrived home. Jorgeson smoked cigars (over Ms. Jorgeson's protests), but Peter wouldn't be bringing him a box of them from Cuba, Missouri.

Dejected, I went to the Book Depot to make sure that Caron was doing my version of community service. The clerk was fine-tuning the window display when I arrived.

Although he'd done a superb job, I felt obliged to suggest a few minute adjustments so that I wasn't totally extraneous. I found Caron seated behind my desk, reading a magazine. "Fancy seeing you here," she said. "Everything was already dusted, swept, cleaned, or alphabetized. I offered to help with the window display, but the guy said that he preferred to do it himself. He wouldn't even let me sort the mail. How long do I have to stay here, Mother? Joel wants me to go over to his house and play a new video game. We're going to a movie later." She sucked in her cheeks and gave me a puckered look. I couldn't tell if she was going for Oliver Twist or Beth March.

"We can discuss a reduction in your sentence if you tell me everything that took place after you went to search for Jordan. No evasions or omissions."

"I thought that that Delmond guy did it. Jordan doesn't even know who he is."

"Get out of my chair and start talking," I said.

She did as ordered, and after I'd taken my place behind the desk, she said, "Jordan was at the graveyard, ripping up weeds and throwing rocks at the squirrels. She was upset and majorly pissed at her aunt, Nattie, and you. She has an amazing vocabulary of obscenities. When she shut up, I told her why we were there. That got her all weepy, which was worse. I promised her that Inez and I would figure out something so she didn't have to sleep there. We were headed for my car when she chickened out and said she'd get in even more trouble if she left. She was afraid that you'd find out that she was at Inez's house and take her back to Hollow Valley."

That was a supposition that I was unable to deny. "Continue," I said coolly.

"So we went to the house to come up with another

plan. When no one had any suggestions, we decided to stay there. We didn't damage the place or anything. I'll pay for the stupid quiche out of my allowance."

"Tell me everything she said about Hollow Valley."

Caron rolled her eyes. "She carried on for hours about how mean they were and how badly they treated her. I expected her to claim that she was chained in the basement every night after she'd had her bread and water. You cannot believe how melodramatic a fourteen-year-old can be."

"Actually, I can," I said. "Try to be more specific, Caron. What was her problem with Ethan, for instance?"

"He didn't exactly do anything to her except make her work. No matter what she did, he'd tell her it wasn't good enough. He was nice about it, but he'd always tell her that she hadn't finished doing whatever and he didn't have time to supervise her. He'd sigh and try to lay a guilt trip on her. It's not like she applied for the job. Honestly, who would?"

"People who need to earn a living. Uncle Charles makes everybody miserable, and Aunt Margaret Louise isn't going to get top security clearance in this lifetime, but what about Nattie?"

"She's the only one who makes an effort to sympathize," Caron said, beginning to relish center stage. "Jordan said that Nattie listens to her, but then all she does is bake cookies or cinnamon rolls. Pandora Butterfly is a mental case. She doesn't listen to anybody except the voices in her head. That is one seriously stupid name, by the way. Jordan's furious at her because she stole the dried pot plants."

"That leaves Aunt Felicia," I said. "What's Jordan's opinion of her?"

Caron paused. "That she's as mean and bigoted as Uncle Charles but stays in his shadow. Anyone who'd marry that awful man has to have a bunch of screws loose."

That covered the family in residence. Jordan wasn't a

neutral observer; she saw them as her enemies. They were probably as tired of her as she was of them. She'd pushed the boundaries with me; she'd tried to breach theirs at every opportunity. There was one Hollow who'd had no boundaries. "Did she go to the graveyard because she was so distressed about Moses's death?"

"I wouldn't use the word 'distressed.' Nobody told her that he was sick. He promised to show her a cave where he found arrowheads, but when she wanted to go upstairs to make plans, Nattie wouldn't let her. The next thing she knows, her Aunt Margaret Louise goes upstairs to take him a cup of tea and discovers that he's dead. Jordan was so freaked out that she ran out of the house to the grave-yard. I think she kind of loved him, and didn't get to say good-bye."

"That's hard," I murmured. I'd let her down, too. "Did she tell you about her unsuccessful attempt to run away?"

"It was a hoot," Caron said with a giggle. "She was stuck in the back of the truck for hours and hours. She took a big bottle of water, so after jouncing for all that time, she absolutely had to pee. When the driver stopped to unload the plants, she tried to slither out while his back was turned. She said it was like she crawled out of a go-pher hole. The driver was so startled that she almost got away. He caught her and let her use the ladies' room and then made her sit in the cab all the way back. He was so mad that he wouldn't even buy her a hamburger. She had to use all her money to buy fries. He had the radio tuned to a country music station and sang all the way back."

"I watched the men load trucks. I don't see how she could have been in the truck without being spotted."

Caron held out her arms and wiggled her fingers.

"Get started on scrubbing the lavatory," I said crossly. "One more thing before you're overcome with self-pity. Is Jordan friendly with any of the workmen?"

"The men made lewd remarks. The women, all Hispanic, called her a *puta*. Do you know what that means?"

"I can guess. Once you've finished with the lavatory,
you can leave. I expect you home at a reasonable hour."

"When's Peter getting home?"

"Tonight, I hope." I took out my cell phone, which was
unresponsive. "I'd better go home and find out if he's left
a message. Scrub your heart out, dear. When you get out
of college and discover that there are no pain-free jobs,
you can apply to be a janitor. You'll have experience."

"You are so Not Funny."

I drove to my duplex, fetched the mail, and then regarded
the telephone warily. The red button was flashing. There
were many people who might have called. I told myself
that I could fast-forward through the tirades and hit
the button. The first was from Peter. The sound of his
voice reminded me of how much I missed him. When he
came through the door, my second order of business would
be to persuade him to extricate himself from the ATF task
force. The message was heartening; he expected to be in
Farberville by eight o'clock. The second message was
from Nattie, thanking me for sending Jordan home. The
third message was from Loretta, a.k.a. Esther, asking me
to come to her house.

It seemed like a plan. I changed back into jeans and
a T-shirt, feeling like a mannequin in a department store.
Traffic was minimal as I drove past the campus and up
the hill. I pondered what to tell her about her mother. The
scene from the previous afternoon had verged on gro-
tesque. All I could do was ease into it and watch her carefully. I'd promised Felicia that I would pass on her message.
Loretta would have to deal with it as she chose. As I
parked, I remembered that she'd called me. Earlier she'd

said that she might have something to tell me concerning Winston. I had an inkling of what it might be.

Loretta met me at the door. "Come on in. Let's sit in the kitchen if that's okay. It's the only room I've ever felt safe in, no matter where I was living. Funny, isn't it?"

"Maybe because it's the only room your father never entered," I said as we sat down.

She thought about it for several minutes. "That may be true. He was very big on a woman's place, and he didn't mean just the kitchen. My mother's place was also two steps behind him, with her mouth shut and her eyes downcast. There wasn't much lively conversation when I was growing up."

"I spoke to her yesterday," I began cautiously and then described what happened, downplaying, but not omitting, the excess of wine. She listened without expression until I limped to the conclusion. I had no clue whether she was going to explode with anger or fall over laughing. "If I shouldn't have told her about you, I apologize. I thought she deserved to know that you're alive and well."

Rather than overreact in either direction, she settled for a broad smile. "My mother, the closet drunk. I love it!" She raised her voice. "Nicole, are you busy? You've got to hear this!"

"I'm working on my closing statement for court in the morning," a voice called back. "You don't want some unlucky guy to be deported, do you?"

Loretta was still smiling as she said to me, "Do you know why I chose the name Loretta? It's not because I'm a fan of country music. I took it from the Litany of Loreto, which celebrates the great queens of the Bible, including Esther. It took me a long time to select it. I don't know what I'd have done if my name was Tiffany."

"What do you want me to tell your mother?" I asked gently.

She bit her lip. "I need to think about it. I don't want her to get in trouble with my father. Her life already sucks."

"If you decide to meet her, let me know and I'll get the information to her. I'm sorry to change the subject, but you wanted to talk to me about something."

"Oh, right. I completely forgot," Loretta said. "I suppose I'm in shock. Yes, I want to tell you what Winston said after he and Terry had been living in Hollow Valley for a few months. He was extremely sensitive to nuances in people's behavior. They pretended to welcome him home, but he knew that was hogwash. What bothered him was that they seemed to be afraid of him. One night when we were well into margaritas, he dragged me outside and warned me to stay away from them. He said it was because both of us are direct descendants, but he wouldn't elaborate. I told him that I would never claim my inheritance. As far as I was concerned, my parents were already dead to me, and the last thing I'd ever do was live in Hollow Valley."

"Why would they be afraid of him? At least half of Farberville knew he was gay, so there wasn't much he could do to hurt the family's reputation. He and Terry were living peacefully in their secluded house. Are you sure he didn't say anything else?"

"He may have, but I was drunk. Like mother, like daughter. The fruit of the poisonous tree. All that crap." She rubbed her temples. "What you told me has knotted my stomach. I need to go lie in the hammock and think it over."

"Keep in touch," I said as I left. I drove slowly down the steep hill, but by the time I reached the stop sign, it came to me.

The solution was buried in the family plot.

CHAPTER 16

All I needed was proof. Jorgeson, the fuddy-duddy, would not take action without it, and I couldn't wander through the meadow gathering bits and pieces of it like daisies. I went home and called Nattie.

After we made the polite noises, I said, "I wanted to see how Jordan's doing. Did she tell you what she, Caron, and Inez did last night? If I'd known, I would have put a stop to it immediately. Please pass along my apology to Margaret Louise."

"You don't need to apologize, Claire. I can remember some of the things I did as a teenager. I'm so grateful that she didn't run away and end up in a bad situation in a hostile little town." She chuckled. "Do I ever remember some of the stunts I pulled. I was clever enough to avoid getting caught—or arrested—but I had some close brushes."

"Me, too," I said, just to be amiable. I'd never done anything that remotely resembled a misdemeanor. Caron was payback. "Have you made funeral plans yet? I'd like to attend."

"It will be a private affair, family members only.

Moses's old friends have all passed away. I appreciate your gesture."

"Has the body been released?"

"We're waiting for the medical examiner to sign the death certificate. That should happen today, since there was no need for an autopsy. I'm going to miss the old coot and his senseless babble."

"It wasn't all senseless babble," I said slowly and carefully. "He had moments of clarity."

"Like I have the body of a ballerina. Tell me one thing he said that was intelligible and remotely plausible."

I counted to five. "Well, you may be right. It'll take me a while to come up with something. My husband's getting home tonight. I need to spend my time making him a lovely dinner and stocking up on champagne. I don't think I have a single candle in the house. I'd better get busy. Good-bye, Nattie."

I sat back and congratulated myself. She would share my remarks with everyone in the family, excluding Jordan. At least one of them would be very unhappy indeed. It was up to me to find out who flinched.

Before I galloped off to unmask the perpetrators, I needed some information. Caron was long gone from the Book Depot. The clerk might not be cooperative. I called Inez on her cell phone.

"How was your appointment?" I inquired.

She sounded as if she had a mouthful of crackers. "The dentist extracted two wisdom teeth, so I've got all this gauze packed in my mouth."

I felt obliged to offer a few words of commiseration, then got down to business. "I need for you to find certain data on the Internet. Do you feel up to it?" When she responded with a mumbled assent, I told her what I wanted to know. I could imagine her widened eyes, but I did not offer an explanation. Three minutes later she called back.

Due to her temporary speech impediment, it required effort and numerous repetitions for her to relay the numbers. "You were right about the truck hijacking," she added in an amazed voice. "Does this have anything to do with Hollow Valley?"

Since that was about the only place I'd been in more than a week, her question was logical. I didn't want to waste time elucidating my latest theory, so I gave her a vague response and hung up. Once the pain medication cleared out of her system, she'd figure it out on her own.

I drove past the Hollow Valley sign and parked where Caron had hidden her car. It required a long slog across an abandoned pasture with waist-high stalks and grasshoppers that whirred into my face. Creatures with wings buzzed me. To make the trek truly intolerable, I began to sweat. My armpits and back were wet and sticky. I was obliged to wipe my eyes. Sneezing did not lighten my mood. I stayed on the far side of the stream from the houses and nursery and finally stumbled into the family plot. I sank down to catch my breath.

As I recovered, I saw that I was sitting on Ethiopia and Lloyd. I wasn't sure if I should have begged their pardon, since I was not a member of the family. I opted for a smile of appreciation for their hospitality. The bridge to the back road was twenty yards away, behind a stand of oak trees and undergrowth. Boards clattered as a truck rolled across it. When the sound died, I made my way to the road, looked around, and then dashed across the bridge. I could hear voices as I crawled up the incline. I felt utterly ridiculous, but I did not want to be spotted by a worker taking a break outside the closest outbuilding. I pulled aside weeds and studied the grounds of the nursery.

Most of the employees were headed for the cars and trucks parked at the back of the graveled lot. They chattered as they crammed themselves inside. Carpooling seemed to be the norm. Ethan went into the office. A few workmen were squatting in the dirt, taking furtive puffs from their cigarettes and passing a bottle in a brown paper bag. Two of the delivery trucks were idle; the other two were on the road with their cargo of plants from the nursery. I had a fairly good theory about what else might be stashed inside.

There was no way to run across the open expanse without being seen. I needed a diversion, but I lacked the contacts to order an air strike. I lay in the prickly weeds, sweat oozing down my back, my teeth clenched. I berated myself for my bravado in assuming I could gain access to a truck. I tried to think of someone else to blame, but I was too distracted by my itchy ankles. I was nearly ready to admit defeat when I heard a tootling melody of sorts. Pandora Butterfly, dressed only in scarves, came capering into the far side of the field, a recorder held to her lips. Her hair was woven with red and yellow flowers. Rainbow and Weevil dragged behind her. I was startled to see that the latter held a hatchet in his grubby little hand. His expression suggested that he was stalking the Pied Piper of Hollow Valley.

Ethan emerged from the office, conferred with the workmen, and walked hurriedly in the direction of his family. The men climbed into their pickup trucks and drove toward me. I put my arms over my head and did my best to look like a fallen tree trunk with auburn leaves.

The trucks rumbled by and went down the slope to the bridge. I raised my head and scanned the grounds. Ethan, Pandora, and the children were gone. The delivery trucks appeared to be miles away, parked near a greenhouse. I waited for five minutes, then brushed unimaginable things off my clothes and stayed by the perimeter as I approached. The open padlocks on the back doors of the trucks dangled invitingly. I reminded myself that I wasn't going to steal anything, which could be used in my defense should I end up in a courtroom. Trespassing was no more than a minor breach of etiquette. When I could think of no reason to stall further, I trotted to the nearer truck, eased a door open, and climbed inside. I felt as if I'd escaped from Alcatraz, but no sirens erupted and no shots were fired. The interior of the van was smaller than its exterior suggested, as I'd noted earlier. In a matter of seconds, I'd slid open a panel in the back to reveal a three-foot space. Jordan would have been cramped, but there was room for her to sit and swill water until her bladder betrayed her.

In mystery fiction and movies, someone would have slammed the doors and engaged the padlock. I would have been driven to a remote locale and ordered to climb out of the truck. The men would have evil grins and large semi-automatic weapons. Depending on the genre, I would have been either gunned down or rescued by a rogue hero armed with a dimple. As it was, I slid out of the back of the truck and ran to a narrow stretch between two of the greenhouses. I found an overturned clay flowerpot and sat down. There was no legitimate explanation for the concealed spaces, only an illegitimate one. Hollow Valley Nursery was importing and exporting goods that were regulated by dear Peter's ATF colleagues. If I hadn't dismissed Moses as a flake, I might have caught on earlier. My brilliant deduction, confirmed in my mind, was inadequate to bring Jorgeson and his troops rushing in with search warrants. If HVN was currently in export mode, the warrants were futile. My next step required finesse. As the council of mice had opined in the medieval cautionary tale, belling the cat was not a simple task. The best approach, I finally decided, was to try to have a private conversation with Nattie. Like Winston, she might have had a hunch that all was not as it seemed in the family business.

When I reached the edge of the green, I paused to assess the situation. The Mercedes and the Mustang were parked under a tree. I could hear loud music in the distance. Margaret Louise was paying homage to Jefferson Airplane. Perhaps the cocktail hour had arrived early. I wondered if Jordan was cowering in her bedroom, appalled by her aunt's taste in a hopelessly dated genre. There was a good chance that Nattie was alone. I looked in the backyard, where I saw her on her knees in front of a flower bed. I cleared my throat and, when she looked back, said, "Do you mind if I sit down?"

"Help yourself," she said. "I'm digging up daffodil bulbs. They were splendid this year. I have a special vase for them that I put on the kitchen table all spring. Do you know anything about them?"

"I can recognize them," I admitted.

"Daffodils belong to the narcissus group. They originated in the countries around the Mediterranean Sea, from Spain and Portugal to the Middle East. Romans brought them to Britain. Now there are twenty-five thousand registered cultivars. Isn't that remarkable?"

"Yes," I said with what enthusiasm I could muster.

Nattie put down her trowel and took off her straw hat to wipe her forehead with the cuff of her shirt. "You'll have to forgive me," she said as she sat down near me. "I'm a card-carrying member of the American Daffodil Society."

"Will you be offended if I ask you about the family?"

"I hope you're not going to bring up Great-Great-Uncle Alvin Shanks Hollow. He traveled in a buggy and sold bottles of unguent that he claimed cured erectile dysfunction. I believe it contained daffodil sap, which is what made me think of him. It caused a rash that kept the men out of their wives' bedrooms for a week. Alvin utilized the opportunity to make sure that the prettier wives produced babies nine months later. He was hanged in Maxwell County in eighteen ninety-four."

"With a smile on his face?"

"So the story goes," Nattie said, chuckling. "Would you like some iced tea? I have fresh mint, and I made some gingersnaps this morning. I need a break."

She went through the kitchen door. I wandered over to the flower bed. Nattie's daffodil bulbs were in a burlap bag, and small marigolds and petunias had been planted in some of the holes. A dozen more plants waited their turn. Red poppies swayed in the breeze while snapdragons bobbled behind them. I pictured myself in cotton gloves and a broad-brimmed hat, wielding a trowel to dig little holes and plant a variety of flowers. I would not be sweating, or even perspiring. I would have the healthy glow of an accomplished horticulturist, responsible for the expanse of exquisite beauty. Peter would choke back tears as he swept me into his manly arms.

"Here we are," Nattie said as she emerged from the Old Tavern. "The cookies are not my best. I was thinking about Moses and almost substituted curry powder for cinnamon, and I couldn't recall if I'd already added the baking soda." She put the glasses and the plate of cookies on a side table. "I feel twenty years older today. Now that Moses is gone, I don't know if I want to live here much longer. My only role was to take care of him." She seemed dazed as she handed me a glass of iced tea. "How pathetic."

"Maybe you can get involved in the nursery," I said. "You have a remarkable talent for growing things. You can expand the variety of stock and offer yourself as a landscape consultant."

"I could, but I'm not sure that's what I want to do. The Old Tavern already feels empty. I used to think that the creaks were from Moses creeping around at night. Last night I couldn't sleep, and I found myself considering the possibility that the place is haunted. I don't want to share the house with Colonel Moses Ambrose Hollow and his deceased offspring." Her smile was forced. "No, I don't believe in that nonsense, but the last slice of strawberry pie was gone this morning. I am not going to bake for a bunch of dead people."

"Ask Jordan before you spend all your money on a ghostbuster." I could think of no way to rely on tact to elicit the information I wanted. "Nattie, there's something going on at the nursery—something illegal."

She put down her glass with an unsteady hand. "What do you mean? Is Ethan growing marijuana? I don't see how he could get away with it. There are forty employees in and out of the greenhouses all day—and don't forget Charles. He would never allow such a thing." She continued to stare at me. "Or maybe those cacti that have hallucinogenic buttons? Mescaline, I think."

"Not something he cultivates. He's transporting stolen property across state lines. That's a felony that will bring down the feds on him—and anyone else who has knowledge of it."

"I don't believe it. Ethan loves the nursery more than anything. He would never do anything to put it in jeopardy."

I told her about the secret compartments in the delivery trucks. "That's where the contraband is stashed, and where Jordan hid when she tried to run away. Ethan was lucky that she didn't demand to know the purpose of the compartment. There's no other explanation."

"I don't believe it," she repeated. "Ethan's not a criminal. He's infatuated with organic pest control and plant food. When he finds a frog in a greenhouse, he takes it to the stream to set it free. He scoops up spiders and carries them outside. If that's not enough to dissuade you, he puts up with Pandora Butterfly. It's easier to believe he might strangle her than deal in contraband. You're wrong, Claire."

"Winston suspected that something was going on. He told . . . a friend that everyone out here was afraid of him."

"Afraid of Winston? That's rubbish. I loved Winston. I grant that there were mixed emotions when he and Terry moved into their house. Charles and Felicia were aghast, of course. Ethan made several attempts to be friendly. Margaret Louise never said much about them, and Pandora may not have even noticed. Why would any of us be afraid of Winston?"

"Because there is something going on," I said flatly. "Think about it, Nattie. I saw delivery trucks come and go late at night, when only a couple of workmen were around."

"I assume it's so the produce can be delivered in the morning. Some of the buyers are hours away. If a driver starts his route at night, he can be in Texarkana by the end of the next day."

"What about the secret compartments?"

"I don't have a clue," she said with a shrug. "Why don't you ask Ethan?"

"I don't—" I searched for a word, but it eluded me. I tried again. "I don't want him to—" To what? My mind was blank. The mountains across the valley were shimmering with an unnatural light. I looked at Nattie, who nodded at me. The last thing I remembered was my face in the cool grass.

I awoke in a dimly lit room. Dark wood beams traversed the ceiling. Sunlight cut through a slit in the heavy drapes. I had no idea where I was, but I did know that my head was reverberating like a gong. My eyes were gritty; my mouth was dry. I licked my lips while I pondered my current dilemma. I was lying on a bed, which meant I was in a bedroom. I congratulated myself for establishing one fact. My mind was sluggish, but I persevered. The beams suggested that I was in the Old Tavern. I clung to the thought as I dozed off.

When I opened my eyes the second time, the beams were still holding up the ceiling but the sunlight was gone. My headache had eased into a dull pain. I forced myself to sit up before I relapsed into sleep. I was pleased to note that my hands and feet were not restrained. The light now emanated from a lamp on a small table across the room. The floor was covered with a braided rug of many colors. I was studying the pattern when Nattie came into the room.

"Thank goodness you're awake," she said as she gave me a damp washcloth. "You must have been exhausted. We were talking, and then you got a peculiar look on your face and toppled out of the chair. I nearly had a heart attack. When I knelt down, you kept saying that you were sleepy. I wanted to call for an ambulance, but you insisted that all you needed to do was rest. Your eyes were open and your breathing was normal. I helped you up, and we staggered inside and up the stairs. I've been looking in on you every ten minutes." She clasped my hand. "I'm so glad that you're okay, Claire. There have been too many tragedies in Hollow Valley."

"I didn't pass out?"

"Only for a few seconds. On our way upstairs, you told me all about your handsome husband and your daughter. Some of your stories are really funny." She gave my hand a squeeze and stood up. "I'll go downstairs and make you a cup of hot tea, unless you'd prefer something else."

I had no memory of telling her stories, although I must

have. I hoped whatever else I'd told her was worthy of my wit. "What time is it?"

"A bit after eight. Do you like honey in your tea?"

"*Merde!* My husband will be frantic if he gets home and I'm not there. I'd better call him. Did you bring my purse up here?"

"It was the least of my worries. You need to make sure you're okay before you try to get up. I'll be back with your tea in a few minutes." Nattie gave me a worried look, then left on her mission.

My body felt heavy, and it was an effort to swing my legs over the side of the bed. The walls seemed to be trembling, as if there were an earthquake of minor magnitude. The side of my face was sore from the impact, but there was no dried blood or hint of a bump. The flawlessness of my complexion did little to mitigate my embarrassment. I considered the possibility that my blood sugar or blood pressure had plummeted for an unknown reason. I'd sweated like a waterlogged sponge during the hike. Dehydration could have caused the light-headedness.

I decided to find a bathroom and slurp water from the faucet. I rose, waited for my knees to assume their duty, and walked to the door. The knob turned, but the door would not open. Telling myself that it was stuck, I yanked as hard as I could. It failed to yield more than a centimeter. I realized that Nattie had hooked it on the other side. She might have worried that I might stagger out and take a dive down the stairs, I told myself as I sat down on the bed. The dehydration theory seemed less and less probable as I thought over the previous events. I hadn't faltered during the sprint to the delivery truck, nor had I felt any discomfort afterward. I'd almost finished the glass of iced tea, which should have revived me. *Au contraire,* I thought darkly.

There was no point in pounding on the door of what had been Moses's bedroom. Presumably Nattie was aware of my predicament, having caused it from the moment she doped my iced tea. I seemed to have recovered with only a headache. I refused to allow myself to think about Terry Kennedy, who hadn't. I scolded myself for being duped by Nattie, with her wide grin and cinnamon rolls.

I crossed the room and raised the window. I leaned out as far as I dared. No rogue heroes with dimples were waiting in the shadows. Within twenty minutes, it would be dark. I searched the room for a makeshift weapon. The lamp was too cumbersome to assure accuracy. I found galoshes in the closet, along with Moses's scant wardrobe, but no golf clubs or lacrosse sticks. Clutching a rolled-up newspaper from nineteen forty-five that trumpeted the bombing of Hiroshima, I put my ear to the door. I heard low voices. In that no one was shouting, I ruled out Charles. Felicia would not be there, either, unless she'd stabbed her husband and rolled his body down to the stream. I was ready to eliminate Pandora Butterfly for obvious reasons but caught myself. Dancing naked in the field could have been a ruse to convince everyone that she was harmless. I'd seen her harder side. It had not been an act.

I heard footsteps coming up the stairs. I weighed my chances of overwhelming Nattie with a brittle newspaper and then hurriedly got into the bed and feigned sleep. Peter had once accused me of snoring, which was absurd. I opted to snuffle just a bit. "Claire?" whispered Nattie. "I brought you a cup of tea."

I breathed slowly and deeply, as if I were entangled in the arms of Hypnos while Morpheus perched on the end of the bed, cheering. Nattie may have missed the aesthetics, but she closed and hooked the door. I waited for a few minutes and then resumed my position at the door. The discussion continued. I had a very bad feeling that I was at the top of the agenda. It did not seem prudent to linger until they arrived at a decision.

The drop from the window was not a viable choice unless I was willing to risk broken ankles. I yanked the sheets off the bed and began to twist them. It was the standard escape technique in fiction, and often successful. I tied the sheets together, tied more knots for my feet to slow me down, and then tossed my makeshift rope out the window. It landed in a jumbled puddle on the grass. "Oops," I said under my breath. There was clearly more to the scheme than I'd remembered. I was leery of pacing, since the floorboards would creak. I wondered if I'd end up like Angela. My car was not camouflaged with branches, and the car keys were in my purse. My car would be found in some deserted clearing in a nearby county. I hoped my body would not be found in the same area. Being buried in Maxwell County was an insult. Nattie might not believe in ghosts, but I would make her life intolerable. Stealing a piece of pie was child's play. She would never drink a glass of tea without looking over her shoulder.

I stopped myself from edging into hysteria. I was glib, I was intelligent, and I was much wilier than they could ever expect. Ethan, who had to be one of the perpetrators, had muscles, but he was mellow. Nattie could outbake me, but I was quicker. Whoever else was downstairs would not anticipate my artful feints. I would make it outside and then run like a bat out of hell.

My adrenaline was pumping when the door opened. I grabbed the newspaper and lunged at the door. Jordan neatly stepped out of the way and caught my arm before I crashed into the wall. She closed the door and pushed me back to the bed. "You'd better sit down, Ms. Malloy. You look pretty awful."

"What are you doing here?" I asked between gulps.

"Letting you out."

"That's not what I mean." I rubbed my face until I felt calmer. "Why are you here?"

She shrugged. "Inez called me and said I should watch out for you. I saw what happened in the backyard. I couldn't use the front door or the kitchen door, so I opened the window in the storage closet and wiggled inside. I had to wait forever before I had a chance to come upstairs. Why did you throw the sheets on the ground? Was that a signal?"

"Of course," I said firmly. "It's a distress signal used by the armed forces. How do we get out of here?"

"Can I spend the night at your house?"

Her bargaining chip was much larger than mine. Once I'd nodded, she said, "There's a back staircase. Once we get to the ground floor, we can go out the same window." She assessed my body. "It may be a tight squeeze."

"I can assure you that it will not be any sort of squeeze," I said, offended. "Who's downstairs?"

Jordan shook her head. "I just heard voices. Do you want me to go eavesdrop?"

"Let's just get out of here, okay?" I gave her a nudge. The back staircase was next to a linen closet. The boards groaned like haunting Hollows as we picked our way cautiously to the bottom. Jordan led the way to a cramped closet and stepped on an upturned bucket. Her body sailed out the window before I could blink. I eyed the bucket. It was plastic and had cracked over the years. The room reeked of ammonia. Unable to take a deep breath, I stepped on the bucket, offered a prayer to Greg Louganis, and propelled myself out the window. My landing was not flawless. Jordan pulled me to my feet and grabbed my hand. I limped as quickly as I could to the edge of the woods.

Once we were safe, I examined my body for protruding bones and copious bleeding. My knee was raw, and my

ankle throbbed ominously. I felt more clearheaded, however. "Inez called you?"

"Yeah, she was stoned out of her mind on pain meds. I
thought she was joking, but she convinced me that you
were here and liable to get yourself in trouble."

Being rescued by a fourteen-year-old was barely palat-
able. "You did a good job, and I thank you. I need to stay
here for a few more minutes. We can meet at Winston's
house. Don't turn on any lights."

"Miss out on the fun? I don't think so." Her smile was
angelic as she gazed at me, but we both knew that she
wasn't waiting for my permission.

"Will you at least stay right here?" I asked.

She ran across the yard and disappeared into the bushy
plants alongside the house. I said something that was unseemly and then limped until I caught up with her. We
crawled under the foliage until we reached the kitchen
window. Jordan peered inside and then sank down. "Aunt
Margaret Louise is drinking whiskey from a flask.
Charles and Felicia look like they've been stuffed. The
taxidermist used yellow glass marbles for their eyes. It's
really funny, Ms. Malloy. Look for yourself."

I ignored her invitation. "What about Ethan and
Nattie?"

"Ethan's sitting at the table, looking pissed. I didn't see
Nattie."

She started to rise, but I caught her wrist. "Nattie must
be upstairs, wondering what happened to me. I engaged
the hook on the door, so she'll assume I went out the window."

"Right up until she notices that you're not sprawled
facedown in the grass, whimpering in pain." Jordan
started to giggle, but I clamped my hand across her
mouth.

"That's enough, young lady. This is serious. Go to

Winston's house and call Inez. Tell her that I said to contact Lieutenant Jorgeson immediately. If you don't, you'll be sleeping in the mill until the geese migrate for the winter."

"What about you? I rescued you once. What if they catch you again?"

I poked her chest. "Go, Jordan. I'm going to wait twenty minutes, then go inside for a chat with those people. I'm counting on you." I gave her a hug and a push. "Stay at Winston's house."

Her lower lip was out, but she ran across the grass and into the woods. I leaned against the stone wall and watched my wristwatch. I heard Nattie asking if anyone wanted more tea. If she'd mentioned my absence, I didn't hear it. Ethan said something that made Charles sputter. His obedient wife said nothing. It was a family council meeting, minus Pandora, who was likely to be twirling in the moonlight or careening down a highway on the back of a motorcycle. I was forced to admit I'd made an egregious error about the power structure—as well as about Danny Delmond. My nearly perfect record was tainted, if not besmeared. I idled away ten minutes trying to come up with bona fide excuses for my minute lapses in detective prowess. The next ten minutes were devoted to putting together the puzzle pieces.

When twenty minutes were up, I crawled out from under the bushes, ran my fingers through my hair, and walked through the kitchen doorway. It was definitely a showstopper. Nattie turned pale and grabbed the counter to steady herself. Charles shot me his customary glare of contempt. Felicia looked down at the floor. Ethan sloshed tea from his cup, splattering his overalls.

Margaret Louise was the only one who seemed delighted to see me. "Oh, hello, my dear," she trilled. "Back again so soon? You must join our little party. Nattie's gingersnaps are divine." She fluttered her fingers at me. "What have you been up to lately, you naughty thing? Nattie told us that you broke into one of the delivery trucks. We're debating about calling the police. What do you think?"

"I've already called the police," I said.

"Let me fix you some tea," Nattie said hastily. "You seem very agitated. Tea is so soothing, don't you think?"

"Especially when it's laced with an herbal concoction," I said. "You should have used something lethal, like you did with Terry."

She approached me. "Claire, you're not making any sense. It's possible that you had a stroke earlier this afternoon. I insist on calling an ambulance. Sit right here and try to stay calm."

"Terry?" said Felicia, startling all of us. "Nattie did something to Terry?"

"To Terry, and to Winston," I continued. "He was a threat to the family business—or should I say the family plot? You all were afraid that he'd realize what was going on and call the feds on you. His family ties were shredded when he was growing up here."

"Balderdash!" Charles thundered. His face turned red, and bubbles accumulated at the corners of his mouth. "Winston Martinson was a sinner in the eyes of an angry God! He had no business coming back here to taunt us with his—his so-called friend. Terry was nothing more than a prostitute!"

Felicia dumped her tea on his head. "Why don't you just shut up for once in your life? Everybody's sick of listening to your bigoted tirades."

"Quiet!" he said, trembling so violently that I had hopes he might levitate.

Her response was terse yet colorful and does not bear repeating. It was adequate to reduce him to rumbling, thus ruining my pipe dream.

Margaret Louise poured a dollop from a flask into her teacup. "Can you back up those accusations, dear?"

"I have all the proof I need," I said levelly. "I thought all of you needed to hear the truth."

Nattie laughed. "My herbs have gone to your head, Claire. I would never harm Winston or Terry. Exactly what proof do you have?"

"Yeah," Ethan said, "tell us."

The spacious kitchen was getting smaller. The air was laden with unspoken threats. It occurred to me that I might be making my third egregious error of the day. I studied their faces for any hint that I had an ally. Felicia, possibly, I thought, although I couldn't count on her to grab a skillet and defend me. I was getting increasingly uncomfortable, but I willed myself not to blink as they watched me. Whatever might happen, I vowed, I would not sweat.

CHAPTER 17

I crossed my arms. "How long have you been smuggling cigarettes from Missouri? Years, I suppose. The state taxes there are much lower than the ones in Arkansas. The markup is more than eighteen dollars a carton. I don't know how many cartons are in a case, but there would be a nice profit for you as well as for the vendors. If you happen to come across a truck with a load of untaxed cigarettes, somewhere in the vicinity of Cuba, the profit's higher. I don't believe that loud thumping noise comes from a washing machine or dryer. You have some sort of machine in the basement that puts on counterfeit tax stamps."

Felicia was the only one who looked shocked. "Is this true?"

"No way," Ethan said. "You're off your meds."

I waggled my finger at him. "I was going to get around to you later, but now's as good a time as any. You were having an affair with Angela Delmond." I paused to make sure I had everyone's attention. "You two met at Winston's house whenever you could. She had to be cautious because of the divorce. I'd like to think that Pandora was home while you were carrying on with Angela. You do have a responsibility to your children." Who might burn the house down, left unattended. "It was convenient, wasn't it, Ethan?"

Charles leaped to his feet, his fist raised. "Blasphemy, Mrs. Malloy! Husbands and wives do not violate the sanctity of their vows! Furthermore, Ethan is a direct descendant of Colonel Moses Ambrose Hollow. He would never sully the family's name!"

This time Felicia bonked him on the head with a saucer. "If you don't shut your mouth and sit down, the conversation's going to get a lot more interesting. I'm not the one who has an account at Victoria's Secret."

Her unspoken threat was effective. Charles plopped down like a sack of turnips and gazed at the floor.

Ethan was not so easily cowed. "You have no evidence. You need to be restrained in a padded room until you're coherent. As Uncle Charles said, I'm a married man with a family."

"You're right about the evidence," I said, "but the police are thorough. Are you going to be able to explain why your fingerprints are on the bedside table? There might be DNA in the silk sheets." I politely disregarded his expletive. "It took me a while to realize that you had to be Angela's lover. You saw her SUV turn on the driveway to Winston's house, and you were worried. You made a call to Angela on her cell, probably demanding an explanation or threatening to expose the affair, and told her to meet you at your house immediately. She must have thought she could deal with you and be back at the house in less than five minutes. Otherwise, she would have fetched me and coughed up a plausible reason for us to leave."

"Ethan?" Margaret Louise said. "Is this true?"

He tried to stare me down, but he was woefully inept. "So we were sleeping together. No big deal. Pandora insists that we adhere to the Kama Sutra. It's fine if you're twenty years old, but I work all day at the nursery, lifting heavy plants and weeding on my hands and knees. It was nice not to have to contort myself like a three-legged pretzel."

Charles's ears quivered, but he kept his head lowered. Felicia covered her mouth to keep from laughing. Margaret Louise felt no such restraints. Only Nattie watched somberly from her position near the sink.

"If I may continue," I said, "Ethan lured Angela away from the house and bashed her with a shovel. Her SUV was put on a truck and abandoned in Maxwell County. Her body was stashed in the outbuilding with the cooling unit. When I started asking questions, Ethan buried her in the pot patch. Did you hope that you could implicate Pandora?"

Ethan was too stunned to offer a rebuttal. I allowed him to squirm while I listened for cars pulling up outside. I heard a whip-poor-will and a tree frog. I furtively glanced at my watch. Jorgeson should have arrived ten minutes earlier. Nattie's unblinking stare unnerved me. I had no choice but to continue.

Meeting her stare, I said, "Winston must have confided his suspicions to you. You lured him to the stream. Everything was fine until you and Ethan found out about the deed that gave Terry the right of survivorship. Maybe Winston had told you about his concerns, or maybe not. Terry was a threat, because he was going to sell the house to the wife of the deputy chief." I was loath to delegate myself to a subsidiary menace, but I had to admit it made for a better story. A story that I needed to keep unraveling until the police arrived.

Nattie raised her eyebrows. "I do think that I should call an ambulance. You're making no sense, Claire."

"Moses rarely made sense, did he? You told me several times to ignore his garrulous ramblings, and most of the time I did. He did, however, have lucid moments. When Terry was on the kitchen floor, writhing from the onset of the poison, I saw Moses on the terrace. I asked him later why he'd been there, and he told me that he wanted to have a word with Terry. He must have known that Terry had arrived the previous night. I could offer a hypothesis of what he wanted to tell Terry, but it doesn't really matter. It was about nine o'clock at night when Terry got to the house, and I showed up soon after that. Moses wandered home to the Old Tavern to have his milk and cookies before bedtime. The only person with whom he might have shared his news was his devoted caretaker."

Felicia, Charles, and Margaret Louise were watching with perplexed expressions. Rather than confront Nattie, I looked at them. "Nattie had access to the house, as all of you did. I don't want to hurt your feelings, but she's the only one with the knowledge to poison the vodka with an elusive substance. Earlier in the week, Lieutenant Jorgeson told me that the lab had ruled out the garden-variety poisons. He meant arsenic, strychnine, and cyanide, things like that. When more testing is done, I believe it will actually be something from the garden. You were digging up daffodil bulbs this afternoon, Nattie. Were some slivers destined for my next cup of tea?"

Margaret Louise stood up. "I can't listen to this any longer. If what Claire said is true, you should be ashamed of yourself, Nattie!" She left through the kitchen door.

Nattie shrugged. "I would never poison your tea, Claire. If you'd ask for a vodka and tonic, well, I can't make any promises. It's not as easy as you think. One has to grate the bulbs, let the pulp diffuse in vodka for weeks, and then meticulously strain it. I keep a variety of my herbal concoctions in a cabinet in the garden shed. One never knows when one might need to . . . modify the situation. Terry would have lived a long and happy life if he'd stayed away. It wasn't my fault that he popped up like a ragweed stalk. That was *your* fault, Claire."

I had a confession, but I had no idea what to do with it. Felicia was gaping at Nattie, and Charles was too stunned to speak. Ethan appeared to be numb. I began to feel rather idiotic, having gone through the steps for a grand denouement that should have resulted in something more dramatic. I was out of accusations. It seemed prudent to stall.

"What did you put in my tea, Nattie?"

"Calendula and a few sprigs of catnip. The proper dosage is soporific. A little too much is fatal. I wanted to find out what you knew and if you'd said anything before"— she shrugged—"I adjusted the dosage."

"When I met you, I hoped we could be friends," I said with a trace of umbrage. "You're not like these people."

She took a step toward me. "Nevertheless, I am a Hollow. That's why I cannot allow you to repeat these accusations to anyone."

"It's too late. The police are on the way."

"Are they? I haven't heard anything outside." Her hand was behind her back as she continued to move toward me.

"Don't make things worse," I warned her as I inched backward, feeling for the doorknob.

"What's wrong with you, Nattie?" Felicia asked suddenly. "Is what she said true? You killed Winston? How could you?"

Nattie's eyes brimmed with tears. "I didn't mean for him to die. I've loved him since I was fourteen. He loved me, too, although he was too awkward to show it. We read poetry together next to the stream. I could hear the emotion in his voice, the yearning to embrace me with all his heart. When he tried to explain why he couldn't, I could see the confusion on his face. All I could do was wait for him to cast away his tangled fantasy and come home to me."

"He was gay," I said.

"No, he wasn't! He was confused, that's all. That's why I waited twenty years for him. He loved me, and I knew he would come home." Her voice grew raspy. "Then when he did, he brought Terry with him. Do you know why he did it? To get back at the family! He wanted"—she turned to face Charles—"to rub their faces in the dirt. Don't you understand that it was a ruse? He wanted revenge."

"He was a pervert," Charles croaked.

Her eyes blazing, Nattie slapped his face. "How dare you! Winston was pretending, that's all. You have no right to speak ill of him. He was a better man than you. That's why you banished him from Hollow Valley. But he came back, didn't he? He laughed at you, he mocked you. You were an object of his contempt. He saw through your pretenses. He knew that you beat Esther until you drove her away."

"That's a lie!"

"Winston never told lies, you hypocrite!"

I decided to intervene before things got out of hand. "Was he lying when he told you that he loved Terry?"

Nattie turned on me. "Winston loved me, but he couldn't admit it. I tried so hard to explain it to him that dreadful day. I got on my knees and begged him to be honest. Instead, he sighed and stood up."

"Then you pushed him," I said softly.

"I tried to grab his arm to keep him from walking away. He jerked back and slipped in the mud. I never meant to hurt him, Claire."

"Then who put the fishing gear and wine bottles on the bank?" asked Felicia.

She rubbed her temples. "I don't remember. Maybe I did."

"Moses probably contributed the wine bottles," I said. "I suspect he saw the whole thing from his vantage point in the orchard and wandered down later to get a better look. That's why he had to die."

Nattie shook her head. "No, he was old and his time had come. He deserved the dignity of dying peacefully in his own bed. I took him cookies and a nice glass of milk. I was a little worried the milk might taste funny because of the poppy sap, but he drank it and fell asleep."

Ethan came out of his stupor and banged a fist on the table. "You put Moses down like an old dog? How could you, Nattie?"

"He *was* an old dog—incontinent, slobbery, smelly. How many times did you offer to take him to the doctor or clean up his puke? I couldn't let him go around blabbing about what he knew."

"Then you should have confined him."

"Where? In your guest bedroom? Margaret Louise didn't offer, nor did Charles and Felicia. Should I have locked him in the attic?"

Ethan was nonplussed. "Well, it would have been better than poisoning him."

"He was the patriarch," harrumphed Charles.

Felicia's smile was wicked. "Will you be wearing a red negligee to your coronation, Charles?"

"What is wrong with you?" he demanded. "Have you lost your mind?"

"No, I've found my spirit."

I was all for them getting into an extended argument. Unfortunately, Nattie did not join in the fun. She took another step in my direction. I took a step backward, wondering where the hell the door was. I was convinced that whatever she was holding behind her back was not a benign tea bag. I shoved Ethan out of his chair. He was so startled that he sprawled on the floor. Nattie smiled at me as she stepped over his body.

"I don't believe that the police are coming," she said. "Perhaps you're not as smart as you think you are, Claire."

"There are witnesses. You aren't going to get away with any more violence, Nattie." Somehow I'd misgauged the location of the door. I bumped against the stone fireplace. "The police are coming. You need to give up, Nattie."

"Do I?" she purred, advancing like a feral cat. She put out her arm to show me a very large knife.

My memory was beyond reproach, most of the time. I felt behind me until I found the poker, clenched it in my fist, and said, "Yes." I then whacked her across the head with calculated force. She crumpled to the floor.

"Well done," said a voice from the doorway. It was not Jorgeson, or one of his minions. I launched myself into Peter's arms and buried my face against his shoulder.

"About time, Sherlock," I muttered.

CHAPTER 18

Two days later, after I'd been sequestered in Jorgeson's office for many hours to explain my incomparable deductions and a few minor glitches, Peter and I escaped for lunch at the sort of restaurant where one does not use one's cell phone without overt disapproval from the maître d'. We'd already had the usual conversation about my selfless, civic-minded contributions to the successful solution of the crimes. For some reason, he seemed to think that I'd promised not to meddle with the subterfuge occurring at Hollow Valley. Peter's only flaw is his single-mindedness. I try to overlook it.

After he'd ordered wine, he said, "How long is Jordan staying with us?"

"Her parents will be home in two weeks. For once in her life, Caron has been a good role model. Jordan's acting like a normal pain-in-the-ass teenager. Besides, we can't send her back to Aunt Margaret Louise. She's probably in Brazil or one of those countries without an extradition treaty. She warned me that they underestimated her. She had ten minutes to transfer every dollar of the Hollow Valley Nursery business account to the Caymans, jump in her car, and peel out before you arrived. Rather impressive. I don't know how to balance my checkbook without a calculator."

"Felicia's the only one in the clear," Peter said. "Ethan and Charles are in federal custody, and Nattie's scheduled for a psych evaluation. We'll attempt to extradite Margaret Louise if or when we find her. Jorgeson's busy dealing with the ATF, the FBI, the ME, and the chief—who is not happy with me."

"I tried to keep you out of it. I fully intended to have everything neatly wrapped up before your plane landed. If Jorgeson had been less patient with the state lab, he would have figured it out himself. I have chigger bites and an excruciatingly painful ankle because he was willing to wait for weeks to get the results. I didn't enjoy crawling through weeds, you know. I could have come face-to-face with a mountain lion!"

The maître d' shot us a dark look as he oversaw the uncorking of the wine. I lowered my voice. "Have the police located Pandora Butterfly?"

"Not yet, but they're watching the bars and dives. Her children are in temporary foster care. Their caseworker put in for early retirement this morning."

I didn't bother to roll my eyes. "It's for the best. Even if Pandora is detained, she won't demand that they be returned to her. Felicia called me this morning. She and her daughter have plans to meet. If Charles gets out on bail, he may find himself home alone, unable to use a can opener or the microwave. At least he can have potluck meals at his church once a week."

A waiter appeared to take our orders. After some prodding from me, Peter told me about the hijacking in Missouri. He gave me an annoyed look when I innocently inquired if it had taken place near Cuba. "Or Mexico," I added. "One of those foreign places."

"The truck was full of cases of cigarettes. The potential profit was enormous. All Ethan had to do was put counterfeit tax stamps on the packs so they would appear to be legal. There's a term for that. It's called 'butt-legging.'"

My laughter warranted a frown from the maître d'. "Is that all you learned at ATF camp?"

Peter looked at me across the table with his molasses-colored eyes. "Let's have a peaceful lunch. I'll be at the PD the rest of the day. Don't you have an appointment this afternoon with a lawyer with a bizarre name?"

"*We* have an appointment," I said firmly. "Cancel your plans for the rest of the day. I intend to be inconsolable." I came close to bursting into tears but caught myself before the maître d' descended on us once again.

Peter picked me up at three, and we drove in silence to Link Cranberry's office. I'd prepared myself by rehearsing mild expressions of disappointment and cramming tissues in my purse. My darling husband seemed grim, although I doubted he would create a scene. I reminded myself that I most certainly would prefer not to.

Once we were seated in her office, she flipped through some papers and said, "Terry insisted on signing a simple will that named me as the executor of his estate. I filed it Monday morning, so it's a matter of public record. Everything of value, including Winston's art, goes to charities."

My composure was going south. Peter squeezed my hand until I was able to say, "That's good."

Cranberry took off her glasses and gave me a quirky little smile. "He left a stipulation that if he died unexpectedly, he wanted you to have the house. I don't think we need to worry about the lawsuit, since the plaintiffs have more pressing concerns. You'll have to pay fair market value."

I bit down on my lip as I stared at Peter. "The neighborhood is much improved. None of the Hollows will sell their property, so we'll have complete privacy. The nursery is bankrupt. We can move in immediately."

"If that's what you want," my handsome, adorable, lovable husband said before he leaned over and kissed me.

There are moments when he can read my mind.

MURDER AS A
SECOND LANGUAGE,

THE NEXT JOAN HESS MYSTERY—
AVAILABLE SOON IN HARDCOVER FROM
MINOTAUR BOOKS . . .

"Why's your shirt covered in blood?" Caron asked as she sat down at the kitchen island and held up her cell phone to capture the moment.

"It's mostly tomato sauce," I said, peering at the recipe. There were twenty-two ingredients, and I was facing number sixteen: "easy aioli." Apparently, it was too easy to suggest directions. I did not have Julia Child on speed-dial. Number seventeen in the recipe was one cup of dry white wine. An excellent idea. I poured myself a cup and leaned against the counter, temporarily stymied but not yet defeated.

"Mostly?"

I waggled my index finger, which sported an adhesive strip. "I'm working on my knife skills. Cooking is not for sissies."

My darling daughter wrinkled her nose. "It smells fishy in here. What on earth are you making?"

"Bouillabaisse. It's a classic French fish stew. I intend to serve it tonight with"—I glanced at the cookbook—"crusty bread and a salad with homemade vinaigrette. For dessert, Riesling-poached pears."

"Are we eating at midnight?"

I refused to look back at the horrendous mess that encompassed all the counters, the sink filled with bowls and utensils, the vegetable debris, open jars and bottles, and a splatter of tomato sauce, sweat, and tears. "I'm making progress," I said loftily.

"Whatever." She took a few more photos, then put down her cell. "You will be relieved to know that I may be able to go to college in a year, despite your lack of guidance. Otherwise, I'm doomed to survive on an annual income of less than twenty-five thousand. I won't be able to go to the dentist, so all my teeth will fall out. No matter how badly I'm bleeding, I'll have to tie a dirty rag around the wound and limp into work. My last manicure will be for graduation. Do you know how expensive fingernail polish is—even at discount stores?"

"I have no idea." I went into the library and looked up "aïoli" in a dictionary. "Garlic, egg yolk, lemon juice, olive oil," I chanted as I returned to the kitchen and opened the refrigerator. Once I'd found eggs and lemons, I set them on the counter. "What specific lack of maternal guidance has imperiled your future education?"

"Community service—and I don't mean the kind that some judge orders you to do. It has to be voluntary. You didn't tell me that you have to show the college admissions boards that you're committed to helping the less fortunate."

"I applied to college in the Mesozoic era. I did so by filling out a form and submitting my transcript and ACT scores." I paused to replay what she'd said. "Shall I assume you're planning to fill that gap in your resume? Did you volunteer at the homeless shelter or a soup kitchen? I can't quite see you adopting a mile of highway and picking up litter in an orange vest."

"Inez found this really cool place where we can volunteer to teach English as a second language to foreigners. It's like four hours a week, and we arrange our own schedules. I figure that if we're there from eleven to noon, we'll have plenty of time to go to the lake and the mall." Having rescued herself from a lifetime of cosmetology or auto mechanics, she moved on to a more crucial topic. "Can I have a pool party this Saturday afternoon? I want everybody to see our new house. I may even invite Rhonda Maguire and her band of clueless cheerleaders."

"Our new house" was also known as my perfect house— a hundred and fifty-year- old Victorian gem with bits of gingerbread trim, hardwood floors that gleamed with sunshine, spacious yet cozy, with twenty-first-century indulgences. It was located at the far edge of Farberville, with a stream, a meadow dotted with wildflowers, and an apple orchard. There had been a few problems with the resident Hollow Valley family members involving malfeasance and murder, but I'd solved the case for the Farberville Police Department (and vacated the valley of the majority of its occupants). We'd moved in two weeks earlier. Now Peter, my divinely handsome husband who had been blessed with molasses-colored eyes and an aristocratic nose, had his own tie rack, his own wine cellar, and his own chaise longue on the terrace overlooking the pool. I'd claimed the library as my haven, and spent a lot of time playing on the rolling ladder that allowed access to the highest shelves of books. I'd also arranged the contents of the walk-in closets, added artwork, located most of the light switches, and mastered the washing machine and the dryer. I'd barely seen my beloved bookstore, the Book Depot, since Peter hired a grad student to be the clerk. My presence was tolerated as long as I approved orders and invoices, and signed checks. Lingering was not encouraged.

After a few days of reading poetry in the meadow, I felt the need to do something of importance. It was too early to make cider, and the idea of knitting made me queasy. Thus I had decided to master the art of French cooking. My *boeuf bourguignon* had been a success, as had the *coq au vin*; the *terrine de filets de sole* had been less so. My *soufflé au chocolat* had sunk. My *petites crepes aux deux fromages* had been met with derision. *C'est la vie.*

"Yes, you may have a party," I said as I attempted to separate an egg. "You handle the food—unless you want to serve *tapenade noire* and *mousse de saumon.*"

"How do you say 'yuck' in French?" Caron was too busy texting to wait for a response. "Do you care how many people I invite?"

I picked up another egg. "I suppose not, as long as you clean up afterwards. I don't see what's so damn easy about aioli. Is there a utensil to crush the garlic? What's wrong with garlic powder?"

"Oh, no!" she shrieked so loudly that my hand clutched the egg with excessive force. "I can't believe this! I've already sent thirty e-vites. Everybody's going to think I'm an idiot!"

I held my hand under the tap and let the gloppy mess dribble down the drain. "What's wrong? Did Rhonda decline?"

"I got a text from Inez. We have to attend a training session at the Literacy Council on Saturday from ten in the morning until six. Eight hours of training to point at a picture and say, 'Apple.' It's not like I'm going to explain the difference between the pluperfect and the imperfect. I don't care, so why should they?"

"You can always be an aromatherapist."

Caron gave me a contemptuous look over her cell phone. "You are so Not Funny."

During the week, I attempted to conquer, with varying results, *gratinee de coquilles St. Jacques, quiche Lorraine,* and *vichyssoise.* My second *soufflé* went into the garbage disposal. Peter was so impressed by my relentless enthusiasm that he insisted on taking me out to dinner on Saturday. As we lingered over *bifteck et pommes de terre* (aka steaks and baked potatoes), he suggested that I might want to spend more time at the Book Depot, learn to play bridge, take a class at the college, or volunteer for a worthy cause. It was very dear of him to worry that I was expending too much time on housewife duties and would enjoy a respite. I gazed into his eyes and assured him that I was having a lovely time in the kitchen, although cooking and cleaning up could be wearisome. My eyes almost welled with tears as he spoke of the wealth of knowledge and experience I could share with the community, were I to sacrifice my nascent culinary goal.

I was thinking about our conversation the next day when Caron and Inez slunk in and collapsed on the sofa. Caron was fuming. Inez, her best friend, looked pale and distressed, and she was blinking rapidly behind the thick lenses of her glasses. I wiped my damp hands on a dish towel and joined them. "Problems at the Literacy Council yesterday?" I asked.

"Yeah," Caron muttered. "The training session was interminable. The teacher basically read aloud from the manual while we followed along, like *we* were illiterate. We broke for pizza and then listened to her drone on for another two hours. After that, the executive director, some pompous guy named Gregory Whistler, came in and thanked us for volunteering. I was so thrilled that I almost woke up."

"Then it got worse," Inez said. "The program director, who's Japanese and looks like she's a teenager, told us that because of the shortage of volunteers in the summer we would each get four students—and meet with them twice a week for an hour."

"For a total of eight hours." Caron's sigh evolved into

an agonized moan. "We have to call them and find a time
that's mutually convenient. It could be six in the morning
or four in the afternoon. We may never make it to the
lake."

I noticed that her lower lip was trembling. It was oddly
comforting to realize that she was still susceptible to
post-pubescent angst at the *très* sophisticated age of
seventeen. Caron and Inez had provided me with much
amusement in recent years, along with more than a few
gray hairs and headaches. Their antics had been inventive, to put it mildly, and always under the guise of righ-
teous indignation. Or so they claimed, anyway. In the last
month alone, they'd figured out a way to bypass a security
system to get inside a residence. They'd abetted a runaway, hacked into a computer, and perfected the art of
lying by omission. There may have been a genetic predis-
position for that last one.

"Do you know who your students will be?" I asked.

Inez consulted a piece of paper. "We have their names
and telephone numbers. We're supposed to call them and
schedule our sessions. I have a woman from Colombia, a
woman from Egypt, and a man and woman from Mexico.
I wish I'd taken Spanish instead of Latin."

"And I," Caron said, rolling her eyes, "have to tutor an
old lady from Poland, a Japanese man, an Iranian woman,
and a woman from Russia. How am I supposed to call them
on the phone? They don't speak English. Like I speak
Polish, Japanese, Russian, and whatever they speak in Iran.
Arabic? Farsi? This is a nightmare, and I think we ought
to just quit now. I say we set up a lemonade stand and
donate the proceeds to some charity."

I looked at her. "That'll impress the admissions boards
at Bryn Mawr and Vassar. Of course, you can always stay
here and attend Thurber College."

She looked right back at me. "Yes, and I can live here the

entire four years. Imagine the size of the pool parties when I meet all the freshmen. They can come out here to do their laundry and graze on bouillabaisse. You'll be like a sorority and fraternity housemother. Won't that be great?"

I went to the kitchen and poured a glass of iced tea. I do not sweat, but there may have been the faintest perspiration glinting on my flawless brow. I'd created some lovely fantasies to explore after I recovered from the empty nest syndrome—which would be measured in hours, if not minutes. In the foreseeable future, scissors and tape would be in their designated drawer, my clothes would remain in my closet unless I was washing or wearing them, my makeup would lie peacefully on the bathroom counter, and I could cease putting aside cash for bail money. I'd resigned myself to one more year—not five more years.

"All right, girls," I said as I returned to the living room, "here's my best offer. I will volunteer at the Literacy Council and take one student from each of you. You can decide which ones after you've worked out your schedules."

Caron pondered this. "That means you only have to be there for four hours a week, while we have to be there for—" She stopped as Inez elbowed her in the ribs. "Hey, why'd you do that?"

"I think that's a fine idea," Inez said to me. "You have to do the training, though, and I don't know how often it's offered."

I shrugged. "I have a graduate degree in English, and I was a substitute teacher at the high school. My grammar is impeccable, and my vocabulary is extensive. I'm likely to better qualified than this teacher you had yesterday. This will not be a problem. Trust me."

The fifteen-year-old Japanese girl purporting to be the program director gave me a charming smile. Her deep

brown eyes twinkled as she said, "I am so sorry, Ms.
Marroy, but the next training session will not be held until the third week in August. I hope to see you then. Now
if you will be so kind to excuse me, I must return some
phone calls."

"If you want me to read a manual and discuss the material, I will do so, although it's a waste of time for both
of us." I kept my voice modulated and free of frustration,
although I was damned if I was going to twinkle at her. "I
speak English. Your students want to learn to speak English. I fail to see the need for eight hours of training to
grasp the concept."

"It's our policy."

This was the third round of the same dialogue. Keiko
Sakamoto, as her name plate claimed, had feinted and
dodged my well-presented arguments with "our policy." I
felt as if I were at the White House, trying to persuade the
Secretary of State to abandon the prevailing foreign policy. My chances in either situation fell between wretched
and nil.

Keiko picked up the telephone receiver, and with yet
another twinkle, said, "We always need volunteers for
our fundraisers. I'll pass along your name and number.
Have a nice day, Ms. Marroy."

I left her office with as much dignity as I could rally.
The Farberville Literacy Council occupied a red-brick
building in the vicinity of the college campus, and had
been designed well. The central area had clusters of cubicles equipped with computers, and a lounging area with
chairs, tables, and bookshelves. Offices and classrooms
lined the periphery. The passageways had black metal file
cabinets under piles of boxes, books, and unfiled files. A
receptionist's desk next to the front door was unoccupied.
Everything was well-lit and clean. I could hear voices. As
I hesitated, a classroom door opened and a dozen students

emerged, talking to each other in several different languages. I recognized Spanish, German, and Arabic. Three young Asian women stared at me and giggled.

A tall, lean, fortyish woman shooed them out of the doorway, then smiled at me. I suspected she was trying to determine my native tongue as she walked across the main room. I was interested to find out how she would address me, so it was a letdown when she merely said, "May I help you?"

"My daughter and her friend are new tutors. They're still trying to get in touch with their students. I was hoping that I could help out, but the next training session isn't until the end of the summer."

"You must be Caron's mother. I'm Leslie Barnes, one of the two full-time teachers, and I was the trainer on Saturday. It was a very, very long day for all of us."

I had no trouble interpreting her look, but I wasn't about to apologize. "The girls are excited about meeting their students, but leery of calling them on the phone because of the language barrier."

"All of their students speak some English, as I told them. However, if they want to come here this afternoon, Keiko can help them make the calls and set up their schedules. I have another class in a few minutes. Nice to meet you, Ms. Malloy." She went into a corner office and closed the door. I hoped her residual scars from the training session had not driven her to alcohol in the middle of the morning.

Two people emerged from an office beyond the reception desk. The man wore a dark suit, a red tie, and an annoyed expression. His hair was beginning to recede, and his features seemed small on his tanned face. The woman had short blond hair, blue eyes, and deft makeup. She was wearing a tailored skirt and jacket and high heels, and she carried a briefcase. "Gregory," she said as though speaking to a wayward child, "we're still waiting for the receipts from your trip to DC two months ago. Are you going to claim your dog ate them? If so, you'd better have that dog at the next meeting."

"They're in my office somewhere," he said. "Why don't you ask Rick where they are? He's been coming by after work to paw through the files. It's a friggin' miracle I can find my desk, much less the manila envelope with the receipts. You've got the credit card statement. I don't see why you want a bunch of bits of paper."

"Willie wants them, not me," she said.

The man now identified as Gregory took her elbow and tried to steer her toward the front door. "You can't have a meeting until you have enough board members present to make a quorum. That won't be until August, will it? I'll find the receipts before then—okay?" There was a tinge of mockery in his voice.

The woman stopped and pulled herself free. "I suppose so. I need to have a word with Keiko before I leave." She swept past me and into the office, muttering under her breath.

I heard a collective sigh of relief from the assorted students, who then resumed chatting or reading newspapers and magazines. Gregory glanced at me before he returned to what I presumed was his office. I stood there for a moment, feeling as inconsequential as I did at the Book Depot. It might be the time for the third stab at a *soufflé*, I finally decided and headed for the door. Purportedly, it was the charm.

Before I could get into my car, the blond woman came outside and said, "Claire Malloy?" When I nodded, she held out her hand and said, "I'm delighted to meet you. I've read all about your involvement with the local police. Tell me, what's it like to confront a murderer?"

"Unpleasant," I replied. "And you are . . . ?"

"Sonya Emerson. I'm on the board of the FLC—the

Farberville Literacy Council. In my spare time, I work for Sell-Mart in the corporate office in the human resources department. What's more fun than a sixty-hour work week?"

I wondered if Mattel had released MBA Barbie in the last few years. "It's nice to meet you, Sonya. I came by to apply to be a tutor. It appears that I'll have to wait for the next training session." I opened my car door, but the subtlety escaped her.

"Keiko mentioned it. She'd love to make an exception in your case, but our executive director is adamant about sticking to our policy. We have to be certain that our tutors are committed. Some of them have signed up, but then lost interest and abandoned their students. Our students can be fragile." She frowned faintly, and then brightened. "But we'd love to have you volunteer in some other capacity. You're so well-known and respected in Farberville. Having you involved in the FLC would enhance our reputation in the community, as well as in the state organization. You're so intelligent and articulate."

I enjoy flattery, but she was shoveling it on. "If you have a bake sale, let me know and I'll whip up a batch of *profiteroles au chocolat*." I waved as I got in my car and drove away at a speed appropriate for someone who was well-known, respected, intelligent, and articulate. If I ever needed a letter of recommendation, I'd call Sonya.

I called Caron and left a message on her voicemail, telling her what Leslie Barnes had said about making the calls. Which, I have to admit, sounded daunting even to Ms. Marroy.

Caron and Inez arrived as we were finishing dinner. "We already ate," Caron said as she went into the kitchen and returned with two cans of soda and a bag of corn chips. Inez nodded and sat down at the table.

"Did you talk to your students?" I asked them.

"Sort of," Caron said through a mouthful of chips. "We went to the literacy council and let Keiko help. It was weird. She understood everybody—or pretended she did, anyway. Ludmila, who's this ninety-year-old obese woman from Poland, about five feet tall, with squinty little eyes and a voice like a leaf blower, came in the office. Guess what? She happens to be my student. Lucky me."

"She was kind of hard to understand," added Inez. "Maybe because she was so upset about something. Keiko took her to the break room for tea. I met my two students from Mexico, Graciella and Aladino. They both speak some English."

"As opposed to my students," Caron cut in deftly. "Besides Ludmila, I got to meet Jiro, who's from Japan and in his twenties. He talks really fast. I smiled and nodded, but I didn't have the faintest idea what he was saying. For all I know, he was telling me where he buried the bodies or what he did with the extraterrestrials in his attic. The Russian woman's English is pretty good. Anyway, we both have our teaching schedules. C'mon, Inez, let's go to the pizza place in the mall."

"I thought you'd already eaten," I said.

Inez lowered her eyes, but my daughter had no reservations about mendacity. "We did, Mother. Joel and some of his chess club friends are celebrating their victory at a tournament in Oklahoma. Inez has a crush on this guy who turns red when you look at him."

"Rory's shy," Inez protested. "Why do you always stare at him, anyway? He thinks that you're going to scream at him."

"That's absurd. I'm merely waiting for him to say something coherent, which may take years."

Peter produced a twenty-dollar bill. "Have a good time."

After they scurried away, he insisted on cleaning up

the kitchen. I took my glass of wine and sat on a stool at the island, admiring his dexterous way with plates and silverware. We were idly speculating about Inez's potential boyfriend when the phone rang. Since Peter's hands were soapy, I answered it.

"Is this Claire Malloy?"

"Yes," I admitted.

"I don't believe we've met, but I have encountered Deputy Chief Rosen several times," the woman continued. "My name is Wilhelmina Constantine. I'm a member of the Farberville Literacy Council board of directors, and I was told that you might be interested in volunteering for our organization. We're delighted."

"I was told that I have to wait for the next training session before I can be a tutor."

"To be a tutor, yes. However, I'd like you to consider becoming a member of the board. You're well-known in the community and have a background in retail. Although the FLC is a non-profit, we're forced to run a business as well. Raising funds, making payroll, dealing with vendors, all those petty nuisances. Your experience will be invaluable."

"I doubt that," I said. "Today was the first time I've set foot in the building. After I've been trained and have tutored for a few months, I'll think about the board. You may not want me. Thank you for asking, Ms. Constantine."

"I wish you'd reconsider, Ms. Malloy. If this wasn't an emergency, I wouldn't be asking. I'm afraid it is, and we're desperate."

I made a face at Peter, who was watching me intently. "An emergency?"

She remained silent for a moment, then said, "I really can't discuss it on the telephone. We have an informal board meeting tomorrow night at seven o'clock. Would you please at least attend?" Her voice began to quaver.

"Otherwise, the FLC may not survive the summer. Our students will have no place to go. They depend on us."

"I'll attend the meeting," I said, aware that I was capitulating to emotional blackmail, "but only as an observer."

"Wonderful," she said, then hung up abruptly.

"Ms. Constantine?" Peter murmured. "As in Wilhelmina Constantine, better known as Willie?" I nodded. "She's a federal judge. Tough lady."

"Her name is familiar, but I'm not sure why."

"She made a controversial ruling a few years ago, but at the time you were distracted by Azalea Twilight's unseemly death."

"I was distracted because I'd been accused of murder and was being stalked by a certain member of the police department."

"You were never accused of murder," Peter said.

"Well, I was most definitely stalked. No matter where I went, you were lurking in the bushes, spying on me."

The certain member of the police department raised his eyebrows. "I was not lurking. You went to extremes to make yourself unavailable for interviews, and the few times I cornered you, you flounced away like Scarlett O'Hara."

"Fiddle-dee-dee," I said. "I have never flounced in my life."

"And I've never lurked."

I thought about it for a moment. "Deal."